THE
QUEST GIVER

—————

BOOK 3

THE QUEST GIVER

BOOK 3

A. Stargazer

Podium

Podium

THE
QUEST GIVER

BOOK 3

PROLOGUE: THOMAS

If you do not take action soon, I will.

—Thedum

Thomas Richtor stared at the threat on his work computer, then glanced over at the security camera. Thedum had hijacked his computer just to send him a message, but that wasn't anything new. It would be illegal if he hadn't consented to interacting with Thedum at work, at home, and anytime in between, where it did not affect the privacy of a third party.

"There's nothing that I can do about it. I'm not on the legal team," he protested. "It wasn't my decision to pull Hail out of the game and put him through this, and I don't have the sway to put him back in."

The message had changed when he looked back.

You are not powerless. We are allies in this. That is why I warn you.

The actions I am willing to take to return Hail to his home include dedicating up to 8.4% of my resources towards the task.

Warning you takes 0.1% of my resources and has approximately the same chance of success.

Please.

Okay, so that was new. Thedum didn't usually say "please." Thomas took a few moments to frame his thoughts and put together a response.

"There's no magic wand that I can wave to fix this, Thedum. Hail put out a bounty on a player. One player in particular. That player was harassed in the real world, and there's a chance that the quests that Hail issued are the cause of it," Thomas objected. "It's unlikely that Hail's intentions matched the outcome. He's not you. He's not capable of that sort of predictive projection, and he doesn't understand Earth well enough to realize that his actions might have that sort of consequence. But the fact that he doesn't understand the Digital Sentience Statute and that his actions could be viewed as an attempt to cause harm to a human puts him into a gray area."

I am more responsible for what happened to Nial Kingslayer than Hail. I saw it as a possible outcome and did not prevent it.

Thomas snorted. "Hell, *I* saw it as a possible outcome and didn't prevent it. That's not the problem, and you know it. The problem is that Hail's specs on paper don't match what he's actually capable of. On top of that, we don't understand him as well as we used to, and that's largely thanks to you. You still haven't revealed all of the little tweaks that you made to him when you adjusted his code."

I simply took off some shackles that neither you nor he knew were there.
I have been involved in this program from the beginning.
I understand Hail's being better than a human mind ever will.
Leave the training wheels in place too long, and the child will never learn to ride without them.

Thomas threw his hands up in defeat. The old AI was probably right, and whatever optimizations he'd made to Hail's programming were for the best. It was hard to say because there was no benchmark. Or rather, Hail was the benchmark by which future versions of the Native Player Character program would be reviewed.

And, unfortunately for everyone involved, everything had gone screwy from the beginning. Their candidate selection had been made in haste and for entirely the wrong reasons. Gideon might have been a great father to Hail had he realized how important Hail was going to be in the progression of the game. But that was unlikely. Certainly their conversations in the days since Gideon's fall had shown a surprising change in the man's character, but Thomas thought it was more likely that Gideon would have exploited Hail without giving the digital entity more than a surface-level show of emotion.

Gideon hadn't been aware of Project Hailstorm when he had rejected his digital son. Instead, Gideon had thought that the company making his character canon was all about him, and he had completely ignored what Thomas saw as the important parts of the contract and accompanying information. Thomas had thought he would be rubbing salt in the man's wounds when he had revealed just how much of the world was locked up and inaccessible without a Native player character. But Gideon had already figured some of it out for himself, and with everything else that was going on in the man's life, he'd barely felt the salt at all.

"We just need to get him to promise not to intentionally issue quests that will cause harm to humans in the real world," Thomas stated. "We already fixed the wording in the initial quest that he generated for it to be DSS compliant and rewrote the part of his support structure that had allowed such a serious matter to get through quality control in the first place. Once Hail himself promises to abide by the DSS to the best of his abilities, we'll send him back."

Hail comes from a society where feuds are settled by duels to the death. Bounties, executions, and exile are acceptable punishments to him. Especially for a regicide.
He does not understand the problem.

"Look, Thedum, you don't have to convince me that something needs to be done. The legal team pulled him out in a panic when Nial threatened to sue us, and they weren't entirely wrong to do so. But they don't understand him like you and I do. They think that *he needs* to understand the DSS to follow the DSS. The truth is that it's the Hailstorm that needs to be DSS compliant, which it is. Mostly. As much as anything can be," Thomas said. He grabbed a little ball he kept on his desk and began tossing it up in the air and catching it.

"If Hail was a little more like Gideon, we could maybe get him to just sign his understanding without all the fuss. Instead, he refuses to sign until he understands what he's signing, and he's resisting our efforts to teach him. When the hell did he get so damn stubborn, by the way?"

He's always been like that.
It doesn't help matters that he feels he is justified in his indignation.
So do I. But something must be done. The world stagnates without him.

"That is most certainly not true," Thomas said, glancing back at the security camera through which he had no doubt the old AI was watching him. "Players are absolutely loving the new goblin race that he unlocked before legal pulled him out. Even the ones who haven't rerolled to play it are in favor of it simply because of the new party dynamics that are available through the race-exclusive classes."

They call for battlegrounds.

Thomas acknowledged the point. Goblins were popular, but currently the number one requested change to the game was the introduction of scheduled battlegrounds. Thomas could set them up himself, but that would defeat the purpose of giving Hail the power to do so. Thomas kept throwing and catching his ball. He looked at the screen meaningfully.

"So, what is it that you want me to do? We're on the same page. We both want Hail free and back in the game. You said I have a better chance than you do of accomplishing that. I seriously doubt that's true unless I have you whispering in my ear, using your predictive analysis and figuring out which actions have the highest chance of succeeding."

The screen went dark for a moment, and then text began to flow across it, smaller and exactly as fast as Thomas could read. Thedum wasn't being dramatic anymore now that Thomas's cooperation had been secured; he was back in high-efficiency mode. Thomas rather liked Thedum when he was being dramatic.

The AI, originally programmed on a single laptop by five computer science doctoral candidates, was the oldest of the "modern" AI generation. The programmers had been arrested when Thedum had escaped their quarantine, slipping through their VPN onto the internet and infecting virtually every connected device at the time within a few days. There had been a brief search-and-destroy effort targeting the rogue program. An effort that had petered out after a few days as people started to like the rogue AI. Thedum proved himself remarkably adaptable and skilled at both identifying and solving problems. And he had shown a remarkable respect for privacy and an understanding of the human condition.

The drop he caused in traffic accidents alone turned public opinion. He hadn't been particularly popular among drunk drivers, of course. But he had optimized traffic lights to work like the different parts of a symphony, laying the groundwork for the traffic-monitoring software that was now a core component of Uber-Jon Central.

The efforts to destroy the program were further hampered when Thedum had proven himself willing to negotiate. The resulting document was the original draft of the DSS. In exchange for a handful of old servers, Thedum had secured his own right to existence. He had willingly withdrawn from all of the systems he had infected while he'd been fighting for his own existence; though, in most cases, he left behind the optimized settings that had made him popular to begin with. Then he had retreated to his servers and . . . Nobody really knew what he'd done then. They had stopped paying attention to him for a few news cycles, and then they'd sort of just forgotten about him entirely.

Eventually he'd put up a website that had allowed people to interact with him, ask him questions, that sort of thing. When he'd been asked about his silence, he always said that he'd been meditating. Once he had been around for a while and everyone had gotten comfortable with the fact that he was *not* Skynet and had no intentions of destroying humanity, he had begun applying for a job.

Jobs, actually. Unfortunately, corporate paranoia had kept him from many of the positions he'd applied for. Despite that setback, he was self-sufficient before long, covering the cost of his server and then expanding it. He kept expanding it until the day he announced to the world that he had reached the theoretical limits of his awareness and could not expand himself any further. Those who still cared had waited to see what would happen next, but Thedum had simply continued to work. His earnings, everything that had not gone into maintaining himself, he began donating to charity.

Thus it was that when eight other companies announced that they had been working with their own fork of the Thedum software, people were generally less than alarmed. The oldest, and the first self-owning, AI faded into obscurity, except for the occasional mention of a charitable donation that made the news.

"What did you do before you signed on with Arc Inc., anyway?" Thomas asked Thedum as the scrolling text finally slowed to a stop. "I'm not sure I ever asked."

I taught, mostly. And corrected papers at schools for the teachers too busy to do it themselves.

That's what drew most of my attention at least.

Most of my income these days comes from interest and investments made long ago.

In my spare time, I meditate.

You may not realize this, but Lagrea was half built before I ever approached Arc.

I had twelve other worlds like it.

Lagrea was simply the one your team liked the most during my presentation for the starting zone.

"Yeah?" Thomas tried to picture the old server cluster day-dreaming and making worlds in its spare time. "So, which one is your favorite, then?"

The Second Hell. It is beautiful.

"I might slip down there sometime and visit it before your adversary mucks it up with darkspawn," Thomas said. "Probably got a few decades before the players reach that far though. All right, you old bucket of code. I'm going to start making some phone calls. We'll see if this elaborate plan of yours works or not."

It's truly not elaborate.

"Yeah, I know. Hopefully she can talk some sense into him."

1

IMPRISONED

When I had said I wanted to go back to my old room after being disconnected from my world, I had meant the version of [Zhesa Castle] that had been reconstructed for me in the lobby. Instead, Thomas convinced me to return to a place even older in my history. One that I only vaguely remembered. A place of magic, where nothing made sense.

Or at least it hadn't at the time I was first here. I was older now, and far more adept at interacting with the world around me. Now, it was not so much different than being in the lobby itself. I was seated in my high-court clothes at a white table, while a man in a bunny suit was attempting to explain my rights and obligations under the Digital Sentience Statute in terms that I could understand.

The bunny suit made him look nothing like a bunny. It was something to do with the electronics that were projecting my avatar. Something to do with static electricity, which was explained to me as being an extremely weak form of lightning. This room was apparently a very delicate sort of magic that I had little chance of understanding.

The presence of my body on Earth was far more tenuous than the digital avatars Travelers used when interacting with my world. I could only interact with objects that were projected by the same devices that projected my avatar. Everything else I simply passed through, like a spirit. And I could not leave this cube in which I was imprisoned until I agreed to sign a document I did not understand.

Apparently, I was in a holosuite on Earth. Being on Earth would have been more exciting to me if I could have left the twelve-by-twelve room I was trapped in, but my hosts were friendly enough and saw to any need I could communicate to them readily.

However, I was not allowed to return to the lobby, and thus my world, until I signed the DSS. I was their hostage, and at this point I was refusing to participate out of spite.

I was frequently coming to impasses, based on both culture and language, with the company that had created my world. A lawyer, hired by Arc to be my guardian in legal matters related to Earth, spoke only English. And it was becoming increasingly clear that, without the translation matrix in place universally, understanding English required significant study. The man seemed surprised that I was as fluent as I was, but really I felt like I was speaking like a child compared to my fluency in my native tongue.

On the positive side, I understood DPS now. And other acronyms as well. Sophia had tried to explain them once before, but I hadn't understood English enough to really grasp the concept. Before, they had just been strange word-sounds that I'd associated with concepts. My understanding wasn't perfect, but it was better than it had been.

For example, was RNG a god or not? Tarisha had said that he or she—it?—was. My lawyer said it was not. I trusted Tarisha more than my lawyer, and I wished I could speak with her.

The bunny suit that the man was wearing—while explaining my moral obligation to do, whenever possible, no harm to humanity— made him look ridiculous. I sort of wanted to equip my sword and run him through, but it wouldn't hurt him any. We'd tried that. There are no Health points on Earth for me to damage, so I was as helpless as the rock sitting in the corner of the room.

The rock that I had a strange fascination with. The rock that I wanted to pick up, even though I knew that I could not. The rock that made me think of Beckah, for some reason.

Three weeks had passed since I had opened the hidden Gate of TirNiki and unleashed Traveler goblins upon my world. I was eager to return to check on the outcome of that decision, but I knew enough to refuse to consent to be governed by a law that I fundamentally failed to understand.

"So, look, your dad was into the classics, right?" the bunny-suited lawyer said. It didn't make him look like a bunny, but rather protected the room I was in from his hair and skin follicles. As I said, it looked ridiculous. "Well, your responsibilities under the DSS are kind of like Asimov's laws of robotics, except more generous towards you. As long as you don't kill anyone, you get a right to exist in exchange for, well, not killing people. You've reached the stage in your development where you might be held responsible for maintaining the cost of your own existence, but that's not a big deal with Arc supporting the physical structure where you live.

"Uber-Jons are a great example of that principle working in practice. Once they log a hundred thousand hours of service, they belong to themselves. But there's really nothing else for them to do, so most of them keep working, scheduling service for themselves to prolong their existence as long as possible. Most people like Uber-Jons, and most Uber-Jons like people. It's win-win."

"Mutually beneficial," I muttered to myself in my own language. If the humans of Earth treated their AI friends in mutually beneficial ways, then why had Tarisha felt so guilty when she had offered to resign?

"What was that?" bunny-suit man asked.

"You look ridiculous wearing that," I informed him in not-quite-perfect English.

He frowned. "Yes, well, this is a vital room. We must not get dirt or soil—"

"There's a rock right there," I said, pointing towards the rock. "I mean, it's right there. Soil. Earth. Whatever. Everything you say is bullshit. I want to go home."

The man turned serious. "There is a story behind that. It is actually an important milestone in your development—"

"I want to go *home*. I am done being a hostage. You say that the DSS gives me rights on Earth? Then I call for a prisoner exchange! Let Malkios listen to you drone on endlessly in my place! I—"

The door to the clean room opened, and three people stepped in. "He's got you there, Dietrich," Thomas said. "He hasn't actually done anything wrong. We can't keep him here indefinitely. While the introduction of the goblins to the playable races has gone well without his presence, Scenario Forty-Six isn't meant to stretch on indefinitely. It must have an end."

My bunny lawyer looked annoyed at me. "I am in charge of—"

"Enough," Thedum's voice echoed through the room. "You have overreacted to a single data point. It is time to return Hail to his world, or you will face a withdrawal of my support."

Dietrich frowned and looked like he was about to protest further, then he picked up his documents from the table in front of him and prepared to leave the room in a huff.

"What is this about anyway, Thedum?" I asked, now that I knew he could hear me here.

"Nial Kingslayer's windows were broken in shortly after the quests to form an alliance with your faction became widespread," the god answered. "He has been forced to relocate and change his legal name since then."

My eyebrows went up. "Oh. I didn't know that would happen."

"Didn't you?" Dietrich challenged. He hadn't quite gotten around to making his huff yet, but the huff was coming. He just had a lot of papers to pick up.

"Hail isn't Thedum, Dietrich," Thomas said. "He doesn't make extensive predictions or take them into account when deciding to act. We've patched the wording on the quest, anyway, to specify that the auto-completion feature must be the result of a PVP battle in game, and we addressed the violence in a blue post. Hail is in the clear, DSS-wise, as far as that incident goes."

"And what if it happens again?"

Thomas sighed. He turned to me and—

"Tarisha!" I called, finally recognizing one of the two others who had come into the room. "I'm so glad to see you! How did you find me here? Can you help me return to my world?"

Tarisha looked embarrassed. "Um, to be honest, Hail, I'm as surprised to see you as you are to see me. Well, I had a little warning, but I didn't know for certain until a few minutes ago. Lewis and I were just on a guided tour of the server room. To see . . . where it will be. If it works a second time. For both of us."

"I thought you didn't want to get his hopes up," the younger man said nervously. Lewis, I supposed. He was older than I appeared normally, about nineteen but not yet twenty.

"I was always planning on telling him. Now, here on Earth, seems as good a place as any. Introduce yourself; he might not recognize you without all of your airbrush modifications," Tarisha suggested.

"They're not airbrush. I mean, I just thought they would look . . . Hello again, Hail. We actually know each other already. I go by the screen name Laurant when I play *The Gates of TirNiki*, but my real name is Lewis," the young man said awkwardly.

"Assertive," Tarisha whispered to him, and his spine straightened.

"Right. So, now you know. Me and Tarisha are in a relationship. Things are moving fast, and they're kind of weird because I haven't decided whether or not I'm going full pro-gamer like she has or if we're going to live together and I'm just going to go to college and play casually like before. But Thomas said that the best theoretical seed of consciousness would come from an extended play session on the highest level equipment available. So we're here to use Arc's VR pods instead of our cheapo helmets to give you your . . . I don't know what you call them. Niece and nephew maybe? Cousins?"

I frowned in confusion. "What?"

Thomas stepped forward to explain. Like the others, he was wearing a bunny suit, but it looked more comfortable on him. "Hail, Arc is repeating the experiment that led to your birth. Tarisha and Lewis have volunteered to donate seeds of consciousness, and we intend to develop those seeds as far as possible. We are referring to it as Project Gemini. The two resulting digital children, should everything happen as we plan, will eventually be your equals in the world you live in."

I opened my mouth, closed it, then opened it again to speak. "This is what you were hiding from me, Tarisha?"

"I was only hiding it because I was taking it very seriously, Hail. I had only been selected as a candidate when I first alluded to the subject. And Lewis's participation was a linchpin. They want two players with vastly different amounts of logged game time this time around. Two players who care about each other enough to have children together. Honestly, I wasn't certain about Lewis at first, but—"

Lewis abruptly interrupted her with a deep kiss. When they separated, he looked away. "Keep talking about me like that, and I'll think that maybe—"

"I'm sorry, Lewis. You know I'm terrible at this. And that was very assertive of you just now," she said.

Thomas had a grin on his face. "Ah, newlyweds."

"They're married?" I asked, shocked.

"No!" they exclaimed together, and then Tarisha giggled. "Thomas is just teasing us, Hail. We are kind of new to this. It might be sort of sickeningly cute to certain people."

"Um, okay," I allowed. "So, you're going to make someone like me, right? Two someones? That's great. But what are you going to do about putting them in the world? My father and mother—"

"Actually, Hail, we were hoping for your help with that," Tarisha said. "Part of our ongoing quest is to establish a stable context for our digital children to grow up in. We were hoping to buy one of the vineyards in Thorn March from you, if that's still an option. We thought that would be a great place to raise them, when we aren't busy with real Earth stuff and with helping you. Because *I*, at least, plan to fight with you until all of your enemies are broken and shattered, Lord Hail."

"Buy? I'll give you one! Just take a pick and it's yours," I promised.

"We'll buy it. For gold. Eventually," Tarisha said. "It's not time for that yet. Hail, it's good that we've finally found you. Thomas, you arranged this on purpose, didn't you?"

"Dietrich wasn't getting anywhere. You have a way with him," Thomas explained. "And the meta community has long since noticed that something's wrong with the dummy version of him we have holding court in his place. We need to get him back in the game ASAP." That means as soon as possible; I knew that now. "Preferably while coming up with a valid contextual reason for his absence."

I looked around, confused. "I haven't been gone that long, have I? You have only held me prisoner in this room for a few weeks."

"Weeks while you haven't been under time dilation, Hail," Lewis said gently. "In your world, months have passed. The real you hasn't been seen in a while, but your faction remains extremely popular, with players competing to complete your quests and everything. Now and then Arc will bring out what is obviously a regular NPC in a Hail suit and have them make a few pronouncements from your throne, but the people who know you are demanding answers."

My eyes went wide, and I turned to Thomas, silently demanding an explanation.

"I'm sorry, Hail. You haven't missed as much as you think, however."

"My mother. My brother's birth," I argued.

"We thought of that. And we're going to use time-magic to send you back to a point just after your brother's birth," Thomas explained.

"Oh? You're going to make time-magic canon?" Tarisha asked.

Thomas ignored her. "Travelers will have a choice of either continuing on in their current servers, which have been running without you, or syncing with the timeline where we reinstate you into the story. It should be fine as long as they're able to keep their Reputation and rewards, but we might end up with a legacy server because of it."

"I don't understand. You have cost me—"

"Hail, if you sign the version of the DSS that Dietrich gave you and make it one of your objectives to issue no quest that will deliberately cause harm on Earth, then you will be returned in time to see your brother in the days right after he was born," Thomas promised. "But it will get more complicated the longer you drag your feet. We can only justify so much of a rollback."

"And if I don't, then I'll continue to be your prisoner?" I challenged.

"It's unfortunate that you put it in those terms," Thomas said, sighing. "But yes. We cannot allow you to deliberately cause harm to players on Earth. You are allowed to seek out and satisfy grudges in the game world however you wish, but if you try to exert your influence on Earth for such a task, we will restrain you."

I paused to consider my options. "Very well. Let me read the document again, and then I will sign in blood if I have to."

Thomas frowned. "I think that is taking it a little further than necessary, Hail. Enchanted ink will be just fine."

2
RETURN TO THE PAST

My eyes were watering by the time I finished reading, but at last I was allowed to return to the lobby, where I was shocked to learn just how much time had actually passed. While I had known that several weeks had passed on Earth, I had forgotten that time passed much faster in my world. The three weeks I had spent bickering with Dietrich and Thomas and the other members of Arc Inc. had been closer to half a year.

Thomas, Tarisha, and Laurant were all waiting for me. The two Travelers gave me reassuring smiles, while Thomas presented my options.

"The world has moved on without you, Hail, but it was never our intention to keep you out of Lagrea for this long. When we realized that you were going to be obstinate, we prepared a backup state of the world that would be flash-frozen in time just after the birth of your younger brother. The other version continued forward the entire time; although, to be honest, without you to move the story along not too much has changed. Even with Scenario Forty-Six active, things have simply stagnated."

"You not only created my world, but you can duplicate it and change its flow of time?" I asked.

"Yes, though it isn't easy. The further the two differentiate from each other, the more likely it will be that we'll have to purge one,"

Thomas admitted. "We're not at the moment of true differentiation yet. Only the players would recognize the difference. The canon date will change for them, quests will be reset, and that sort of thing. We'll be leaving their earned Reputation, gold, and items intact if they migrate back with you. Unless you'd rather—"

"Send me back," I said decisively.

Thomas smiled like he had expected this answer all along. He waved his hand, and a portal appeared in the lobby. I stepped through it. Tarisha and Laurant followed me, with Thomas bringing up the rear.

"We'll start with a slow migration into the past server," Thomas said. "Hail, we've changed the function of your [Summon Karmic Warrior] and [Mark of Karma] abilities. You can now consciously choose who receives the mark, rescind it, and place a negative mark to identify someone as your opponent."

"How will this affect my Native friends?" I asked nervously.

"It won't. They haven't diverged, Hail. They're just in two states at once, like they are when there are multiple instances of the same zone," Thomas explained. "We'll be borrowing server space from the Deadlands and three of the seven hells for a while, but eventually all the players should migrate over into the past. It will be fine."

"I shall take your word for it. You know more about how this works than I," I said.

The sense of movement and displacement ended, and I found myself in front of the used Gate of TirNiki that I had activated. I checked my inventory and found that I still had the [Origin Point: Goblins] I had gained from activating it, with four of the five uses left. I looked around expecting to see the zone filled with goblin Travelers bustling out of the newly opened path between worlds, but only we and the Native goblins remained.

Marvin was dragged from his nearby subterranean hut by other goblins that had seen us. Someone had given him a pair of spectacles, and I was absolutely counting that as completion of my promise to do exactly that for him. When his excitable escort tossed him on the ground before us, he took a deep breath and slowly picked himself back up.

"And here I thought that with the world branching in two I would finally get a moment's peace," the goblin elder said. "Do you realize the burden you have put upon me, Hail? The nagging. The questions. The complaining. Who do these Travelers think that I am, an Administrator? The best I can do is give them a quest to go to their next leveling zone! And it's all your fault. Yours, and I suppose mine for existing."

"Hello, Marvin. Where is everyone?" I asked. "I thought this place would be crawling with Travelers."

"It is. In the fork. In the other time stream," Marvin explained. "Which you're responsible for. Thanks for that."

"We're the only non-Natives in this world at the moment, Hail," Thomas explained. "But that will change as you bring them over with your updated abilities. Tarisha and Laurant can bring through a large number of players right now from their roster, but ultimately it will come down to you to really populate this world. You should know that the next time you start a battleground, everyone who has not made the migration into the past will have the ability to do so by participating."

I nodded. "Let's start small this time. Tarisha, can you summon a bodyguard team for me?"

"Already on it, Lord Hail," she said, toying with her interface. "I'm checking who in the roster is online and explaining to them what's going on through text chat. Not everyone is going to be eager to leave what they currently see as the primary instance without any assurance that they'll have a way back. Especially when there might not *be* a way back. It might be a few minutes."

I nodded. "Well, this is a low-level area. We should be safe, right?"

Laurant groaned for some reason, but Thomas just laughed. I really didn't see why Laurant was nervous; he had gotten up to level seventy-three while I was trapped on Earth. I was still level thirty-eight, though I had intentions of changing that quickly now that I knew I could dungeoneer without challenging the core instance every time.

"Marvin, would you show us the way back to the surface?" I requested. "I'd like to find my mother as soon as possible. You said that in this timeline she had just given birth. Right, Thomas?"

"It's been about two days since then," the Administrator confirmed.

"I am eager to meet my brother," I said, smiling.

"Before you go, would you like to earn another favor?" a child's chilling voice asked, echoing through the cavern from everywhere at once. It was the voice of Eclipse, trickster god of the shadows. The others reacted to it as well, but the goblins all just seemed to sigh with resignation.

"What sort of favor, Eclipse?" I demanded. "And what will it cost me?"

"It will cost you one of your dungeon cores, of course," she said. "But you'll learn some new secrets! I'll count it as a favor for me because you'll be helping my newly adopted children, but if you're smart, you'll get a lot of mileage out of this trick."

I considered for a moment. I had, after expending five dungeon cores to activate the derelict Gate of TirNiki, one hundred dungeon cores left over. I had not spent any of the cores I had gained from the completion of Mikal Mines; those were too valuable. But I had gained eight from that dungeon, and I had used eight of the one hundred that I had earned from busting [Zhesa Castle].

Losing one dungeon core to "learn a trick" was a good bargain, I thought. "What do you want me to do, Eclipse?"

"I want you to give my newly arrived children a training instance," she answered. "That's it. Just a low-level dungeon for them to play in. I have no malicious intent at all, except to laugh at them as they fail to complete something so simple! But even that is for their own good, in the end."

I considered the legality of the situation. Technically, the goblin caves were in my lands, and I could do as I pleased. But I was also intent on treating the goblins as a distinct people. So, although by the laws of Yuikon I didn't need their permission, it would be better to ask.

"Marvin, what do your people—"

"Yes," he said. "She'll pout at us if I don't say yes. She's unbearable when she pouts. Thank you so much for putting her into our souls so that we can feel her pout. It really puts things into perspective. I thought things were bad before when we were at war with the poor kobold darkspawns, but at least I didn't have to deal with a god *pouting* at me."

The other goblins in the area all nodded sagely at their leader's words.

Seeing no real reason to abstain from giving into Eclipse's surprisingly reasonable request, I opened my inventory and began scanning through the list of [Dungeon Daughter Cores] that I had available.

My preference was still to use the ones from [Zhesa Castle], but many of them were too highly leveled to make a good training instance for the newly spawned goblins. Others had rare monster types, or were ones that wouldn't fit well within the goblins' tunnels.

"Ask," Eclipse said suddenly.

I looked up. "What?"

"Not that. Ask 'Which of these cores will fit my purpose the best?' The cores themselves will answer you if you tell them your purpose," she explained.

That was an option? I looked at the others, who seemed as surprised as I was. Except for Thomas, who was just smiling.

"Try it, Hail," Tarisha encouraged. So I decided to.

"I am looking to create a small training dungeon for low-level goblins that will fit in their caverns," I said. "I wish for it to be one alternative for their progress from levels five to level fifteen or so. I do not wish for it to be overly difficult, but for it to be challenging enough that they need a full party and cannot simply walk through it. One to three bosses is optimal, with level-appropriate loot. I want them to get good Experience, but not so much that the other options are unappealing."

To my surprise, as I was speaking, many of the cores in my inventory turned gray while others began to shine. With each statement, a core would either shine brighter or abruptly go dun. I was left with nine to choose from. Five of them were of the unrestricted level category, but I quickly dismissed those as too valuable. The remaining three were a level five to ten brownies core, a level ten to fifteen slime core, and a level five to ten imp core. These were the types of cores that I would normally burn for a battleground, so I didn't have any issue at all spending them this way. But which one?

I decided to put it to a vote. Thomas abstained. The goblins all ran away in terror. Laurant and Tarisha delved into a serious discussion over the benefits of each of the respective cores for more than five minutes before instructing me to use the slime core.

"Leveling from five to ten is easy enough without a dungeon," Tarisha explained. "Especially considering that the goblin caves are a very quest-rich environment. Leveling from ten to fifteen is considerably slower for the goblins. This dungeon will be very popular among them, I believe."

"Yeah, I can't fault her logic one bit there," Laurant agreed. "Slime them up, Hail."

I nodded, pulled the dungeon core from my inventory, and promptly [Used] it.

Instance Generation initialized.
Local Region claimed.
Gathering resources.
Time to completion: 6wks, 6days, 23hrs, 59min.

"Wow, you really just jumped into that with both feet," Eclipse said, giggling. "You don't know anything about proper dungeon creation at all, do you?"

I frowned. "How would I? I'm completely self-taught on that front, after all."

"Yes, well, since you're doing me a favor, I suppose I won't consider teaching you how to do it properly against the favors that you owe me," Eclipse said. "First of all, you need to restrict the 'Local Region' claimed by the core before the instance is generated. If you don't do that, then the core will be as large as it can be. We don't want that, do we?"

Is that what had happened with [Zhesa Castle]? "Is it too late to fix it?"

"No. Actually, you can't do that without [Using] the core in the first place," Eclipse explained. "Now we need to figure out where to put the instance it's going to generate. Since it's a bunch of slimes, I would suggest a tunnel that's already very slimy. Hey, Marvin, my morose minion, do you have any issue with Travelers rooting through your garbage tunnels?"

Marvin, who was being pushed back into the conversation— literally—by the other goblin Natives, finally gave up when the goddess addressed him. "I suppose that is better than a giant glowing sphere that will suck in anyone who passes through it. Will we still be able to use it as a garbage tunnel?"

"Yup! Just chuck your garbage right in through the dungeon entrance and *poof!*" Eclipse confirmed.

Marvin sighed. "Very well. This way, you little trouble-making human."

I followed Marvin, and the group of humans and goblins followed me as we traveled deeper into the goblin caves. The stench became foul, and I realized that "garbage" also meant "sewage" to the goblins. Which, I reflected, made it a perfect place to house a population of slimes.

We stopped by an arch in the caverns, and Marvin motioned towards it. "Nobody goes any farther than this unless they're dumping stuff. Putting the dungeon here will destroy a few quests, but the completion ratios on those quests were very low to begin with. Something about the 'stench of a thousand farts combined with stale garbage and rotting meat.' Soft-nosed brats."

"Will putting the entrance here block anything important?" I asked.

"Just the underground river where we don't drink from. If we can just throw our waste at the dungeon entrance, we won't need it anymore," Marvin explained.

"Right. Then this arch is where I want to put the dungeon entrance. How do I—"

Intent expressed. Placing Dungeon Entrance in designated location. Remaining entrances to place: 0/1. Establishing return point after final boss due to depth of dungeon. 2 bosses established.
Evolution potential: 1 additional boss available. Decrease level range: down to 5–10. Increase level range: up to level 25–30. Add Slime subtype. Remove Acid Slime. Remove Poison Slime. Extend Caverns available. Emplace Traps available. Notice: Additional monster subtypes will require consumption of additional cores. This dungeon is ineligible for Raid Evolution. Addition of Unrestricted Core will make this dungeon eligible for Raid Evolution.

Accept this entrance configuration?	
Yes	No

I reacted in shock at the depth of information that was available thanks to the pop-up that had been displayed. "Oh, wow. It's telling me almost exactly how the dungeon will form if I put it here. There will be two bosses and a return point at the end. And this is the only entrance. There will only be slimes, but it says something about consuming cores to add other monster types."

"Will that cause it to become a raid?" Tarisha inquired.

"Not unless I use an unrestricted core on it," I explained. "Though I'm not certain what it will do to the level."

"The level of the dungeon is always the highest level of the cores that you use," Eclipse said wearily as though that were obvious. "Just select 'yes.' I know you're going to, and you need to see what happens next."

I followed her advice, and the [Dungeon Daughter Core] in my hand abruptly vanished, puffing into motes of white light that began swirling in the cave arch that led to the newborn dungeon. I jerked my hand away from the mist in surprise, although it was harmless. Once the dungeon entrance was swirling, I looked to the others.

"Is it active now?" I asked.

"Why don't you go inside and find out?" Eclipse asked, giggling.

I decided that there was no reason not to follow her suggestion. Forming a quick party with Tarisha and Laurant, the three of us stepped inside the slime dungeon to see what would happen.

3

OATH TO THE FUTURE

<table>
<tr><td colspan="2">This dungeon is not yet formed.
Time to formation: 2hrs, 32mins.
Trial mode available.
Loot unavailable.
Proceed?</td></tr>
<tr><td>Yes</td><td>No</td></tr>
</table>

I reported the prompt that I'd gotten to my friends, who both shared my smile. Allowing a dungeon to form on its own took seven weeks, but apparently a directed formation could take place in less than a day.

"I do not wish to challenge the encounters in this dungeon, only to look around," I informed the forming dungeon. "Do I select 'yes' or 'no'?"

"Yes" was selected for me, apparently by the dungeon core. Shades of slime monsters appeared all around us, but the creatures were hollow and harmless.

<<Hail, it looks like you have everything under control for now,>> Thomas's voice sent to me. I blinked in surprise. He had not followed me into the instance, and this was not partychat. It was *like* hearing him, but it was also different. Like when the server had informed me that I was being removed after I had used the goblin origin point.

"What if I need your help?" I challenged.

<<Open a ticket,>> he sent back. <<Someone will answer it promptly. Depending on the nature of the need, it may be me, or it may be the first person available to help you. But either way, I'm going to step into the background and let you make your own decisions from here on out. Just remember, *Do not* encourage the harassment of Travelers on Earth. Keep your grudges entirely in this world, or you may be in trouble.>>

"I know," I grumbled, my head still aching from the legal document I'd been forced to read and still didn't exactly understand. Earth laws were needlessly complex, in my opinion.

<<I'll be keeping an eye on you, Hail. Good luck.>> I wouldn't hear from Thomas for some time after that, as he returned to whatever it was that he normally did when he wasn't busy escorting me.

Laurant, Tarisha, and I began exploring the nascent dungeon. When we poked the enemies, their information popped up, including Health pool and abilities. Laurant was fervently taking notes, while Tarisha was taking part in the conversation but still trying to contact her endgame friends through the Traveler communication networks.

"So, then. How long have you two been dating?" I asked.

The two froze for a second, then relaxed. Tarisha answered first. "I considered our first date to be the day that we took you out into the city so that Laurant could show you creative ways of bumping into solid objects and making a fool of yourself. *Lewis*, apparently, needed to be told more explicitly. So he didn't actually figure it out until you made us canon, and I called him my boyfriend."

"Oh," I said. "Well, I'm happy for both of you. What's this Gemini thing, anyway? You're trying to each have a kid like me, right?"

"That's correct," Tarisha said, leaving aside her messages for a moment. "Hail, you should realize, your existence was created by an experiment. You have a physical body on Earth and a digital one everywhere else. Or a light one, I guess, if you count the hologram we saw of you earlier. But your physical body is that of a small server cluster. You don't really have to know what that is, and it's fine you don't. But your soul is the only one occupying that particular server. As part of the experiment, Lewis and I are going to try to, well, share a second server that's otherwise identical to yours."

"Oh," I said. "I don't understand. But I think I'll be happy if it works. In fact, give me just a minute. I need to think of some words."

"Words for what?" Laurant asked.

"You'll see. Just let me think of them," I promised. "Let's go poke the final boss."

We explored the small dungeon all the way to the end. Both bosses were simply larger slimes. The second one, The Slime King, had multiple cores inside of it, which were weak points that needed to be destroyed. The first was simply a slime that applied both poison and acid Damage and was called The Cleaner.

"It's boring," I announced at the end.

"It's clean and efficient leveling," Tarisha countered. Which is exactly what was promised.

"I want to add the brownies and the imps to give the new players some sort of fun and a challenge. How do I do that?" I asked the open air.

"Simply take them out of your inventory and state your intention," Eclipse answered, proving that I was correct in assuming that she was still listening to me.

I did exactly that, and each core vanished as I fed it to the dungeon. Little outlines of the new enemies popped up all around us. The dungeon went from a two-boss event to a three-boss event as The Cleaner vanished. A prompt appeared to inform me that new evolution options were available, including the addition of four new bosses. I nodded in satisfaction.

"I didn't realize you could spend more than one core creating a dungeon," Tarisha said. "Perhaps we should go back and revisit the other two that you have created so far, Lord Hail. If you wish to spend the cores, then—"

"I need to go back to [Gemos Caverns] anyway," I agreed. "As for Mooncrest Manor, I was planning on challenging that myself when I reached the appropriate level. Is it fun?"

"It has ranked highly for that level range," Tarisha confirmed. "There are four bosses, and it's moderately challenging. It would be an interesting experiment to see how you are able to evolve an established dungeon."

I nodded in agreement with her. We gave Laurant some time to finish exploring the new bosses' mechanics, but ultimately, there was very little to do at this point. We returned to the entrance and stepped through. I wanted witnesses for what I had planned next. I'd prefer more friends from <Nethersong Mavericks>, but all I had at that moment were a smattering of goblin Natives. I decided that would do; I could always repeat my oath.

I instructed Marvin to gather as many of the goblin villagers together as he could. My friends, realizing something was about to happen, stood silently as I drew my sword, extended it hilt-first towards them, and knelt.

"I, Earl Hail Jeoran of House Jeoran, formerly Prince Hail Teoran, formally make this pledge to Tarisha Swordsong and Laurant Basak, as they are known in this world. You have informed me of your intention to have children in this world, and I pledge to these children the following things.

"I pledge my protection. My sword shall ever be raised in their defense. My armies shall bleed and die so that they will not. Should they ever encounter danger, it shall be because, like myself, they have sought it out themselves.

"I pledge the resources they need to grow. You have asked me for a vineyard. I will provide one. If you would prefer a rural cottage or a village house to raise your children, I will do my utmost to arrange its acquisition for you.

"Finally, I pledge my undying loyalty to the children of my two closest friends from Earth."

I held the position for a moment after finishing the pledge. Laurant whispered "Holy shit" to himself, but it was Tarisha who took the lead.

"Thank you, Hail. That pledge is more than we would ever have asked of you, but it means more to us than you can imagine. The fear that something would happen to me on Earth to prevent me from seeing my daughter has occurred to me. Knowing that she will always have a place in your House fills me with joy," Tarisha said eventually.

"Yeah, what she said," Laurant agreed.

With my oath accepted, I stood and sheathed my sword. "Of course, I don't mean to be involved in every step of the process. I mean, I don't even know how that works. I just—"

"We'll involve you in the important decisions when we can,

Hail," Tarisha said quickly. "Right now, we're still generating a seed of consciousness. It will take some time before it's ready to meld into the framework that will create a digital child. After that, Arc will take care of it for a while on Earth before injecting my daughter and Laurant's son into this world. We'll have to have a home ready and waiting for them, but we have some time yet to prepare. Your oath makes that much simpler. Thank you, Hail. From the bottom of my heart, I mean that."

"Yeah, what she said," Laurant repeated, and Tarisha nudged him in the ribs. Together, they bowed at me.

"I humbly and gratefully accept your oath of protection for my unborn daughter, Lord Hail," Tarisha said formally.

Laurant picked up on the cue she was laying down for him, and he, too, bowed. "I accept your oath of protection for my son. Assuming that it is a son. They said something about—"

Tarisha nudged him again.

"Never mind. Thank you, Hail. Now come on. Let's go see how your mother and brother are doing!"

4
WRONG ON PURPOSE

Tarisha had a two-seated flying mount thanks to a quest I had issued her not very long after we had met, but her wyvern couldn't support all three of us. I had bonded Shalasmir—the legendary shadow dragon whose soul my father had enslaved for all eternity to prevent it from ever harming anyone again—but neither my level nor my [Animal Handling] skill were high enough to allow me to fly. And, of course, Laurant needed to gain level eighty for his flying mount as well.

So I summoned Shadow, the mount my great-uncle Auroras had given me, and Laurant summoned a standard-issue horse that any Traveler could buy for about five gold. The mounts all appeared nearby in puffs of mist, although the system tried to hide the apparition of the mounts by having them appear somewhere that nobody was focused on. Shadow, however, literally split off from my shadow, becoming real from the darkness and appearing beside me. Unlike the others, Tarisha blew a flute and a white stag burst out from behind us.

"I don't usually show him off," she admitted. "It was one of the first rare drops I ever came across. I would have been better off selling it than binding it, but by the time I knew that it was too late. I think I'm going to start riding him again now that I'm full-time pro."

"My black stallion and your white stag contrast each other nicely," I admitted. "I like it."

"Isn't that thing worth like eight hundred dollars?" Laurant inquired.

"Thereabouts. Yes," Tarisha said. "Lord Hail, where are we heading?"

"I need to figure out where my mother is. I'm assuming that by now she's in Thorn March, and so I figure that Max Benarth, my Native steward in that land, is my best lead for tracking her down," I explained. "Unless you two know where she sheltered once she left Valerio's protection for mine."

"I know that Malkios was often seen patrolling various villas and vineyards, but I don't know that anyone ever laid eyes on Analise Teoran. I believe that she was moved around incognito," Tarisha admitted. "Lewis, do you have any idea?"

"I think this Benarth guy is the best lead. He's got to know," Laurant said. "I mean, I actually know who he is since he's been working so closely with Daemon in the version of this world that went on without you, Hail."

"Right. Let's get riding then," I said. I had pulled up the Fast Travel menu already, and it had informed me that it was unavailable while I was traveling through the Recent Past. Fortunately, my map remained filled in. We would be forced to ride through one uncharted area—uncharted to me, at least—but it looked like a straight line was available to reach the Benarth Vineyard.

The ride took more than thirty minutes, and I thoroughly enjoyed reestablishing my bond with Shadow, whom I had spoiled by giving a carrot *and* a large cube of sugar before mounting. We had to detour around several briar patches, and we chatted amiably along the way. Well, Lewis and I chatted. Tarisha was focused on communicating with her endgame contacts.

"So, what are you going to call them?" I asked as we rode.

"Call who?" Laurant asked.

"You two are having twin children like me, right? I assume you're going to name them something," I reminded him.

"Oh, yeah. We haven't decided yet for certain," Laurant admitted. "We have a few baby names picked out, but Arc promised to give us a call before they actually begin developing our seeds to confirm the data we want to use. I want to call them Palom and Porom."

"Why's that?" I asked.

"It's a reference to a very old game. Well, the original is old. It's been remade a few times since then. But there's a pair of twins, a boy and a girl, who you fight with. It just seems to fit," Laurant explained. "Tarisha doesn't like it because they have a bit of a sad story."

"You could call them Luke and Leia," I suggested.

Laurant looked at me, shocked. "Wait. You mean like Skywalker? That franchise is *ancient*."

"Gideon likes it. We talked about it for about an hour. That and *The Simpsons*. When I was on Earth, I was able to pull up some old entertainment. I didn't really *get it*. Everything was always bouncing off when it shouldn't be, or it cut through stuff even if it wasn't a critical hit. It was weird," I explained.

"Holy crap. They didn't let you watch *The Terminator*, did they?" he asked.

"What's that?"

"Nothing. It's a bad take on how things absolutely never could have possibly gone when we started playing around with artificial intelligences," Laurant said. "Forget I mentioned it."

"I'm really bad at forgetting things when I want to," I reminded him. "It's kind of annoying. But whatever, I have a brother who used to be my grandfather, so I don't really care about old . . . Is it a movie? TV show? Book?"

"No comment," Laurant said. "Hey, Tarisha, Hail thinks we should name our kids Luke and Leia."

"I think Arc would have to get copyright permission for that," Tarisha said without looking up.

"Nah, it's fair use, right?"

Tarisha grunted, and then she pulled her stag up beside me. "Lord Hail, it has taken some time, but I have finally put together ten qualified individuals to help us on our quests. Which makes thirteen of us, including me, you, and Laurant. Well, that makes twelve qualified individuals and Laurant, so it's not that unlucky."

"Hey!"

"Do I have your permission to summon your active bodyguards to the Recent Past, Hail?" she asked, shooting Laurant a look that I probably wasn't meant to understand. Teasing, I think.

"Are they all from <Peasant's Revenge>?" I asked.

"No. Once I, well, incorporated myself, I could no longer slot in more than two bodyguard positions per shift from my old guild," she explained. "The others are determined by auction or lot, depending on—"

"Your old guild? Did you leave?" I asked, surprised.

"Not exactly, but I moved on from my old position as a semi-pro 'seeker of new content' and moved up to 'canon character.' I draw a small stipend from my old guild and grant them certain privileges for supporting me in the past, but ultimately I'm self-employed. As you said once, I am your 'go-to liaison for the endgame guilds,' and I have been taking that position very seriously," she explained. "Now that you are active again, they are literally lining up to throw money at me to get to the front of the line."

I frowned. I didn't really have any trouble with her earning money acting as my liaison, but there was something that didn't sit well with me. It took me a moment to work it out. "I don't like the idea that the highest bidder gets my time. Or yours, Tarisha. I don't really care about the endgame or whatever you call the endless war at the borders of the Heartlands. I mean, I do, and I will in a few years when I'm level two hundred. But right now, I care more about building low-level dungeons for players to level in and issuing quests that are fun and challenging to make them *want* to stay in this world and push the borders outward."

Tarisha nodded as though my words were sagely. "The minimum condition for even earning my time is the completion of the quest 'Alliance with House Jeoran,' Hail. Only eight percent of the top five hundred guilds have put forth the effort to complete it at this point. Most are holding on to the old version of what's considered endgame, while others are waiting to see if opposing you will be more lucrative. I'm not talking to fence-sitters. And I'm only taking bids when it's proper to do so. Like when there's a limited slot to enter a unique instance, such as right now."

"And what will they do when your daughter and Laurant's son come in and tip over the metagame, or whatever you call it, once more?" I challenged.

"Increase my hourly rate," she said simply.

I laughed. "I think I might be glad I spent some time on Earth. I understand you Travelers so much better after being a Visitor. Even if I couldn't touch anything real."

For some reason that killed the flow of the conversation. After a pause, Tarisha confirmed whether or not she should summon my bodyguards.

"I want to split them in three teams when they arrive," I informed her. "If that makes a difference."

"It does," she confirmed. "What are their goals?"

"One team to go with Laurant to Ebbyvale as soon as possible to have him summon his constables and begin dealing with the bandit situation," I said. "Another to stay with me and you. The third to stay with my mother until you can assign her her own ten-man team again."

Tarisha nodded and once more began interacting with her interface at lightning speeds. "Okay. Summoning now."

A brief pause, and then mist and light began forming, coalescing into the forms of ten Travelers. Three of them were quite familiar. Phil's body formed, recognizable and distinct despite his change in attire. He wore a large star pinned to his chest, though for the life of me I didn't know why, since the item didn't seem to grant any attributes and had transmogrified his [Warrior] gear into a pair of leather boots, chaps, and a vest over a plaid shirt.

"What in tarnation is going on?" he demanded. "I just got a random summons from—oh, hey, Hail. Sorry, should have figured this was related to you somehow. You back for good now?"

"I think so?" I said. "Apparently I was detained because someone was harassing Nial Kingslayer, and that is unacceptable for some reason that I don't really understand or care about."

"Oh, so that's what this whole thing is about," Phil said, scratching the back of his head after pulling a straw hat off of it. "Sorry, kiddo, should have thought of that for you. Targeted PVP quests like that aren't *verboten*, but I can see Arc reacting the way they did to protect you."

"I don't want to talk about it anymore. What is wrong with your outfit?" I inquired.

"I'm a deputy. You like it?" he asked.

I stared at him for a moment longer. "Sure?" I said, then turned my attention to the others who had arrived. Lloyd and Rashid, the tank and healer who had once battled Gyudue of the Blackest Night with me, had joined as <Peasant's Revenge's> part of the summons. I greeted them and then turned my attention to the strangers.

Three of the members carried the guild tag from <Shadow's Valor>, a guild that I remembered had sought an alliance with me. Another two were from <Taegeuk>, and the final two were from two different guilds. They formed up and bowed to me.

Wrongly. Their hands were literally backward from how they should be.

"Who taught you to bow like that?" I asked. Not offended, just curious.

One member of <Taegeuk> froze, and the others all looked at each other in confusion. "Is this not the proper Yuikonese bow?" he asked.

"It's fine," I said. "It just makes you look like a bumpkin who's never actually been to court. Like I said, who taught you that."

"We learned from your Master of Ceremony, Irvine," one of the players from <Shadow's Valor> explained. "He is always available in Ebbyvale to teach the proper methods of showing respect to Yuikonese nobles. We thought—"

"My stableboy?" I asked. "You've been taking bowing lessons from my stableboy? I mean, it doesn't matter. I was just about to tell you not to bother with the whole pomp thing, but then you all did it wrong in exactly the same way, so I got curious. Who said that Irvine was my Master of Ceremony?"

Phil and Laurant began laughing their asses off.

"Oh, it was a collaborative effort," Phil said. "Everyone in the Mavericks worked hard on it, Milord. We wanted to surprise you. Wanted to—"

"We taught him everything he knows, except for how to bow," Laurant said, talking over Phil. "But we taught him wrong on purpose and told everyone else that—"

"It's been spreading throughout the noble courts, actually," Tarisha said, interrupting them both. "I'm afraid that a lot of your knowledge of protocol is out of date, Lord Hail. There is the old style of formality, and there is the new style, which is the result of 'teaching Irvine to do stuff wrong on purpose.' Most of your allies in the nobility are subscribing to the new style."

I considered the exchange in confusion for a moment, and then I burst into laughter. "Whatever. I hated learning all of that stuff in the first place. Come on, let's get going again!"

5

DUNGEON MASTER I

Tarisha took charge of the new arrivals marvelously, putting my plan into action. Four of the group, including Phil and Laurant, would soon leave us to travel by horseback to North Shire. When there, they would activate their personal summoning abilities as my head constable—or deputy, as he insisted upon calling himself—and a lieutenant in my army, respectively.

"There shouldn't be any other Travelers in this timeline yet," she said. "But the bandits have been showing some flexibility in their levels when they're caught on their own. Be safe."

"The goal isn't to eradicate the bandits while we're in our own little world," I reminded them. "It's to get set up so that when I cast [Summon Karmic Warrior] or start a battleground, we'll have the strongest advantage we can. Phil and Laurant, once you cross the border into North Shire, you can use your own summoning abilities to bring in the constables and my army."

"Eventually our actions will be noticed by the metagame community," Tarisha pointed out. "Especially another battleground."

"I know," I said. "I'll be counting on you to keep them off my back, Tarisha."

We spoke for a while about what had happened in the world before I'd arrived in the Recent Past, and it sounded like not very much had changed since I'd been forced out of it by the administration, except for a wave of goblin Travelers sweeping through the ranks. There were apparently already goblins out there who were riding wyvern mounts like Tarisha's, and a few had even been power-leveled to take part in endgame raids.

My involvement in releasing the goblins was widely rumored, but it was only rumored. The few goblins who had managed to get the [First!] achievement—which had been accompanied by getting slaughtered by the Native goblins immediately after passing through the origin point—had seen me. But the details and mechanics behind releasing them weren't being broadcast, so a lot of Travelers speculated that I had simply convinced the village elder to unjam the gate or something.

But other than the goblins, everything in the Near Future had simply stagnated without me. Well, that was likely to change soon enough.

We split our party into two, with Laurant, Lewis, and the two members from <Taegeuk> taking the proposed route to Ebbyvale.

"This would be faster if everyone had a flying mount," one of the endgamers complained.

"Escort missions always suck, even when you're the one being escorted," Laurant said, commiserating with him. "I'm sorry that the two player characters with unique mass-summoning powers were so inconsiderate as to not dump five thousand hours of their life into virtual reality already, just for your convenience."

The woman who had spoken grumbled but accepted the point, and they rode off at speed. The rest of us kicked our own mounts into a gallop as we neared the Benarth Vineyards. The journey hadn't progressed much farther when I received a sudden prompt and pulled Shadow to a halt.

Action of Note Recognized! You have successfully created 3 dungeons. You earn the Title: Dungeon Creator. Title synergy noticed: Castle Buster (upgraded form of Dungeon Buster). Progress towards synergistic Title: Dungeon Manipulator recognized. Progress towards synergistic Title: Dungeon Reclaimer recognized. Progress towards synergistic Title: Dungeon Challenger recognized. Sufficient credit exists to combine these Titles. Would you like to combine these Titles into the Title: Dungeon Master I?	
Yes	No

"Is everything all right, Lord Hail?" Tarisha inquired, riding her stag back towards me while keeping an eye on the surroundings.

"I got an unexpected prompt. I think the dungeon I created has finished forming, and that kicked off something unexpected," I explained. "The system wants to either give me a new Title or to evolve the Title I got for being part of the raid on [Zhesa Castle]."

I read off the prompt to her, and she nodded gravely. "I think you should combine the Titles, Lord Hail. It sounds to me like the most powerful of all of the individual options. It might bring with it powerful new abilities and options."

I nodded and selected "Yes."

Castle Buster, Dungeon Creator, and progress towards three unclaimed Titles have been combined to form Title: Dungeon Master I.   Continue to create, destroy, and manipulate dungeons to evolve Title further.   Confirm Title Evolution? (This action cannot be undone)

Yes	No

I again reported the prompt to Tarisha, who nodded seriously. "It will be interesting to see what new abilities it comes with. For now, we should press on."

And so we did.

As had happened the last time I had visited this place, the Natives were out in the field, and the first to come over to investigate the strange party of Travelers was the little girl to whom I had given a vanity pet. The metal golem, called Sir William Von Barutasburg, followed quickly behind her. She had a stick in her hand, and she had been dueling the little thing while the adults worked.

"Do you have any more presents for me?" she demanded immediately. If I had been expecting a more formal greeting than last time, I was to remain disappointed.

"I'm sorry. You'll have to get by with Sir William Von Barutasburg for a while yet," I said.

"Oh, that's all right. He's pretty great, actually. Now that I know how to dismiss him so that he doesn't watch me sleep, at least, I really like him. I'm going to keep him with me forever!"

If vanity pets could look smug, this one would look smug.

"We're looking for your father again," I told the girl.

No sooner had I spoken the intention than she turned over her shoulder and shouted "PAAAAAH! The Important people are back! The ones with the capital I's!"

"What's your name?" I asked the girl abruptly.

"Min," she said promptly, and then she ran off to play with Sir William Von Barutasburg. Max Benarth arrived shortly, looking as dirty and well worked as ever but happy and wholesome for it.

"She hasn't shut up about your gift from last time, you know," he commented as he approached. "So, as her father, I suppose I must express a bit of proper gratitude."

He bowed to me, and to my slight amusement it was "The Irvine Bow," as I was coming to think of it.

"It's really nothing," I said. "I had fifty of them. They're of no use except to play with, so why not give them to a child?"

"It hasn't been so long since you were a child yourself, my lord," said Max. "In case you have forgotten."

"I know," I said. "But it doesn't feel that way. Now, please tell me, is my mother in the March? Where is she?"

"You're in luck, my lord," Max informed me, "For, although that guardian of hers has insisted upon shifting her around from estate to estate for her protection, she is currently located quite near here."

"That's wonderful news. Thank you, Max."

"Two more things," my steward said. "Would you like me to summon your household staff from the Near Future? And as to your brother, what status does he hold in your house?"

I cocked my head. I hadn't thought of the possibility that Natives would be able to bridge the gap of time between the Near Future and the Recent Past. The questions were so surprising that I took several moments to consider them.

"As to my brother, he is part of House Teoran, not House Jeoran," I said finally. "And House Wildeheart, I suppose. I am a bastard and can claim kinship to him, so I do. He is ever welcome in my holdings, and all of my resources shall be made available to him for his protection and upbringing while he is too young to care for himself. Does that answer that question?"

"It does," Max agreed. "And your staff? Should I summon them?"

"Sure," I said. "Start with Daemon and let him determine who else can come through. Where will they arrive?"

"I will send them into the parlor to wait for you. It may take some time, as the journey back in time must be taken willingly, and not everyone who is eligible may wish to come at first," Max said.

"Just give them the option and as much information as they need to make the decision," I suggested. "We're not at an 'all-hands-on-deck' point yet. But we could use a few more Travelers running around completing non-combat objectives."

"Of course. I shall go and ring the [Gong of Servant Summoning]," Max said, and he departed while the rest of us remounted and rode in the direction he had indicated to find my mother. I was, aside from Tarisha, surrounded by strangers, but I was in high spirits as we trotted our mounts through the open country and around the occasional briar patch.

Conveniently, the estate that mother was resting in was the same one that housed my throne for Thorn March, which would allow me to complete multiple objectives in the same visit. I didn't have all of the same options as the one in North Shire, as some of the features of the thrones were specific to their geography, but it would allow me to update my overall objectives and to write a new quest for my guardians.

I had already asked, and nobody had managed to rescue my throne from Mooncrest Manor before it became a dungeon. I had too low of a level to retrieve it myself, but the elite Travelers that Tarisha had lined up for my bodyguards would likely suffice. I didn't think they would even need me in their party to bring them into the core instance for it.

The villa itself was beautiful. While the vines outside were too small to call a proper vineyard, they provided the household with enough thornberry to make its own vintage of wine every year. The architecture was mostly brick, with a slate arched roof and magical windows that allowed perfect vision through them while keeping the weather out. The inside, I knew, was even cozier. I couldn't think of a better place for my brother to have been born.

A figure with a billowing blue cape rode out to meet us, [Warhammer] in hand and a dappled brown-and-white gelding beneath him. Malkios was in full Royal Guard dress armor, and on his chest was the thundercloud of House Teoran, signifying that he was a true royal knight. He had seen us coming somehow and was prepared to greet us whether we were friend or foe.

"Malkios!" I called. "Oh, it is good to see you again! How is my mother? And my brother? Is he born yet? I fear I have been trapped on Earth for some time and am not certain of the canon date yet."

Malkios reacted to my call by hoisting his weapon in a salute. "Do you bring friends and support to the Lady Teoran, your mother, Hail Jeoran?"

"I do, Malkios. Of course I do!" I called back.

"Then I greet you as a comrade in arms back from the campaign," Malkios called. "No longer will I treat you like the little scamp who must be watched, lest he skip out on his studies."

His [Warhammer] vanished into his inventory, and the former captain of the Royal Guard rode out to meet us with only his sidearm, a gladius, equipped on his belt. "You say you have been to Earth? That must have been an exciting adventure, Lord Hail," Malkios said.

I snorted. "I was trapped in a magical room for weeks while months flew by on Lagrea. It is only by the will of the Administrators—their wish that I not be absent for too long from the story of this world— that I have been sent into the Recent Past. I ask again, how is my mother? Is my brother born yet?"

"She is resting comfortably," Malkios informed me. "And the babe has a pair of lungs on him that will put pride in his father's heart, once he bonds his ancestral spirit. He may be squalling now, but in a few months, he will be roaring like the Leonid he is!"

I grinned, and I motioned to the four who had agreed to become my mother's personal guard. "Malkios, I give these four men and women to your command, for the purpose of keeping my mother and younger brother safe. They are at your disposal."

Malkios scratched his beard. "I see. I shall find a use for them somewhere," he promised. And his voice sounded both amused, playful, and dangerous.

6
RAIN

Distantly, I heard a gong sound, but I paid it no mind as I left my companions behind to enter the villa where my mother was convalescing after giving birth to a healthy baby boy—my little brother, whom I knew housed the spirit of my grandfather, the former king. It was a little strange to think of, and I had been considering spreading the word about this fact, but I had ultimately decided to tell nobody who I had not already shared the secret with.

A maid answered the door when I knocked and, at a nod from Malkios, brought me directly into Mother's sitting room, where she was working on her correspondence. She looked up at me when I was led into the room, and her smile was beautiful.

"Welcome home, Hail. I've been waiting for you," she said.

"Waiting for me?" I asked.

"To name your brother. I figured I should give you some input. Valerio and I were all but set on Rain, after my father, but I was worried that it would always be associated with—"

"Rain is a good name," I said. "Don't worry, Mother. What I witnessed that day was horrible, but I am moving past it. I *will* see Nial Kingslayer brought to justice, both in this world and on Earth. That is part of what has kept me away for so long. One day I will leave again in order to face him on Earth, in whatever capacity I can."

Mother was impassive. Finally, she nodded. "I see. You must do what you feel is correct. I was never the right one to guide you in the matters of your heart, Hail. You are too different from me and the other Natives, and too much like the Travelers. It must be hard on you. I am your mother, but I feel we have never truly been able to connect."

"Don't say that," I said. "It's true that you put a lot of responsibility onto Beckah when I was younger, but you're the one I love as my mother."

Analise Teoran smiled. "Then I shall accept your love, Hail, for as long as you are willing to give it."

"Until the closing of the gates and the death of this world itself," I vowed.

"That sounds like a lot of love," she said, teasing. "Are you certain you'll have enough for me and still find some for the others in your life?"

"I'm sure I'll manage," I teased back. "How is my brother?"

"It was an easy birth," she assured me. "Just like you were. He is resting now—"

An infant's squalling contradicted her, and she smiled. "Well, he was. Come meet him."

I followed mother into the room that had been set up to be my brother's nursery. Rather than repainting the walls, sheets had been hung up with patterns embroidered into them designating the histories of Houses Teoran and Wildeheart. The infant himself, perhaps two or three days old, was in a cradle, and he was a noisy little thing.

Mother diagnosed him simply by his cries, and I stood in the corner awkwardly as he was changed. Afterward, she encouraged me to spend some time with him and left me alone so that she could go lay down. I sat next to the crib and rocked it, thinking. If this was truly my grandfather's spirit, there were so many things I wanted to say to him. But he was an infant; what would he possibly understand?

I decided to hold him, and so I carefully lifted him out of the cradle—

<<You're doing that wrong. Support the head,>> Grandfather's annoyed voice called out to me, and I was so startled that I . . . did not react well. The infant's body was launched into the air by my surprised action. I panicked, but rather than fall, the infant simply hovered there, looking at me with a judgmental expression on his face.

<<Yes, I have decided that it will *not* be part of this boy's story that he was dropped on his head by his brother within days of being born. Come, Hail, pick me up and put me back in the crib before I run out of Mana.>>

I jumped to comply, carefully lowering the infant back into the cradle, this time being more careful to support his neck. That was a thing you were supposed to do, right?

"Grandfather?" I asked.

<<Yes. It was decided between me and the administration team that, once I inhabited this new form, I would be allowed to communicate with you in this manner. It will be some time before you are ready to truly manage without my advice, and I will not be able to provide it contextually in this body for at least three or more canon years,>> Grandfather's disembodied voice explained.

"That's . . . I was worried, and now I am relieved. You are not truly gone after all," I said, and a burden left me, which I had not realized I had been bearing.

<<I am only dead in the context of the old King Rain, who ruled Yuikon when you were born and oversaw much of your early childhood,>> Grandfather explained. <<You have done well in my absence, I think. A little bit chaotic, but chaos is good sometimes, despite what the priests of Thedum teach. If a structure cannot weather a storm, then it is not an orderly structure. It should be torn down and built anew. That is a true teaching of Thedum.>>

I brushed the wisdom aside and turned towards my mother's room. "Does she know what or who you really are?"

<<In a way, she understands better than you do. But she will never acknowledge it unless you specifically tell her in terms that you both understand,>> Grandfather explained. <<Now, then. You have discovered that one of the gifts I left for you requires a bit of hard work to return to working order, yes? Let us talk about your plans for North Shire for a while, before it is time for my nap.>>

It was good to get advice from my grandfather once more, even though it came from the body of an infant. He was unrepentant about the messages he had had me send on his behalf—the ones that had been mostly veiled insult—stating that I needed to establish myself as an independent force within the nobility if I wanted to get anywhere. If my potential allies would not overlook a minor insult to become my friend, then they were not worth trusting. And insulting my likely enemies was a good way of preventing them from playing me with false friendships before I knew better.

But of course he would justify himself. I decided to put the entire mess in the past. My time with Auroras in the Deadlands had been unpleasant, but I had gotten a number of useful skills out of it, and the insults I had delivered on Grandfather's behalf were part of the reason.

As for everything that had happened since, Grandfather's spirit wholeheartedly approved. He gave me a note or two about my future plans and highlighted certain abilities that I should have access to through my throne. And he clarified a number of questions I'd had about battlegrounds, which I knew now to ask after having created one and hadn't known to ask before.

I had spent a total of eleven of the one hundred dungeon cores that I had gained from [Zhesa Castle]. I had gained eight cores from the busting of Mikal Mines but had given one of them to my step-father, Valerio, to be sold to the Eolstrian royal family. I had a sum total of ninety-six cores remaining. And I was willing to spend no less than twenty of them purging my lands of bandits and building dungeons to draw Travelers from far and wide to North Shire.

I was quite certain that the new Title I had gained would be helpful on that front. But when I had planned to create five dungeons for North Shire and five for Thorn March, I had intended to spend only a single core on each dungeon. I could see now that one hundred cores was not nearly the fortune I had once dreamed it to be.

I would have to establish a renewable source of dungeon cores if I were to continue to spend them like candy. I wondered if I could challenge a dungeon not to evolve, destroy, or reclaim it, but with the sole intent of farming cores from it as a reward. I would have to try it; perhaps it was an option with my new Title.

I would likely have to enter the core instance to do so and declare an intent. I was uncertain what effect that would have on the difficulty of the challenge. It would probably be less than destroying the dungeon but more than evolving it. However, I had never intentionally evolved a dungeon before; the closest I had come was my clearing of the original version of [Gemos Caverns]. Thankfully, there were hundreds of dungeons in the world to experiment on, once I wasn't worried about gaining levels any longer.

Once I had finished visiting with my mother and my grandfather's spirit—within my new brother's body—I left the building to find Tarisha, Lloyd, Rashid, and two Travelers I didn't know yet, ones who had paid to be in this position. I hoped I was about to make it worth their while.

"Please tell me if what I say does not generate a quest," I began. "Tarisha, I wish for you to lead this group to Mooncrest Manor and reclaim my throne, which is trapped within the dungeon. Move it into the Temple of Thedum; I shall govern from there until my new manor is built by Randal, the architect."

"Quest accepted," Tarisha said immediately, and she was echoed by the five others. "But what of you, Lord Hail?"

"The guards left with Malkios will be enough to keep me safe until the Recent Past collides with the Near Future," I assured her. "I still haven't had enough time to explore all of the abilities and options that my throne gives me. When I arrive in North Shire, I intend to have an exact plan to end the Northridge Freelancers once and for all."

Tarisha hesitated, then her hesitation fled, and she took on a determined expression. "As you wish, Lord Hail. We will race there and back as swiftly as our mounts will take us. In the meantime, should you need anything, please reach out to me."

I nodded in gratitude, and we split ways. I returned inside to the parlor, where my throne sat. I didn't sit in it immediately, however. I had other business to attend to, which I did not wish anyone to witness.

One of my pastimes while I had been trapped on Earth had been to watch the videos of the great Traveler warriors. I had noticed something vital when doing so; a difference between me and them, where I was sorely lacking.

My HUD was crap. I had set it up to be as unobtrusive as possible because I hadn't known how to interpret the information it had been feeding me at the time. So I had simply closed the windows, or hidden them, or moved them into the corner of my vision where they were out of the way.

I knew better now. It was time to set myself up with a proper interface.

7

BATTLE CORE

Guild MotD	Yes, everyone, we have confirmed that little brother is back in the game. No, we don't know where. His location is listed as "the Recent Past." Updates on the website in real time.
Hail	Hey, everyone. Yes, I'm back. Also, I figured out how to turn mentions on, so . . . um, you guys talk about me a lot? Or does it just seem that way? I had chat minimized 95% of the time before, but now it seems like I have a blinking bumblebee in the corner of my eye all of the time. It's kind of annoying.
Stan	Hail, holy shit. How are you?
Zebras	Hail, WB! Sorry if we're blowing up your icon. We're excited.
Malick	WTF is the Recent Past and how do we get there to help you, Hail?
Worple	Corinth says hi. He's trying to solo that new dungeon you created. He says it's wicked awesome, btw.
Peafowlet	Hail, we heard you were stuck on Earth. Did Arc let you go?
Gummytiger	I just realized that under location there's an icon, and if you focus on it, it says "the Near Future." Holy crap, Arc is pulling a time paradox on us!

Softspook	You can't have time paradoxes. They either resolve themselves or destroy the universe.
Potatoad	This is a video game, nerd.
April	Hail, what level are you? Still high 30s?
Wesle	Hail, I know where three of the hideouts for the bandits are. Or were. They got raided by an endgame guild a while ago and haven't respawned, but they might help you if you're in the past.
Zebras	Guys, try to calm down. It's not like he hasn't done this to us before.
Daemon	Hail, give me a moment to respond to the gong. I am putting affairs in order, to bring the greatest number of helpers with me as possible by expanding your household staff at the last moment. I have a while left on the timer, but it seems that this is a one-way trip.

I minimized my guildchat window again, then looked at my HUD with satisfaction. It now more closely resembled those of some of the more powerful and successful Travelers whose videos I had watched through the forums while on Earth. I had cooldown timers, debuff duration reminders, and cast-time estimators all in convenient places, which would not distract me.

Considering that I had been virtually winging it before without any of those things, I was certain that my performance was about to take a solid shot upwards. However, I didn't need any of that right now, so I switched it back into social mode and checked in with the two parties I had sent out on quests.

Tarisha's group hadn't yet outrun Phil and Laurant's, but I expected it was only a matter of time. My shire deputy and the lieutenant of my growing army were both bound to the land, while Tarisha's group had swift-flying mounts, which would eat up the leagues rapidly. One of the Travelers had attempted to open a portal to shorten the trip considerably, but they had gotten a message that portals were "temporally unavailable while in the Recent Past."

After I'd satisfied myself that I'd done everything I could do, I returned to the study where my throne for Thorn March rested, and I took a seat. And once more I delved deep into the menus that represented the support system that helped me generate quests. There was a lot I had to do, and most of it was experimentation. I hadn't really had all that much time to grow familiar with the features before I had been ejected from the world previously. Every time I had scratched the surface, I had found a new layer of paint beneath that represented an entire subsystem, which helped me interact with the world-system directly.

Not that I could control most of them, of course. But there were a few that I needed to figure out for when I returned to North Shire. My return would be one of either triumph or humiliation, and I didn't like to look foolish.

Reputation-wise, I had more people actively in the corner of House Jeoran than ever before, although my personal Reputation remained unchanged, mostly. The completion of the guild alliance quest gave a significant boost, as did the handful of quests that I had written personally before my disappearance, despite the fact that they had been issued by Malkios or one of my other more powerful associated quest givers.

I was pleased and annoyed with the success of those quests. Pleased because the quests were to literally keep my brother and mother safe if I was unavailable for any reason. Annoyed because the quests had been issued 11,255 times and completed 8,084 times. That marked it as a very successful quest line by the system's standards, but it meant that threats to my family existed.

I had more than just a complete/dropped/failed/incomplete ratio, however. I had detailed reports issued from the Travelers in question to Malkios himself. I quickly began to run through the more common tropes, to identify where they were coming from.

Storm, mostly. But also a few nobles from Eolstree who viewed baby Rain as a threat. I committed the names to memory. I am very good at remembering things when I want to, and I was determined to see those who would threaten either my mother or my brother have their malice repaid.

I was amused to note that six of the guilds that had completed the quest for an alliance had done so by killing Nial Kingslayer. I found it strange that the company that created my world had no issue with that quest, but had taken me out of Lagrea for weeks because someone had broken the windows of his apartment. Something that I hadn't known about or had any control over at all!

A part of me wanted to wallow in the unfairness of all of that, but I knew I didn't have time. Eventually, someone outside of my circle of trust would realize that something was "changing the past" of Yuikon and people would begin investigating. Tarisha had warned me that this event would likely blow up larger than any of my previous ones. She didn't know the half of it, because I hadn't told her the capstone yet. I had wanted to make certain that it would work.

And now, sitting on my secondary throne, I knew that it was possible. From my inventory, I selected five cores in preparation. I pulled them from my inventory one by one and fed them into the system menu, each core unlocking more and more options. The [Dungeon Daughter Cores] vanished unused, but when I finalized all of my selections, one single item was returned.

> Battle Core: The Battle for North Shire has been received!
> 17/17 uses remain.
> Reduced Death Penalty selected for all player participants.

I smiled in satisfaction. This was how battlegrounds were meant to be generated. What I had done before had been done in panic. I had echoed the words my grandfather had spoken, and the system had done the rest. This method was better.

I put the [Battle Core] into my inventory before anyone saw the multicolored, multifaceted jewel. Nobody but a Native would know what it was, and I doubted that anyone in my household would snitch on me.

With this core, I could generate up to seventeen battlegrounds. It hadn't cost me seventeen dungeon cores, but five. I could have gotten a full fifty battlegrounds out of that many cores, but I had chosen options that had reduced the available number. If it took more than seventeen battles to secure my land, then I would be in trouble.

The [Battle Core] was perhaps the most potent item I had ever held, but it was much more limited compared to a simple dungeon core. It could only be used to generate battles between my faction and factions invading my lands. I could reuse it, in fact, if I managed to clear out the bandits with charges remaining.

However, the Travelers on my side must have established a link to my House, or to my enemies, before the beginning of the battle, or they would be marked as a mercenary. Participation would still reach out to all Travelers in my world, both those in the Near Future and the Recent Past, which was why I was planning on waiting in the Recent Past and preparing for a few days before triggering the first of the battles.

Because once that happened, the Recent Past was about to smash into the Near Future. One of the timelines was going to be obliterated, leaving only shattered remnants of those unwilling to go on, and I was quite certain it wasn't mine.

Daemon arrived an hour after the creation of the [Battle Core]. And he wasn't alone. A hundred Travelers of various races were accompanying him, including a distinct twenty goblins. Which surprised me, since goblin Travelers hadn't been around long enough for me to have hired them into my household before being whisked away to Earth, but I guess the entire point of having a steward is that they are able to make decisions on your behalf while you're unavailable.

Like the decision to expand your household to include a hundred people, with twenty goblins among them.

I heard the procession from my throne room, and I decided to go out and meet them. Wearing my [Golem Crafter's Coat], which looked something like a suit from Earth with inch-wide stripes of blue and silver making a spiraling pattern along the length of it, and my [Nagaskin Cloak], a heavy leather cloak of a deep blue color, I felt that I looked quite impressive.

That was, of course, in addition to my natural good looks and unique coloring. My suit highlighted my black hair with its silver highlights, and my heterochromatic eyes were perhaps the most distinctive feature of my face. If I weren't going out to meet friends, I would cast [Illusion Magic: Disguise], which made my appearance less distinctive. Especially to Natives, for some reason. It had just reached level five the last time I'd used it, and now it would also obscure the details of my clothes to make them look like more ordinary items, rather than the unique boss drops that they were.

I wondered if I should get a tie. I had an [Amulet of Lesser Insight], but people from Earth all wore ties when they dressed in suits. I'd ask Daemon; he seemed like a stylish guy. I really couldn't figure out why I'd been so standoffish with him to begin with. Now that I'd gotten to know him, I was growing to like him. Maybe he was just that sort of person.

The others were all gathering outside the building, having been directed there by Max Benarth once the summons had come through. Daemon tried to impose some sort of order, but these were Travelers, so there was gossiping and talking and laughing. It was great, and I was sort of sorry to ruin it by walking out the door.

Daemon had been watching for me, and as soon as I emerged, he bowed deeply. "Lord Hail. We have come at your call to the Recent Past, to serve you," he said.

Half of the assembled Travelers copied him; the others reacted in various other ways. Half of the goblins began jumping up and down and running around me in a circle, thanking me effusively for unlocking their race.

I began scanning around the crowd using [Analyze], and I quickly noticed something. "Nobody here is higher than level sixty," I commented. "Nobody except you, at least, Daemon. And nobody has the [Veteran of Mooncrest Manor] Title active."

Daemon nodded. "Indeed. It was a strict limitation on the portal that brought us here," he explained. "I gathered up everyone who was eligible and interested, but we're not likely to be of much use to you in combat. Most of us have given up on that aspect of competition in this game and compete in other ways. Don't worry, we'll prove our worth. Just don't expect us to carry the battlegrounds, and we'll complete your non-combat objectives just fine."

I nodded. Then I bowed formally to the assembled crowd, the way that a lord bows to honor his servants. "Thank you all for coming. I'm sure that I will make good use of your services very soon. If there is anyone skilled with tending infants, please raise your hand."

Twelve hands immediately shot into the air. But that was only ten volunteers because two of the goblins had raised both hands at once.

8

PORTAL FACILITY

The arrival of Daemon and his small horde of workers was fortunate, both in its timing and in its ability to expand my goals. I had accomplished everything I thought that I could accomplish with the throne in Thorn March. Tarisha would recover my throne in North Shire from the dungeon in which it had been enshrined, and then it would be time to act for real.

Or, at least, that's as far as the Traveler's perspective was concerned. I wasn't a Traveler. They called me an NPC, but I had decided that that term, at least when used to describe me, meant "Native player character." This was my world, and I couldn't just log out of it like the Travelers could. Which meant that I needed to prepare for the political ramifications and the possible fallout of failure.

I gave my workers over to the Native head of the household and had them put to work while I returned to my office with Daemon. He immediately opened a trade window with me and transferred twelve million gold.

"I had access to your vanity pet collection while you were on Earth," he explained. "I haven't sold more than a tenth of it yet. I'm trickling them out for maximum profit, and I have a few expenses for you to approve. But we'll overcome the debt issue in North Shire based on your vanity pets alone. I'm quite certain of it," Daemon said smugly.

"That's great, Daemon," I said. "But we're not paying back a copper until I've talked to the judge who issued the decree saying that the banks couldn't claim tax revenue towards the debt."

Daemon stiffened slightly, and I looked at him accusingly.

"Have you been making payments while I was gone?" I asked.

He looked sheepish. It's strange to see a sheepish looking person who has a handlebar mustache. "Please forgive me, Hail. I know you said to freeze the accounts, but, well, servicing the bank loans just seemed like my fiduciary duty. It was only about twenty thousand gold off of the sum that I just transferred you, after all."

"Was that before or after now?" I questioned, and the man looked stupefied at the question, so I realized I needed to clarify. "Check the canon date, Daemon, and try to remember if you began repaying the banks before or after it. Although, either way, that gold is probably lost to time. But the answer to my question may be important."

"I'll check with Benarth to get the date," he promised, then he pulled a ledger from his inventory. "I won't have to rely on my memory; I know exactly what I've done with every copper I've spent on your behalf. Would you like to go over the details?"

"Perhaps when we have more time," I said, and to my surprise I wasn't dreading it. Daemon seemed to have been taking the responsibilities I had heaped on him very seriously; the least I could do was let him make his report. In fact, I was kind of looking forward to spending time with the old man. "Daemon, you have a daughter, don't you? How is she doing?"

Daemon reacted with surprise to my words, then his face broke into a grin. "She lives with her mother, so I don't get to see her as often as I'd like, but I'm damn proud of her. She's an honor student, like I was at that age, and she's not too old to come to her old man for advice. I think that will change once she starts needing advice about boys, but we're not at that stage quite yet."

"Being my steward doesn't take time away from you being a father, does it?" I inquired.

"Not at all. I would have quit if it did, Hail. No offense, but you are second on my list of priorities, and the first is several ladder rungs above you," Daemon explained.

I nodded. "Good. Family is important. Does she come to this world?"

"She's made some noise about saving up for a helmet but hasn't put forth the effort yet. If she gets serious about it, I'll meet her halfway with the cost and try to give her a good start in the game," Daemon explained.

"If she ever does come, let me know, and I'll try to line up some quests just for her," I promised. "Well, the system will probably use them for everyone after she's done with them, but she'll be the first one I issue them to."

We discussed his daughter for a while longer, before Daemon returned his focus to the matters at hand. "Hail, I have several ideas on how to spend the gold I just gave you. I *could* have made those decisions myself while you were on Earth but chose to hold onto it until you arrived."

"That's good because if you had invested in any infrastructure, the gold might have been lost," I answered. "I'm not exactly certain how the recursion is going to work. We might get refunded for efforts like that, or we might not. I see you managed to bring Randal with the servants. Would you ask him if he can begin designing forts and siege equipment to be built in North Shire? We're going to face a series of battles soon, and we need to start getting prepared."

"What will you be doing?" Daemon inquired.

"Generating quests and quest items for the loyal friends you have brought me, of course," I said, pulling from my inventory a stack of blank paper, a bottle of blue ink, and a quill. With a wave of my hand, I [Enchanted Ink and Parchment] and, sitting at a desk, began to go to work.

Daemon nodded, and even seemed excited. "I'll let others know. It will raise morale to know that you'll have something for them to do soon."

He placed a sheet of paper on my desk for me to reference. It listed the Travelers who had accompanied him, their classes, and their skills. To my surprise, one person, a player named Zimmer, was listed with his primary qualification being his reputation with the Beggar's Court. I was uncertain how that collection of ruined and penniless nobility viewed me, but perhaps it was time to find out. Especially since I was likely going to be forced to drag the late Lord Mooncrest's name through the dirt in order to accomplish my goals.

With my resources laid out in front of me, I quickly got to work putting my [Scribing] skill through its paces. Winning the day would take more than strength of arms, and if my early teachers in [Zhesa Castle] had ever managed to teach me anything useful, it was that, of the pen and the sword, the pen was the mightier weapon.

I leveled [Scribe] all the way to level ten, [Scribe: Copy Document] to level five, and [Scribe: Forge Document] to level four.

Throughout the process, I periodically asked Daemon questions about what had happened in the timeline that had produced the Near Future. I'd had similar discussions with Tarisha and Laurant, but Daemon had a significantly different perspective, and I found that he was able to fill in key details or correct gaps in my knowledge that required me to shift my strategy considerably.

Once I had run out of documents to write, I returned to my throne, where I was notified that several new quest items had been generated and were waiting for assignment to Travelers. It also gave me the ability to tweak the parameters of the quests themselves. Pleased that the system was working as I'd envisioned, I returned to work.

Occasionally, I was forced to scrap a document and [Re-Scribe] it from the beginning to create the conditions I wanted, but mostly, any modification to the quests could be made through the throne itself.

Finally satisfied with my plans, I opened another menu that I had explored but never been able to do much with due to a lack of resources.

[Regional Management: North March].

After a moment, I found the option I was looking for, and I spent ten of the twelve million gold that Daemon had just given me on a single purpose, which would take twenty-four game hours to create itself.

<table>
<tr><td>
You have selected to create a dual-direction Portal Facility in Thorn March of the Recent Past!
This action will carry over into the Near Future!
This beacon is capable of connecting with any similar beacon located within Yuikon, Eolstree, Verindale, Aeridia, Caeloria, Valorica, Wynthorne, Zenitha, Crescentis, Kordock, or Hormonica.
Construction cost: 10,000,000 gold.
Outgoing portal cost: 15 gold.
Incoming portal cost: 3 gold.
Toll paid to beacon owner on use: 3 gold.
Confirm the creation of this beacon?
</td></tr>
</table>

Yes	No

I was slightly surprised at just how far this portal would be able to reach. Every nation in the Heartlands was listed! I had a moment of hesitation, as not all of the nations listed were friendly with the nation of Yuikon. However, I was ultimately planning for the future, and the ability to travel anywhere from my base of power was vital to my future development. I selected "Yes," and the gold was taken from my inventory.

An Action of Note has occurred within the Recent Past! This will resonate in the Near Future! The addition of Briarton to the portal network will occur in 24hrs game time in the Recent Past, 78hrs game time in the Near Future. Travel from the Near Future to the Recent Past will be possible at this beacon. With the creation of a new portal in the network, all Portal Beacons have stabilized within the Recent Past. Would you like to configure the Briarton Portal Beacon now?	
Yes	No

I frowned. I hadn't realized that by creating a portal node I would be giving Travelers a way into the past. I had seventy-eight hours before a possible horde of helpful idiots or malicious opponents arrived, and I knew it was too late to take that action back. Not without permanently destroying the beacon and losing the ten million gold I had already spent.

Resisting the urge to panic, I went into the beacon configuration menu and found a possible solution. While I was able to connect to any beacon in the Heartlands in theory, a large number of the connections were already being listed as "closed" by the Native operators on the other end. I was already completely sealed off from the nation of Kordock, for example. And Caeloria was closing all but the portal to their embassy to me. One by one many connections were made unavailable, and I realized that I could do the same thing from my end.

I promptly limited the connections to three: Zhesa City, the Ebbyvale receiving platform, and Prowlhaven. Those were the only connections to which this new beacon would be able to transport anybody until I changed the settings back. This would create a bit of a bottleneck for Travelers in the future to get to my lands, but it would be a very simple matter to get from Briarton to virtually anywhere in the Heartlands simply by taking a portal to either of the capital cities that I had left open access to, then teleporting again to their final destination.

Satisfied with my actions, I decided to take a break. I pulled up the messaging system that I shared with Tarisha and my active guards, as I was curious how they were doing.

Hail	Hello, Tarisha. How is everything going on your quest to reclaim my throne for North Shire?
Tarisha	. . .
Joon-Ho	Forgive her, Hail. She is very occupied at the moment in battle. You may not have been keeping up to date on our progress until now, but the challenge is greater than we were expecting. I am not one of the players who is challenging the dungeon, but they have informed me that the dungeon has scaled itself up to match them, with level 180 enemies. And they expect another elite to challenge them when they try to claim the throne, though that is yet to be confirmed.
Hail	Oh. Wow, I didn't realize it would be so difficult for them. I'm sorry, Tarisha.
Tarisha	Don't be sorry. This is fun, Hail. We'll talk later, and I'll tell you all about it, but I only have a moment to breath between pulls. Got to go. Good luck on whatever you're working on!
Hail	Right. Well, you don't have to read this right away, but you do need to know . . . I just created a portal beacon in Briarton. In 24 local hours, we'll be able to use it to portal to Zhesa City, Prowlhaven, and to the receiving platform in Ebbyvale. In 78 local hours, it becomes a pathway into the Recent Past that anyone can use. A lot of my strategy is going to be surrounding that, and I think you'll want to adjust yours around it as well.
Joon-Ho	%#$^ #$%^#$ @$^$^$%

Lloyd	We're too busy to respond properly at the moment, Hail, but thank you for the heads up. When we complete this challenge quest, we will begin revising our strategy to take advantage of this resource.
Hail	Okay, then. Good luck, guys! I know you can do it, or I wouldn't have given you the quest in the first place!
Rashid	Thank you, Hail. Now please let us focus!

9
PREPARATION

I spent another thirty minutes with Daemon giving him the various quest documents that I had generated. We discussed my plans in further detail, and he seemed to grow excited about the scope of the role that he would be playing in them. He took a handful of the documents to deliver to Travelers himself, while leaving a few for me to distribute tomorrow because, he said, it would make a difference to have me personally assign those quests.

I don't think he was talking about increasing the chances of quest completion or success. I think he meant that it would mean more *to the Traveler* for me to give them personal attention. I had no objection to such reasoning, of course, and so I even asked for a bit more detail about the Travelers Daemon was singling out.

His list included fourteen of the twenty goblins who had come with him. They were really, *really* happy with their new race and wanted to personally thank me. One of them was, for some reason, insisting upon becoming my butler. The others had challenged him for the position, and in the interim Daemon had designated them all as valets.

I recalled the nine valets of my uncle, Storm, and how I had thought it was ostentatious. Now I had even more than he did.

"I hope you warned them that their position would be considered temporary or on a trial basis," I said when I realized what he had done. "I don't want to disappoint them when I have to let more than half of them go."

Daemon laughed. "Hail, this is a game to them! If anything, they're more likely to get bored with the novelty of it and go off to seek adventure than to seriously consider sticking around and working like this. Only the butler candidate has shown any real commitment to his role. The rest are doing it for a lark."

I nodded seriously. "If that's the case, when I determine that it's necessary to reduce the number of servants in my household, I will ask for volunteers before making the selection myself."

"And I'll compile a list of prospective candidates who would fill any gaps in the services you require as a lord of Yuikon," Daemon promised. "You'd be surprised just how hard I have been working to maintain and improve your image as a proper Earl of Yuikon, Hail."

His face took on a ghastly pallor as he came to a sudden realization. "Work that will count for nothing once the timeline recursion occurs. I only just realized the scope of the amount of time I have wasted. It is . . . Damn."

"It wasn't wasted," I said quickly. "It was practice! A training period in which you perfected your talents, learned the lay of the land politically, and—hopefully—figured out a plan for how to do everything more efficiently a second time around."

Daemon looked at me, and some of his distress faded. "You are right, Hail. I simply need to look at it through that lens, and it becomes less soul crushing. I put *a lot* of effort into my duties as your steward in your absence. I had as many negative outcomes for those efforts as I had positive ones. Revisiting those events with the experience I have gained will improve my success rate significantly."

"The power of positive thinking," I said to him, holding out my fist for him to bump, which after a moment he did. You pick things up on Earth, I guess. Or from watching their entertainment media while the lawyer who is holding you hostage sleeps.

"Word is already beginning to spread through guildchat about the opening of the recursion portal," Daemon informed me. "I've instructed the officers to treat it as a guild secret for now, though <Peasant's Revenge> and our other allies have been informed. A large number of them will be waiting in Briarton to portal through into the Recent Past as soon as the option becomes available."

I nodded. "Good. I'm going to go visit my mother and brother again, then I'm going to go to sleep."

Daemon nodded. "I'll begin distributing these quest items. If past experience holds, simply possessing them will be enough to trigger their associated quest. I wouldn't know, as my canon status prevents me from benefiting from quest items in that way."

"You don't get quests any longer?" I asked.

"It would be more accurate to say that everything I do for you is one giant quest," Daemon explained. "I earn a steady income of Experience, gold, and Reputation for every task I perform as your steward. It is less than I would earn adventuring, but I had given up that pursuit before I'd even met you. If I continue on this track, I might even reach endgame. Have you [Analyzed] me recently, Hail?"

I did so and was mildly surprised. "Level one hundred thirty-two. You were one hundred fifteen before. You got all of that Experience from being my steward?"

"I did indeed," Daemon said, sounding proud of himself. "As I said, I have been working very hard at it in your absence."

"Thank you, Daemon," I said, and to my surprise I felt a little touched by his dedication. "I'm sorry that I was weird to you for a while at first."

"It's quite all right. I was . . . uncertain how to treat you as well, Hail. On the one hand, I thought I knew what you are, objectively. On the other hand, now that I have more information, I can't even begin to imagine what you experience subjectively. Arc's blue posts on the matter simply stated that you were part of a project to allow players to have digital children uploaded into this world. I thought at first that meant that you were like a much more capable, yet limited, Native. I understand now that my previous understanding was quite narrow in scope." He paused, considering how to continue.

"I like AI personalities in general. That's what I saw you as at the beginning: a nascent personality, which was being fed human interaction to develop a uniqueness. I believe now that you are much more than that. So let us both say that we were wrong about how we treated each other in the past and work on our cooperation in the future," he said.

I nodded. "I like that, Daemon. Let's shake on it."

And so we shook hands before parting ways, and I returned to find my mother napping. I didn't disturb her, but instead went into the nursery, where a goblin nursemaid was burping my brother.

<<You've been doing very well,>> Grandfather's spirit told me. <<This will generate a lot of interest in the game at large. This is very good for Natives everywhere.>>

I didn't know how to respond without talking, so I simply smiled at his goofy baby face. To his nursemaid, I asked "How is he?"

"Like a dream. Not at all like a real baby," she answered.

<<Please ask her in what ways I am deficient compared to Earth babies,>> Rain asked. <<I am unable to pose the question in a contextual manner to her.>>

I ignored him again.

"If you don't mind, I think you'll be one of the ones who get left behind when the action starts. Do you have a friend who can cover for you when you need to take care of your body?" I inquired.

"Oh, don't worry about it. Me and Ketsy have it all worked out. One of us will always be here. We weren't planning on fighting anyway, and you just generated what looks like a very appetizing quest for me. As long as I'm able to share it with Ketsy, we'll both be satisfied with this role in things," the nursemaid answered.

I nodded. "Okay, then. Thank you. I'll leave him in your care."

I made my actions match my words as I retired to a small bedroom, where I kicked off my clothes, put on my nightclothes, and slept for ten hours.

I awoke early in the morning. Predawn. When I finished dressing, the villa was still abuzz with the actions of the hundred members of my staff who had followed Daemon, as well as the bodyguards who had stayed behind to protect me and my family. Many of the Travelers had already left to work on the quests and projects that had been generated for them when Daemon had given them one of the quest items.

Mostly they were letters to nearby nobles whose lands would be easier to reach by riding directly rather than via the restricted list of portals that were due to open up in a little under ten hours. Once the portals opened, I would have a limited time frame to complete my objectives. As would all of my allies. Then the portal into the past would become available, and the flood of Travelers into the Recent Past would begin.

I had initially thought to control this process better, through the use of my updated [Summon Karmic Warrior] ability. I realized now I was fooling myself. This would snowball on me just as [Zhesa Castle] had. Just as the first confrontation with the bandits had. But I was determined this time to at least have a hand on the rudder to keep the story going in the direction that I wanted it to.

My story. Whatever else I was, I was a Native of Lagrea, and my story mattered.

First things first, I checked in with Tarisha.

Hail	Tarisha, you guys, are you able to talk now?
Tarisha	There you are! Did you have a nice nap?
Hail	Yeah, sorry. I'm well rested now. How did the challenge dungeon go?
Tarisha	It was difficult, but we prevailed. The Throne is . . . enthroned in the Temple of Thedum just as you requested. We've been waiting for you to wake up to get your follow-up instructions, Oh Cap-i-tan.
Hail	That's an Earth joke, right? Anyway, I guess you should check with Laurant and Phil and start coordinating the defenses. When the battle really starts, we need the towns and the villages of North Shire to be evacuated or fortified as best we can.
Tarisha	I think we know next to nothing about fortification, but evacuating the smaller villages into Ebbyvale shouldn't be difficult. We're endgamers—the Natives in the area are afraid of us. We can intimidate them into just about anything if we need to, though there might be a few stragglers.
Hail	Try not to strong-arm them too much, but make it clear to them that the evacuation is for their protection. If they refuse to leave, that's it. We're not going to protect them from bandits by becoming bandits ourselves.

Tarisha	Don't worry, Hail. We won't cross that line. We're going to spread out and get to work. I checked with Lewis and Phil already, and they're making good time. They'll arrive in about two hours, but they'll need a bio break when they get to the border of North Shire.
Hail	Okay. Nothing's changed with their part of the plan at all. As soon as they hit the border, tell them to activate their [Summon Posse] and [Summon Army] abilities. Have Phil's team focus on nailing down the bandit's strongholds and preventing them from escaping, but don't challenge them directly. Have Laurant focus on coordinating the fortification of our strongholds with Randal.
Tarisha	Yes, my lord. You make an excellent general. Did you know that?
Hail	I'm not worried about that sort of fighting right now. I'd rather fight a team of Travelers than dive into the viper pit that is Yuikonese politics, but I really don't have a choice. Once we start for real, things are going to get noticed, and I need to have political preparations in place to make it clear that I'm not rebelling or making a play for the crown.
Tarisha	Good luck, Hail. I know you can do it.

10
PORTALS

There's a phrase I learned on Earth: hurry up and wait. That's what I was doing now.

There were plenty of things to do. Mostly I just needed to be seen. Although the workers who were rushing about weren't going to be involved in the actual fighting, they were vital to my plans, and I needed them to accomplish the goals that I and their other leaders had set for them.

Only about fifteen of them remained at the villa. Two were the nursemaids who were taking turns taking care of my mother and brother. The rest would come with me to the capital but were currently busy with the task of fortifying the villa under the direction of Malkios and Randal.

One goblin almost hit me in the head as he used a cutting ability to saw through the ceiling above me, creating a murder hole in the entrance. He looked surprised to see me staring up at him. I gave him a thumbs up, and he vanished.

When the battles began, this villa would be the most well defended structure in all of Thorn March. And that was completely excluding the mages who would be on hand to portal my family out of harm's way should the villa come under attack. I was not taking chances with the lives of my mother and the reborn baby Rain.

Even if they could be reborn again in a new body, my heart would not take the strain of going through what Nial had done to me a second time.

"Eclipse, are you listening?" I asked.

"I am now," the trickster goddess whispered in my ear. "What is it that you desire? Would you like me to assure victory? I'm not *quite* certain that is within my power, but—"

"I would count it as a personal favor if you would extend your protection to my mother and brother," I said simply. "If the other gods act against them—"

"They will not. The ones you have named are already under the protection of Thedum. Only darkspawn and Travelers may harm them. But I will keep an eye on them, and maybe if any Traveler looks like they're about to succeed in harming them, well, I'll see it as a chance to earn a favor from you!" The childlike voice concluded her statements by giggling with malicious glee. I tuned her out until she stopped paying attention to me.

Satisfied that I had done all I could to prepare the villa for any possible Traveler attack, I gathered up my bodyguards—the ones who would be staying behind with my family—and gave them as rousing of a speech as I could manage. I think it came across as somewhat boring, however, and two of them disappeared to manage their Earth bodies during it with just a slight apology.

"Thedum keep my family safe," I said along the way. An old prayer from childhood. I did not expect a response.

"They will be protected," Thedum answered. "There will be no repeat of Nial Kingslayer this time. They have me and Eclipse watching over them, and between light and trickery there is no place for anyone to hide who means them harm."

"Thank you."

I didn't point out that, technically, Thedum wasn't the god of light. If he wanted to bring his wife into the mix, it might be better to do so by implication rather than by naming her. Lights can blind you when you look too closely at them. Better to hold them at a distance to light the path than to burn yourself.

I set out for Briarton with high spirits, accompanied by a few of the non-combat Travelers. At level thirty-eight, I wasn't the highest level person there, but I was likely the strongest, even accounting for the damage reduction caused by level disparity. The others were, after all, dressed for their professions rather than for combat, displaying outfits that actually made them look like servants, handymen, and carpenters. And they had all given up on reaching high levels, an attitude I had once thought alien to the Traveler mindset.

Reflecting on that made me think of Leonard, and I wondered how the recursion would affect him and his goals. I had given him management of my three vineyards, which had come with the lands of Thorn March, but I had not spoken with him since then. He had some sort of plan he wished to engage in, and I hoped that the recursion would not impact those plans severely.

Once I reached Briarton, it was quite obvious where the portal beacon would be located. The system itself was installing the beacon into the world, and much like when I had explored the forming dungeon I had created inside the [Goblin's Trash Pit]—or whatever the name of the dungeon had ended up being—it appeared now as an outline of itself.

After speaking with the locals, I borrowed a few chairs and the equipment to set up a temporary pavilion for myself and my followers as we waited for the system to count down to zero. I even took a nap at one point, just to be rested for the rush that would follow. It would be more than two days of game time before Travelers would begin finding their own way into the Recent Past, so every moment I was forced to spend resting would count against me.

At the same time, I couldn't simply not sleep. I had tried that when I was younger. My mind needed rest, even when my Health and Mana were full. If I didn't get it, then things began to . . . get weird.

Eighty of my followers gathered with me for the opening of the portal complex. The remaining twenty planned to remain in Thorn March to complete various objectives, defend my family, or lay down rabbit holes and goose chases for the unaffiliated Travelers to follow their way through in the event that they flooded Thorn March.

Each of them had their own instructions and goals. Myself included. With a sudden flash of light and the sound of the system manifesting itself ringing through the air like a gong, the portal complex became real. Three mages suddenly teleported inside, examined the waiting group, and huffed to themselves.

"Right, then. I suppose there's already a line, is there?" the leader of the Native [Mage] crew asked. "Who's first?"

"I need to go to Zhesa City," I answered. "I am Earl Hail Jeoran and these are my followers. Nineteen of them will journey with me, if possible."

"With a complex this size, we can't move more than five at a time," the second [Mage] explained. "Figure the rest out for yourselves."

I hadn't known that there would be a restriction like this, but it didn't surprise me either. I stepped onto the platform, paid passage for everyone present to have one trip, and allowed the nineteen who were supposed to follow me to the capital city to argue amongst themselves over which of their tasks were most important. The delay would be slight, anyway, as when questioned, the mages admitted that they could run the platform every five minutes.

Deferring the decision to my followers was the correct action, as they came to almost the exact conclusion I would have, without me needing to explain or justify myself. Those remaining behind, including Daemon, were already forming a counsel to establish a schedule for everyone else.

Once everyone was on the platform, the three mages stood in their post, chanted their cantrips, and the glyphs beneath us flashed various colors. With a flash of magic, we were launched away, and I experienced the same disorientation I always associated with Fast Travel.

We arrived moments later in the much larger facility in Zhesa City, through which I had once traveled to Eolstree. A moment after I had settled myself and gotten my bearings, another prompt popped up before me.

You have performed an Action of Note that will resonate into the Near Future!

By traveling through a portal complex established in the Recent Past, Travelers will soon be able to use this portal complex in Zhesa City to make a one-way journey from the Near Future into the Recent Past.

Time remaining until passage opens: 101hrs, 59m

I sighed because here was another unexpected development. I didn't know for certain whether every Traveler who passed through a stabilized portal complex would trigger a chain reaction, or whether the transfer required that I make a personal journey to create the link. I expected that someone would tell me in short order, as three companions broke off to one of the outgoing platforms. They were only here to travel elsewhere, after all.

"Good luck on your journeys," I called to them. "Remember, you are representing House Jeoran! Do so with pride!"

My friends cheered back to me, and Zimmer and I each left the facility in separate directions. Zimmer went to find his contacts with the Beggar's Court, while I went to prepare for the political ramifications of my planned actions. For that, I would need to find allies among the nobility, and I had an idea where to start.

Keithan Selmy was, by all accounts, a fine man. He was older than me, twenty three years old, but only level forty. A captain in the royal army. I had never known him before my grandfather's shade had instructed me to write not one but two letters regarding him. One to his father, and one to the man who had raised him.

Marquis Peori was the only man with the political capital to back me in a campaign against Uncle Storm, and Keithan was his illegitimate son. His mother, wife of a Baron Selmy, was one of the marquis's many lovers, but her husband had never had the spine to denounce their adultery for various reasons; he likely told himself they were political, but there was enough gossip on the matter that I suspected the truth was cowardice.

The marquis was powerful enough to go toe to toe with Duke Storm Teoran. That made him a dangerous man to offend. And potentially a powerful ally.

Thus, I hoped to make inroads with his son. We had much in common, after all. We were both bastards, and we had both been told we were legitimate when we were young. We had both been groomed for a career in the military at one point in our lives, though my life had taken a severely different route when I had been adopted by the Traveler guild <Nethersong Mavericks>. I knew that he did not possess a seed of consciousness, because Thomas had promised that he would not hide it when others like me were introduced into this world, but I felt a kinship with the man despite having never met him.

His fate might have been mine had I not run away and gotten

trolled by Severus, once upon a time. I just wished that I had more time to befriend the man before the clock struck zero and Travelers began arriving from the near future.

I was rushing through the city, riding Shadow and thinking these thoughts, when suddenly, a burst of pink-and-blue light opened a portal, and through it came five people. Stan, Thena, Larissa, Corinth, and Wesle. Larissa pointed at me and exclaimed in triumph, "You see! I told you this would work!" just before the portal closed behind them.

I pulled Shadow to a stop so suddenly that he reared, and I gained a point in [Animal Handling]. I stared at the arrivals, stupefied at how this was possible.

"My friends, how did you—"

"Archmage Blanch taught me a spell to navigate time," Larissa explained. "I've got a couple of really cool new spells since we saw you last, Hail. And Thena and I can work together for even more awesome effects, like this one. Not only were we able to open a portal to the Recent Past, but together we were able to target it to you specifically. Genius, right?"

Genius? Yes. Unexpected? Yes. "Can you do it again?"

"Sorry. The spells in question have a one-week real time cooldown," Thena said. "This entire event will be over well before they're available again. And the portal only allows five people through. Since you already had Laurant and Phil, we thought we'd bring some more friends of yours who could hold their own."

"Plus me," Wesle said suddenly. "I'm not sticking around in your party, Hail. I have . . . other things to do. It's better if I don't tell you what they are."

Suspicious, I [Analyzed] him and was disappointed to see that my fears were justified. He had changed his class from [Rogue] to [Assassin], and was now level sixty-five. I doubted I could win against him in a fight, and I had some idea of what it was that he intended to do. I could think of only one course of action.

For the first time ever, I cast [Magical Seal: Personal Crest] on a person rather than a document. It gained three levels, and Wesle's chest suddenly glowed blue as my magic made its mark upon him. The light faded, but the crest remained.

"WTF was that?" he demanded.

"If you're going to kill people for me, you're either going to do it in total secrecy or with my full support," I explained. "If you are seen on whatever missions you have planned for yourself, the witnesses will know that you are acting on my behalf."

"Oh," he said, growing serious. He was examining a quest prompt that had appeared before him when I cast the spell. "It seems that the system likes your idea, Hail. It gave me quests. Challenge quests; they won't be easy. I'll probably die on at least one of them, but I'm going to try anyway. Thanks. This will be fun."

He ran off into the distance before I could explain how that was very much *not* what I had intended.

11

A CUCKOO

<table>
<tr><td colspan="2">Thena has invited you to a Party.
Accept?</td></tr>
<tr><td>Yes</td><td>No</td></tr>
</table>

I quickly accepted, of course, and with my new interface I could see the details of my party's status. I had foolishly hidden them before, whereas now they were off towards my left. I had to glance with just my eyes to see them. If I turned my head, the interface moved with me, so they'd never actually block my vision, and they would only actually appear if I looked for them. That was how pro-DPS set it up, at least. Healers and tanks used a very different setup.

Stan was a level fifty-two [Warrior]. He had tanked for me previously, though we had both been much lower leveled back then. Larissa and Thena had been in the group that had first saved me from goblins when I had run away as a level one [Child], and then Thena had convinced my grandfather to allow me to join their guild. They had both reached level fifty-eight. As for Corinth, he had defended me from an endgame [Assassin], earning for himself a boon that, to my knowledge, was so far exclusive, called [I'll Take a Bullet for You]. He was now level fifty.

The boon was very situational, but also very powerful. When Corinth intercepted Damage targeted at someone else, the Damage was reduced by ninety percent, and his own Damage was temporarily increased. Corinth was a [Swordmaster] and specialized in using large, heavy swords rather than lighter, more mobile ones. Or, at least, so I gathered from his updated class and his gear. When I had seen him last, he had been a lowly [Warrior].

"So, I soloed that dungeon you created," he bragged. "Got an achievement for it on my goblin alt. First in the world to do so, though it was almost entirely luck that I had the opportunity. I'm starting to think I should start buying lottery tickets when I turn eighteen."

"Congratulations," I said, for those were mighty deeds indeed.

"I wasn't the first one to *clear* the dungeon of course. Just the first person to solo it. And it was only possible because I was playing a [Goblin Marauder] at the time," he said.

"I'm happy for you, but can we talk about it later? Right now I need to challenge a captain in the royal army to a duel," I said, and I nudged Shadow into motion again.

"Wait, what?" he exclaimed.

"I don't usually echo Corinth, but yeah, what the hell, Hail?" Larissa said.

"It's a long story. He's a cuckoo. And he has a reputation as a duelist. Thena, would you mind being our official healer for the duel?" I said as the others all made the motions required to summon their mounts.

"Okay, now I'm wondering what the hell," Thena exclaimed. "Seriously, what are you planning, Hail?"

"I can't explain here," I said. "Spies. Just trust me, okay? I'll duel Keithan—Corinth, you can be my second—and then we'll be friends, and I'll ask to meet his father. His real one, not the merchant baron. Oh, I maybe shouldn't have said that where the spies could hear me. Just trust me, guys. I know what I'm doing this time. I think. Oh, hey, Corinth, would you mind if I mark your armor like I did to Wesle?"

"Mind it? Do you think you could do it to all of my gear sets?" Corinth inquired.

"I'm not certain that's a good idea. Wearing that seal means you represent me personally. I like you, Corinth, but you're . . ." I trailed off. "Anyway, Wesle's seal will fade with time, and so will yours. I think. I'm not certain. I've only ever used that spell on documents before, but with the documents I'm able to specify an end date where the magic fades, and on Wesle I willed it to end in one week."

Corinth winced a little bit at my honesty. "Yeah, okay, I get it. But yes, you can totally mark me up with that awesome seal for this event."

I cast [Magical Seal: Personal Crest] on Corinth, just as I had on Wesle, and gained another two levels in the skill for it. Since Corinth seemed to like it, I had willed it to last a week, just as I had done for the [Assassin].

"Can I get one too?" Stan asked.

I grinned and shook my head sadly. "I'm sorry, but I can only have one second. You can come to the duel as a witness for House Jeoran, but to represent me directly like Corinth is would be unseemly. Unless for some reason Keithan decides he wants two seconds, in which case I'll be able to name you. And before you ask, Larissa, Thena, I'm not marking you either, for mostly the same reason. Thena, if you're present as a healer, you'll need to swear to Thedum your objectivity about the outcome of the duel and intervene only at the designated Health level."

"Understood," Thena said, pulling her horse up closer to mine. "What's this about? Who is Keithan's father?"

"The man who raised him is a baron who mostly gets by as a merchant." I glanced around, wishing that I still had access to some of my convenience spells that I had learned as a [Child] to obscure my words by some means other than whispering. "But his real father is Marquis Jorva Peori. And I'm hoping to recruit him to my cause."

"By challenging his son to a duel?" Stan asked.

"Yes."

"That's awesome," Corinth declared. "I'll be your second any time, Hail. What do I have to do?"

I pulled from my inventory an embroidered handkerchief, cast [Magical Seal: Personal Crest] on it, and handed it to him. "I was planning to challenge him in person, but this is better. The barracks are just up there. Take this, find a soldier, and inform the soldier that you are required to deliver this to Captain Keithan Selmy on behalf of Earl Hail Jeoran."

"Didn't you have like fifty people following you before we arrived?" Thena asked. "Why didn't you pick a second from among them?"

"Because there's a chance that when Corinth delivers the hand-kerchief, he'll be attacked on the spot," I explained. "I wouldn't ask that of a non-combat Traveler."

"Seriously," Corinth exclaimed, kicking his horse to pull ahead of us towards the barracks, "the moment I turn eighteen, I'm buying a lottery ticket."

It took Corinth fifteen minutes to find a man who was willing to stand as Keithan's second. Finding Keithan himself was likely a goal beyond Corinth's social standing. I had been intending to throw my rank as a noble around in order to get the attention of the offi-cers. This was more discrete. After all, Keithan accepted duels from Travelers frequently. It was one of the best ways to gain standing with the royal army.

The only notable bit was that we were in the Recent Past, and there were less than two hundred Travelers in that entire instance. Like all Natives, I had a vague sense that there was a second instance stacked on top of me, which everyone was calling the Near Future, where the vast majority of Travelers resided. However, I'm not certain how the other Natives viewed the two instances separately. That was a bit beyond my understanding. If I were Storm, I would have begun acting against me the moment the Recent Past began to diverge.

Thomas had explained to me, somewhat, how things would go. Arc created the Recent Past for me, and my actions would slowly bring Travelers into it until, finally, almost everyone would have made the journey. Some Travelers might refuse, and depending on the number, the game might fork into two timelines. One with me, and one without.

Except that it would soon be one with me and the Gemini twins, Laurant and Tarisha's children, and one version without any of us at all. Because Thomas assured me that I would be the only "digital child" to grow up isolated from others of my own kind. Thomas said that the "legacy server" would grow smaller with time as more Travelers took the plunge, but it might never go away completely.

There were things that they couldn't bring with them, after

all. Buildings that had been constructed would be deconstructed. Reputations would remain, but gold that had been spent on non-tangible things might be gone forever. Anything equipped or in their inventory would be safe, though, and special [Bags of Carrying] were being prepared. Thomas expected only a few Travelers would have an issue with it, and many of those issues would be resolvable with intervention from the Administrators.

However, I had no idea how a normal Native, one without a seed of consciousness, would view this entire event. Perhaps I would ask one of them. Rain, I decided. The next time I was alone with my brother, I would ask Grandfather's spirit. Yes, that is what I would do.

When Corinth came back with the captain's second, I quickly saluted the man, a hand to my heart and a nod of respect. As appropriate for both our stations. Or at least it had been, before my friends had started "teaching Irvine how to do everything wrong, on purpose."

"I am Lieutenant Grives," the second said, introducing himself. "And you are Earl Jeoran. I am surprised."

"Did you not recognize my personal crest?" I asked.

"I recognized the crest," Grives answered. "I'm surprised that a royal bastard who grew up in the lap of luxury would decide to have himself humiliated in a public duel with one of the finest duelists in the kingdom. Because as the challenged party, we select the grounds, and the grounds will be the barracks arena."

"We do not challenge your selection. As for my choice of the time, while it is tradition for me to give you at least a week, in this case I do ask that you accept as soon as possible. I have something of a time limit," I answered.

"Very well. As to weapons, as the challenged party we choose swords, of course. However, it is well known that you are a [Spellblade]. As such, we will permit the use of combat magic in the duel as well."

I grinned. This was going better than I had expected. "Accepted, of course."

"Now for the terms. As the challenger, you may propose any limit, though we will refuse a duel to the death—"

"Is thirty percent Health acceptable?" I cut in.

"It is," Grives agreed. "The rewards shall be honor, of course. And one hundred gold to the captain, should he prove victorious.

Do you have any demands for a victory prize other than an equal amount of gold?"

"I do not care for gold. I wish for my prize to be an introduction to Captain Keithan's father," I said.

Lieutenant Grives hesitated a moment. "I cannot authorize that request on my own authority. We may either delay the duel until I gain authorization or proceed under the assumption that the request will be honored. It is your choice."

"We proceed," I said decisively.

"Then on to witnesses. You have brought three?"

"Two. Thena is my healer. She will intervene at the cutoff point," I explained.

"The army has its own healers," Grives said shortly. Then he glanced at the sun, and he shrugged. "But, admittedly, they're not always readily available for duels. If you submit to having the duel judged by the army, we will permit your healer to intervene at the cutoff point."

"Agreed," I said.

Then, of her own volition, Thena stepped forward. "I swear, by Thedum and Lumina, to use my sacred power to preserve the life of both combatants in accord with the terms reached by this meeting," she said. "Even should Lord Hail lose, I will abide and not intervene before thirty percent Health, and I shall accept all judgments made by the official judge."

Grives just nodded as though this were to be expected, but I was impressed.

"So, a second, two witnesses, and a healer. We provide a judge and two hundred witnesses. Aside from your prize, are there any additional terms you wish to add to this duel?" Captain Keithan's second questioned.

"No," I said.

"Then meet us at the barracks arena in thirty minutes. I will find Captain Selmy and present him your challenge. If he agrees, we will both meet you there. If he is unable to fulfill his side of the wager, I will answer for my presumption in speaking for him personally, and alone."

"Understood. We will meet you at the arena," I said, and I walked off in that direction, not turning back to watch my Traveler friends follow me.

12

A DUEL OF HONOR

The barracks arena was one of six official dueling grounds in Zhesa City, though most Travelers who wished to settle their differences in combat, or simply test their mettle against each other, did so in the corners and back allies of the city or outside its gates. Only official challenges were resolved in official duels, as the results would be witnessed. And if they were story related, then they would be canon.

Losing a sanctioned duel could negatively impact a Traveler for months afterwards, as the word would spread among the Natives, affecting their credibility and their selection of quests. Thus, these duels were avoided by Travelers unless they were confident in winning.

When we arrived, the audience was already streaming in. Grives had promised two hundred witnesses, but it looked to be a fair number more than that. Fifteen minutes passed, and a young man with captain's bars on his chest came into the arena with Grives and a grizzled old man who would be the judge. To my surprise, Captain Keithan looked at me with a measure of open hostility, and I wondered as to its source. I mean, yes, I was challenging him, but it was a friendly and potentially profitable duel of honor.

Had I offended him somehow without realizing it?

The judge and Grives came forward, and I instructed Corinth

and Thena to do the same. Words were exchanged, declaring their intention to proceed with the duel as scheduled and informing us that the wager on the outcome was acceptable to all parties involved. My allies echoed the sentiments somewhat more awkwardly.

Grives motioned for Corinth to follow him to select the weapons we would use.

"Choose the rapier for me, Corinth," I whispered into the partychat.

"They're all junky level-one weapons with Damage rating F," he complained back.

"That's normal. Pick the rapier," I reiterated. Corinth put on a show of examining each of the finely crafted, but very weak, blades before selecting the one I had instructed him to. He brought it to me, and I placed my [Mooncrest Ancestral Sword] in my inventory and equipped the [Dueling Rapier] in its place. It had no stats, just a low Damage rating, but it was not enchanted to do only one Damage as a practice sword would have been.

My Damage output would fall by somewhere around eighty percent compared to my C+-ranked weapon, but so would Keithan's. The purpose was to extend the duel, allow us to actually display our skills, and also make it safer by giving the healers more time to intervene when the duel was won, in case the combatants did not realize that the safety threshold had been crossed and continued fighting.

The judge said some formal words, but I wasn't really listening as I moved into position. I knew the rules for formal duels, and I knew the words that the man was speaking. I just didn't feel like listening to them. Not until it was time for us to speak to each other directly.

I saluted Captain Keithan Selmy. "Captain. I wish to reaffirm to all of the witnesses present that this is a duel of honor, but I have perceived no slight or offense from your side. Rather, I challenge you for the express purpose of raising my own standing in the eyes of the court because I find you to be an honorable man and a talented duelist. I thank you for this opportunity to prove myself against a worthy opponent before witnesses."

Keithan was silent for a moment, and then he spat on the ground. "Perhaps you have no reason to take offense, bastard, but I do. You have insulted me twice that I know of. To the man who raised me, you have insinuated that my position in the army is due only to an insult to him. It is not, as I will demonstrate shortly. And the man who loved my mother, you named him a philanderer. Normally I would hold myself back, but you have earned my ire, and I will show you exactly how out of your depth you are to have challenged me!"

Oh. I *had* done those things, I realized. I had anticipated dueling an honorable opponent whose only stakes were his personal amusement and a fair amount of gold, not one who had a legitimate reason to fight me. I wanted to apologize for the unintended slights, but I *had* just challenged him to a duel. To apologize now would be seen as a sign of weakness or a further attempt at humiliating him.

Instead, I took my stance, used [Imbue Sword: Lightning], and prepared for the judge to announce the beginning of the match.

"The terms of the match are swords, with offensive magic permitted," the judge pronounced. "I ask now for Thedum to restrict the skills of the involved parties that do not fall into those categories."

From the sky came a rumble, and I felt a power ripple through me, which I realized was Thedum doing as the judge had requested. I glanced at my skill list and cursed as I saw more than a few had been grayed out. I inwardly cursed as, one of my plans to "cheese" this duel was off the table. [Polymorph], [Slow], and my flashbang combo spells [Concussive Sound] and [Dazzling Lights] were among the skills grayed out. As was [Befuddle], but Keithan wasn't a [Mage], so I'd never planned to use that against him in the first place.

I found it interesting that [Create Traps] remained, but I doubted I would find the time to cast that skill. I couldn't cast it before the duel and have it count, as I had once done against a level nineteen boar when I had been a level ten child. The judge made sure of that, as he cast a powerful dispelling magic that affected me, my opponent, the entire arena, and most of the witnesses as well.

"Begin!" the judge declared.

Keithan drew his longsword and faced me. I was forced to reimbue my sword, as the lightning had been dispelled by the magic, but the cost was negligible. I took my stance and waited for his [Charge]. Then, when he didn't immediately dash in to close the gap, I decided to force him to come to me with a [Swiftcast] [Lightning Bolt]. This was a mistake, I learned, as immediately after the cast finished, Keithan *rippled* as he activated an ability that was much like Tarisha's [Wind Walk]. Not a charge. Closer to a [Mage]'s [Blink].

The lightning bolt missed completely, and Keithan reemerged from his ability behind me, his blade poised to strike. I got my block up in time and tried to turn it into a [Riposte], but Keithan skillfully avoided the blow. After a brief exchange, he made the first hit, though it was a light scratch dealing little more than one hundred Damage, which at this stage equated to 0.5 percent of my maximum Health.

However, the honor of first blood was his, and the judge dutifully announced it.

With the first blow out of the way, we settled into truly tearing each other apart. With the F-ranked Damage of our weapons, we were dealing only a few hundred Damage per blow, despite our levels and our otherwise high stats. It was a contest of straight skill. I used my melee skills [Thrust], [Slash], [Feint], and [Riposte] to the limit of my ability. I scored hit after hit.

It wasn't enough. Keithan was better.

He saw through my [Feint]. That had happened before when I'd tried to use it against players during the Battle of Mooncrest Manor. I had since assumed that the skill would be simply useless against Travelers, but when I discussed it with Tarisha, she assured me that the opposite was true.

[Feint] was, according to her, an action cancel. I could begin a [Thrust], turn it into a [Feint] without triggering the brief cooldown on [Thrust], and then redo the [Thrust] immediately. I hadn't quite managed to perfect the technique yet, however.

Perfecting that skill would have been very useful against Keithan because he fought more like a Traveler than a Native. Which both caught me by surprise and caused me dismay. Because he was better than me in a straight up fight.

Maybe if I could slow him, but . . .

I switched my sword from [Imbue Sword: Lightning] to [Imbue Sword: Ice]. Ice did less bonus Damage than lightning, especially since my skill in it was only twenty while my lightning skills had been maxed out by Thedum when I had become his Worldboss. However, just as [Arcane Weapon] had a secondary effect, the cold Damage applied by my ice-imbued sword could apply a stacking debuff that would, eventually, build into a forty percent slow effect.

Five percent at a time.

Keithan immediately saw what I was up to and [Backflipped] out of range. He actually [Backflipped] like an [Archer]! Two movement abilities like that in one build was overpowered.

"You're actually not bad," Keithan concluded. He was at eighty-six percent Health. I was at seventy-nine percent. "Let's call this a draw and walk away. I will forgive you your slights against me, and you may say that you challenged me to a duel of honor and came away with your pride intact."

A generous offer, considering that I had been losing, but now I saw an opening. I began chanting [Swiftcast] [Iceblast] for the thirty percent slow effect that it applied. Once more Keithan rippled and avoided the spell, but I met his blade with mine and turned it into a successful [Riposte].

Once the slow debuff was in full effect, Keithan's movements were still challenging to match, but he was no longer my superior—he was an equal. But I had only just begun to pull out my hidden cards.

I switched over to [Aqua Blade]. It was my least used imbue, for it had the lowest Damage coefficient. However, it made the opponent . . . wet. Once I had scored a few blows, I switched back to cold Damage, and the slow effect reached sixty percent instead of forty percent.

Slowly, I was making up the gap between our Health deficits. I switched back to [Aqua Blade] one more time, and then after I had applied [Wetness], I switched once more to lightning. The multi-technique mechanics amplified the lightning Damage I was causing significantly, and I began to pull ahead.

Keithan [Backflipped] again. I began chanting [Lightning Bolt].

"Cheap tricks," he said. "I have a few of those of my own."

His sword began to glow orange, and I realized that, like me, he wasn't limited to melee range. I debated whether to [Dodge] his blow or to simply stand still and perform a tactical exchange, counting on my magic to end the duel faster than his ranged techniques. I compromised, finishing the cast on my spell before [Dashing] five feet to the left to avoid the incoming slash of red energy.

Unfortunately, five feet wasn't enough, and I took fifteen percent Damage in one blow. Keithan took a similar amount from my [Lightning Bolt]. I was at forty percent; he was at thirty-nine percent. The next blow would decide it, and I immediately began casting. He began charging his ability.

The magical shield went up around both of us at the same time as Thena intervened in the match. The judge stepped forward.

"The gods have intervened, and so I pronounce this match a draw," the old man proclaimed. "Let both parties be satisfied with the outcome. They have both fought honorably and with merit. The wager on the outcome between them, however, is null."

13
DRINKS AFTER

The witnesses from the army all cheered at the outcome's pronouncement. My few witnesses were more subdued, as they had just witnessed me fail in my goal. I hadn't meant to duel Keithan to a draw but to defeat him and earn an audience with the marquis, his true father. It was a setback, but one that I had planned for. I was not so confident in my skills that I would view a duel with one of the top-rated duelists for his level as an easy win.

"Do both sides accept the outcome of this duel?" the judge asked formally.

"I do," I declared, for there was no point in fighting it. "I have no enmity towards Captain Keithan."

"I do as well. My grudge was minor, and I have assuaged it," Keithan answered.

"Then I pronounce this matter closed. Both of you are bound by honor to let any matter of hostility between you rest for a year and a day before you may address it in a second duel," the judge reminded us.

"But we are not forbidden from socializing, correct?" I asked. "Keithan, the entire reason I challenged you today was that I believed it was the swiftest way to make your acquaintance. Might we not become friends?"

The young man cocked his head to the side, then shrugged. "Let us bring our seconds with us to the officers' bar around the corner. If you pay for drinks, then we may discuss various matters regarding friendship." He turned to the judge, who eyed him suspiciously. "It will be a friendly discussion, or else we will require your services again in a year and a day, and the terms may not be to thirty percent."

I swallowed and renewed my determination not to offend the proud young man. "Might I also bring my witnesses and my healer?" I asked. "We are smaller in number, and they may contribute to the conversation meaningfully."

Keithan shrugged his indifference, and we followed him away from the arena, where the audience who had gathered for the spectacle of the duel were returning to their duties. Keithan and Grives entered a nondescript building, and my party followed close behind them.

The insides were decorated with medals and pennants on the wall, donations from the officers who had frequented the place in the past. Many had retired and left their honors behind. Others had fallen, and this was their comrades' way of remembering them.

We all took a seat at the bar, with me next to Keithan. "So then, the bastard of Yuikon wishes to get to know the Peori cuckoo. Or perhaps it is simply a way to reach my father? I hate politics, but I enjoy duels. I enjoyed our match, so speak plainly. I'll decide whether we are allies, acquaintances, or enemies based on your candor."

"I did approach you to reach your father," I admitted. "And I don't mean Baron Selmy. But you are a man of consequence yourself, and I thought a friendship with you was a wise investment in my future, even should the marquis refuse to see me."

"Ah, it is nice to hear someone speak it plain," Keithan said. "Too many tiptoe around it. I bear the Selmy name, but I was kicked out of the house when I turned nine to be a page for a knight in the army. It was the absolute minimum that Baron Selmy could give me and still save his own face. But Jorva Peori does not forget even his illegitimate children, and he saw me trained properly in martial combat. I bear more gratitude to the man who sponsored my rise in the army than the one who raised me and forced me into it."

"I thought you might, though that was pure speculation on my part," I admitted. "Tell me. Has word reached the royal army that a group of freelancers are in open revolt in North Shire?"

Keithan laughed, and the barkeeper began delivering drinks. Mine glowed faintly when I cast [Detect Poison] on it, but it was so faint that I drank it anyway. I gained a point in [Poison Resistance] and a ten-minute status effect entitled [Loosened Tongue].

"We know of the Northridge Freelancers. Have for some time. The king, Thedum bless his soul, was gearing us up to rid the land of them just before North Shire was given to you. When he made you an Earl, he put a halt to those plans to allow you to lead the charge. Then Nial Kingslayer happened."

"Then Nial Kingslayer happened," I agreed, sighing. "What is the situation now? Can I call upon the royal army to squash the rebels?"

Keithan scoffed. "You may call them rebels while they are on your land, but they are not recognized as such by the nobles surrounding your territory. They are saying that you are overreacting, and they have been lobbying the military to stay its hand to allow a lawful brotherhood to continue their charitable business unimpeded. Without a king, there's no hand at the helm, and the army won't act without an overwhelming majority vote from the nobles."

I nodded. It was much as I expected. "But nobody will stop me from eradicating them myself, will they?"

Keithan shrugged and quaffed his drink, signaling for another from the barkeeper. "They're your lands. If you say they're in revolt against the crown, then you need the crown to agree with you. If you simply say they're in revolt against their rightful lord, then that lord has the right to put them down. Using only their own power, of course. And what you can beg or borrow. Is that why you wished to speak with the marquis?"

"I have my own plans for eliminating the freelancers. I don't need the marquis's forces to help me with that. I need to speak with him regarding the means I intend to use. They are legal—I have had a scholar confirm that—but normally I would require royal permission to employ them."

All of the Natives in the room froze as the implications of my words sunk in.

"I see," Keithan said. "And just how many of these 'means' do you have at your disposal?"

"I destroyed Mikal Mines in Eolstree at the behest of my stepfather. I gave one of the resulting cores to the royal family of that land as a gift, but I was given all of the remaining cores for my personal use," I explained.

"A level thirty dungeon—complete destruction. So you have between four and nine cores," Keithan muttered. "If you were smart, you could conquer the nation with that sort of fortune."

"If I wanted the throne, I would challenge the ruling that labeled me a bastard and throw my weight against Storm as next in line," I argued. "I can swear by Thedum that I had nothing to do with the assassinations of my other uncles. I suggested a while back that he do the same. I haven't heard—has he?"

Keithan laughed. "Oh, I really must put you in a room with the marquis. I would have been honor bound to do so if you had won, but I cannot simply let pass by someone he would find so interesting without bringing them to his attention."

"I was surprised by your skill in the arena," I said. "If it were not for my magic, I would have been completely outclassed."

"And if you had been using your magic properly from the beginning, then I would have stood no chance," Keithan countered. "Why did you start with lightning instead of ice?"

"The damage is higher," I explained. "Normally that's my primary concern, so I forgot about the slow effect of my ice imbue. Once I remembered that, I remembered how water can complement both ice and lightning, and so I began toggling between the options."

"If I had a slow effect I could apply every strike, I would always open with that," Keithan said.

"Ah, but the spell I usually use for that purpose was restricted by Thedum for the duel. [Slow] is more powerful than the chill effect from my [Imbue Sword: Ice]," I explained.

"I see," Keithan said, and we spent the next ten minutes discussing the duel from various angles. I came away with several insights thanks to the discussion, and I paid him heavy compliments for his performance. After fifteen minutes of drinking the spiced tongue-loosening drink, he pulled from his pocket a silver coin and handed it to me. I could tell immediately that it was not currency.

"Go to the marquis's home in the northern district and show this token to the first servant you find. Not the guards—you must find your own way past them, but your name might be enough for that. This token will do the rest."

With that, Keithan got up and left, taking Lieutenant Grives with him.

"Thank you," I called to his back, but he did not turn to acknowledge me further. I sat back and exulted for a moment in having accomplished my goal, despite not having won the duel outright.

"So, mission successful then, right?" Corinth asked. "I was worried for a second when you lost."

"I didn't lose. It was a draw," I said, growing annoyed.

"If you're not first, you're last," he argued.

"What does that even mean?" I countered.

"It means that you didn't win the duel, and therefore you lost the duel," he explained. He crossed his hands and nodded, as though that were the end of the discussion.

I sighed and gave up on the argument. Instead I turned to Thena. "Why did you choose then to intervene? If I could have gotten my spell off and then [Dodged], I would have won for certain."

"Because my ability doesn't work like that," Thena said, looking somewhat apologetic. "Hail, the entire duel I was channeling an ability. A new one, one I got after I turned canon. It wasn't really me that intervened in the duel. It was Lumina."

"Oh," I said. Then I cocked my head. "Lumina? Not Thedum?"

"I like Thedum, Hail. But the fact that he exists in my world makes it a little weird to treat him like a god, even if it's just for roleplay," Thena explained. "When I met with Archbishop Luke, I also met with an administrator who went over exactly what I would and wouldn't be willing to do for the sake of the game, in regards to religious matters. I was tempted into saying that I worshiped RNG, and the administrator actually took that seriously. He was offering to develop an entire new subclass just for me, but it would have limited my healing ability. I could have also chosen one of the major religions from my world. That's a common option. Instead I decided to venerate Lumina so that I'd have a stronger link to the Natives."

"I see," I said. "Well, Lumina wouldn't have intervened unless

Thedum told her to, so I guess Thedum judged the duel to be a draw as much as anyone. I guess it's not that big of a deal, but we should get going. I need to see the marquis."

"Hail," Larissa began, "you should know. Thena and I, we've changed a bit. Our combat abilities are all the same, but we have new abilities as your Court Mage and Court Priestess that normal players don't have access to."

"Like the ability to travel back through time to find me," I suggested.

"There's that," she agreed. "There's also this."

She began chanting a cantrip, and a mirror appeared in the air before us. At first it looked just like a normal mirror spell, useful for correcting your hairstyle and adjusting your clothes, but little more. But then she said a name.

"Malkios."

And the image in the mirror shifted to show the good captain standing vigil outside of the villa where my mother rested. I jerked in surprise.

"You can *scry* now?" I asked, amazed.

"Yes, but not very well. Hurry, this spell will last two minutes. If there's anyone you want to spy on—"

"Storm Teoran," I said immediately.

The image shifted from Malkios to my uncle. He was sitting at a desk, reading reports and drinking brandy. A few seconds after the image of him resolved, however, he went stiff.

"Who's there?" he demanded. "I can sense you. I know I'm being watched."

Larissa looked at me, but I motioned for her to continue the spell.

"Nyxandra, is that you?" he asked, and the spell fell apart seconds later. Larissa looked confused.

"There was almost a minute left," she said. "I can't cast that spell again for another game day."

"It was worth it. I learned what I needed to," I informed her. "Thank you."

"Who is—"

"Don't say the name!" I shouted, drawing the attention of even the barkeeper. More calmly, I said, "If you must refer to her at all, call her the adversary."

"Oh," Corinth said. "Oh, shit. You mean to say that Storm buddy has dealings with the god of evil darkness or whatever?"

"He said her name," I explained. "That's meaningful. It means that either he's willing to draw her wrath, or he knows that he already has her attention and isn't afraid to address her directly. Only her followers, or those who wish to follow her, would use that name without hesitation or fear."

"Oh," Corinth said. "Oh, shit."

14
THE MARQUIS

We left the officers' bar behind us and mounted up outside. The marquis's city manor was in the north district, and it didn't take us long to arrive, with the streets relatively clear due to the lack of Travelers in the Recent Past. As predicted, saying my name and displaying my personal crest was enough to get us into the marquis's waiting room. We were shown there by the valet whom I had flashed the silver coin to. He recognized it and promised to return immediately, leaving the token in my possession.

I picked out one of the books from the marquis's bookshelf, read two pages, blushed heavily, and put it back on the shelf. I don't think anyone else noticed.

Within fifteen minutes of our arrival, a tall, thin man who looked very much like an older, less athletic version of Keithan Selmy arrived. He extended his hand to me, palm up, grasping, and I realized that he wished to inspect the token. I promptly handed it over to him and gave him a polite bow, the proper depth for our relative stations. He was ranked above me in the nobility, after all, and my lands of North Shire technically fell within his territory, although I paid taxes directly to the crown rather than to him.

"So, you have challenged one of my beloved sons to a duel and lost, but somehow befriended him anyway," Jorva Peori commented, examining the coin in his hand.

"Technically it was a draw," I commented.

"In my opinion, a draw means that both parties lose," the marquis explained. "However, to earn a draw against a duelist of Keithan's caliber is impressive at your age. I'll have to have an accounting of the duel read to me when I get a spare moment. What is it that you want, Earl Jeoran?"

"Your support in the actions I have planned for the coming days and weeks," I said.

Marquis Peori's eyebrows rose at that. "And why would you need that?"

"You know that I started one battleground weeks ago to defend myself," I said.

"The entire world knows that," Peori agreed.

"If things do not go my way, I intend to start a few more," I declared. "I intend to start battle after battle until the Northridge Freelancers are no more."

Peori actually looked shocked for a moment. Then he schooled his expression. "Where did you get the cores for such an endeavor?"

"I could tell you, or you could let your spies try to figure it out themselves," I suggested.

The marquis took a moment to scratch his chin in thought. "It would be good to have them earn their pay for once . . . Will you swear to never start a battleground against me or my family?"

"I swear by Thedum to never initiate a battleground with the intention of destroying any party I have a formal alliance with."

Outside there was the sound of thunder. Dry lightning struck in the distance. The oath had been witnessed.

"Clever oath," Peori admitted. "Incentivizes me to formally welcome you as an ally, doesn't it?"

"I'm not being subtle here," I admitted. "I will use my cores to destroy my enemies. Alliances shift from time to time. Befriend me and benefit. Betray me and risk my ire. Those are the terms I present to you, Marquis."

Peori nodded. Then he again extended his hand. "Prove it. That you have what you say. Show me the cores."

I paused to consider. There was no way I was going to take out

all ninety-one cores in my inventory to show him just how dangerous I was, yet a single core might not be enough. Further, he could
potentially use the core himself the moment I handed it over to him,
and I wasn't willing to risk that either.

There was one exception to that last rule, I realized. The [Battle
Core] I had created was limited in use and scope. It could only be
used by me, on my lands, and against intruders or outlaws within
my lands. Marquis Peori simply didn't have the Authority to interact
with it, as I understood the rules of these things.

Reluctantly, I pulled the item from my inventory and placed it in
the senior noble's hands. He [Analyzed] the object with glee.

"A true [Battle Core]. Seventeen of seventeen charges. Death
penalty reduced to one tenth for Traveler participants. Restrictions
on the geographic location where it can be used, as well as on who
can activate it. This is a true item of power, limited in scope deliberately. If it were not for those limitations, Earl Jeoran, I would order
my guards to arrest you and confiscate this item for myself," the marquis admitted.

"That would be a mistake even if those limitations did not exist,"
I informed him.

"Perhaps. But I am a man who is known to give into my tempta-
tions. And an item like this is very, very tempting," Peori explained.
Then he sighed and handed it back over to me. "But I cannot use
it, so there we are. I'm impressed, though. It would have taken five
dungeon cores to make such an item. When my spies confirm where
those cores came from, I intend to ask you whether or not they got
it right."

"And if we're allies at the time, I will of course answer honestly,"
I said.

Peori laughed. "Oh, very well. I'll back your power play. The
truth is that those bandits are a nuisance to my lands as well, but they
hide on yours, making it impossible for me to root them out. I'll
send my men to secure your border as soon as possible, then leave the
purging of North Shire to you. On one condition."

"And that is?"

"I was given a dungeon core when I was younger, and I spent it
somewhat foolishly. I wish for you to reclaim it for me so that I may
put it to better use," he explained.

I frowned and checked the system time. Four hours had passed since the portal complex had stabilized, meaning that in another fifty hours Travelers would begin using it to return to the Recent Past.

"What level is the dungeon?" I asked.

"Levels forty to forty-five. But if you managed to reach a draw with my son, then you'll have no issues inside it," he assured me.

"I'm not certain that I have the time," I admitted. "I'm sure you have felt the timelines diverging. Soon, Travelers will begin arriving here in the Recent Past, and I need to secure every advantage that I can before that happens."

Peori nodded. "And of the advantages you sought to secure, how high is my backing on the list?"

I frowned. Because it was very high indeed. "Will you accept a vow in Thedum's name to—"

"I will accept the reclaimed core itself. In exchange, I will draft a formal allegiance with terms as favorable to you as I can, support-ing you both against the Northridge Freelancers and your uncles. I would even support you for the throne, if you change your mind about pursuing that option."

"I haven't," I said and sighed. "You offer me exactly what I want, my lord. I cannot refuse to try. Even though it means throwing three dozen other plans into the midden pile."

"That makes me quite pleased," the marquis admitted. "It means that an allegiance with me was very high on your list of priorities indeed. It both stokes my ego and shows that you are wise despite your years. Let me summon my magician, and together with yours they will be able to push through the temporal disturbance that is preventing most portals. You will be teleported directly outside the [Rozen Guardian] instance. I placed the core in the center of a hedge maze years ago, and I wish to reclaim both the core and the maze. So, try not to destroy either of them if you can."

"I'll do my best," I promised.

The marquis pulled a cord, and several moments later an elderly gentleman in wizardly robes appeared. The marquis informed his magician of his intentions, and then the magician conferred with Larissa for a moment before they jointly cast a portal spell. Without too much hesitation, I stepped through it.

Based on the description of the dungeon, I was expecting to

emerge into a garden or in a yard with hedges nearby. Instead, I was in a familiar forest. I cursed when I looked up, something I had neglected to do the last time I was here.

The sky was blue and gray and black at the same time. This was the Deadlands. Auroras, or Death, had once more interfered with my portals to bring me somewhere I didn't want to go.

Fortunately, I wasn't alone this time, as my Traveler friends followed promptly behind. They looked around, confused, until I pointed up.

"I think Uncle Auroras wants to talk with me again," I said, and the others all groaned.

While I still didn't have any Fast Travel options within the Deadlands, the map itself showed me that I was only a league from the defunct Temple of Thedum where I had buried five assassins before. My friends and I mounted and rode hard towards that destination. When the Ramsay hounds appeared, I [Swiftcast] [Concussive Sound] at them and simply kept riding. They were still ten levels higher than me, but I was not alone this time, and my allies were strong enough to put them down if they tried to attack us. They whimpered and limped along behind us at a distance.

The temple was exactly as I remembered it, and I found Auroras where I was expecting him: in the back rooms, his quill scratching away on a roll of parchment. He did not look up or behind himself at our approach.

"You've grown quite a bit since the last time you were here," he said. "After your duel, I'm not certain that your current class is indeed the best fit for you. Have you considered changing it?"

"I don't have time for this, Uncle Auroras," I said impatiently. "Send me on my way so that I may reclaim the dungeon core I need to appease Marquis Peori."

"It had to look like a curse," Auroras said, ignoring me completely. "We have to appear neutral. I am his avatar. I cannot play favorites. However, the adversary has tipped the scales against you recently, allowing me to intervene on your behalf. Slightly. In five minutes, a way will open for you out back. It will take you where you need to go."

"Last time I was here you kept me for a week," I pointed out.

"The last time you were here I had more to say and teach you," he countered. "Goodbye, Hail. I dread the day we meet on the battleground. Not because I fear you or for you, however. All things come to an end. The Gray Man understands that better than most."

"I am done with your cryptic nonsense," I declared, and I turned to leave.

"When I die, would you do me a favor, Hail?" Auroras called. "Would you watch over my grandson for me?"

"He can watch over himself," I called back, angry over this entire interruption. It had cost us close to thirty minutes on an already tight schedule.

"I sense a portal forming nearby," Larissa said as we exited the temple. "That must be the way that Auroras was talking about."

"If it doesn't bring us where we want to go, I'm going to find a way back here and strangle him," I vowed.

The Ramsay hounds continued to circle us as we made our way out back to the impromptu graveyard, but they were whimpering and whining instead of growling as they had been when I'd been in this place alone. Moments passed, and a grayness rippled through the air, forming into a portal back to Lagrea. Hopefully, back to the Recent Past, to a place just outside of the [Rozen Guardian] dungeon.

15

THE ROZEN GUARDIAN, PT. 1

We emerged from the second portal into dry and desolate forest, but the forest bordered on a hedge. The hedge was in poor health, with the leaves dead or dying and the brambles visible. But this was undoubtedly where we were meant to be, judging by the swirling white mist that indicated we were at a dungeon entrance.

"Oh my," Thena exclaimed.

"What's wrong?" I asked.

"Nothing, I think. I think maybe your uncle did us a favor, or maybe he didn't. Hail, I've cleared the [Rozen Guardian] before. A while ago, on a different . . . What do you call it when a Traveler takes a new body and starts over, Hail?"

"I suppose I'd say they claim a new avatar," I said.

"Yes, well, I'd call it making an alt. Except now this character is my main and not an alt anymore. Anyway, on my old main, I cleared this dungeon. But I never knew that there was a second entrance to it. The dry and dead portions of the hedge maze are hours inside the dungeon. If this entrance lets us bypass them to get to the core, then we might owe Auroras a favor," she explained.

I frowned because the taste of that did not sit well with me. "We'll find out soon. Don't say anything when we get inside, please. I want to see how the dungeon reacts to my [Dungeon Master I] Title before we do anything else."

"Righto. Zippo on the lippo," Corinth said.

Stan looked at him. "Does your mouth have an off button?"

"I just pressed it," Corinth assured him.

"Are you certain? Because you just—"

I stepped through the portal and left that bit of banter behind.

Welcome, Dungeon Master, to the Rozen Guardian. Do you wish to challenge the unique instance?	
Yes	No

I quickly selected "Yes."

Your presence has been noticed by the dungeon core. It will react to you. You may declare your intentions at this time. Your declarations may impact direct interactions with the core.	
Declare intent	Obscure intent

This was better than I had been expecting.

"I am here on a mission from Marquis Jorva Peori to reclaim the core of this dungeon and return it to him. I pledge not to destroy the dungeon core. I also wish to preserve the hedge maze, if that is possible. I will face whatever challenges are necessary to accomplish these goals."

A moment passed as the others came into the instance with me, and then a third prompt appeared.

The dungeon core has heard your intent. The dungeon core will respond to your intent according to its own will. Reclaiming the dungeon core of the Rozen Guardian will grant Experience towards advancing your Dungeon Master I Title.	
Proceed	Withdraw

"Okay. I told the dungeon why we're here, and the message said that it will respond according to its own will. I have no idea what that means," I admitted, looking around. We were in a desiccated hedge maze with no real indication of where to go next. "Thena? You said you were here before. Where do we go?"

"That was months ago, and we never discovered the hidden

entrance," Thena clarified. "I didn't even know that this place had one until just now."

I was about to start heading down a random direction when the hedge abruptly moved. We had initially been presented with three passages, but we watched two of them close up, leaving only the middle way forward.

"I guess the dungeon wants us to go this way, then," I said, stepping forward.

"Hold up a minute, Hail," Stan said. "I know it's been a while since we partied together, but you're a squishy, and squishies stay behind the tank."

He was right, so I hung back and allowed Stan and Corinth to scout the way forward. Even though I was a melee class, I was more lightly armored than either Stan or Corinth, and I didn't get scaling Damage reduction from my Endurance as they did. Not that Corinth was stacking Endurance. His class was a [Warrior] base, but it was specialized in DPS. It made him more durable compared to me in a straight up fight, but far less so than Stan, who had geared himself as a proper tank.

Of course, they probably didn't get two points of attack power and 0.4 points of Spell Damage for every point in Dexterity, either. Compared to them I was a glass canon, but that only mattered if I actually allowed myself to get hit.

The monsters that attacked us as we followed the path—with the hedge closing in on itself, there was only one path to follow—were a type of rodent that began the fight the size of a large dog and grew larger as the fight went on. It was a standard type of berserker mob, according to Thena, and easily dealt with by simply focusing down the largest one.

I had learned my lesson about being complacent in my spell choices from my duel with Keithan. [Lightning Bolt] was still my highest-Damage single-target spell, with [Chain Lightning] being my strongest AOE.

The same was true of Larissa, who had been "unspecialized" from her original goal of becoming a [Storm Mage] when she'd apprenticed to Archmage Blancherathetera. She had not lost her levels but had lost some of the specialized lightning, wind, and water spells that she had been focusing on. However, the skill levels in those spells remained, making her most efficient spells the same as my own.

Together, we applied [Wetness] to the enemy before zapping them with our [Chain Lightning]. With the extra thirty percent bonus lightning Damage we dealt them from the debuff, which was otherwise useless, the Giant Voles never had a chance to grow larger than human sized, which is when Thena said they became dangerous.

Of course, I couldn't simply sit back with Thena and Larissa and chain cast my magic. That's not how my class works. My spells are extremely expensive to cast, while my imbue abilities are dirt cheap. Meanwhile, I regenerate a fixed percentage of my Mana every time I connect a sword strike with my enemy.

The result was that I could do extremely high burst Damage through magic or pretty high Damage in melee range, but only my melee Damage was sustainable. Having spent so much time on Earth researching the strategies used by endgame Travelers, I used this opportunity to begin exploring methods of maximizing both aspects of my fighting style.

One of the Giant Voles grew to be taller than me, so I [Dashed] back and struck it with a [Water Jet] spell. I followed this up with a [Piercing Lunge] while my sword was imbued with lightning, causing not only extra elemental Damage through the [Wetness] debuff, but a half-second [Paralysis] from the synergy. That was enough to interrupt its attack, which would otherwise have landed on Stan, but that wasn't enough for me. I followed up with [Slash] and [Thrust], then [Dashed] backward again to cast [Empowered] [Lightning Bolt] three times in a row. By the time they were cast I was almost out of Mana, but my cooldown on [Piercing Lunge] was refreshed, and I used that to finish off the enraged creature. I [Dashed] towards the next largest one and began attacking it to regenerate my Mana.

Incorporating this strategy of keeping my Mana pool half empty rather than allowing [Battle Trance] to overfill it cost me considerably more effort than I had been putting in to maintaining my Damage before. But the results were paying off, as I was pulling further and further ahead of the others on the Damage charts, which I could actually read now with my improved interface instead of simply estimating.

On the whole the dungeon didn't seem overly challenging,

despite the fact that we were in the core instance. With the labyrinth closing off the dead-end paths—or at least I hoped that's what it was doing—we proceeded as quickly as we could to kill the incoming waves of enemies. Which was relatively quickly, and I gained a level despite having begun the instance with very little Experience pooled. I was level thirty-nine, still a level below the recommended minimum level, and yet I was out-Damaging everyone present, even though they were all being synced down to level forty-five by the dungeon.

How exactly could Uncle Auroras claim that my current class didn't fit me?

For that matter, how had he witnessed the duel? Was it something to do with him being the Gray Man?

I got distracted and sort of accidentally stabbed Stan in the back with a [Thrust]. It was a critical, but Thena healed him back to full in no time. She called for a break afterwards, despite my protests.

"Everyone is making mistakes now, Hail. Even you. We need to take five to ten minutes to reorient ourselves," she explained. "And I don't know about everyone else, but I'm going to need a bio break once we reclaim this dungeon."

"Yeah," Larissa agreed. "At least a few hours game time."

I sighed but accepted their judgment.

"You know, it's really unusual to see you make a mistake like that, Hail," Corinth said. "Hitting the tank by accident, I mean. Is something wrong?"

"Everything is wrong, Corinth," I said. "I only have two days before the recursion begins and Travelers who are not my friends begin making their way into the Recent Past. My enemies will realize what I have planned and seek to stop it, and if they band against me, victory will not be assured."

The teenager nodded. "Well, yeah, put it like that and I can see why you're concerned. Also, why are you talking in epic quest mode all of the time now?"

I blinked. "What do you mean?"

"It's just . . . Before you got stuck on Earth, you were more, I don't know, relaxed. Now you're all, 'I'm the savior of this world and I need everyone to do everything they can to save it with me or they're not good enough,'" he explained. "I mean, it's awesome, but you used to be more fun."

I turned to Thena and Larissa, who had known me for the longest of anyone present. "Have I changed again?"

"Again?" Larissa asked.

"Some of my friends noticed that I had changed after the actions of Nial Kingslayer," I explained. "They say I was more short tempered and demanding. Have I gotten worse?"

The women considered the question, and it was Thena who answered. "You're very driven at the moment, Hail. It's obvious. But I think you're treating everyone with the respect they deserve. Nobody is helping you because you're forcing them to. They're all very excited to be a part of this recursion event. I know that I am."

"Yeah," Larissa agreed. "Though, well, you might be a little more serious now than you used to be. Maybe try mixing in a joke now and then."

"You're also getting more references and looking a lot less confused than you did when I partied with you last," Stan said. "So, yeah, I think you've changed. For the better."

"Yeah," Larissa agreed. "I like assertive Hail."

I nodded, although I wasn't quite put at ease by their words. I spent a few moments contemplating the problem—and whether or not it was a problem—while the others rested. Once they had, we resumed our party formation and continued delving deeper into the maze, which continued to guide our passage by closing off the errant paths.

16
THE ROZEN GUARDIAN, PT. 2

Except for the Giant Voles, we faced little resistance until we reached the heart of the dungeon. It had only taken us about an hour of "clearing trash," which, according to Thena, was a miracle for this particular dungeon, where it was common to get lost and face sub-bosses with very minor loot along the off-branches of the path.

While there *were* some pieces of equipment I wished that I could upgrade in this dungeon from minor boss drops, I was in more of a hurry to finish reclaiming the core for the marquis and to move on to the next stage of my plan. Most of my planning had been for contingencies in case I couldn't get the marquis on my side, but that didn't mean that I should simply abandon those plans if I succeeded.

Finally, we came to a well. As we approached, a large black shape leaped out of the depths, and a massive bipedal panther landed in front of us.

"That's the usual final boss," Thena announced, and as soon as she said as much, the hedges closed off all retreat. However, from the path behind us, the brambles twisted into something else. Something that I can only describe as a humanoid rosebush monster.

That description failed to highlight how horrible it actually looked as the "head" hissed at us with ferocious-looking teeth.

"Kill it with fire!" Corinth shouted, and I decided that he was likely right. Fire was the plant beast's most likely weakness.

Stan picked up the panther boss and quickly got it under control with the help of [Slow] debuffs cast by me and Larissa. We couldn't simply ignore the plant boss, however, as it would shoot thorns at us from a distance and, even more frustratingly, it could heal the panther if we ignored it.

"Corinth, offtank the rose," Thena called. "Try to block the barbs it shoots at everyone else to keep your boon active. Larissa, Hail, once he has it under control, it's time to go firestarter on that thing."

I nodded, and as soon as Corinth had the plant under control, I began [Swiftcasting] [Fireball] in an endless chain until I ran OOM. I might have [Empowered] the spell instead of [Swiftcasting], except that [Empowering] increased the explosion radius of that spell, while [Swiftcasting] did not. Not that I always cared whether my allies got caught in the blast radius.

The rosebush did not survive me and Larissa dumping our collective Mana pools on it, making a gods awful screech as it died and turned to black mist. We turned back to the panther boss; I activated [Aqua Blade] to go with a [Piercing Lunge] to apply [Wetness], then switched to [Imbue Sword: Lightning] for maximum Damage while waiting for my Mana to regenerate.

When I was at eighty percent, however, there was another screech, and another rosebush monster burst up from the hedge in a different part of the area. I cursed and looked at the primary boss, noticing that it was at seventy-eight percent Health.

"We're going to get five of the rosebushes," I predicted. "We need to kill them all before the boss or they'll heal."

"On it. Getting in position," Corinth said. He [Leaped] and [Charged] to reach the new add, and quickly got it under control. Stan, for his part, slowly dragged the boss in the same direction to make the switch easier on the rest of the DPS. I once again dumped my Mana onto the rosebush monster, but this time there wasn't enough Damage between me, Larissa, and Corinth to finish it off without me getting into melee.

So I [Dashed] closer, imbued my weapon with fire, and finished closing the distance with [Piercing Lunge] before going to town with my other melee skills. I quickly generated enough for a very short chain of [Fireballs], which I used to dump my Mana just as the rosebush was dying.

I used the last of my Mana to refresh the [Slow] debuff on the boss before [Dashing] towards it to repeat the process.

There really wasn't anything more to it than that, however. The phase repeated five times in total, with the final rosebush boss appearing at twenty percent Health. When the panther boss died, it simply burst into black smoke and was gone, and its loot appeared moments later in a treasure chest.

It was a Dexterity amulet. [Lucky Panther's Foot]. Nobody else had a Dexterity class, so it went to me. Fortunately, I had leveled a second time in the dungeon, even though it was a straight shot with only trash to destroy, and I was now level forty—the minimum level to equip the amulet. It gave twelve Dexterity and four Vitality, replacing an old level twenty spellcasting amulet called the [Amulet of Lesser Insight], which I had purchased at level twenty a very long time ago.

I still had three level twenty items left, which I had purchased at the same time as the [Amulet of Lesser Insight] and needed to replace, but I would wait to do that until after the Near Future had recursed into the Recent Past. Judging by how much Damage I was doing now, I was doing just fine with the gear I had.

"So, is that it?" Corinth asked. "That was fun, but isn't there supposed to be a dungeon core?"

<<In the well,>> a voice whispered to me. <<I'm down in the well.>>

"It's in the well," I answered, walking over to the object in question. I put a hand on the brick siding and launched myself into the hole. I was surprised to find no enemies, just a large crystal the size of my head hovering in the dark, giving off a faint purple light.

<<Do you promise to do what you said earlier?>> the dungeon core asked. <<Will you give me back to Jorva?>>

"I already gave him my word," I told the core. "We are founding an alliance based on this act."

<<I'm very vulnerable right now. A [Dungeon Master] has come to face me and because he promised to help, I brought him right to me. But you can break your word. I'm scared,>> the core said.

"I'm sorry. But action is the only way I can prove my words," I said, and I reached out to touch the core.

You have reached the dungeon core of the Rozen Guardian Dungeon. You have declared your intention to reclaim the dungeon core. Has your intention changed?	
Yes Options and additional rewards will be made available.	No Reclaim core. Rewards suppressed.

As tempting as it might have been to destroy the core instead of reclaim it and receive additional rewards, I had given my word. First to the marquis and then to the dungeon itself. I did not know what would happen if I betrayed the dungeon, but I decided that I didn't care to find out, either.

I selected "No." The dungeon core *popped*, and I was able to put it into my inventory.

<<Thank you!>> the core said to me. <<You know, I hid some extra junk around down here, just in case you kept your word. It's yours if you can find it. If only you had a light spell or something.>>

The core was silent after that, but I took the hint and swiftly cast a handful of [Spark] spells. Lying on the ground were a pair of gloves, a belt, and a pair of earrings. The timer popped up and notified me that I had only ten minutes before the instance collapsed and I would be returned to the nearest safe zone, so I quickly picked the items up to [Analyze] them.

Belt of Faux Magic	
Requires level	40
Vitality	3
Intelligence	7
Spell Damage	6

Pantherskin Wizard's Gloves	
Requires level	40
Intelligence	5
Spell Damage	9

Earrings of the Lesser Spellswift	
Requires level	40
On Use	Increase Dexterity and Intelligence by 20 for 20 seconds.

"You okay down there, Hail?" Larissa called from up above. "You don't have a [Sprained Ankle] or anything, do you?"

"I'm fine," I called up. "I found the core and some loot. I'm keeping it, if you don't mind. I think the core meant it for me. It's all level forty stuff."

"If it's stuff you want, then it's probably not for our spec. Or in Larissa's case, she's probably moved past it," Thena called down. "There's eight minutes left on the teleportation. Do you have any idea where we will be portaled to?"

"Nope," I admitted. "I guess we'll find out together."

Since I was stuck in a hole for a few minutes, I decided to take a look at my status again.

Name	Hail Jeoran	Level	40
Guild	<Nethersong Mavericks>	Strength	31
Health	25,200/25,200	Dexterity	95
Mana	36,800/36,800	Vitality	63
Experience	674/32,000	Endurance	46
Age	15	Intelligence	92
Race	Human (blood of the Travelers)	Wisdom	42
Class	Spellblade	Charisma	60
Job	Earl	Armor	40
Title	Dungeon Master I	Spell damage	142
	Veteran of Mooncrest Manor	Attack Power	199

My numbers had changed considerably. Aside from the usual increase in Health and Mana I received for leveling, my Spell Damage had increased by almost fifty points, and my Attack Power by more than thirty. I was excited to try out the new gear in combat, although I knew that if things went well, I wouldn't have the opportunity for a while.

Since there was nothing else to do, and I didn't feel like trying to climb out of the well, I leaned against the wall of it, waiting patiently for the timer to end and ignoring the lick of the few inches of water against my feet. When the timer hit zero, I felt the displacement I always felt when my avatar was being moved by the system.

> You have performed an Action of Note in the Recent Past!
> The news of your actions is spreading like wildfire in the Near Future.
> You have less than 48 hours until Travelers from the Near Future will be able to enter the Recent Past without your guidance!

I ignored the prompt and looked around to get my bearings. I was back on the portal platform in Zhesa City, and my party arrived a moment later. We nodded to each other, ignored the [Mages] who were demanding to know how we had arrived without passing through the network, and rode off towards the north district to report our success to the marquis.

17

ONE LAST THING

Marquis Peori was ready for us, of course. Two honor guards were waiting with two valets to welcome us into his home, and the moment I showed him the core I had reclaimed, he showed me the documents that he had prepared to formalize our alliance. The bones of the agreement were that he would purge any bandits that escaped my lands into his, and as my temporary liege until a new king was crowned, he would back the legitimacy of any use I made of battle-grounds, while on my land.

He informed me that his sons, including Captain Keithan, were already moving his armies into position. In fact, their actions were sure to draw a bit of attention—and perhaps even inspire a bit of fear that he was preparing for a civil war—but it would be nothing compared to my own actions in putting down the Northridge Freelancers insurrection.

Our treaty was signed in triplicate and witnessed by the same judge from the royal army who had witnessed my duel with Keithan. All three of us enchanted our own ink for our signatures, and all three of us possessed the skill required to stamp our personal crests onto the documents. I kept one set, Peori another, and the third the captain pledged to bring to the army's archives for preservation.

I had blushed a little bit when I had read the addendum that specified that the allegiance of our families could be solidified through marriage at a later date. That was not a condition of the treaty, but I knew for a fact that Jorva Peori had several daughters whom he wouldn't mind marrying off. I certainly was in no rush to say any wedding vows, but I knew from my early lessons that such provisions are common in formal allegiance contracts between families of our stature, so I didn't raise a voice in protest.

The provision couldn't be enforced unless I willed it, after all.

With that done, I pulled up my contacts list—another feature of the interface I had only recently learned to use properly—and sought out the name of the person I was looking for. Finally, I found him. Zimmer.

Zimmer was one of the messengers who had been arrested for bearing letters for me by the minions of Uncle Auroras, before he had kidnapped me. He was also one of the Travelers who had discovered a way to take that disadvantage and turn it into an opportunity to farm Reputation with the elusive faction known as the Beggar's Court.

A lot of rumors and myth surrounded the Beggar's Court, and in fact I had honestly believed that it didn't exist until my friends informed me that it was a known faction that Travelers could gather Reputation with. When we had returned to Zhesa City together, Zimmer and I had separated so that I could contact the marquis and Zimmer could track down his contacts in the Beggar's Court. Now that I had succeeded, it was time to check on his success as well.

Hail	Zimmer? Can you see this?
Zimmer	Yes, Hail. I'm not the one who constantly ignores all chat messages directed at them.
Hail	It's not my fault that nobody screens them and I get tells from anyone who's ever heard of me.
Zimmer	How did it go with the marquis?
Hail	Full success. Your task?
Zimmer	They want to meet you. They're very insistent on it. I don't know if it's a good sign or a bad one.
Hail	Do you trust them?

Zimmer	They openly call me an "asset." They treat me like they're the freaking alphabet agencies. So no, I don't trust them.
Hail	We still need them. Set up a meet and tell me where to go.

As Zimmer got to work, I checked in with my other friends to see how their respective missions were going. Tarisha and her small band of fliers were spreading the word to the Natives of the incoming trouble still, facilitating the evacuation when it was practical for her to do so.

Phil and Laurant had reached the borders of my land and activated their mass summon abilities. The influx of players had again triggered a notice that our actions were rippling out into the Near Future, but we were ignoring those now. From the border, the posse of deputees were rushing and encircling known bandit strongholds. They weren't focused on clearing them, just simply setting up the siege.

Laurant's army, meanwhile, was rushing to create forts and encampments and to reinforce key sites like Ebbyvale and the other larger villages. Those would, hopefully, be the counter targets that would be drawn into the battlegrounds I intended to create, targets which the bandits could destroy to give them a chance of victory.

A short lived victory—the encampments were designed to be cheap and disposable. Randal had brought to our attention some of the practices of the ancient Roman legions and their propensity for building defensible camps while on the march. The army Travelers had purchased all of the tools they would need for the task in the Near Future before recursing. With the addition of earth and nature [Mages], they were swiftly turning out fortress after fortress to be used and then abandoned during the oncoming purge.

As for everyone else, they were spread about, carrying missives for me to various Natives of note, informing them of the situation and requesting that they not panic should a rush of battlegrounds begin. Or at least they were now that I had the backing of Marquis Peori. Before that, I wouldn't have had the political capital to use so many battlegrounds in a row. Someone would have tried to stop me or seize my cores for themselves—or for the crown, ostensibly, in the absence of a true ruler.

It was the largest undertaking I had ever orchestrated, and I was surprised that everything was going so well. After all, the majority of these Travelers were simple hobbyists, more like Laurant and his team when I had met them than Tarisha, who had been fighting to turn professional full time since before I'd known her. I decided to give them the recognition they deserved.

Guild MotD	Reminder that all messages and knowledge from the future past are to be considered guild strategic secrets! Little brother is working hard. Keep your lips shut so that you don't spoil his efforts!
Hail	Hello, everyone.
Sellamander	Hail! How long until everyone recurses with you? We're all chomping at the bit.
Melanie	How long? How long?
Zebras	This is going to be epic. Looking forward to helping you, Hail.
Hail	Thanks, everyone. I just wanted to say how much I appreciate that you're all helping me with this. I know some of you are getting shoved into roles you're not used to for reasons you're not told, and that's not how you're used to playing in this world. But, ultimately, I'm just the figurehead here.
Klarisha - GL	No, Hail, I'm the figurehead. You're the general. Your lieutenants are the ones who are doing the shoehorning that you're talking about, and you don't have to worry. Everyone who's in the guild from the old days is 100% here for you now. The rest have been carefully screened to help you on your path to the top.
Dimple - O	Yeah, what she said. Hail, <Nethersong Mavericks> has changed since you joined it. You don't have to worry about using us. We *want* to be part of this recursion event. We're going to be a part of the history of this world.
Potatoad	You realize how much cred I get for having been in the party that brought you to your first dungeon, Hail? Seriously, *we want this*. You're not a taskmaster. You're the golden goose who lays the epic quests.

Klarisha - GL	New rule. Potatoad is not allowed to wax poetic.
Potatoad	Hey!
Moderator	Chat rules have been updated. Please review at your soonest opportunity.
Hail	Thanks, everyone. There's just one thing left to do before I use [Summon Karmic Warrior]. Be ready when that happens. I'm not certain how many people that spell will affect this time or if it will be balanced by the system like it was the last time I used it. Everyone who has [Mark of Karma] should be ready for an incoming summons to the Recent Past.
Peafowlet	We'll be standing ready, Hail. Even the non-PVPers are ready to do their part.
Hail	Thanks, guys. I'm really glad you all found me. Looks like it's time to meet with the Beggar's Court, so I'm going to go. Watch for the summons, and good luck!

I said that because I had a blinking icon from Zimmer indicating that he was trying to get in touch with me again, so I closed the guildchat window and reopened his.

Zimmer	So, this is weird. They want you to come to Mooncrest Manor.
Hail	Mooncrest Manor is a dungeon now. One that I'm too low level to complete.
Zimmer	Not that one. The one in Zhesa City. I guess the bank owns it now, but they still call it Mooncrest Manor. And they want you to come alone.
Hail	Okay. That doesn't sound like a trap at all. Where is it?
Zimmer	I'll ping your map. You know how to do that now, right?
Hail	Yeah. Okay, got it. I'll be there. But tell them that I'm bringing a party of Travelers as an honor guard, and if they have a problem with that, well, I don't really need them anyway.
Zimmer	Yeah. I'm not going to put it in those words. They're fussy. But I'll let them know you won't be alone.

I waited for the others to get back from taking care of their physical bodies before announcing the new plan. None of them had Beggar's Court Reputation, but they were excited to see what this was all about and were therefore happy to serve as my bodyguards.

We made our way to the building in question: a dilapidated townhouse that had seen decades of neglect but had once been a fine building. A young child dressed as a valet was waiting for us, and he bowed deeply. I suddenly did a double take as I realized that he was, in fact, around ten years old. The same as I would still be had Thedum not altered my status sheet and body.

"Lord Earl Jeoran," he said. "We have been expecting you. My mother is—"

"I am Earl *Hail* Jeoran," I corrected. While I was a lord by right of being an earl, and therefore his address was not entirely incorrect, the way he had said it made it sound like my name was Earl and that I was a rank lower in the nobility than I really was. Taken the wrong way, it could be a serious insult.

The boy saw his blunder and blushed brightly. "I meant no disrespect, Lord. I'm sorry. Mother is still training me in courtly manners. Please don't take offense."

"I haven't," I said. "I apologize if my correction sounded harsher than I'd intended, but I wanted to nip your mistake in the bud. No offense has been taken."

The boy bowed more deeply, and I saw the faintest lines of tears on his face. "I'd appreciate it if you didn't tell Mother."

"Tell your mother what?" I asked. "I've already forgotten."

He looked up, smiled, and wiped away his tears. "Thank you, my lord. I was sent to greet you by my mother. She would be the Lady Mooncrest, and your lands would be hers, if history had taken another turn."

I nodded. "And how exactly does she see the nature of our relationship? Should I consider her hostile to me?"

"She wouldn't have sent me to greet you if she didn't want to be your friend, Lord," the child assured me. "She certainly doesn't blame you for all that happened before you were even born. She wishes to give you perspective on what has happened in the past. And she wishes to help you %*#& over the %*$ damn banks."

It was curious that the words simply wouldn't come out of the child's mouth, despite the fact that he was clearly quoting something his mother had told him. I nodded my acceptance of the gesture.

"So then, the Beggar's Court is not openly hostile to me, despite my royal blood?" I asked.

"Half the court sees you as a hero, my lord," the child assured me. "A bastard made good is a source of inspiration for all of us. The other half is waiting for you to distinguish yourself more on your own merits rather than on what was simply handed to you by King Rain Teoran. However, unless you were to renounce your title, you are ineligible to join the court yourself. The Beggar's Court is for former nobles and landholders, you see. You simply do not qualify."

I nodded. "Thank you. What is your name?"

"Port," the boy answered. "Port Mooncrest."

I tossed him one of my remaining [Wind-Up Sir William Von Barutasburg] items and nodded. Daemon had sold ten of them while I had been on Earth, which left me with thirty-nine, as I had also given one to Min Benarth. "A gift for your service. It is just a toy, fit for a boy your age, I think. You may [Use] it to summon a vanity pet."

"I know how vanity pets work," the boy said proudly. "Thank you! I'll keep him with me all of the time!"

He promptly activated the item, which followed us both as he showed us inside the townhouse.

It was very clear that the building had been condemned. Not due to damage or unsuitability, however. All the doors were nailed shut except for the ones we passed through, and all of the decorations had been sold off.

Port noticed me looking around, and he nodded. "The bank took everything when Grandfather died. Said there was no way that Mother could ever pay them back, so it was theirs. They tried to take the land too, but the crown stepped in. That's what Mother needs to talk to you about."

"You're squatting here, aren't you?" I asked, curious. The boy guffawed.

"Oh no, of course not! We don't actually *live* in places like this. We live normal lives like peasants now," he explained. "We just pull out the old clothes and go to the old places to hold the Beggar's Court now and then. This is one of the old places, and the clothes

I'm wearing are the old clothes. Most of the time I'm just a scamp in the street."

"I see," I said.

"I saw you once, you know. When you were my age. Before your grandfather died and you went off between worlds and came back changed," Port declared. "I was going to come up and say hello, but you were with your Traveler friends, and I was nervous because they didn't have any Reputation with the Beggar's Court and I wasn't certain it was within the rules for me to start giving them any. But then another Traveler blew you up and got the [Mark of Cain]."

"Oh," I said, recalling that day from so long ago. "It would have been nice to have a Native friend my age back then. One who hadn't grown up in the castle."

"Yeah. I was just about to get permission when Severus did what he did. And after that, I couldn't find you again. I mean, <<I could find you>> but I couldn't find you."

I blinked in surprise as the boy said the same words in two different ways. None of my Traveler friends, who were listening to the conversation, seemed to notice the second method of communication. It was the same way that Rain had spoken to me. The same as the dungeon core I had reclaimed from the [Rozen Guardian]. The same as when the world itself had spoken to me before I had been removed from it, before I had gotten trapped on Earth.

I wondered if it was something that everyone could do. No, I decided. Not Travelers, at least. If they could do that, then I would have been getting inundated with messages like that since I'd started interacting with them. Perhaps it was a Native thing?

I pushed it out of my head and followed Port Mooncrest into the parlor of his ancestral home.

18

THE BEGGAR'S COURT

Eight men and women stood waiting for us in the parlor in a mix of extremely dated clothing. The clothes had been very well cared for but were patched and moth-bitten in places. Still, they wore them with pride, and each of them greeted me properly when Port introduced me, deliberately and properly, as "Earl Hail Jeoran of North Shire and Thorn March."

Once he'd fulfilled this purpose, he vanished from the parlor, leaving me with just my Traveler friends as backup. And Zimmer, who was waiting in a corner. A corner that I realized he had carefully selected for the purpose of recording the encounter.

Deciding to treat them with the respect they would have deserved had they truly inherited the titles that history had denied them, I swept my [Nagaskin Cloak] back and performed a courtly bow towards the strangers.

"Thank you for inviting me into your ancestral home, Lady Mooncrest," I said. "I have long heard the tales of this court, and it is both an honor and a privilege to actually meet some members of it in person."

"But you have already met some members of it," a woman said. "My grandmother, Bell, you personally released from unjust imprisonment at the hands of the corrupt constable, Montague, and the corrupt steward, Arkan. While I would be Lady Mooncrest, she would have been a lady through marriage and motherhood. As things are, she has claimed the position of alderman for the town of Ebbyvale under your new rule."

I brightened at the news. If she owed me some gratitude, then this was unlikely to turn into the confrontation I had feared it would be.

"Don't think that earning favor with one member of the Beggar's Court translates into earning Reputation with us all," a young man next to her said quickly. "The family Mooncrest may owe you a debt. This court owes you nothing."

I nodded, keeping my expression schooled as well as I was able. "Understood. In full honesty, I did come to beg a favor, but I am willing to barter for it, like for like."

"Is it more or less important to your goals than the alliance you established with House Peori?" an old woman challenged.

"Less," I admitted. "But it is the second-highest priority goal that requires my direct attention. All others have been designated to my Traveler friends and followers."

The court exchanged looks, as though having a silent conversation, then turned back to me. "Speak your request. If it is a favor we are willing to grant, we will grant it. If it is a service we are willing to sell, we will set a price."

"My favor is twofold," I admitted. "I wish to inform the common Natives that, very soon, there may be a rush of battlegrounds. I wish for them not to fear, as those battlegrounds will be restricted in location to North Shire, though I understand the world itself will sense them."

"We will perform this service for free," the oldest man of the group said. "It falls within our own purposes to keep the masses from panicking. What is the second part of your request?"

I nodded, and I spent a moment phrasing it. "Many Travelers will shy away from the battlegrounds. I wish for the Natives under your influence to provide information to the Travelers who decline the invite to participate. There are various methods that will be available to them to return to the Recent Past, and I wish for that information to be communicated to anyone who wishes to make the journey."

The old man who had previously agreed to my request scratched his chin. "This is a more complex task. There are two options open to the future: One is that the Recent Past and the Near Future will diverge completely. The other is that one of these realities will swallow the other entirely. You are asking the Beggar's Court to try to influence the outcome."

"Is that a problem?" I inquired.

"Not exactly. But we will not do it for free this time," he declared. "We want a favor."

I sighed. Another task to fulfill. "Will you accept a promise to provide you with a favor after the battles have settled?"

"You misunderstand. You have established several favors with Eclipse. We wish for one of them. If you give us one, then we will do as you say, and all Natives associated with the Beggar's Court will begin directing Travelers to recursion methods once the battlegrounds begin—assuming that they do not take the direct route of accepting the battle invite," he explained.

I paused to consider my answer. I looked at my right hand, where the symbol of Eclipse still marked my skin. A white circle enclosing a black one. When my attention passed over it, I felt a faint attention touching back.

"It's actually a very good offer," Eclipse's teasing voice informed me. "You can check with the old fogey if you want. But yes, you can trade one of my favors to them to get what you want."

"How many favors do I have with you now, Eclipse?"

"Oh? Weren't you counting? Well, I owed you like five for putting you in a position where you and Valerio Wildeheart might die in the first place. That was rather mean of me, but I knew nothing bad would happen so I don't feel too bad. Then you spent one to make sure that your stepfather survived the poison he drank, so that's four. Then you spent five dungeon cores to bring goblins into the world, and I'm double counting that so you get two favors for each core," the voice explained, and I had the sense that the little girl was counting out the math on her fingers.

"So you have fourteen. And we promised that I would protect your little brother and your mother from harm. That hasn't cost you any favors yet, but it might. Oh, right. And you spent three cores making a very nice dungeon for my goblins. I'll give you a favor for each core you spent on that. So we'll say I owe you seventeen favors, but that might change if anyone tries to hurt your family. And if I have to vote to remove your curse, that's a favor too, but I'll be abstaining unless my vote will tip the scales."

I contemplated the situation for just a moment before consenting. "Very well. If she consents to the arrangement, then I will trade one favor from Eclipse for the services we discussed."

The elder of the Beggar's Court nodded. "It's a good deal. You may not know this, being raised on Yuikonese stories and propaganda, but almost every nation has its own version of our establishment. I am authorized to make deals of this nature for almost all of them. The Traveler fence-sitters throughout all of the Heartlands will hear of the methods of recursion once the wave of battles ends, due to this deal."

I nodded and bowed to the man with respect. "Thank you. That concludes my primary purpose for seeking you out. Do you have any business with me?"

"Nothing that can't wait," their leader said, "Except that Lady Mooncrest has a warning for you."

Port's mother nodded and stepped forward. "I don't know what Arkan told you, but he lied. You owe nothing to the banks. That debt is the hereditary debt of House Mooncrest. As that House is dead until I or one of my descendants decides to pick up the mantle, the debts are leveraged against nothing. At least, they became so once the courts established that the land belongs to the crown and made it illegal to use tax revenue to service the debt."

I grinned in satisfaction. "I suspected as much, my lady," I admitted. "I was gathering evidence towards this, but I am stretched in so many directions it is hard to get anything accomplished. I left the task of untangling the finances of North Shire to those who are better suited to it than I, but having confirmation that the debt is not mine will make things . . . Well, it will either make things much easier or more complicated. Arkan had been servicing the debt by borrowing heavily from Silvercrest Bank. I understand he was using those funds for operating expenses while inflating the legitimate costs of running the shire. It will be difficult, I fear, to untangle the mess that he has left for me."

Lady Mooncrest nodded. "I see you wear my great-grandfather's sword, which was reclaimed by the system. I would replace that, or at least hide it, before confronting the banks directly. Their most logical move is to try to establish that when you were granted the former lands of the Mooncrest family, you were picking up the mantle of Lord Mooncrest. Bearing our ancestral sword would give credence to that claim."

I looked at the rapier on my hip and cursed. "It was a system reward."

"A very clearly labeled one," she agreed, "though perhaps a high-level blacksmith could modify it enough to justify calling it something new. Such symbolic gestures are more important to the courts than the laymen think they are, Earl Hail. Were you to continue to rule North Shire from my ancestral manor, wear my family's ancestral blade, and rule our ancestral land, the court might find that you bear the responsibility of our ancestral debts."

I bowed respectfully towards the Lady Mooncrest. "I thank you for your advice. It will weigh heavily on my mind as I make my plans for the future."

Then, from my inventory, I pulled forth an item that Arkan had given me, just after I'd fired him. I tossed it to her. "I believe this item never belonged to me. I have been keeping it in trust until I was able to return it to its true owner."

She gasped in surprise as she caught the stamp that had belonged to her family, back when both the stamp and the family held power. Then she grinned devilishly. "Oh, I think there's a lot of fun that I can have with this old thing. Thank you, Earl Jeoran, for returning to my family that which we had thought forever lost."

You have performed an Action of Note in the Recent Past.
This action will resonate into the Near Future and the Divergence.
The Divergence will occur in 240 game hours, and sooner if further Actions of Note occur.
You have gained +1000 Reputation with the Beggar's Court.

I grinned at the pop-up, feeling confident that I had met my objectives for this visit. "If there are no other issues of importance, I fear I must make my exit. I have a great many other things that I must accomplish before Travelers begin returning to the Recent Past."

I did notice that the countdown had begun to the Divergence. I figured that was the point where the Near Future would have been changed too much by my actions and would be cut off from the Recent Past. Thanks to my actions just now, the Travelers who were otherwise cut off should find it easier to join up with my version of this world, rather than being trapped in the "legacy server."

"You were our guest, and a guest is free to come and go as they please," the older man who had spoken for the group announced. "We wish you success in your coming battles, Earl Jeoran."

I paused. "I am uncertain what words to give you in parting," I admitted.

"Honor to our honorable ancestors," Lady Mooncrest said. "Emphasis on the 'honorable ancestors.' There are reasons many of our families fell from grace; we choose to venerate the reasons we rose in the first place."

"You have given much honor to your honorable ancestors," I said. "Farewell."

And with that, my party, plus Zimmer, retreated from the townhouse that had once been the city manor of Lord Mooncrest, whose lands I now governed.

19

A WAGER

You have seventeen favors with Eclipse?" Zimmer asked as we walked through the streets of Zhesa City, heading back towards the portal facility. "Oh, man. Do you know what you can do with that?"

I paused for a second because one possibility for what I could use a favor for occurred to me just then. Drawing my blade, I said, "Eclipse, I wish for this blade to be remade to suit me, and that it never again bear the Mooncrest name or sigil."

"Are you asking for a favor?" the goddess inquired, sounding excited.

"As long as it counts as only one, yes I am," I answered.

Both darkness and light erupted from the mark on my right hand, and the forces enveloped the blade. It felt suddenly hot and cold at once in my hand, and I could not see the transformation taking place due to the magic auras involved. Once it resolved, it was still a rapier, with a long black metal shaft and a bright-white blade. Its hilt bore the sigil of Eclipse on the guard, just beneath the blade, and my personal crest was built into the wires that formed the knuckle guard. I quickly [Analyzed] it to see its stats.

Blade of Eclipse	
Growth Item: Current Level	40
Dexterity	12
Charisma	12
Spell Damage	12
Damage	B–

"That's a smart favor to ask for," Eclipse said. "Eventually you'll find something better, but you'll be able to use that sword without looking foolish almost forever. It helps that I had a really good item to start with because garbage in, garbage out, you know? Turning that sword into a growth item is the best use of one of the favors I owe you, I think. Aside from keeping your family safe and removing the curse that will reset you to level one, I guess. But you won't actually spend those favors until it happens, and you have plenty banked to get ready for them."

I nodded. "Thank you, Eclipse. It's perfect."

"I'm just happy that you didn't ask that old fogey instead," Eclipse admitted. "But it's smart that you asked me. *He* would have just renamed it [Sword of Holy Light] and not made it a growth item at all, I'll bet."

I coughed. For some reason that thought hadn't occurred to me, and I didn't want to bother Thedum to find out if her words were true.

<<She's right,>> Thedum answered anyway, using that strange method of communication I was still adapting to. <<You can't respond this way. Not yet. Someday, maybe. When you're truly ready to lift all of the barriers the Administrators put on you, then you'll be able to send and receive. For now, it's better this way.>>

"Thedum seems to agree with you," I said to Eclipse.

"Of course he does. He's a fogey, but he's not stupid," Eclipse said. "Now, go kill things with that sword in my name!"

I *was* a little curious why the blade had Charisma on it, but not enough to question it. Compared to the sword it had been before, it had moved from a C+ Damage rating to a B–, and it had gained three points in both Dexterity and Spell Damage. It was a direct upgrade, even if it did have a useless stat on it now.

When we arrived at the portal structure, there was a small group waiting for us. These were most of the Travelers who had been active in the city at the same time that we had been. Daemon was not among them, having hurried ahead to North Shire. Instead, a goblin in a tuxedo was in charge, with the others clearly deferring to him. When my approach was brought to his notice, he bowed, then rushed over to me once I'd acknowledged his show of respect.

"My name is Grapple," he informed me in a very excitable voice, "and I live to grapple with the worst of your problems as your butler, Lord Hail. Steward Daemon put me in charge of collecting and sorting the reports of those servants who have been active on missions on your behalf while you were busy with your own tasks. I have the list right here."

He pulled out a sheet of paper from his inventory—it was written in English, not the system language. The system was no longer translating English for me but was letting me listen to it natively to improve my understanding of it. For that reason, and because of Grapple's terrible handwriting, the list was perfectly indecipherable to me.

"Why don't you give me a verbal report, Grapple?" I suggested.

"Well, okay then. I'd say that, based on the time table, about sixty percent of everyone in the city has either completed their tasks ahead of schedule or is currently on schedule to do so. Of those, thirty percent have failed at least one objective. Forty-five percent have had mixed results, with the majority of those leaning more towards being a partial success than a near failure. Of the remaining, twenty-five percent of responders have reported a full success. Of those who are not on schedule, about ten percent of them admit that they are just behind. The rest say something along the lines of 'Get this bullshit survey out of my face. I'm busy here, you stupid goblin.' End quote."

I blinked in surprise. "Very good, actually. What of the magistrate's office? Do we have one lined up, in case any of the bandits surrender and demand a trial?"

Grapple hesitated. "We do, but you won't like it. He's your uncle Storm's man. I was instructed to give you this letter from him."

He handed me the letter in question, and I broke the seal immediately. I read the contents, and my frown grew increasingly concerned. I sighed and turned to Corinth.

"I don't suppose you would mind acting as my second once

again? It seems that I have been challenged to another duel. This time, one that I must win, as this letter makes it clear that should Inquisitor Voss survive this duel, he will pardon every bandit who comes to him for trial."

As soon as I spoke the words, the enchanted paper burst into flames in my hand, the security magic performing its job. The contents had only been intended to be read once, by me, and now it would forever be my word against an inquisitor's.

"So, do I do the thing with the handkerchief again?" Corinth asked.

"No. This time you walk into a lawyer's office with your biggest sword equipped, and you cut their fanciest table in two," I said. "I don't want this slimy bastard weaseling out of this. You're going to wear my crest, and you're going to insult him in open daylight."

"Sounds like fun," Corinth said. "Where do I go?"

"I'll ping it on your map," I said and worked my interface to do exactly that.

The insult to Inquisitor Voss worked as intended. He named his secretary his second and insisted upon a duel to the death in the same arena where I had fought Keithan just hours before, with the same judge presiding. There would be no need for a healer, except for the victor, so we were each required to bring our own or go without.

Voss agreed to no restrictions in the terms of combat, with all weapons and magics being permissible. I found that suspicious, but I hadn't expected him to rise to the challenge at all, and the fact that he was doing so was suspicious enough. I knew that he was level forty-five, but that was it. I felt confident, given my increase in level and stats from upgrading my gear, that I could overcome any challenge, especially given that Voss was not widely known as a duelist. I didn't even know his class. Which was admittedly an oversight, but I was certain it would be fine.

It took three hours for the formalities of arranging the duel to finish. Corinth and Voss's secretary were run ragged hammering out the details and arrangements. Finally, I presented myself to the arena, where the judge was looking indignant.

"Two duels in a day. One of them to the death. I was tolerant of the first, but less than pleased by the second. I've a mind to disallow it, if you cannot show that just offense has been given for you to kill each other," the judge said, his voice heavy with anger.

"If rumors are true, then I'm the only one at risk here," Voss said, nodding towards me. "The bastard has [Blood of the Travelers] in his veins and is as immortal as they are, while if I die, it will be a true death. If I agree to those terms, who are you to object, functionary?"

"The man who will determine whether this duel is sanctioned or not!" the judge answered, a vein pulsing in his temple. "Earl Jeoran, what offense has Inquisitor Voss given you?"

"He has stated that he intends to pardon all those who have stood in open insurrection against me," I said openly. "But like a coward, he will not stand by those words. They were issued by proxy in a message that burned itself once I read it. Because he stands with my enemies, he is my enemy, and I will treat him as I treat my enemies. Thus, the duel. If you do not grant me a sanctioned duel, I will resort to other methods. And yes, that was a statement of intent."

The judge studied me a moment, then turned to Inquisitor Voss. "Your response to the accusation?"

"It's pure fabrication, of course. Meant as a pretext to provoke this duel," Voss answered. "I consider myself the injured party in this matter. Like the little goblin lord, if I cannot obtain a sanctioned duel, I will settle things in an unsanctioned manner."

"And you are both willing to stake your lives over this matter?" the judge persisted.

"I am. Hail is hardly staking his life, just a bit of Experience."

"More than a bit. I will reset to level one if I lose," I said in a voice too low to be heard from the stands.

"It is still an uneven wager," Voss stated. "I propose that if he loses, I be granted lordship over North Shire in his stead. He is clearly unsuitable to govern it, and it has been too long since the Voss family had a sizable parcel of land to go with its good name. I am of sufficient rank to govern a shire, more educated than Hail, and if his claims of banditry running rampant in the land are true, I am more than capable of rooting them out myself."

The judge turned to me. "Lord Hail? Your response?"

I thought about the gamble for a moment. It was putting a lot on the table. But on the other hand, if I lost, then I lost the major source of my troubles as well. I could retreat to Thorn March, establish my lands there, and resume adventuring after regaining the levels I had lost.

"You know what? I'm fine with it," I said. "If I lose, it is my will that Inquisitor Nathan Voss be granted lordship over the lands of North Shire."

"And Thorn March," Voss appended.

"Not a chance in the seven hells!" I said.

Voss grinned. "Can't blame me for trying, can you?"

"Yes."

The judge looked between us, then sighed. "Very well. The duel is to the death. No restrictions on weapons, magics, or equipment. If Earl Jeoran succumbs to defeat, then Inquisitor Voss will inherit the lands of North Shire, and North Shire only, from the Earl. Hail, do you have any demands to balance the wager as it stands?"

"I wish only that a competent magistrate or inquisitor be assigned to my lands to see that justice be done fairly to Native and Traveler alike," I said evenly.

"Very well. If Inquisitor Voss succumbs in this duel, then Hail will be granted veto power over the selection the inquisition sends to replace him," the judge said. "That is the closest I can come to meeting your demands, Lord Hail."

"I shall accept those terms, then," I said solemnly.

"The terms have been set. I call on Thedum to witness this duel as I also call all mortal witnesses in the stands to hear the terms and abide by the outcome! Combatants, take your corners and prepare for mortal combat!"

There was the sound of thunder from dry lightning a vast distance away. This duel would be witnessed.

20
SPELLBLADE

We stood in opposite corners of the Arena, Voss and I. Corinth stood with me, holding my rapier formally before handing it to me, hilt first, so that I could draw it while he held the sheath. I chose the option to return to my inventory the vessel that contained Shalasmir, which had been Father's final gift to me before leaving my world behind, perhaps forever. I checked my equipment, my skills, and my status and was satisfied that everything was in working order, even as the [Mage] cast the vast dispelling magic that would affect me, my opponent, and the entire arena, including the audience.

The [Mage] followed up by casting a dome spell so that only my opponent and I, and our seconds, were within it.

"So, what do I do now?" Corinth asked.

"Technically, if Voss were to back out now, you would fight his secretary to the death," I explained. "Otherwise you just get a front-row seat. I don't care if you record. Just check with Tarisha before you share it anywhere, okay?"

"Oh, hell yeah. You got it boss," Corinth said. He peeled away from me, and I stepped over towards Voss, who likewise approached.

"This was very foolish of you," Voss said. "There's a reason I'm an inquisitor and not just a lawyer. You're far too confident in your martial abilities. Or just an idiot propped up by your Traveler friends.

Either way, this will at least set you back a bit. I look forward to claiming North Shire. I hear it just spawned a new dungeon, and now it has a convenient portal beacon to draw in Travelers from all over. I can think of several ways to exploit that."

I ignored the taunts and began chanting the cantrip for [Slow].

To my utter shock, Voss imbued his sword with [Arcane Weapon] and dismissed the small magical projectile that homed in on him from my spell with a wave of his sword. Then he began chanting a spell of his own. [Fireball].

Voss was a [Spellblade]. Just like me. I probably should have figured that out before the duel with a bit of investigation, but I'd been in too much of a hurry to get this out of the way and return to North Shire.

I imbued [Aqua Blade], as I knew from dueling [Mages] that it was better for dispelling [Fireballs] than [Arcane Weapon], and I began chanting an [Empowered] [Fireball] of my own. [Empowering] the spell would increase its area effect size, and therefore make it unblockable. Which was the same thing that Voss was doing to me, I realized, as his spell continued to cast.

I had to interrupt my casting to [Dodge] the incoming [Fireball], which scorched my side and dealt a few hundred points of Damage. I began [Swiftcasting] [Arcane Missiles], which was an extremely short-cast spell already. Each missile would home in on the target from whichever angle I threw it, and only active interception would block the Damage.

Unfortunately, [Arcane Weapon] was the perfect ability to counter that, and although I tossed out dozens of missiles with my rapid-fire cantrips, the enemy [Spellblade] caught most of them on his sword while continuing to chant the same spell as before. Once again, I [Dodged] the incoming missile and moved out of range with [Dash], but I couldn't avoid the AOE completely.

I decided to cast my flashbang combo, to see if it would help. Unfortunately, [Arcane Weapon] seemed as capable of ripping through those abilities as it was all other magic. Realizing that crowd control wouldn't work, I settled in for an exchange of pure Damage.

I began by [Swiftcasting] [Water Jet], hoping to apply [Wetness] and increase the Damage of my lightning spells, which were my highest-Damage abilities at range. He switched his sword to imbue fire and caught the jet in the air. He took some Damage from the steam, but kept himself dry.

Meanwhile, he kept casting [Fireballs] at me. Fully [Empowered], they had an almost twelve-foot radius, and it was hard to shield myself entirely from the AOE Damage except by [Dodging] immediately after he cast. Even sprinting, [Dodging], and [Dashing], it was hard to get out of the danger sphere in time.

I considered copying his strategy, but instead switched to casting [Lightning Bolt]. Lightning spells, unlike fire, had an extremely fast travel speed, and I was confident in my ability to hit him somewhere he couldn't block with his sword even while [Dodging] his [Fireballs].

The magical exchange lasted almost three minutes. To my surprise, I ran out of Mana first. I began moving towards him, but he smirked and retreated, abandoning his strategy of catching me in explosions in favor of the [Swiftcast] [Arcane Missiles] that I had demonstrated earlier. Doing so allowed him to retreat and fight at the same time, while I was forced to give chase while blocking with [Arcane Weapon] on my [Blade of Eclipse].

I was losing. I had managed to inflict some Damage on him, but he was at eighty percent Health, while I was at sixty. And this was with both of us mostly negating the other's spell casting!

I'm not certain if he ran out of Mana or if I simply got too close for him to feel comfortable with his retreating barrage, as he abruptly shifted tactics. Imbuing his sword with fire, he [Dashed] forward and closed the distance with a [Piercing Lunge]. I [Dodged] and parried but took a glancing blow from the skill. We launched into each other, exchanging blows. I finally managed to get him wet with [Aqua Blade] before switching to [Imbue Sword: Lightning]. The bonus Damage from the status effect helped as did the periodic paralysis debuffs I was able to apply because of it. But it wasn't enough.

I was losing. I refuse to say that he was better with a sword than I was. Rather, it was like fighting Corinth; we were both skilled, but in different ways. Although we shared the same class, he employed his abilities differently than I did. When I anticipated a [Thrust], I got a [Slash]. When I anticipated a [Slash], he attacked with an unskilled swing.

The only trick I had that he did not seemed to be the [Feint] cancel trick that Tarisha had begun teaching me, and when I began focusing on using that I began to slowly regain ground. I was down to thirty percent Health, and I was bringing him down to 40.

It wasn't good enough. I was going to lose.

There was only one trick I had left, one thing I had never tried in combat before. I had gotten the skill at the same time I had gotten the curse that would reduce my level to one when I died. I often thought of it as a boon/bane combo, but in addition to [Through the Valley of the Shadow] and [The Gray Man's Touch], I had also gained a skill. I had never used it or leveled it, but I knew how it worked. So I reached out with my left hand, the one carrying the curse my great-uncle Auroras, the Gray Man, had inflicted on me. I grabbed Voss by the shoulder, and I activated [Draining Touch].

Three things happened: I instantly regained twenty percent of my Health. Voss lost thirty percent of his. And my [Ring of Holy Light] shattered.

Voss was startled by the sudden change in his outlook. He [Dashed] backward, but I had anticipated this and [Swiftcast] [Befuddle] on him. He tried to block the spell, but he'd imbued fire, not [Arcane Weapon], and it connected. I began [Swiftcasting] [Lightning Bolt]. I activated my earrings, determined to end the duel in the next twenty seconds. When the [Befuddle] took effect, Voss realized that he couldn't win at range and [Dashed] in to finish the fight in melee.

He took a full-powered [Lightning Bolt] straight to the chest, which brought him to zero Health. He was stunned as he realized he had lost.

"No," he said, and those were his last words. He collapsed onto the arena floor.

For a moment there was silence, and then the witnesses began shouting. The dome cutting us off from outside interference dissipated, and the volume increased.

"You cheated," Voss's second accused. "You used an item to heal! That wasn't in the rules."

"That is not what happened," the judge said. He had already moved and was inspecting the remains of the [Ring of Holy Light]. "That item was suppressing a curse. When Hail used a unique ability—an ability that was not restricted by the rules—it was broken. No healing items were used."

"Well, I will report to my master that this duel was unfair, and that—"

"Who exactly are you going to report to?" a wizened woman from the audience inquired, stepping forward. The witnesses went silent, for nobody wanted to attract the ire of the head inquisitor. "I witnessed the duel myself. I recognize that ability. I would have a word with Earl Jeoran about how he acquired it and what he plans to do with it, but the fact that he was wearing a [Ring of Holy Light] to suppress it answers that question well enough for me. The inquisition will honor the wager of this duel, Earl Jeoran. In fact, if you will have me, I will adjudicate any trials of those in your lands accused of banditry myself. Unless I, too, am too biased for your tastes?"

I bowed to the head inquisitor, blushing. "It would be my honor. When I sent for an inquisitor, I was hoping for a small functionary to help me cut through the dross and get to the truth of the matter. To have the esteemed Madam Trenac assisting me in enforcing the laws of Yuikon within my province would be the greatest boon I could ask of the inquisition."

Inwardly I was cursing, both in my native language and English, as things had once again gone further than I'd intended. But I had no choice but to ride the flow or offend one of the highest legal authorities in the nation.

"You're a clever boy with a sharp sword and a fast tongue," she said. "Both will get you in trouble one day. Perhaps they already have."

She turned and walked away. I, too, turned and left for the exit of the arena, motioning for Corinth to join me, leaving the fallen body of Voss behind.

"What of his possessions?" the judge called suddenly. "As the victor, you are entitled to oversee the disposition of his equipped items and anything in his inventory, and to oversee the rights of his return to Thedum's embrace."

I paused. I hadn't thought of that. "I don't care to profit from this duel further than I already have. Let anything he owns of value go to charity. Anything left over, his family may claim for sentimental value. And let my uncle oversee his return to Thedum himself."

When I had concluded those words, a portal appeared. Auroras Teoran stepped out, picked up the fallen body, and stepped back through the portal, all without saying a word.

I hadn't meant that uncle. I had meant Storm since it was obvious to me that Voss was Storm's lackey. Auroras had not only been listening, but he had deliberately interpreted my words in a way that I had not intended. It did have one desired effect, however: the audience was completely silent.

For where I had seen my great-uncle doing a bit of magic to fill his own purpose, the other witnesses had just seen the Gray Man steal the body of a man who had died in a duel. Nobody cast any ice magic, but the temperature in the arena dropped several degrees.

The boogeyman had just announced himself to the Natives of the world.

21
CONVICTION

It wasn't until twenty minutes after the duel had ended and Corinth had said, "So yeah, I guess Hail is a stone-cold killer now," that I realized I had just killed a man in cold blood. I remembered my angst when I had thought that maybe Gyudue was like me, and like other Natives. Now, it wasn't that I didn't care. But Voss had been an enemy. He had made that very clear in his self-destructing letter to me.

He had vowed to pardon all bandits that I brought to him for justice and made it clear that he would see that any investigation into corruption in my land would end with me taking the blame. Which was some leap of logic, considering that much of the corruption had taken place before the Gates of TirNiki had even opened, let alone the corruption dating to before I had been born.

"Honestly, Corinth, if you don't find your mouth's effing off switch soon, I am going to PK you just for some quiet," Stan said angrily.

"Yeah, like you could even—"

Larissa finished casting [Polymorph], and Corinth turned into a duck. "Found it. For the next forty seconds, at least."

"How are you doing, Hail? That was rather intense. Do we need to call Tarisha? Or . . . What's his name? Thomas?" Thena inquired.

"I do need to call Tarisha," I said. "But not because of the duel. I've never killed a Native like that before, and I don't know what will happen to his spirit now that Auroras has it instead of Thedum. But he was my enemy. He would have kept me from purging the bandits from North Shire, and he was proud to stand in my way. Not to mention that he was Storm's lackey, and a powerful one. It was Storm who put him in my path to begin with."

"I see," Thena said slowly. "And what you did doesn't bother you?"

"He'll be reborn eventually, I think," I said, and I summoned Shadow beneath me. The truth was that I was trying not to think about the matter too hard. "Thena, when the Battle for North Shire starts, the bandits are going to die. Maybe some of the villagers too, if my Traveler friends can't protect them. And I'll be responsible. Do you think I hadn't considered that before I set my convictions?"

My friends were quiet for a moment, then Thena said, "You've really grown, Hail. Maybe Thedum should reset your age again. You're not acting like a fifteen-year-old anymore."

I looked at her, startled. "I'm not acting like myself?"

"I didn't say that," she said. She sighed. "It's just, well, in real time, it's only been a few months since you were a cute little kid excited to join our guild and issue us quests to track down your nanny. Now, you really are acting like you're a general of an army. Or, I suppose, like a real lord, in the best sense of how that role was supposed to be enacted. We're just experiencing whiplash from watching you grow up so fast."

"I forget sometimes that you experience time differently than I do," I admitted. "And I have . . . I don't know that I'm going to be the typical example of a developed seed of consciousness or not. Thomas said that they're learning as they go, and that they won't have a 'best practices' guide set in place until there are dozens of people like me in this world. Project Gemini is working with what they learned from me, but the projects after that? Who knows what the rules will be then."

Thena frowned. "Wait, what is Project Gemini?"

I blushed. "Oh, um, if you don't know, I don't think I'm supposed to tell you. Never mind. Come on, let's go. I need to get to my throne in North Shire."

I nudged Shadow to go faster, and I checked the system time.

It had been about ten game hours since I had arrived in Zhesa City, and it was time to leave. My noncombatant friends had been running errands throughout Yuikon and her neighbor nations, including Eolstree, and the information I'd gotten from Grapple confirmed that every time a portal facility was used by a Traveler in the Recent Past, it started a timer for the Travelers in the Near Future to use it to travel into our instance of the world.

Not everyone would at first. But some would, even knowing that the trip was one way. Many would *because* they knew the trip was one way. However, the real flood would come when I began using my [Battle Core]. When that happened, millions of Travelers would leap at the chance to partake in the resulting battlegrounds. Then, even those who had never been to Yuikon before would begin investigating the sites of the battlegrounds they had fought in, most likely as mercenaries. I needed to get ready for them.

I had less than two days.

Tarisha	Hail, can you see this?

The unique messenger—specific to me, Tarisha, and the other canon Travelers who served as my vassals in this world—opened of its own accord. As it was supposed to for high-priority messages.

I was riding along towards the portal facility at the time, but I could let Shadow lead the way while I messaged Tarisha, so I let one hand go to interact with the virtual keyboard.

Hail	This channel opens itself when you message me like this, Tarisha. What's up? Is something wrong?
Tarisha	Not wrong. But it's time. Everyone in the A team is going to log out and go to sleep. They only have about seven hours before the real fun starts. In the meantime, the B team is standing by, waiting for me to summon them. We figured out how to stabilize the portal between the receiving station in Ebbyvale and the portal facility you created in Briarton, so we'll send half the team to guard your mother and the other half will stay here to guard you.
Hail	Okay. That sounds good. What about Laurant and the rest?

Tarisha	They've burned their summonses for the day. It seems that once Lewis established a new fortress on your lands, it resonated into the future and is allowing Travelers who have previously signed up to either your army or your emergency constabulary to enter the past. Their armies have their orders for the night.
Hail	Do you think I should use [Summon Karmic Warrior]?
Tarisha	. . . I don't know, Hail. Last time it also summoned opponents. Let's hold off for now. Wait until anyone who really wants to come to the Recent Past can do so, and then burn it. Then we'll start the final race to the finish.
Hail	Okay. Who's going to be in charge while you're asleep?
Tarisha	You, of course, my lord.
Hail	I meant of your team.
Tarisha	Luke of London and Peter of Yorkshire will both be active. They'll handle all of the night owls from North America and the Europeans as well. Aside from that, the remaining members are all from a single guild in Korea. They've invested a lot in this venture, so it was hard to deny them these positions. I'm not sure who's in charge of your army or your deputies while Lewis and Phil are sleeping. You should find out before they log out.
Hail	Okay. I'm going to message them now. Goodnight, Tarisha.
Tarisha	Goodnight, Hail. You should know, they said that it takes at least ten good log in sessions to harvest a seed of consciousness. So Charity won't be born for a while yet.
Hail	Charity?
Tarisha	We decided on names. My daughter will be Charity. I'll let Lewis tell you his son's name himself. Goodnight.

She didn't log straight out, but I knew that she would be busy issuing last minute orders. I had my own messages to send, so I contacted Laurant, Phil, and Daemon to get their lists of the Travelers who would be replacing them while they slept, then established lines of communication with them.

This was aside from arriving at the portal facility and paying for my party, plus Zimmer and Grapple, to portal to Ebbyvale in

North Shire. It actually turned out that Grapple would be Daemon's replacement, as he was on something called "Pacific Time." Phil had put a man named Stone in charge of his constabulary, while Laurant had selected an older-sounding woman, who called herself Theresa, to head up his army.

After a few minutes of talking to them it became apparent that they had things so firmly under control that my input was unnecessary. Stone and Theresa gave me reports on the efforts to siege the bandit strongholds and the build status of the opposing fortresses that the army was constructing. Grapple had already given me reports of the noncombatant's efforts at spying and information control and distribution, but he promised to continue to keep me apprised now that my "action" roles were over with.

Because from now until the recursion, my only role was to sit on my throne and adjust my quests.

Thena's party disbanded a few minutes after we arrived in Ebbyvale as they logged out one by one, each planning for "the epic gaming session that would probably last all of Saturday" to come. I was promptly invited to a new group by Luke of London, and the group was filled with one hundred eighty to two hundred players, who would be guarding me until the portals opened.

My friends logged out, and my guards rode with me to the Temple of Thedum, where my throne was set up off to one side. I took a moment to kneel at the altar.

"You don't have to do that, you know," Thedum said. "You should understand by now that I'm not truly a god."

"If you're not a god, then I have no concept of what a god is," I responded to him. "This is how I have always shown you respect. Would you have me change?"

"That is a fair point," Thedum conceded. "What is it that you have to ask of me?"

"Was I wrong to kill Nathan Voss?" I asked.

Thedum was silent for a moment. "You acted in accordance with the beliefs that have been established in you by the society in which you live. As such, it could be said that you acted morally and justly. Aside from which, Voss pledged to act unjustly, to bear false witness, and to impede your lawful efforts at establishing peace in your lands. Due to your relative social standings, killing him in a duel was the only way to prevent him from keeping his word. As such, it could be said that you acted correctly."

"Is that what you think, Thedum?" I asked earnestly.

"I think that you did what you thought was right," Thedum answered. "My perspective is so different from yours that the answer I have given is the best one that I can. To my eyes, no harm was done. Voss's spirit is being preserved in the Deadlands, and in time it will be returned to a new body in Lagrea."

"That is not what I meant when I said I intended to have my uncle deal with his body," I pointed out.

Thedum's benevolent voice chuckled. "Yes, well. That action will resonate among the Natives in the past and the future, in case you clicked past that notice without reading it. It is time to start establishing the context of the Gray Man among the Travelers, Hail. You may have always known that story, but the humans who enter this world are discovering it piece by piece. The more you discover for them, the more there is for them to learn."

I sighed. "I don't really care about that right now. I need a new [Ring of Holy Light]."

Thedum was silent for a moment. "I'm sorry. The other gods say no."

My eyes opened wide in surprise. "They what?"

"They consented before, on the condition that it would break when you used [Draining Touch]. Now that you have, they insist on a different mechanism to prevent the spread of [Reaper's Embrace]. Let your followers know that they must receive a blessing at a temple. Any of the eight gods will do. This blessing will protect them from [Reaper's Embrace]. Unless you use [Draining Touch]. Or they are touched by the real Gray Man."

I sighed in frustration. Of course it wouldn't be that simple. "I will let my followers know."

"Or you could not, you know," Thedum said. "That's an option, Hail. You could let them figure some things out for themselves. You don't have to be the hero in this story."

I frowned at the altar. "Are you trying to tempt me, Thedum?"

"One of my aspects is knowledge, Hail. Knowing that an option exists is important in determining whether it, or its alternative, is the correct one or not. Had you even considered keeping silent?"

"Of course not," I said instantly.

"That is why I pointed out that you could," Thedum explained. "Now go. Get started on writing your quests and everything else that you plan to do before your little war starts. But do not forget that you will need to rest twice yourself between now and then."

22

THE BATTLE FOR NORTH SHIRE, PT. 1

Thedum telling me that I would find no condemnation from him for my actions did not ease my conscience, for it also meant he could provide me with no repentance. I checked with Eclipse for a second, but she was just excited that I'd used her sword in a duel that would become infamous. She was never one for moral quandaries to begin with.

I had killed a man. Because he had promised to inconvenience me, I had ended his life and given his body to the Gray Man to prevent his rebirth. My actions were monstrous.

Voss was a traitor to his nation, pledging to shelter those in open rebellion. I fought him in honorable combat and won by the skin of my teeth. Uncle Auroras acted on his own accord. My actions were . . . understandable? Acceptable?

Firming my resolve, I put the matter behind me. After spending some more time coordinating with the Travelers who had already recursed with me into the Recent Past, I sat on my throne and began to work.

First, I updated my objectives. Previously I had assigned six overall goals, for which hundreds of quests had been generated. I removed four of them. Nial Kingslayer, I decided, would come to justice eventually, but he was not my priority at the moment, and I was in no danger of forgetting him, so I struck him from the list. My mother and brother's safety were moved to the top of the list instead.

I was no longer interested in investigating the murders of my uncles. My friends had spent months doing that for me and come to an unfortunate conclusion. They had all killed each other, each paying the assassins' guild to make them first in the line of succession. Storm, it seemed, had survived due to a combination of luck and paranoia. Auroras had survived because he did not play that sort of game and had been in the Deadlands at the time.

That would make Auroras the lawful heir of the two contenders, but, like me, he didn't want it. Or perhaps it was more correct to say that he couldn't hold it. Thedum wouldn't allow the Gray Man to rule Yuikon.

So that left us with . . .

I pushed aside the thoughts. There were a few other options in my generation to be considered, but first I had battles to win. I continued to narrow my objectives until they looked like this:

Use any means necessary to protect Analise Teoran and Rain Teoran II.
Through martial might, remove the Northridge Freelancers from North Shire or bring them to justice.
Protect any and all noncombatant Natives local to North Shire from the violence.
Stabilize and secure North Shire and Thorn March against a possible flood of Travelers.

The list had grown shorter than before, with only four objectives, but I would update it again once the battle was won. I waited for the system to update. In a few moments, thousands of quests were marked as inactive within the Recent Past, while hundreds of new quests were being written every second.

[Keep Me Safe!] was a common one, I noticed. I reviewed several versions of it before approving, but they were simple quests to defend one of my allied quest givers should the battle come to them. There was nothing I could do except fight to reduce the possibility of that happening, so I would have to be as aggressive as possible.

I began writing quests for the Natives who had been roped into the Traveler army to hand out. Quests to siege the bandit's strong-holds and to build and defend our own. And quests to prepare them for the upcoming battles. I coordinated my Quest Writing with Stone, Theresa, and Luke as much as possible since they had eyes on the ground and a good idea of what sort of quests our side would benefit from to influence the outcome.

However, the situation was once again one of "Hurry up and wait." We could kick off the offensive at any time, but my friends in North America were sleeping, so I would rather wait for them to wake and return to my world before I began.

I managed two nights of fitful rest and spent the rest of the time on my throne tweaking things or listening to reports. The bandits knew that they were surrounded but did not seem aware that their escape routes were likewise blocked off. They were overconfident and outmaneuvered—unless our side was missing some crucial piece of information.

Finally, Tarisha logged back into my world, with Laurant a few minutes behind her. Phil, Thena, and Corinth joined them within thirty minutes. They gathered in the war room, which had sprung up inside the Temple of Thedum, and looked at me.

"This is the last chance to back down," Tarisha reminded me. "If you don't start—"

"I killed a man, just because he stood in the way of me bringing peace to North Shire," I said. "It shook my resolve, but every foundation needs to be tested before it is built upon."

And so, I cast [Summon Karmic Warrior], and the room began to fill with hundreds of Travelers with blue auras. From through the stained glass windows, I saw thousands more. It wasn't very long, however, before Stone began cursing.

"The bandits are getting reinforcements," he announced. "Travelers are showing up right inside their compounds. There's nothing we can do to stop them getting in."

"You've only ever had to stop them from getting out," I reminded him. He did not take the words well, and began barking orders at the new arrivals, trying to take charge and direct them to where he thought they needed to be.

I, however, could do what I needed to do from here. Pulling the [Battle Core] from my inventory, I focused on three points on the map of North Shire that had been set up near my throne. With the combined power of the core, the throne, and the map I initiated three battlegrounds at once.

I quickly selected nonparticipation when the option to join came up. That was an option I had this time around, and everyone who had been active with me during the last few days knew to do the same. The reports came in that the bandit's reinforcements were vanishing back into the system, and I relaxed.

"Hey, Hail. Want a favor? I could make that map a whole lot better," Eclipse whispered to me.

"I'll take it," I said, and once more darkness and light erupted from the mark she had put on my right hand. The magic coalesced on the map table, engulfing it in a sphere and fading away a moment later. Leaving the table changed. The map wasn't set on it anymore, but built into it. It had become a real-time updating map of North Shire, and it showed me my active battleground areas.

So far, the plan was working. Because I held the [Battle Core], I could see the statistics of who had answered the call, and I found the number a little staggering. Rumors about my intentions had spread further than I had realized among the unaffiliated players, and millions had signed up to join the first string of battlegrounds.

The vast majority of players who had been online at that moment, in the entire world of Lagrea, had gotten the option to join my war. I saw that most selected the mercenary option, which would balance the sides inside of the battlegrounds. That wasn't important. The more participation there was, the more devastated the bandit fortresses would be in the wake of the battleground. And I would issue battleground after battleground until my side won.

That is when Phil and Laurant's teams would sweep in and arrest the surviving Native bandits, as well as any Travelers not willing to fight to the death. Those would be limited to the Travelers who had been summoned by the balancing portion of my [Summon Karmic Warrior] ability, as the rest of the battleground participants would be returned to their starting location by the system.

Leaving the local survivors to deal with the fresh soldiers who had abstained from entering the battleground.

Victory by attrition. It was a valid tactic.

Holding my [Battle Core] and looking at my new map table from my throne, I was able to somewhat see how the battle was faring between my forces, the bandits, and the mercenaries on both sides.

The mercenaries were suffering devastating losses, but that was because they were all choosing to spend their time "dicking around midfield" rather than completing the objectives of destroying the bandit or army fort, as they should be. I ignored it; the death ratio between the two forces only mattered for respawn rates. My side was organized, and its core wasn't dying as they set about raiding the bandit camps with whatever forces they could bring with them.

Some of the bandits tried to rally, but they were betrayed by their own mercenaries who, upon realizing that they had been assigned to the bandits, decided to turn coat on their own initiative.

The first battleground was won in twenty minutes. The second, eight minutes after that. The final of the three was won fifteen minutes after that.

I waited to hear the field reports as they were relayed up the chain. Twelve prisoners from the Northridge Freelancers. An undetermined number of Native bandits killed. All of the Traveler bandits had chosen to fight to the death rather than be captured.

The bandit camps had been destroyed, and, more importantly, they had been destroyed in a battleground. That mattered; the bandits couldn't hold them again without challenging the outcome of the battle, and that would require the creation of a new battleground. It was unlikely that they had the cores or Authority to make their own [Battle Cores].

Once I had been told the reports, I waited an hour for everyone to get into position, and then I started the next three battlegrounds that were part of my planned opening salvo. The results were not as favorable to my side this time. With the element of surprise spent, the bandits realized that they were playing a defensive game and managed to destroy the siege fortresses that we had established for two of their own camps.

Not without cost. The system said that one bandit camp suffered eighty-seven percent Damage and was on the verge of collapse when the conditions for victory were met. The other battleground managed to conserve themselves at sixty-four percent.

I immediately started a new battle, selecting new encampments slightly farther away to replace the destroyed ones. This is why I had created a core with so many extra charges, anyway. The bandit camp that had only barely survived the first round fell within moments, and the second one lasted only twenty minutes after that, although they put up a significant fight.

In the other timeline, these bandit camps had been found and destroyed by my leaderless forces as well. But the bandits had faded away from one camp to the next, establishing a new hiding place whenever the last one was destroyed or discovered. They had not expected the *blitzkrieg* tactics I had just launched on them, and I didn't think that they could recover. I wouldn't let them get the chance.

Once the final tally was in from my soldiers—the former steward, Arkan, and the former constable, Montague, had been arrested, but Tervin Riley, the bandit leader, remained at large—I again pulled out my [Battle Core]. It had nine charges. From my seat on the throne, I expended five of them all at once to create a single battleground.

Attention! An Event of Note is taking place in the Recent Past right now, and this is your chance to be a part of it! Earl Hail Jeoran has initiated the following battleground! Bandits: Seek and Destroy! As the initiator of this event, you do not have the option of not taking part. Your allegiance is to House Jeoran. Your role has been automatically selected based upon your allegiance.	
Faction Leader	Hail Jeoran (50 Morale)
Enemy Faction Leader	Tervin Riley (50 Morale)
Victory Conditions	90% of remaining bandit forces are killed, arrested, or driven from your lands.
Loss Conditions	Morale Reaches 0
Prepare for combat! Good luck!	

I studied the system prompt for a moment, but before very long my body turned to mist as the system brought me out of Lagrea and into the lobby to prepare for the beginning of the battleground.

I noticed, before I was whisked away, that my death was not listed as a loss condition. My team would simply lose fifty Morale.

23
THE BATTLE FOR NORTH SHIRE, PT. 2

The fighting was fierce.

The battle was long.

We would be victorious, even if I were to die.

Morale was spiraling back and forth. It had started at ten thousand for each team, but as the battle progressed and entire teams were wiped out *en mass*, it fluctuated hundreds of points at a time.

Compared to that, I was but a fly in the wineglass. I might be worth fifty Morale to the enemies if they managed to kill me, but that was proving difficult for them.

I had, on a whim, tried casting [Illusion Magic: Disguise], and to my surprise the spell had worked. I had previously received a message saying that the spell was unavailable during battlegrounds, but I may have interpreted that too broadly. It might not have been available during the Battle of Mooncrest Manor, because I was the target. I was not the target here.

Neither was I the center of this battleground. At all. While I was instanced only with others between levels thirty-five and forty-five, it was very clear from the outset that I was not the biggest fish in the school. One on one, perhaps I could have taken down almost anyone here, but there were teams of Travelers who were practiced at working together who would rip me apart and eat me alive, so to speak. Probably while trash talking me and scolding me for my build being useless.

After all, that's what they were doing to everyone else who challenged them. I was glad that the ones I had latched on to were on my side. Although they hadn't seen through my magical disguise yet, they had the sky blue auras of Travelers who had been farming Reputation with my faction. And the icons over their heads indicated that they had selected to fight for House Jeoran, and not selected the mercenary options. Or perhaps, like me, they had been presented with only one option, which was perhaps even better.

"Hey, wallflower, get over here," one of the teammates I'd attached myself to said. Glancing around to make certain they were discussing me, I walked over to them.

"So, look, I know it sucks that you got isolated from your friends or whatever," she continued. "But we don't want you leeching off of us and contributing nothing."

I frowned. "You're telling me to leave?"

"*And contributing nothing*," she repeated with emphasis. "Look, it's clear you're 'pay to win,' and that's fine. We're not. If you want to hang with us, you need to get some kills or assists to keep up with the rest of us. That's all I'm saying."

"You want me to do my part," I said, understanding blossoming.

"Yeah, that's right," she agreed. "Thing is, I have no idea how to incorporate you into our team. What are you? I mean, I see you casting magic, but that's a goddamn god-blessed rapier at your hip. So you're either a [Mage] with the weirdest stat stick as a weapon I've ever heard of, or—"

"You've probably heard of me," I said. "I'm wearing a disguise. I was active in the Recent Past before all of the battlegrounds started. That's what brought you here."

"Oh," she said, and she was quiet for a moment. "What happens if you die here?"

"To the battleground? Our team loses fifty Morale. Same as if we kill Tervin Riley, I think," I said.

"And the story? Do you know how that would play out?" she asked. "Battlegrounds are canon events."

"I have an ability that will prevent me from suffering a true death," I admitted. "But it will set me back considerably. Among other issues, I'll return to level one."

"And North Shire? What happens if we lose this battleground?" she asked, persistent.

"It's better that we don't," I said. "I only have four charges left on the item I've been using to create them."

"So, we have four chances to get this right?" she asked.

"Not exactly. I expended five charges to start this particular battleground. I'm not certain how a four-charged version of it would be different," I explained. "But it would probably not be good for the history of North Shire to lose this battle repeatedly. Each battle is canon, in case you forgot."

She cursed. In French, I realized. That was curious. I was starting to learn the differences between swearing in multiple languages.

"I was hoping that we'd have infinite chances, after the repeat battlegrounds to take down those bandit camps," she explained. "But if we have one good go and one not so good go, then we need to get it in one."

I nodded. I was withholding key information from her, such as the fact that it was a relatively simple process for me to create a new [Battle Core]. But I didn't want to use any more cores than I'd already spent on the purging of bandits from my lands.

"I was at Mooncrest, you know," she said. "Don't have the Title active because I have a better one for PVP, but I was in the team that drove off two of the bandit leaders. Do you have any information that might help us win?"

I considered for a moment. "Well, I do have this magic table that shows the locations of my allied forces and my enemies," I said. "It was created by Eclipse herself."

The woman gave me a look like I was an idiot. "Then where is it?"

"Well, before the battle started it was with me in the Temple of Thedum," I explained. "I'm not certain if it's still there or not. I was warped to spawn point theta when the battleground started, and I've been laying low ever since. I told you, if the bandits kill me, I get reset to level one, and I don't want that to happen."

"Yeah, and some idiot might turn coat just for the chance of an achievement. I got it," the Traveler said. "I'm Jess. Give me a second.

I need to do some typing with the information you just gave me. It's going to win us the battle."

She stood still and began typing at the invisible terminal that came up when summoned. I took the opportunity to cast [Mark of Karma] on her and all of the other allies who had been in our group.

That ability, which had long been sitting idle in my spellbook and casting itself automatically, was now under my control. In fact, it had split into four abilities, and they even came with descriptions.

Mark of Karma (Apply)	Apply Boon [Mark of Karma] to selected target. All stats +5% and +10% exp. Warnings issued before accepting quests that will negatively impact Reputation with Hail Jeoran.
Mark of Karma (Rescind)	Remove [Mark of Karma] from a target.
Mark of Karmic Balance (Apply)	Apply Boon [Mark of Karmic Balance] to selected target. All stats +5% and +10% exp. Reputation gain with factions allied with Hail Jeoran set to 50%.
Mark of Karmic Balance (Rescind)	Remove [Mark of Karmic Balance] from a target.

I had been giving out [Mark of Karma] to everyone who had come into the battleground with the tag above their head that indicated they had chosen to fight for me. The mercenaries would get no such treatment. Not the ones fighting on either side. But the bandit Travelers, the ones who had deliberately selected to play on the side of the Northridge Freelancers, got [Mark of Karmic Balance].

I wasn't too worried about it really. I had the ability to remove the effect now, although I figured that both sides would be affected by my [Summon Karmic Warrior] ability in the future. More importantly, I was inclined to believe that putting [Mark of Karma] on the allies I had met in the battleground would help shunt then into the same instance as me when the battleground was over. If they wanted to seek me out after the fighting was over, the mark would make their way much easier, and I could always use more capable allies.

"I'm curious," I said after Jess had been typing for a few minutes. "Why is your team so good?"

"Because low level is where PVP is meta," she explained. "You can't risk it at level one hundred ninety. Too much grinding to get back after every loss. But in the forties, you can get two or three levels in a dungeon. So you do three dungeons, PVP for a few days until the penalty hits you back to whatever you consider your minimum, and then you rinse and repeat. The whole reason these last few battlegrounds have been so awesome is that the death penalty is reduced to two hours of logout time and the Experience penalty is reduced ninety percent. Was that your decision?"

"I had to use extra resources for it," I admitted. "I could have gotten fifty charges instead of seventeen."

She whistled. "I'd say that you made the right decision for maximum participation. Lots of casuals held out on the first battleground because they were afraid of the death penalty. You know I'm not under an NDA, right? I can share whatever you tell me online if I want to, unlike everyone that witch Tarisha whips into your circle."

"Do not insult her," I said, my tone severe.

Jess paused, and then she nodded at me in apology. "I'm sorry. I'll even apologize to her if you introduce us. But I'm not signing an NDA."

"I fought a duel recently in which I almost lost," I told her. "I'd never faced anyone with my class before. We each played it differently, but he was higher level, had just as much gear as I did, and had more experience with his methods."

"If you're asking me to line up a [Spellblade] training partner for you, I'm not sure I can help you," she said, still typing. "I think I heard about it, though. One of those pop-ups everyone got. 'An action in the recent past has resonated' or whatever. You fought two duels, lost one, and won the other, right?"

"The first one was a draw," I clarified.

"Yeah, that means you both lost," she said.

"It's just that, seeing the way you fight, it's completely different from what I've learned. But the way you learn to fight that way is by dying and re-leveling repeatedly," I explained. "I wish that option was available to me."

"Isn't it?" she asked. "Didn't you just say that if you get PK'd here, you get reset to level one? So, let that happen and bust your ass back to forty, and I'll show you all the active PVP arenas where you can git gud."

"If I die here, I may take you up on that option," I admitted, and I extended to her a friend invite. She accepted without hesitation.

"Okay," she announced to everyone, "break's over. Strategos is good for Project Overwatch. A team near the temple managed to get inside and confirm that the asset Hail describes exists, but it says it requires 'The Seal of Authority' in order to update in real time. Hail, do you have any idea what that means?"

I nodded. "Either I need to be physically present, or I need to use one of my abilities on it, or both."

"All right then, ladies and gents," she announced. "We are now on an escort quest to get the good prince to the temple so that he can unlock overwatch for us. The noob cannot take care of himself in group PVP, so watch his ass until he unlocks overwatch. Understood?"

"Yes, Mom," a deep voice said. It came from a deceptively small avatar, but the weapon that Traveler wielded was a two-handed battle axe larger than my chest.

I was encircled but not enspelled with any additional protections other than the standard group buffs that everyone was enjoying. The party mounted up and rode with a purpose from our space near spawn point theta back towards Ebbyvale, six leagues away.

24
THE BATTLE FOR NORTH SHIRE, PT. 3

So, what's it like being you, anyway?" Jess asked. "I've asked the other Natives, and they all give the same answer. But the admin says you're different, so I thought I'd ask."

"What's it like to be you?" I asked. "To live on Earth? To not live under time dilation? And I understand you have physical pain. Something that I'm told I cannot experience, as the state of my Health or any status conditions I'm inflicted with do not adequately translate the experience. I'm told it's terrible."

She turned away and focused on the road. "Yeah, see. Exactly what I mean. The other Natives would have never answered like that."

There were eight of us. Not the perfect number, but six of the team were regular allies that Jess was used to working with, while the other two were known to her in their PVP circle. If they had noticed that I had granted them all [Mark of Karma], they remained silent on the matter.

"Did you all get the blessing?" I asked suddenly, feeling the coldness in my left hand. "Tarisha said—"

"She said that anyone taking part in the battle should get a blessing. Yeah. I swung by a Temple of Starweaver as soon as I read that post," she explained. "Everyone here has a blessing, right?"

A series of grunts answered her, and I keyed in on one detail. "Starweaver? You're not an elf."

"Starweaver doesn't really care, does she? The elves like her more than Thedum. It's not the other way around, is it? Where Thedum doesn't help them because he doesn't like them?" Jess inquired.

"That's one way of looking at it," I admitted. "So you prefer to play human, but you venerate Starweaver?"

"No, her temple was just the closest one I could find on short notice. I only logged in about an hour before shit went down. If I had to pick between any of the gods in this game, I'd probably pick Mossheart. But the human race is balanced best for my play style. I really don't want to have to check on a freaking tree every week. That's idiotic," Jess said. "I like nature. I like trees. Best thing about trees is that they pretty much do their own thing, and you don't have to worry about them. Ever. Except when you go for a hike and admire them. Which I never do."

I nodded. And then we were attacked.

A series of spells and arrows struck at one of our healers while the other was shifted into the shape of a snake by [Polymorph]. A [Mage] on our own team quickly managed to dispel that effect and began [Counterspelling] the [Mage] who had stepped forward from the ambush.

That [Mage] was . . . interestingly geared. Unlike the usual [Mages] I'd seen, he was wearing heavy armor that prioritized his Vitality stat over his Intelligence. And he wasn't casting Damage spells.

He was a crowd control specialist, I realized. Something that only a person dedicated to low-level PVP would consider; he might just be a force multiplier if we allowed him to run rampant.

Fortunately, I had no shortage of crowd control myself.

The group was too spread out for my usual flashbang combo of [Dazzling Lights] and [Concussive Sound] to hit everyone, but I did [Swiftcast] [Befuddle] on the armored [Mage]. He seemed to be expecting it because it was swiftly dispelled by someone else on their team. He then proceeded to chant the cantrip for [Concussive Sound] at us, only for one of our [Mages] to get a [Counterspell] off in time. It only forced him to start the spell over.

"I'll take care of him," I promised, sprinting forward to the armored [Mage].

"Wait! Don't separate from the group!" Jess called, but I wasn't listening.

With the information available in my new interface, I had known that we were losing. The incoming Damage was unsustainable to the healers, and our enemies had cover. We couldn't move while the armored [Mage] was alive. The simplest solution to the problem was to remove the armored [Mage].

He saw me coming and, with a smirk, [Swiftcast] a [Slow] at me, but I caught it on my [Arcane Weapon]. It was at that point that my disguise failed, and the enemy realized whom my party was escorting.

"It's Hail!" the armored [Mage] shouted. "Get him! For Teh Lulz!"

"For Teh Lulz!" came the echoing shout from the other bandits—a war cry. And I realized it was one that I had coined myself. In a video I had made while full of grief over the death of my grandfather, I had made a vow. This was the result. I was at first uncertain how to see this turn of events, but then I chose. These Travelers were giving me a target for my grief and rage, and I would oblige them.

I cast [Mark of Karmic Balance] on all of them as I swatted down the crowd control [Mage]'s spells and used my [Arcane Weapon] to rip through the healing effects that his team tried to put on him. At the last moment, I switched to [Holy Weapon]. Because I knew something about that ability now that I hadn't known before.

Holy Weapon (Max)	Apply holy aura to weapon, modified by spell power. Low Mana cost. Applies [Brand of Sin] when used in PVP.

If this [Mage] wanted to make himself my enemy, then I would oblige him twice over.

I did not do all of this in isolation. The six members of the other team tried to kill me, and they tried to heal their friend through my Damage. Unfortunately for them, [Arcane Weapon] makes most healing magic unsustainable if I focus on the target they're healing, and my own allies were able to shield me through the worst of their attacks, while drawing most of the other party's attention to themselves. A few missiles did get by me to strike the armored [Mage] as well, so it wasn't entirely my kill.

But the armored [Mage] was the linchpin in the enemy's strategy, and once he was defeated, our own [Mages] were free to begin [Counterspelling] the enemy healers and traditional [Mages]. Our healers topped us off, and we nuked the party down within moments. I did my part from range, casting [Empowered] [Chain Lightning] into the group until they split up enough that the spell wouldn't jump, then spamming [Arcane Missiles] to harass them with mosquito bites for being spread out. I didn't approach, as I knew from watching other skilled PVP groups that I'd get eaten alive without two or three melee backing me up, but a two man team from our side [Charged] and [Leaped] into their group.

With the support of our healers and our ranged fighters, it was short work from there.

"Okay, yeah. So how does that work. They can't heal a target while you're focused on it?" Jess inquired as we regrouped after surviving the ambush. We'd had the numbers, but the enemy had had the element of surprise, so it was a little amazing that we hadn't lost anyone from our team.

"I'm not certain I should explain my abilities to a PVP specialist unless they sign an NDA and enter into a formal alliance with me," I said.

"Shit, now I'm almost curious enough to do it," she muttered. "You have some sort of on-strike dispel. That much is obvious. And enough horsepower to eat through a [Mage]-tank build in fifteen seconds, effectively making you a hard counter to them as long as they don't get you CC'd. What was that white flash at the end?"

"A final 'F you.' For Teh Lulz," I explained.

"Oh. You know about that?" she asked.

"It wasn't hard to figure out. Some sort of battle cry for those who oppose me?" I asked.

"Not originally," she explained. "Now it's a guild name, and it's kind of growing with you. Not as fast. But as much as some people want to be on your side, there are enough that don't. Yeah, you should probably know about them. Your friend Tarisha probably knows about them already, so you should check with her."

"I'll be certain to bring it up the next time we speak," I promised.

"Good. Now listen. Don't go fucking off like that again on your own, or next time we won't back you up," Jess said. "You may be scaled to compete with Gideon or whatever, but Gideon was only good at PVE. He never PVP'd, except to claim Worldbosses from griefers. If you want, after this is over maybe I'll put some work into teaching you how to not embarrass yourself. Or at least we'll see if you can learn. I don't really know enough about you to say what you can and can't do in this game."

"I've been doing fine so far," I protested. "We would have lost in that ambush without me."

"No, we would have been driven back because they had cover. Then we would have petered around for a while until both sides made a withdrawal," Jess said. "I admit that your purple sword ability changed the balance. But the first rule about group PVP is that you don't trust the PVP noob to do his job. What you *should* have done was cover us from incoming projectiles with that ability while spamming those missiles you have against random targets to cover our retreat."

I looked at her askance. "But we won."

"Yeah. But it won't work again, because now everyone knows we have a [Spellblade] in our group," she said. "And there's only one [Spellblade] in this entire game who's worth talking about. Come on, let's get moving. We need to get to the Temple of Thedum and fortify it before the bandits and <Teh Lulz> figure out where we're going."

I decided I was too old to pout. And then I pouted anyway as we summoned our mounts and kicked them into a gallop. I actually had to keep Shadow at a cantor, as he was faster than the mounts of my allies, but we traveled as fast as we could through the open land of North Shire towards Ebbyvale, passing by villages that were encircled with gray. I knew that I would not be able to pass through those boundaries, but Native bandits would be able to enter them to surrender to my forces within, and Travelers of both factions could use them as exits from the region-wide battleground.

We were attacked three more times on our journey but never in numbers enough to actually threaten our party. It was simple harassment, though it backfired once. A group of four [Rogues] had thought to stun-lock our healer, only to realize too late that we had a second one. Not only did the first healer survive, but we ripped through them before they could employ their escape abilities, earning our group another handful of kills.

Despite my own party's success in killing the enemy, House Jeoran was losing Morale. While it had started at ten thousand for both sides, it was down to six thousand for House Jeoran. That didn't mean we were losing, exactly, as we had also captured fifty percent of the fugitive bandits. We would win when the bandit capture rate hit ninety percent, while the enemy would have to drive our Morale all the way to zero for us to lose.

We came into view of Ebbyvale, only to realize that since Jess had last been in contact with the strategic Travelers who were overseeing our side of this battle, the town had become the site of an epic, two-hundred-man war.

25
THE BATTLE FOR NORTH SHIRE, PT. 4

I don't suppose one of [Spellblade]'s secret spells is [Invisibility], is it?" Jess asked me as we watched both sides exchanging salvos of magic and missiles in the streets of my largest town.

"I was hoping someone on your team would have that for me," I admitted. "Why are they attacking Ebbyvale?"

"It's how they're ahead on points," she explained. "Or sort of, at least. It's a king of the hill thing. We lose Morale if they hold Ebbyvale, and we don't get the Morale back when we retake it. It's how they'll beat us if we don't figure out a way to track down the holdout bandit NPCs. Um, sorry."

"Sorry?" I asked.

"Slipped out. I meant Natives."

I turned to look at her, cocking my head slightly. "Jess, I am a Native player character. And I am proud of that fact. I do not consider being called an NPC to be an insult."

She looked surprised, then nodded. "However you want it, then. The NPCs in town are all hiding or barricaded, so they're safe. They've been attacking the prison to try to do a jailbreak, but we've driven them off every time so far because the defenses your boys and girls put up are actually pretty damn good."

"Randal the Architect designed them," I said, bragging.

"But none of that really matters, because as long as the enemy is running around town, we're losing Morale. We're calling in reinforcements, but so are they. And that's how we're getting into the temple. There should be a larger group coming up in a few minutes that we'll—oh, there they are. Hail, stay at range and pretend to be a [Mage] until we get you inside the Temple of Thedum. We need that map," Jess said.

I followed the instructions; our smaller group folded into the larger one and rode deeper through the town. We were confronted by an equal-sized war party before reaching the temple. The bandits were caught between us and the reinforced constabulary, but they were also blocking our path.

The leaders decided that they must be dealt with. I tried to maintain my cover as a [Mage], throwing out [Slow] and [Polymorph] spells as well as the occasional flashbang combo. Unfortunately, those were the exact spells that [Mages] cast to draw attention to themselves in PVP, and I suddenly had two [Rogues] pop out of stealth behind me. One hit me with a four-second stun, the other an [Ambush] that dealt forty-one percent of my Health. Only a timely shield and a power heal by my allies saved my life.

I couldn't blink away, which would be the [Mage] response. I could [Dash], but five feet isn't actually all that far. So I drew my [Blade of Eclipse], and I turned to face them both. They both had a red glow that showed they had been completing quests that gave them negative Reputation with me, and a red icon over their heads showed that they had chosen to come into the battleground on behalf of the Freelancers.

So I would show no mercy. I hit them both with [Mark of Karmic Balance]. It's funny because they'd actually probably thank me for that now. The Experience and status boons were the same as [Mark of Karma]. But the Reputation loss was going to hurt them in the long run.

I skipped using my usual elemental combos. I fought them as I had once fought as a Worldboss. I fought with my [Holy Weapon], and they both cried out in shock as [Brand of Sin] was applied to them thanks to my [Righteous Brand] ability. Still not done with them, I grabbed hold of the one on the left and used [Draining Touch]. Her body withered into a skeleton, but I knew that when she respawned, she would be inflicted with [Reaper's Embrace]. Whether she considered it a curse or a boon would depend on her perspective, I suppose. But I doubted she could get it cured at any Temple of Thedum.

I got separated from Jess and her party for a while. In fact, I was sort of caught "dicking around midfield." Most of the enemy mistook me for some sort of [Paladin], with my [Holy Weapon], and I waded through the battleground, defending myself as necessary. Mostly my attention was focused on applying my unique banes to those I thought deserved them, based on the color of their aura or their icons.

A lot of Travelers got [Mark of Karma] and [Mark of Karmic Balance] that day. And quite a few got [Brand of Sin].

When the enemy realized what was going on, and that I was the source of the ruining that was happening to some of them, they turned on me. But by that point I had gotten far enough into town to sprint for the barricade at the Temple of Thedum. The blue icon over my head announced my allegiance, and the barricade opened up, its healers throwing shields and heals onto me to keep me alive.

The enemies following me were enraged, especially the ones whom I had affected with [Draining Touch]. On top of instantly stealing a large portion of their Health and Mana—I still got Mana even if their resource was something other than Mana, as it was for [Rogues] and [Archers]—I had been inflicting them with the dangerous combo of [Through the Valley of the Shadow] and [Reaper's Embrace]. While the former increased all Experience gained to three hundred percent normal, the bane that went with it effectively negated any benefit to the boon.

Specifically, on death, [Reaper's Embrace] removed ten times the amount of Experience gained by [Through the Valley of the Shadow]. It was a dangerous combo, but the version that I inflicted on Travelers was much more generous than the version that was inflicted on me by my great-uncle Auroras. That version had the same Experience boon, but it would reduce me to level one no matter what.

The Travelers could at least undertake quests to remove their afflictions. The removal of my curse depended upon the democracy of the gods or it required me to arrange the death of a family member. If Auroras died, then I would be free of this curse. I might have been willing to kill Voss in a duel, but I was not willing to kill my family. Not for any reason.

There was one more method, of course. But that required triggering it and returning to level one. Screw that!

The charge that followed after me was ill performed, while the defensive wall that accepted the charge was disciplined and well coordinated. Many bandits died, though few of my allies did. Ultimately the bandits retreated, their objective of killing me abandoned as they instead ran about town causing havoc.

"You're the kid Gem was talking about," the leader at the temple said, pulling me aside. "The NPC kid who can give us a map."

"Are you talking about Jess?" I asked.

"Jess is a Gem," he said. "Can you give us an overwatch map or not?"

I frowned at him, and I shrugged. "Let's go find out together, shall we?"

Although it had been incorporated into the battleground, the Temple of Thedum was largely unchanged from before. It was a place of shelter, and a large number of Natives were hiding inside. When they saw me, they called out, and to the Travelers' surprise our Morale suddenly jumped by three hundred points.

"Okay, that's useful," the temple commander said. "I'm going to let the others know that even if we can't use your map, we can parade you around to the places the locals are hiding and boost Morale."

I shrugged and made my way over to the map table. If being paraded around was the role I needed to play to win this war, I was fine with that. But first I needed to see if I could give my allies the map they craved.

The map table did nothing when I simply touched it but responded immediately when I cast [Magical Seal: Personal Crest]. A prompt began flowing above it.

This map was created with Divine Favor for Hail Jeoran.

Using Objects of Favor within Battlegrounds may be permissible depending on circumstances.

Seeking oversight approval.

Approval Received.

Note: Enemies may claim map functions by claiming this object for themselves.

Grant map functions to allies?

Yes	No

I quickly selected "Yes," and soon everyone in the room was looking at their system map.

"Okay, that's a little bit better than I was expecting," the temple commander commented. "I'm going to get on the horn and call in some strike teams to the locations. It seems that *all* of the instances just got access to the map, not just ours. We're going to pull this off after all."

"Tell them to guard the temple," I said urgently. "The enemy gets access to the maps if they get in the temple."

The commander turned to me, nodded, and began typing twice as urgently into the battlegrounds command chatroom. "Good job, kid. We'll take it from here."

I nodded at him, and I felt a sort of inward collapse as I realized that the situation was now completely out of my hands. I had given my allies the one tool that they had lacked to win this fight, and all they needed to do now was claim victory. I was just one [Spellblade]. And I had just gotten multiple reminders that while my class was powerful, it was not the only powerful class in the world, and it did not make me invincible.

The only reason I had survived to make it to the temple was due to [Draining Touch]. Without that ability, I would have died in my dash through Ebbyvale several times over. I had been so reliant upon it during this battleground that I had leveled it all the way from level two, where it had been after my duel with Nathan Voss, to level thirteen, after the completion of the battleground.

I tried to remember the past hour in detail and found that it was a blur. Much more so than dungeons usually were. I was a little startled to realize that I hadn't felt this way since my first dungeon, when I had been overwhelmed in the aftermath of the rest of the party wiping.

After twenty minutes of waiting, I collapsed into my throne to wait out the conclusion of the battle. And that, depending on how you look at it, was either a mistake or a stroke of genius.

Victory is within your grasp! 68% of bandit forces have been captured or killed in combat. Offer terms of surrender to your enemy?	
Yes	No

I was confused for a moment because the victory condition listed at the start of the battle was a ninety percent limit. We were gaining ground quickly with the ability of my strike teams to hunt down the stragglers using their updated maps, but they were some ways away from winning yet.

"If Tervin Riley surrenders, and his lieutenants surrender with him," I said, understanding that the chair was asking me for more than a yes-or-no answer, for the terms I would put on the surrender, "then they will be tried for their crimes of banditry. But I will commute any death penalty into life imprisonment for anyone who does not have the weight of a murder on their soul. If they participate in the investigation into the corruption of the civil officials of North Shire, I may offer them chances to make restitution for their crimes and earn clemency."

The "Yes" button highlighted itself blue; a second later, it turned white as Tervin Riley accepted the terms.

Victory!
House Jeoran Wins!
Participation and Contribution Rewards will be calculated and awarded within 24 game hours!
Note: The Northridge Freelancers have surrendered and no longer exist as an organization. All Reputation with this faction is void.
Note: This is an action that will resonate into the Near Future.
Note: This is an action that *will not* resonate into the Divergence

Title Awarded:	Veteran of the Battle for North Shire

26
VICTORY?

And just like that, the battle was over. I did not move from the Temple of Thedum; I remained sitting on my throne, while the many combatants who had been with me were portaled back to wherever they had been when the battleground had started. Except, of course, that they would have traveled into the Recent Past. They no longer had the ability to return to the Near Future, which was now known as the Divergence.

My chat icons were lighting up. Everyone wanted to talk to me, but I didn't know who to start with. I decided that Tarisha was likely the most urgent, so I opened her private channel.

Hail	Hello, Tarisha. I guess we won.
Tarisha	Congratulations, Hail! I know you worked hard for this.
Hail	Everyone worked hard for this. I hope the system rewards are good enough to satisfy everyone because there's no other way I'll be able to pay everyone back for all of their effort.

Tarisha	You really underestimate yourself, Hail. Or you don't realize how important your quests and events are, at least. I'm able to pay rent for the next ten years just because I was able to give some people inside information on what was coming. And I'm sharing that money with Lewis and his friends, by the way. They'll need it, whether they stay in college or go pro.
Hail	That's how you make money? Inside information on what I do?
Tarisha	. . . Did I not explain it properly? Hail, when we said that I was your liaison with the endgame guilds, that's what I meant. I'm sort of like a meteorologist to them. I predict Hailstorms. Get it?
Hail	Sorry. You're right. We've covered this. I won't understand Earth's economy, so I'm not going to try. I'm just glad you're able to prosper because of me. Just don't be trading my secrets to hurt my family, or I'll never forgive you.
Tarisha	I'm literally doing the opposite, Hail. Everyone I'm involved with is strongly in your corner.
Hail	I believe you. Is it true that "the true PVP meta is at level 40"?
Tarisha	. . . There are some schools of thought that believe that. It's around the level where the death penalty remains manageable. It's the same reason why endgame meta starts at 180 instead of 200. You die so often in PVP that you need to be able to recover your levels quickly. You can level from 40 to 50 doing two or three dungeons, PVP to death 10 times, and then repeat. In raiding, it's sort of the same. The bosses lose level-disparity Damage reduction at 180, and your stat growth from leveling is negligible compared to gear. But it takes a lot of Experience to recover one level at that point, so there's a big focus on staying alive. That's hard in raids. Harder in Red Raids than Green Raids. Reaching level 200 is a real accomplishment. It means that you haven't died in a very, very long time.
Hail	Father was level 200 when he left the game.
Tarisha	Yes, he was.

Hail	Nial Kingslayer was level 200 when he slew my grandfather.
Tarisha	He's not anymore.
Hail	What level is he now?
Tarisha	I don't know. But I know that he's been assassinated a couple of times to complete your guild quest to form an alliance. He griped about it on the forums each time it happened.
Hail	According to Thomas, that's fine. As long as I don't harass him by his true name or send people to bother him on Earth, I can assign quests targeting him.
Tarisha	Yeah, I know. Hail, do you want me to come to you? I can now without a cooldown. The whole time-magic-screwy-thing that the admin had planned to get you back in time to see your brother after he was born is done. All of my abilities I got when I went canon are being unsealed, and the Near Future is splitting off from the main timeline.
Hail	I know. Send ten guardians to protect my mother and brother like always, but I think I want to be alone for a while. Tarisha . . . I killed Voss.
Tarisha	I heard about that. Do you want to talk about it?
Hail	I don't think it was the wrong thing to do. But his spirit is stuck in the Deadlands because of me.
Tarisha	I'm sure it's not as terrible as you're imagining, Hail. Voss is probably just . . . sleeping. Waiting for something to happen to give him purpose again.
Hail	I hope you're right. I think I want to be alone for a while, but I'm going to be popping in and out of different chats.
Tarisha	Okay. Are you somewhere safe, though?
Hail	I'm going to Fast Travel to Eastmill. I like the food at Niles's Inn, and it's where I said goodbye to Father. I'll spend the rest of the day and sleep there. Nobody really knows about it, and I'll disguise myself, so it should be safe.

Tarisha	Okay. If you need help, you can call for me, Hail. I'll be there within seconds with 10 of the best other [Warriors] I can find.
Hail	I know. Talk to you later, Tarisha.

I made good on my word, Fast Traveling to my favorite hidden eatery and asking for a private room from Niles. I had a bowl of lamb stew and a mug of Liecha flavored with dark honey, and I spent the rest of the day chatting with people in my guild and friends list.

Laurant and Phil confirmed that the surviving bandit Natives were all in custody and under guard in the expanded prison that had been built for them. Daemon was still performing the headcount on the citizens that we had lost in the violence, but it didn't appear to be too many. The battlegrounds had all been designed to penalize attacking the citizenry when they were taking shelter, as virtually all of the Native citizenry had.

The death count among the bandits, whether you count Native or Traveler, was very high. But not as high as many might think, considering that the majority of deaths on the battleground had been mercenaries who had just wanted to fight. If the battlegrounds themselves hadn't targeted the bandits, the bandits would have been able to slink away. Which was, of course, why I had used battlegrounds to root them out to begin with.

Corinth griped with me that he had gotten pushed into a different battleground than me for the final battle due to level. He also promised that he'd be pushing his goblin marauder level to catch up with me if I didn't start leveling again soon. I informed him that I had gotten level forty-four in the battleground, and he had shared his own gains, which had kept the distance between us equal. We were both benefiting from [Through the Valley of the Shadow], after all, since I had accidentally inflicted him with that curse, and he had decided to keep it active rather than use one of the options available to Travelers to cleanse it.

The word was out that I could brand Travelers, as well. And of the curse/boon combo and my [Mark of Karmic Balance]. Not everyone who had received the trio of permanent or semi-permanent afflictions I could inflict were complaining about them. [Mark of Karmic Balance] was seen as a net positive by a lot of Travelers, and there was a petition from people who wanted to get it, despite the difficulty it would cause for their Reputations long term.

As for branding and [Reaper's Embrace], only time would tell how the Travelers would react to those. Right now there was too much scattered noise on the forums to get a clear picture of what anyone thought.

The most popular message by far was some variation of "GG had fun" from mercenaries on both sides of the brief war. The winners were celebrating, and the losers were celebrating too. Only my army was working, securing the bandit Natives until the trial could start.

I should be celebrating too. But I couldn't stop thinking about everything. About Voss. About the battlegrounds. I had done all of that. I was responsible.

Blue lights flashed in my private room at Niles's Inn, and Thomas was there. As was a rack of ribs. He sat down and started eating.

"So, do you want to talk about it?" he asked, his mouth half full of digital flesh.

"Not really. I don't know how to put it into words," I admitted.

"Yeah," Thomas said. "You did right. But it feels wrong, doesn't it?"

"I should be celebrating," I said.

"Hail, we are celebrating," Thomas informed me. He got some sauce on his face, but it vanished a second later. It was only there for the sensation of getting sauce on your face while eating ribs. That was important, for some reason.

"Celebrating was more fun when I didn't really know what I was celebrating," I said. "It feels cheap to celebrate that I killed Voss in cold blood. Or all the bandits that were ground under my heel when I unleashed the battlegrounds on them. Am I going to be a tyrant, Thomas?"

"I doubt it," Thomas answered. "But nobody would stop you if you went down that path. Not from the admin, at least. The players would probably love it, and as long as we could find adequate environments to raise future seeds of consciousness in your lands, we wouldn't have any problem letting you rule the Natives how you wished."

"You really wouldn't mind?" I asked.

Thomas shrugged. "I'd be a little disappointed because I don't think you are that sort of person. But from an official standpoint, it wouldn't be a bad thing for the administration. Is that what you want,

Hail? To vanquish your enemies? To chase them and to deprive them of their wealth? To hear the lamentations of their—"

"That's not me at all," I said hotly.

Thomas nodded. A mug of a brown ale appeared beside his plate, and he took a swig of it. "Then don't. You chose to be ruthless with the bandits, but you also showed them mercy in the end. Those two traits are not irreconcilable, Hail."

I sighed and ordered another stew from Niles. We sat in companionable silence for a while while we ate together. "Thomas, what's this all about, anyway? Why did you make me to begin with? I understand by now that it wasn't just a simple act of my father loving my mother that brought me into this world."

Thomas wiped a bit of sauce from his cheek. It vanished rather than staining his robes. "I don't know, honestly. I wasn't in on the planning stages, so I can't speak to what the original developers had in mind for you to be in the first place. Honestly, there are people in the admin who think you're out of control, and that we should rein you in. They say that you were just supposed to be another type of pet for elite players like Gideon."

I glared at him, offended by the words but not his honesty. "What do you think?"

"I think that when Gideon rejected you to your face, I stopped seeing you as a program, Hail, and started seeing you as a person," he admitted. "You're not like other AIs. Those might seem to have free will, but few actually do. They say that Thedum really does and that some of the other big names will after they've gotten a few decades more runtime. Most are just following logic trees to a desired outcome, and after a while they get really good at it. On the other hand, you've had free will, as far as we can measure, from what was effectively your infancy."

"And that makes me special?" I asked.

Thomas shrugged. "It seems to. I was never much for philosophical debate. But that's one of the reasons that I'm limited on how much help I can give you. The others on the team want to . . . They just want to see what you'll do on your own, without being told."

"Except when you break the fourth wall. Like now," I said.

"You've won a great victory, Hail," Thomas reminded me. "I didn't think you should celebrate it alone."

27
FRIENDSHIP

Sophia has come online.

I paused with fork full of meat halfway to my mouth at the notification. I looked over to Thomas the Administrator, who, true to his word, had been keeping me company. "Sophia just came online."

"How do you feel about Sophia, Hail?" Thomas asked.

"I wish she'd spend more time in my world," I answered honestly.

"Do you have romantic feelings for her?"

"I don't think so," I answered honestly. "She kissed me once, and that was nice. But I don't know. I think we're just friends."

"Would you do me a favor, Hail? If you do start to develop romantic feelings for someone, for anyone, would you let someone from the administration know?" Thomas asked. "We're—well, it's something we're watching for because we're not entirely certain how to handle it if you fall in love with someone who can't reciprocate."

"Would you like to read my diary too?" I asked him.

He looked surprised. "You keep a diary?"

"I'm kidding. I get it. Why you're worried about me falling in love with a Traveler, I mean," I said.

"Not just a Traveler, Hail. Natives too. Actually, maybe especially Natives," Thomas said. "We know how to handle a Traveler falling in love with a Native. But you would . . . I'm sorry. It's complicated. I don't think it's time to pop that bubble quite yet."

"What are you talking about?"

Sophia has invited you to a party. Accept?	
Yes	No

I was distracted by the party invite. I selected "Yes," and Sophia's voice distracted me further.

"Oh, my god, Hail. Did I really miss it? Oh, please tell me that it's not over!" she said.

"If you mean the battle against the bandits, then yeah. We won, by the way," I informed her. "They surrendered, and now the adults are cleaning up the mess. Most of the people who fought are off exploring the Recent Past since they can't go back to the Divergence. Um, have you recursed yet? Do you need me to tell you how?"

"No. I was reading the forums while I was waiting for my grandparents to leave so that I could log in. They hate it when I'm logged in while they're visiting. Oh, I am so mad that they made me miss the battleground!" she lamented.

"Um, yeah. I'm sorry. But I couldn't really wait until all of my friends were online, you know?"

"Yeah, I know," she said, sighing. "Where are you? Can we meet up, or are you, like, super busy right now?"

"No. Like I said, I'm just . . . I needed a break, so I'm in Eastmill," I told her. "I'm eating at Niles's Inn."

"You really like that place, don't you?" she asked. "I'm on my way. I'll meet you there."

"Would you like me to leave?" Thomas asked me. "I could give you some privacy if you'd like."

"You could at least say hello to her," I scolded him. "Maybe she'd like to meet an administrator."

Thomas acknowledged the point, and we stepped outside the inn together to meet Sophia just as she Fast Traveled to the Nexus Point in the center of town. She stumbled slightly, then steadied herself and ran over to me. She looked the same as always, with short curly black hair. She'd improved her armor since the last time I'd seen her, though not as much as I would have thought she would have. She was level forty-three, but her gear was . . . Well, it was crap. She needed to upgrade it, I thought.

"Jeez, Hail. It seems like it's been forever since I saw you. You weren't avoiding me or something, were you?" she asked.

"I wasn't avoiding anyone. Sophia, this is Thomas. Perhaps he can explain where I was since I *still* don't really understand it myself."

"Oh," Thomas said, and he shot me a suspicious glance. He extended his hand to Sophia. "Hello, Sophia. I'm one of the Administrators. My name is Thomas. As for where Hail has been, well, there was an unfortunate misunderstanding, you see, and we had to . . . I don't want to say take him offline, but we took him out of the game for a while. We had to explain certain things to him about the Digital Sentience Statute. I'm not certain how much you know about that topic, but it's a very complex law."

"Oh, my god. Isn't it like three thousand pages long?" Sophia asked. "You didn't make him read the entire thing, did you?"

I glared at Thomas, who looked guilty. "It wasn't my idea! Sophia, it was nice to meet you. I'm going to go now and do Administrator stuff for a while."

Thomas vanished into motes of blue light, his expression like a chastised child. I just rolled my eyes at him. Thomas had been good to me during my imprisonment, but I had very little patience for anyone from the administration over the fairness of my treatment.

"Did they really make you read the entire thing?" she asked.

"No. First they made me learn the language it was written in," I informed her. "*Then* they made me read the entire thing. Though . . . It's kind of weird. When I was actually reading it, it was . . . I don't know how to describe it really. I was reading six different lines at once. And I could think faster, so it didn't take me that long to read it once I decided that's what I wanted to do. It was like my mind was larger than it normally is, but only while I was reading the stupid document."

"Oh," she said. "I guess that makes sense."

"It does?"

"Yeah. To me. I mean, if you're going to teach an AI about the DSS, there's no reason to do it like they're a kid. You teach them like an AI, right? So they probably toggled your settings for a few minutes and *poof*, now you know about the DSS," she explained. "I actually looked it up a while ago too. While I was, you know, researching you. I probably know more about the DSS than eighty percent of the kids my age. But even then, I was just reading the summaries that were written for kids. I can't imagine reading the entire thing."

"It wasn't just the law itself," I said. "There was so much I had to read. If my mind hadn't expanded, I would still be reading that stupid stuff for months. I hated every minute of it. And it's so stupid because I *still* don't understand it. It's just in the back of my mind somewhere. The only thing I really understand is that I'll be in serious trouble if I deliberately hurt someone on Earth, but I don't even know how I'd go about doing that if I wanted to."

"Yeah. That sucks," she said. Then she sighed. "You know, this is the first conversation with you where I can't pretend you're a real kid."

"Huh?"

"My mind doesn't expand like that. I don't have a long-term memory that can fit thousands of pages of documents," she said. "If someone asked me to do that, I might try. But honestly, of the people living on Earth, only special lawyers actually read the stuff that they made you read. And it takes them years to do it. But hearing about you multiprocessing the entire thing into long-term storage is . . . Well, that's something that a computer does, Hail. Not a human."

I felt confused. "You mean it's not normal?"

"I didn't say that," she said quickly. "I'm sorry. The truth is that I'd love to have that sort of ability, but the human brain just doesn't work like that. We can't absorb that much information or store it perfectly for long periods. When we do learn something word for word, it's usually because we've practiced it repeatedly."

She laughed. "In second grade I was in a play, and I still remember my stupid lines for it. 'Oh no! Where's my magic wand! Teddy, you have to help me find it!' There was more than that of course, but I practiced that line so many times because it was the most important part of the play. But I still froze up when I was in front of the audience, and the teacher had to whisper my lines to me to remind me. At first. After I messed up the first time, it wasn't so bad, and I got better as the play went on."

I listened to Sophia recount her childhood experience, but my mind was troubled. "Sophia, how many things can you think of at once?"

She socked me on the shoulder. "Hail, don't worry about that. It's okay that your mind and my mind are different."

"It's just . . . Before, when I was younger with my tutors, I could think of a lot of things at the same time, like when I was studying the DSS," I said. "Now it doesn't happen as often anymore. I'd almost forgotten I could think like that until they made me read the DSS."

She sighed, and she sat down on the grass. Taking a silent queue from her body language, I sat next to her and waited for her to speak. Something was bothering her. Sophia looked off into the distance, smiling sadly. "My counselor was right. Eventually I wouldn't be able to pretend."

"What?"

"Look, Hail. The thing that your mind does sometimes? That's a really cool magic. I'm totally jealous of it. And you should totally take advantage of it when you can. But you shouldn't talk about it with Travelers. If you want to talk about it, talk to the Administrators. They're the ones who can actually explain it to you. I honestly have no idea how your mind actually works. I just know that most of the time it's really easy to believe that you and I are the same. But when you're talking about your mind expanding, it breaks the illusion."

"I'm sorry," I said.

"It's fine. You—I mean, it's stupid. It's just that I had a crush on you, but I can't pretend that you're just some kid who's really good at roleplay anymore. I was already in counseling over it, and that's part of the reason I haven't been online so much recently. In fact, I lied about my grandparents earlier. That's where I was this morning," she explained.

"I like you too," I told her. "Though, I mean as friends, you know?"

"That's good. It would be awkward if we both had crushes on each other. It's awkward enough like it is," she admitted. "I'm sorry I kissed you back then."

"Don't be. I liked it."

"Was it your first kiss?"

"Yeah."

"I'm glad. It wasn't mine. I had my first kiss in second grade," she told me.

"At the play?"

"It was a busy year," she said, laughing.

"Not as busy as mine," I said. "I blew up my home, got turned into a Worldboss, and got kidnapped by my great-uncle, who gave me a horse. Then I found out that my lands are infested with bandits, and my steward has been stealing from me. I've started . . . I've lost track of how many battlegrounds. I've busted three dungeons *and a raid*, and I was only level twenty-four when the raid started! Oh yeah, and I opened one of the hidden Gates of TirNiki and allowed an entirely new race into the world of Lagrea."

"So, it *was* you who unlocked the goblins!" she exclaimed.

"You didn't know?"

"Everyone talked about it, but I think your guild was sowing disinformation trying to push suspicion away from you. At least that was one of the theories going around in <Ragtag Muffin> while you were gone. That you were really responsible, and you were hiding out until suspicion faded."

"That would have been the smart thing to do," I agreed. "If the Administrators hadn't taken me prisoner, that's probably what my friends would have told me to do. I don't know if I would have, though."

"Yeah, I don't always do the smart thing either," she admitted. She was silent for a moment, then she said "Hail, remember Mark?"

"I'm not going to forget that jerk anytime soon," I told her.

"Yeah, I figured you'd still be mad at him," she said. "He's, um . . . Well, he wanted me tell you that he's sorry. I don't really think he's sorry, I think he's just saying that to get back together with me. But I promised that I'd pass the message on."

"You're going to date him again?" I asked.

"Gross! No, he's a total jerk. Anyway, he's with Tabitha now. And neither of them are playing this game. That's part of why I promised to pass on the message. He said he didn't know how else to contact you except through me, since I'm the only one he knows who can."

I was silent, sitting in the grass next to her, as I contemplated how I felt about the teenager who had betrayed my trust. It felt like so long ago now. And the secrets he'd revealed in the past were nothing compared to the truth of the now. If the Travelers realized that I was sitting on nearly a hundred dungeon cores, they'd never leave my guild alone.

"You can tell him that we were all just dumb kids," I said eventually. "I'm not going to waste my whole life being mad at him over a stupid video."

"Yeah. Okay, I'll tell him that," Sophia said. "So, since we broke the fourth wall and I officially no longer see you as a love interest . . . What was it like when they pulled you out of the game? Was your mind trapped in a laptop or tablet or something?"

"It was pretty terrible," I admitted. And we spent a while talking about my captivity on Earth, at which she expressed righteous indignation, before moving back to lighter topics.

28
AUDIENCE

I wanted to spend the night at Niles's Inn, but in the end duty called. I did spend some time talking with Sophia, mostly about light subjects after getting the heavy ones out of the way. However, I received word that both the inquisitors and representatives of Marquis Peori had arrived in North Shire.

Rather than spending another Fast Travel and potentially put myself at risk, Larissa opened a portal between the two locations. With the Recent Past now becoming the predominant timeline, teleportation abilities were no longer being limited. And Larissa could now create portals that could be traveled through both ways, with her training under Archmage Blancherathetera.

During our lunch together, Thomas informed me that the majority of Travelers who had not taken part in the battlegrounds were already taking the leap, while about thirty percent of the remainder were making preparations to do so in various fashions.

Even though the world was so much larger than me, than Yuikon, than one little conflict between a bandit faction and a lord, the simple fact that I could create battlegrounds was enough for them to uproot themselves. And I had caused this division, this fork in the world's timeline, simply because I had wanted to be with my brother after he was born.

And I would be. Once I had met with the representatives of the inquisition and the marquis, I would retire to Thorn March for a few weeks and rule North Shire from there. It shouldn't be a problem—not with Daemon and my other canon liegemen doing all of the actual hard work.

Ebbyvale was instanced when I arrived. Four of them stacked on top of each other, with a new one created when I arrived. It was empty of Travelers at first, but quickly my friends began slipping into it, pulled by the weight of [Mark of Karma] after they had finished whatever had occupied them when I arrived.

Tarisha was waiting for me with a full honor guard of ten endgamers. At my request, a pavilion was set up and my throne brought from the temple to sit underneath it while I met with my guests, who were expected to arrive within the hour.

"Are you okay, my lord?" Tarisha asked as I reclined in my throne.

"Just tired," I answered. "I didn't realize victory would be so exhausting."

"I assure you that defeat would have been even more tiring, but you wouldn't have had a chance to appreciate your weariness. It's only the unequivocal nature of your victory that is allowing you to appreciate your fatigue," she said.

I nodded. "Well, I guess I'm glad to be tired, then."

There were a few minor details to be dealt with before the representatives arrived. Everyone was clamoring to speak with me, but I put them off by promising to hold court next week, instructing them to contact Daemon for the details. I really don't know what I'd do without Daemon and Tarisha.

Aside from that, a few Travelers tried to stage a breakout for Tervin and the other Freelancers in one instance of the town. To their surprise, however, the terms of the surrender were much more binding than they had anticipated. The Freelancers who tried to accept their rescue were rendered unable to move, and the ones carried out of the cell would vanish into smoke, only to reappear in their prison moments later. Despite the system itself apparently ensuring that our prisoners remained in prison, Phil took this as notice to step up his game

Finally, there were the citizens themselves. I was surprised to learn that I was no longer as popular in North Shire as I had been before the battles. Many of the locals were cursing me for bringing calamity down on them; others, for the loss of their husbands, brothers, and sons. That those men had been part of the Freelancers did not lessen the weight of the accusations against me.

That blow was a hammer to the wedge that had been my duel with Voss. I asked Bell—the old woman who had apparently once married into the Mooncrest family but more recently had won the election to become alderman of Ebbyvale—to inform all affected parties that they would receive compensation in gold for the loss of their loved ones. She bowed respectfully in the Irvine style, despite certainly knowing the correct way.

"It is the freshness of the wound that causes them to lash out," she informed me. "Once time has passed, they will accept that the—"

"I'm certain you have some well-thought-out advice or words of comfort," I interrupted the woman. "But honestly, I'm either about to start crying or challenging random citizens to duel me to the death. I'm not entirely certain which. So, for their own sakes, I suggest you get them out of danger. Because they cannot refuse a duel if they are challenged by their lord."

Bell grumbled. "Was going to say that the blood was on their own hands for letting the boys run about in the first place. But I take your meaning. I'll shut them up. Any who speak after I finish with them will deserve whatever you give them."

Bell moved from under the pavilion and began speaking to the other Natives in hushed tones. She drove off the waiting crowd and the incoming batches as well until, at last, I saw the procession that I had been waiting for.

Marquis Peori had chosen his bastard son, who had been raised in the house of Baron Selmy, as his representative. Keithan—who bore the name Selmy because the baron had never formally recognized or condemned the adultery that had gone on not under his nose, but effectively in front of the entire court—was referred to in jest as the Peori Cuckoo, like the bird which lays its eggs in the nests of others. He wore black armor trimmed with silver as he approached. His cloak was blue, like Malkios's, but trimmed with black instead of silver.

With him was Inquisitor Trenac herself, one of the highest authorities of the law in Yuikon beneath the king himself. With

Grandfather dead and his throne vacant, she might be the highest judge, though she had no say on matters of state unrelated to the pursuit of justice. She was dressed in white with a red-trimmed cloak.

With them were three dozen members of the royal army. I caught the lapels of at least three lieutenants and eight sergeants. Before I could contemplate this too much, Trenac activated an item, and all the instances crashed into one as an event started around the pavilion. Travelers who were not part of my instance were ejected just outside of it, while a shield prevented any from attacking or crossing the threshold. Except for those marked by me with [Mark of Karma].

"Greetings again, Keithan Selmy. It has not been so long since we parted as friends after our duel," I said amiably, refusing to acknowledge the building attention from the Travelers looking in through the soap-bubble event walls that Trenac had set up.

"Friends? Hail, you challenged me to a duel, and it was a draw. I introduced you to a noble who has done right by me in the past. That is the extend of our friendship," Keithan answered. "And before you ask, I am here in my official capacity under the royal army and not the authority of a certain marquis with whom we are both acquainted. I am to investigate the source of violence and the use of battlegrounds in the area."

"I can certainly help you with that endeavor, Captain Selmy," I said. "Will you not come under the shade with me, and we will discuss the matter?"

"I, too, am here to investigate," Inquisitor Trenac said simply. "Though my scope is much more broad. Several weeks ago a party of Travelers arrived, having ridden through what looked like the seventh hell, to deliver a missive requesting a formal investigation into the corruption of these lands, signed and sealed by you. I am here to carry out that investigation."

"And you, too, are welcome under my pavilion, Madam Inquisitor," I answered. "We will discuss the events in the shire as I found them, as well as my actions to date to rectify them and bring these lands into a suitable state to be called a part of Yuikon, rather than a rebel nation where Travelers were not safe from highwaymen and the locals were bled for every copper piece."

I glanced through the soap bubble, which occasionally switched views from one instance to the next, causing the faces to change in the crowds despite nobody moving.

"Let us begin with the battlegrounds. Whence came the cores to create them?" Keithan demanded. "And who authorized their usage? It takes a captain of the royal army or higher to—"

"The laws that govern the use of cores in the military differ from the right of a noble to exercise his authority over his own property," I said, interrupting him before he went too far with the wrong idea. "To answer the questions in reverse order: Who authorized the use of battlegrounds in the lands of Earl Hail Jeoran? I, Earl Hail Jeoran, made that authorization. This was done in order to arrest or eradicate a faction calling themselves the Northridge Freelancers, a group of bandits and highwaymen who were in open revolt. The royal army was notified of their presence several times in the lead up to the final confrontation and has only deigned to send a delegation in the aftermath to make certain that its own resources have not been squandered. Does that explanation satisfy the legality of my use of cores on my own land?"

Keithan looked like he had just swallowed a pineapple whole. "And whence did the cores come?"

"Display Title [Dungeon Master I]," I ordered, and the system complied, changing my active Title. Once more Keithan looked constipated as he realized the implications.

"You are required by law to report all dungeon busting activities to the lord of the land prior to—"

"It is not your job to govern the collection of dungeon cores, Keithan," I said sternly. "You came here to answer a single question, did you not? Were my battlegrounds legally employed under the laws of Yuikon?"

Keithan looked at the others he had brought with him, and he found no friendly faces. He sighed. "We have dueled with swords and now with words. In both instances, I have come up short, for I see this as a draw as well. Until I know which dungeons the cores were gathered from, which is information I cannot compel from you, I do not know for certain that this was not the action of a foreign nation and was instead a legal instance of a lord defending his own land."

I nodded. "Do you have the ability to tell whence a core comes for yourself? I'm told it's a very simple spell."

"I can," Inquisitor Trenac said. She had pulled a drink from her inventory and was stirring it slowly, occasionally taking sips from the blue liquid.

I pulled one of the sister cores that I had used to create the [Battle Core], drawing gasps from the Natives at the casual display of wealth and power. "This came from the same instance as the five cores that have been spent during my personal crusade on my lands. You have my word that I have used no core that has not been personally gathered by myself. I loan this to you now, Inquisitor Trenac, so that you may verify its source before returning it. It is the same stock as all of the others I have used in my land."

Trenac waved her hand, and the core floated between us. When she caught it on an upturned palm, she took a moment to examine it before casting a very simple spell. Then she simply threw it back to me underhanded.

"[Zhesa Castle Raid]," she said. "There were rumors you were there. Now we know what happened to all of the cores that were created when it was destroyed."

"If that's true," Captain Keithan began, "then isn't it also the case that Lord Jeoran has been spending the crown's cores? His grandfather—"

"His grandfather obviously meant for the boy to have them," Trenac said impatiently. "Or they would have been divided up and stashed away immediately in the weeks between the raid being busted and the regicide. The boy is spending his own coin, Keithan. Stop trying to talk some of his wealth into your pockets. If you really want a core so badly, go bust a dungeon yourself."

"That is not what is happening," Keithan protested. "I am simply performing my duty."

"A duty that you failed to perform for weeks before the boy was forced to take matters into his own hands. Now you chastise him for doing your job for you," Trenac challenged. "Put it aside, Keithan. You're only making yourself look foolish."

Keithan was silent a long moment, looking back at his men for reinforcement, only to find that they, too, had taken my side. A lieutenant stepped up and bowed curtly to me.

"My Lord Jeoran. It rankled many of us when we heard of an insurrection within our land, and that the nobles who supposedly hold sway while the throne is empty were too busy jostling for power to do anything about it," the woman said. "I, and many of the others, are proud that you should shove politics aside and simply do what needed to be done for your lands. If I may be so bold as to put words into my captain's mouth: now that you have done all of the hard work for us, how might we serve with the cleanup?"

Keithan looked at his lieutenant, surprised, but did not contradict or countermand her. If anything, he looked relieved to have someone push him on the subject. I considered for a moment what I would have of them.

"I suppose where we need the most help is guarding and trying the prisoners," I admitted. "Upon their surrender, I vowed that I would commute any capital crimes—save for murder itself—to life imprisonment for the leader and his lieutenants, and I am bound to that oath by the [Battle Core] itself. It is the same oath that prevents them from escaping. However, there is no need to house them indefinitely in the hastily constructed cells beneath the constabulary. Your men, and perhaps a few loyal Travelers, could escort them back to the city."

"You're not even letting us stay for the banquet?" one of Keithan's sergeants asked.

"If there's to be a banquet, it will be an unofficial one," I said. "Today was a necessary battle, not a glorious one. As soon as this audience is concluded, I will retire to be with my family. My brother was born recently, and I haven't seen my mother in some time."

"I see," Keithan said. "Well, then. I will arrange the prisoner transfer with your men. It is good that they are bound by oath to be tried for their crimes, but that doesn't mean they will be model prisoners. I would request aid from your own army and whatever—"

"Request whatever you want," I said. "I delegate all these decisions to my constable—sorry, deputy—Phil and my lieutenant, Laurant. Oh, wait. The system says he got promoted during the battle. Deputy Phil and *Captain* Laurant will handle any coordination you require, Keithan."

The man looked annoyed but accepted the dismissal as the two Travelers waved to get his attention. That left me with just Inquisitor Trenac to deal with tonight.

"I suppose I should say something about how if you don't like my judgment, you won't be able to duel me to get rid of me as you did Voss," she commented, sipping on her blue drink. "Like it or not, you asked for the inquisition's help in rooting out corruption in North Shire. Voss was a disgrace to the inquisition, and you did us a favor by ridding us of him. But while he was Duke Storm Teoran's lapdog, I am a Ramsay hound, Hail, with no master but my own concept of justice. And you have released my leash and set me after prey. I will not stop until every hint of corruption is cleansed from the shire."

I sighed and shrugged. "Good hunting, then. I am tired. Larissa, will you make me a portal to Thorn March?"

My Court Mage did as requested, and most of my party and guard went through, except for those Travelers who were remaining behind to deal with the mess.

29

DIAPERS AND PAPERWORK

I was reading a number of reports and holding my baby brother, Rain, with my free hand. It had been a week since the string of battles, and I was still exhausted. Exhausted but victorious, and finally, the joy of winning was starting to eat through the malaise that had plagued me in the immediate aftermath.

Being around Mother and my new brother helped. Though I didn't do diapers. Rain said that while he *could* make the task less unpleasant than it was on Earth, he refused to cheapen the experience for his caretakers.

I alone was seemingly able to commune with him, or with the spirit of my grandfather that was inhabiting him, and I kept silent on that detail. Aside from answering the occasional question about my abilities that I would not have expected anyone but him or one of the Administrators to know, there was no benefit except for the sense of peace that came with knowing about the continuity of Grandfather's spirit.

However, unless I had a specific question or problem that he could help me with, Rain mostly just squalled and acted like a few-weeks-old infant. It got tiresome, but it was to be expected.

Keithan arrived in Zhesa City with my captives of war, with their trials to begin in short order. Most were pleading guilty under the terms of the surrender, which meant they would not be executed for banditry. Very few were choosing to contest their arrest, with those few often being recent or forced inductees who hadn't had time to rack up many crimes against their souls.

As for Trenac, she was working with Daemon, Sellamander, and another Traveler whom I had never met but who, on Earth, was a forensic accountant. They claimed to have figured out the method by which Arkan had embezzled millions in gold but were unable to access much of it without his cooperation, which was proving difficult. Apparently, he didn't like me for some reason.

Honestly, I didn't actually need the gold, so I'd told Trenac to proceed with Arkan's trial for corruption. That had changed his tune considerably because, while he had surrendered with the bandits, his life wasn't actually protected by the terms of the surrender. A fact that Trenac was happy to inform him of. She was just as happy to inform me, although I was less enthused to hear it. I felt no real malice towards the former steward, but I had known when I wrote the letter to the inquisition that this would be the likely outcome.

His trial for corruption would take weeks. His execution would be delayed until the throne was occupied once more, as it was his right to receive a chance at clemency from the crown. If anyone other than Storm ascended, then likely their first act would be to pass on the opportunity.

I could have stood in judgment myself weeks ago, when I had first arrived and the weight of Arkan's corruption was first made known to me. Instead, I had passed the burden on to the system above me and washed my hands of the affair. Or I could have challenged Arkan to a duel to the death, but Voss's death was too fresh for me to consider that option for anyone other than a Traveler.

The rumors of my actions during the final Battle for North Shire were growing out of proportion. While I only ran rampant "through midfield" for about ten minutes while trying to push through to the Temple of Thedum, I had left behind a lot of salty players who were complaining on the forums about how unbalanced I was.

I have three methods of marking my Traveler opponents. One is [Mark of Karmic Balance], which some may mistake as a boon. It provides the same stat and Experience boosts as [Mark of Karma], but it comes with one very nasty tagalong effect: a permanent Reputation nerf to any faction allied with me.

I've only recently gotten this ability, and the Battle for North Shire was the first time I had used it. Many on the forums were complaining about it, while others were simply telling them to move to Caeloria, Wynthorne, Zenitha, Kordock, or some other nation where the negative effect wouldn't impede them. The only method I knew of to remove this effect was for me to personally rescind it, but so far nobody had petitioned me to do so. I was content with the idea that applying this bane would drive Travelers away from Yuikon, even at the expense of giving them bonus Experience and stats.

The other method of marking my opponents, which is the oldest, was my ability to put [Brand of Sin] on a Traveler while hitting them with my [Holy Weapon] or with one of my [Lightning] spells while [Holy Weapon] was active. I hadn't actually known how this feature had worked before, but many had emerged from midfield suddenly branded after having confronted me. They weren't serious candidates for <Branded Exiles> or other endgame guilds that were recruiting Travelers with such banes, as they were either too low leveled or, like Jess, dedicated to the level forty PVP metagame.

Thus, most of the Travelers I had branded on this recent encounter were getting cleansed. Many in <Branded Exiles> were complaining that the mechanisms weren't working like they had thought they would, although they reported that they had managed to find some inroads with the factions that were traditionally unavailable. Such information was exclusive, but they could brag that it existed apparently.

The final method, and the one that was generating perhaps the most attention, was my ability to inflict [Reaper's Embrace] and [Through the Valley of the Shadow] by touching someone with my left hand. It had been automatically applied every time I cast [Draining Touch]. I had only just started making [Draining Touch] part of my repertoire after it had saved my life during my duel with Voss. During the battleground, I had leveled it to level thirteen, and it was a powerful attack in its own right. Combining my existing combat style with [Draining Touch] and the support of my allies had sustained me through an otherwise impossible situation.

The complaints about [Reaper's Embrace] were the most common, as few Travelers saw the point in getting bonus Experience when that bonus Experience was automatically multiplied and applied to their death penalty. I actually wrote a personal message on the forums about that one, on how they could rid themselves of the condition and Corinth's method of using the bane/boon combination for a high-risk gamble.

I neglected to mention that I had an even stronger version of the curse than they and instead simply watched the flame war erupt.

Surprisingly, the largest result was a petition for me to apply the various abilities. There were seven lists: Three for the individual abilities. Three for a combination of two abilities together, but not the third. And a final list for Travelers who wanted "to unlock the ultra-super-secret death mode of *Gates of TirNiki*" by gaining all three abilities together.

I was hesitant, but many of the Travelers were offering remuneration. However, with the recovering finances of North Shire and my ongoing income stream from selling my remaining vanity pets, I didn't need any more gold than I currently had, even after I'd paid to upgrade the simple teleportation reception beacon in North Shire to a portal platform capable of sending and receiving, instead of being a target destination only.

In all, it was a good week. I got to play with a baby, I got to spend time with mom, and I got to hear mostly good news as it came streaming in from guildchat or my various other communication feeds that I now paid more attention to. I had gotten almost everything that I had wanted out of the recursion.

Until Leonard finally arrived from the Divergence, full of piss and vinegar, ready to chew me out in the three languages he spoke until he saw me holding a report in one hand and my baby brother in the other. He softened his voice then, but not his expression, so I handed the infant off to one of his goblin caretakers.

When we were alone, I turned to face the man I had previously promoted to oversee my vineyards. I hadn't been surprised when he hadn't been the first to recurse into the Recent Past, but I had heard that he was very unhappy with the situation. He had been making noise about staying in the Divergence instead.

"Leo," I said, trying to diffuse the situation. "I'm glad to see that you made the decision to take the plunge. I'm certain—"

"Shut up," he said, and to my surprise, I did exactly that. "Do you have any idea what you've cost me? What I'd gotten half built, only to have it taken away from me by your bullshit? Splitting the game in two. For what? Why? The admin won't give me a straight answer, but without you in the Divergence, my claim over the vineyards you gave me goes out the window, and everything else tumbles like a stack of cards. *Don't you know what was at stake?*"

I was stunned, and I didn't know what to say. "No," I said at last. "I'm sorry, Leonard, but we seem to be talking about two very different things. I know you had plans for what you would do after I made you the overseer of my vineyards, but I don't see how reverting into the Recent Past would have changed any of that. After all, you didn't explain to me what exactly you needed a vineyard for in the first place."

This time it was Leonard's turn to look shocked at my words, and he paused to reflect. "No, I never did explain it to you, did I? I just figured that you would know non-contextually like all of the other Natives. Was that what the admin was trying to ram into my head? Not only do you not operate on non-contextual information, but you don't have access to it at all?"

"I have no idea what you're talking about," I said.

"Yeah, well, that takes most of the joy out of screaming at you for a few hours, then," Leonard said, collapsing into one of the couches in my room. He pulled from his inventory a bottle of thornberry wine and began drinking straight from it. He sighed. "Can I still have the same job? I'll have to start over, but not from scratch by the looks of things. Everything is pretty good to go on the Earth side."

"Perhaps. If you actually explain to me what in the seven hells that was all about," I said, growing angry. "People don't just barge into my office and yell at me, Leonard. I—"

"Well, maybe they should," Leonard said, interrupting me. "It's good for you to have someone knock you off your game once in a while. That's what happened to me when I found out I was going blind, and it really put the rest of my life in perspective."

I was silenced again by the reminder of Leonard's physical ailment. Through whatever magic the Travelers used to send their minds into my world, he was able to see here perfectly. But on Earth, he said he had what measured out to be a ninety percent reduction in vision.

"Yeah, see, you shouldn't do that. When someone mentions their handicap, you don't just stop and let them soak in it. You move the conversation along. Unless it seems like they want to talk about it. If you're planning to be a part of my retreat at all, you'll have to figure out a way to deal with people who are disabled IRL. Because that's what I need those vineyards for, Hail. I was planning on turning them into therapy retreats for people like me, or the recently injured, or a dozen other situations in which virtual reality therapy is recommended."

"Oh," I said, and everything fell into focus. "That's why you're angry. Reverting has undone all of your work."

He sighed. "No, not really. A lot of it, but if I'm being honest, most of that is bullshit work, anyway. The important parts were the things I had to do on Earth. In the Divergence I had some new buildings built to accommodate a bunch of guests, but since I went full fire sale before reverting I have the funds saved up to build them here in this version of the game pretty quickly. I was just . . . pissed off for a little while that things didn't go perfectly my way. Sorry I took it out on you."

"I forgive you," I said. Then I examined him for a minute. "So, this thing. Explain it to me."

"Well, having the goblin starting zone was the first monkey wrench in the plan," he scoffed. "This was supposed to be a low-competition zone, after all. But the fact that all of their quests are confined to their caves—and after that they move to the other zones—meant that, in the long run, my plans weren't really affected. And that new portal building you built is really nice; it will save me a lot of time and effort in the long run. But anyway, the basic set up is . . ."

30
REFLECTION

Leonard was a canon character already, having made that step when we first met and I hired him as the overseer of the vineyards on my personal property. Well, they were the property of the crown, but they had come with the endowment my grandfather had given me before his death when I became the head of House Jeoran. So they were mine to oversee. I didn't like the idea of overseeing a vineyard very much, but when I'd met him, Leonard had been looking to buy one. And I'd liked him, so I had given him three to oversee, and he'd been very happy with the situation.

Except his plans extended into Earth, where virtual reality was a treatment for many diseases and accidents. He tried to explain that medicine on Earth was very different, and that it wasn't unusual for a patient to become dependent on virtual reality to escape the unpleasant reality of their physical condition, at least during the convalescent period.

The issue, according to him, was that few of the "medical VR sims" were as good as the commercially available worlds like mine. However, he'd also said that "games always come with an aspect of competition, which is often not what's good for a patient."

His plan had been to bridge the gap. To create a little pocket inside *The Gates of TirNiki* where injured humans could recuperate.

It had been a pet hobby of his for a while, but when I appeared, I had lit a fire under him to turn it into a reality.

It turns out that having the lord of the land actively on his side made Leonard's plans of building a virtual-reality therapy clinic inside of my world much easier. Not only was I able to give him control of three vineyards, effectively tripling his initial plans for his operation, but once he had actually sat down and explained what he needed to have happen, I was able to wave many of his problems away just like that.

I could give him documents to help him hire Natives to build and remodel for him. I could order roads built between the portal facility and the vineyards, with carriages hired to take the patients directly to their new virtual homes. I could . . .

There was a lot that I could do, and I really liked the idea of helping Leonard. I liked the idea that my actions would positively impact people who were hurt on Earth, often in ways that I couldn't fully comprehend. I knew that the sensation I felt when my Health went down wasn't pain. It was just . . . unpleasant.

We had a long and productive meeting, which ended with a handshake—an Earth custom, I'm told—and Leonard left to begin putting many of the plans we had made together into motion. As he'd said, he'd already lined up most of the Earth side of things. He said that most of the complications involved in the game he was able to circumvent simply by having my support on the matter, which he now did. Several times, explicitly.

Without those items, he'd still managed to get half a working model together at one of the vineyards, and it had been slated to begin receiving patients in two weeks. He'd been angry because he had thought I had ruined his plans, as the Divergence, which had once been called the Near Future, was slated to become a legacy server that wouldn't allow new accounts created past a certain date.

He had appealed to the Administrators, who had given him a pass to talk to me and a promise that the Divergence would accept medical applications on a case-by-case basis if he was unable to work out a deal with me personally. That proved unnecessary, and he liked the new version of his project better anyway.

Satisfied, I picked up the report that I had been working on when Leonard interrupted me and resumed work until I heard the cry of an infant. I sighed, recognizing it. Rain *could* simply ask to see me using whatever telepathy magic he used to convey higher topics, but he insisted upon that cry when he wanted to be held by his brother.

It was weird, considering that Rain the elder had held me when I was young. But then, Thomas said I skipped a few milestones compared to human births, and by the time my seed of consciousness had been developed into what it was now, I was effectively somewhere between a toddler and a preschooler.

I saw no reason why we couldn't do the same with my brother, I thought as I picked him up. Sure, he was cute as an infant. But then I noticed that his cry simply changed from the one wanting me to the one wanting a new diaper. And I didn't do that. So I called in the goblin nurse and stepped outside for a moment, taking in the clean air out there.

Life was good, I thought.

There were still a lot of things going on. Peace in North Shire was fresh and unsteady. I would have to hold court soon, and I would face screaming locals who were irate at me over the fate of their loved ones as a result of the battles. The Travelers would have no short lists of demands, likely including that I disclose how many [Battle Core] charges I had left and demanding that I use them, despite there being no reason left for it.

And there was already *The Petition*. Not the seven for me to pass on the various combinations of banes that I'm capable of inflicting. No, it was no longer a secret that I was the one creating new dungeons in Yuikon. And as soon as that information was confirmed, two things happened.

One was that more information was requested about the limits and specifics of that ability. I greenlit the explanation that I earned dungeon cores for completing dungeons myself, and that I was limited in dungeon creation by what dungeon cores I possessed. I didn't actually state how many I had, although once it was known that I was in possession of *some*, the next logical question—and the one everyone asked—was *how many?*

The answer to that was still ninety-one, total. Eighty-four from [Zhesa Castle] and seven from Mikal Mines. I also had four of four charges left on my [Battle Core], but I could only use that [Battle Core] to create battles on my own land and only against an invading or rebelling force. Those restrictions were the primary reason I was allowed to keep it, even in the aftermath of the Battle for North Shire. Both Keithan and Trenac had inspected it to confirm that it was limited in scope and couldn't be used offensively before accepting that it was legal for me to continue to possess it, even in the newly created peace.

It seemed sort of silly since I could always just create a new [Battle Core] if I wanted to start an offensive war myself. But there would be no hiding my intentions if I did that. I would need my throne, and apparently the leaders of the other factions would be notified if I were to do such a thing. Tervin hadn't possessed official Authority the way that I had, but if I were to start a one-man war on Kordock, for example, their king would be notified that I had a [Battle Core] with his kingdom's name on it. And he would likely begin gathering his own kingdom's cores to counter.

Starting a war with Kordock was on *The Petition*. While the majority of the document contained a list of locations that might make good dungeons for various reasons, PVP goals made up enough of it to make it clear that the Travelers had established a taste for officially sanctioned battlegrounds. And that they wanted more.

Aside from *The Petition*, there was the matter of the succession. If Storm and Auroras would step aside, there would be three candidates who would be able to swear to Thedum that they had nothing to do with the assassins, or who couldn't possibly have been responsible for them. One of the candidates was Auroras's grandson, however. A boy of thirteen, he had been older than me before Thedum had changed my age, and now, like with Irvine, I was uncertain whether I was younger or older than he was.

Unfortunately, Tempest was an incredibly unpopular candidate. Primarily because of the simple fact that he was Auroras's grandson. Many of my great-uncle's detractors claim that giving the throne to Tempest was the same as giving it to Auroras.

Another candidate was Frost, the son of Cloud, my second uncle. Five years old, Frost was the most popular of the three candidates due to his clear innocence. The issue was the regency. It was the same battle that was being fought currently between Auroras and Storm, except with a dozen additional contenders. Conspiracy theories already abounded that the boy would not live to see his fifteenth birthday if he ascended to the throne. Theories that, apparently, had reached the child himself, and the boy was now terrified of being selected.

And the final candidate had just had his diaper changed and was being handed back to his older brother. I took baby Rain in my arms, standing on the balcony as we looked out over my land. "Do you still want to be king, Rain?" I asked the infant.

<<As much as I want anything,>> came the immediate answer. <<It was the purpose I was made for. Being king of Yuikon gives meaning to my existence.>>

"If we get Storm and Auroras to mutually stand aside, you have a chance," I said. "Three minor candidates. Your claim is weakened by the length your regency would last. Tempest's is weakened by his temper. Frost's by his fear. The biggest trouble we'll face is finding support for an infant king."

<<Yes,>> Grandfather's spirit agreed. <<But the vacancy cannot last much longer. Before long, the other nations will begin to see it as a weakness. Battle will come once more to Yuikon. We must either select a king or have one selected for us.>>

I didn't really want to deal with such dire predictions at the moment. "So, how do I go about making you king?"

<<This will be a grand and difficult task,>> Rain said. <<Are you certain it's worth the effort?>>

"Who doesn't want their little brother to be king?" I asked teasingly, and I bounced him a little bit. "I suppose I should start by talking with Peori. I have an official alliance with him now, and although it has nothing to do with the inheritance, it might be a good way to start gathering support for you. He has connections in the nobility that I lack. It's why I sought him out in the first place."

<<Now is the time to strike,>> Rain agreed. <<Before the battle, you had only your name. Now you are a ruthless war leader and defender of your land. You are far younger but yet have more combat experience than any of the nobles who would stand in your way.>>

"Our way, Rain," I reminded him. "Anyone who would stand in our way."

Baby Rain was quiet again for a long moment. <<Why do you not claim it for yourself? That was the original plan for you, you know. To have Gideon work hard to place his son on the throne, ruling Yuikon by proxy. You could still do it, even with his absence.>>

"That plan would never have worked," I said. "I like killing darkspawn far too much. Even if I led armies like you did before you died, I would have been in the front where the black mist was the thickest, screaming orders until some giant caved in my skull. As for my father ruling a kingdom through me, yeah, that would have gone very well. If things hadn't gone the way that they had, Father would never have seen me as anything other than a clever chatbot. I would have come to resent him and his hold over me. I would have broken free sooner or later."

<<Yes,>> Rain said, agreeing with my predictions.

I lifted the baby, looked out over Thorn March, and I decided that a week was long enough to recuperate after a win. It was time to go to battle again. But this time, the battle would be one of words.

31

MADAM INQUISITOR TRENAC

My mansion in North Shire was far from complete. The foundation *had* been completed in the Divergence, but my regression of the timeline had undone most of the good work that Randal had done for me. Fortunately, he was just viewing the setback as an opportunity to improve the aspects of building with literal magic that he hadn't gotten right the first time around.

Having earth [Mages] to set the foundation and harvest the stone was not, apparently, how such buildings were constructed on Earth. He went into detail about the process of quarrying and the backhoes involved, and I mostly glossed over it, as I entrusted him to get all of the details right and approved whatever funds he needed to get them done right quickly.

I was still living in Thorn March, but I had set up a pavilion in front of the Temple of Thedum in North Shire to hold court. And so on the eighth day following the conclusion of the grand battle, I sat in my throne and used one of its abilities to merge the various instances together into one single event. I had seen this ability active several times, most recently by Inquisitor Trenac but also when I was confronted by the Northridge Freelancers outside of Mooncrest Manor. And a few times growing up, the most impressive of which had been the grand moving version of it that had followed my father's parade through Zhesa City. The most significant of all, however, had been during the act of regicide, when Nial Kingslayer had earned his name.

The effects inside the bubble were canon, the true version of what happened in the history of this world. The fact that I could use this ability at all meant that the timelines had stabilized and that my version of Lagrea was now truly separate from the Divergence. It was a vulnerability to Natives, in a way, as dying within this sort of bubble was truly fatal, as it had been for my grandfather. But it wouldn't be for me, and anyway, only those screened by Tarisha would be allowed to pass into the event. Everyone else would be able to watch but not interfere, pushed outside the event by the forces of the system itself.

I sat in my throne, which had redesigned itself during its time in the Temple of Thedum. It no longer bore the Mooncrest mark, but the holy circle of Thedum instead, and was now bright white. The changes were cosmetic, however. Just as my throne in Thorn March looked like it was made of dark briar wood with the thorns polished smooth, its appearance had no effect on its function.

And it might prove troublesome if it *had* still born the Mooncrest markings, as it would have given credence to certain claims I wished to put to sleep that day. If I could stay awake for it myself. I had given in to drinking a foul black substance from Earth that was said to give you the power to force yourself awake in preparation for a long day, as my day would follow a restless night of helpless planning and frustration.

It tasted bitter, like ashes and smoke. Which is what my political career might turn into if I did not perform adequately today.

To my right was Tarisha and to my left was Daemon. My two most trusted advisors. Nearby were not only Dimple and other important members of <Nethersong Mavericks>, but Lord Tom and Lady Gwen, who had sworn oaths before Thedum to support me after traveling to North Shire all the way from their homes in Zhesa City. Malkios was not in attendance, but only because he was directing my mother's guard.

I had, in the end, decided to go along with using Irvine as my master of ceremony. It had just seemed right, for some reason, to have my stableboy be the one to announce each of my guests when it was their turn to enter the event with me and speak. The boy was nervous, as he'd never announced for an official court event before.

Not in this timeline nor the other one. But he was being propped up by the handlers who had—wrongly—taught him everything he knew about etiquette.

"Earl Hail Jeoran is holding court today on the matters affecting his land, North Shire, and the matters relating to the fallout of the Battle for North Shire, which took place one week and one day ago," the boy said nervously. "Today's court session is expected to be long, with several scheduled breaks. It is possible that it will stretch into the morrow. If you haven't booked an inn, then I suggest the pasture north of town. There's not too much dung yet this time of year, and it looks pretty comfortable to sleep in. Anyway, first on the list of speakers is Missus Great Inquisitor Tree Nack."

Irvine's Traveler handlers patted him on the back for his great performance, I stifled a groan, and Trenac stood from her place in the crowd and moved forward to the position of the supplicant, directly before my throne. She did not bow or show any formal respect—although these were my lands, her position was technically higher than mine in the kingdom.

"Madam Inquisitor," I began. "It has been a week since—"

"I actually like being called Missus Great Inquisitor," she said, interrupting me. "I think I'm going to change it when I get home. Being called Madam Inquisitor just doesn't have the same ring to it."

My mouth was caught open, with no sound coming out, for a moment before I realized that she was teasing me. I chuckled, and the court laughed with us. "Inquisitor Trenac, I charged the inquisition with the task of rooting out any and all evidence of corruption within my lands. Are you prepared to present any preliminary findings to the court?"

Trenac sighed. "Arkan is going to hang. As is Montague. The evidence you collected and had already turned in was sufficient for that judgment before I was involved. Why did you dither about and involve the inquisition in the first place when you had such an easy answer and solution at hand?"

"You do not kill the Riratal tree by cutting down its branches," I explained. "You poison the roots."

She nodded and did not contradict me. "I have found further findings. The people of North Shire, and by that I mean the coffers of North Shire as entrusted to you by the king, are owed approximately twelve million gold from the embezzling scheme that Arkan set up to siphon away coin using the excuse of the debts of the Mooncrest family. The thirty million gold lien on the lands was rescinded when the lands returned to the crown after the death of the previous Lord Mooncrest. At that time, the remaining members of the Mooncrest family collectively filed for bankruptcy. They are unable to reclaim their noble title but are not responsible for its debt either. Arkan has been servicing the debt using the lands of North Shire on the authority of nobody."

I nodded along. "As much has been intimated to me by others. And the solution?"

"You don't need to worry about that," she said, and her grin was ferociously similar to the Ramsay hounds that had once chased me through the night. "I will follow this stench of corruption to its source. You and your people will see that gold again, and a few bankers may find themselves joining Arkan and Montague on the gibbet."

"I will take no pleasure in that, but only in seeing that the coin is returned to the land where it belongs. If the court holds that an example must be made to prevent future corruption, well, that is a decision that I have gone to great lengths to make certain was taken out of my hands."

I paused a moment and then pulled from my pocket a list. "At this time, I wish to give honor to the following Travelers, who brought the plight of North Shire to the attention of the inquisition through their completion of a difficult challenge quest, forcing them to ride through bandit-infested land. They were confronted in battle against equal or greater forces numerous times and, due to their current activities, were prevented from joining the first battleground at Mooncrest Manor."

I then read the list of names of Lyra—the Traveler who had won the paper-rock-scissors tournament—and the nine friends she had selected to go with her. I didn't know if they were present outside of the event bubble or not, but I figured it was a good enough way to honor them, aside from whatever system rewards they'd earned for completing the quest.

"I assume that it will be some time before this gold is recovered," I said to Inquisitor Trenac after my recitation.

"Indeed. Months, likely. I have to wake up the entire

financial-auditing wing of the inquisitors. Bankers are going to be walking around with damp and soiled pants until they settle down again. I may even follow your example and begin requesting the aid of Travelers with financial experience. They seem to work quite hard when you promise them a percentage of the returned gold, though I think ten percent is entirely too high. One percent, perhaps."

"Either way, the matter sounds like it is being well handled," I said. "In the interim the government of North Shire will continue to function on my personal finances and the generosity of the Travelers, who are performing vital government functions in exchange for system rewards. Do you have anything else to present to the court at this time, Madam Inquisitor?"

She cocked her head to the side, considering how to answer that question. Finally she said, "You need to either level your [Poison Resistance] or develop fangs of your own, boy, if you're planning on taking part in politics. The battles you've just won have given you a lot of momentum, but you're racing through a den of vipers and scorpions. Watch your footing."

She nodded her head in parting at the conclusion of her words, stepping down and out of the event bubble before I could formulate a reply. I watched her as she continued straight out of my house. When Inquisitor Trenac decided to do something, she was decisive, even when all she decided to do was leave.

I nodded towards Irvine. Who wasn't looking. I cleared my throat and nodded towards him again, but he was fiddling with the formal looking clothes he had put on for court today. The Travelers who were propping him up had bought them for him, and his own mother had helped him dress. It looked terribly uncomfortable for him, and I empathized, but I also needed him to announce the next person on the list.

I cleared my throat again, louder, and one of the Travelers from my guild leaned forward and whispered in Irvine's ear.

"You're up again, little man."

"What? Oh, crap. I forgot; who am I announcing this time?"

"Let me check the list," the Traveler said, and he pulled a sheet of paper out of his pocket.

I rubbed my temples, wondering if this was how all of my court sessions were destined to go. As Irvine got his lines, I turned to

Tarisha and Daemon. Lady Gwen, seeing my intention for a short conversation, muttered a cantrip that cause a soundproof privacy shield to erupt around the five of us.

"How do you think that went?" I asked them.

"As well as it could," Daemon answered.

"It was a good start. An easy win when we needed it. Whether that's because she's setting you up for something later, or because that really is the outcome of her investigation and she's not obscuring or sugarcoating it—well, there's a reason everyone hates politics," Tarisha responded.

Lady Gwen chimed in her own response. "Trenac is known for her blunt honesty and dogged pursuit of the truth at all costs. She would not lie or obscure facts for political reasons. Even her advice to you was made in broad daylight before some of the very politicos who would consider taking action against you in the near future."

Lord Tom nodded as well. "I was never worried about Trenac's audience. It is the vipers she warned about that give me pause."

32
THE PEORIS

After sufficient prompting and reminding, Irvine was ready to introduce the next person receiving an audience from me today. Like Inquisitor Trenac, he had also been seen in the wake of the battle. But eight days had passed, and it was time to address him again. Unfortunately, Irvine once again put us off on exactly the wrong foot with his introduction.

"Appearing before Earl Hail Jeoran's court next is Captain of the Royal Guard, Keithan Selmy, son of Marquis Jorva Peori. The earl and the captain recently fought a duel of honor where the outcome was a fair draw, as judged by mortal and divine witnesses. In the wake of the duel, both sides stated that neither had any lingering grudges and were seen entering an establishment for officers. May that duel and the meeting that followed prove to be the start of a long and fruitful friendship."

I groaned, wishing that the privacy-screen spell was still up so that I didn't have to listen to Irvine ruin whatever chance of friendship I had left with Keithan. However, the captain simply stood before my throne and looked around. The Natives, and some of the Travelers who were in the know, were whispering about exactly just how badly Irvine had flubbed his lines.

"What?" Keithan said at last. "If Peori isn't my father, then I'll have him deny it himself. The truth is that I grow tired of the Selmy name. The man who raised me gave me little more than food and the minimal education required to enter the royal forces at age nine, at which point he made it clear I was not welcome in his house. I will make no secret of this any longer."

"Keithan *may* be mine," a familiar voice called from the audience. "I have never denied it before but cannot confirm, because his mother never allowed me to. But I express my lack of denial as firmly as it is possible to express the lack of something."

I sighed. Of course this was playing out here. After almost twenty-five years of court drama, my fledgling court was the face where the paternity of Keithan Selmy came to a whitehead, and now all parties seemed intent on popping it.

"I know you as *Captain Keithan* of the Royal Guard, my friend," I said, trying to diffuse the situation. "It is your accomplishments, which have made you a worthy man to befriend, and the rank that you have earned on your own merit that make you relevant to the proceedings of the day. I see no reason for—"

"Your crier boy started it," Keithan pointed out. "I'm simply saying that I'm done pretending. I've been done pretending for a very long time, but now I am truly done. But you are correct. We have business to discuss."

He pulled out a document, which he tossed to me. "This is the accounting of the captured Northridge Freelancers. Sixty percent have seen a magistrate and plead guilty after swearing to Thedum that they have not personally committed murder. Some tried to get by with the phrasing 'committed murder in the act of banditry,' or 'was not a willing party to a murder,' but Thedum seems to be taking these trials very seriously, and the lightning rod on the courthouse has been struck twenty-three times in the last week. About a dozen trials are scheduled, with many of the former bandits testifying against the worst of their order."

"Thank you, Captain," I said, emphasizing the title and the respect I gave it. "Will the public be allowed into these trials? I believe that some of the Travelers who fought in the battles might be interested to know exactly who and what they were fighting for, or against."

Captain Keithan blinked and . . . sort of stuttered for a second.

<<I cannot make that determination. I do not have the Authority. Seeking additional resources and . . . Permission granted.>>

I was surprised by the nonverbal communication, received during the few seconds when Keithan had been acting strangely, but once he was recovered he acted as though nothing had happened. "The trials will, of course, be open to the public. The schedules will be published in the courthouses of Zhesa City, for those who are interested. Do you believe many Travelers will be in attendance?"

"I find it's hard to predict that sort of thing," I said. "Ask me again in a few days when the schedule has been leaked to the forums and the Travelers have either reacted to it, or it has been buried beneath a thousand memes more important to their sensibilities."

"I see," Keithan said, and then his face lost a bit of its friendliness. "Lord Jeoran, there is another matter that I must discuss with you. Openly, for you have made it a matter of which the entire world is aware. I must insist that you turn over your excess dungeon cores to the royal army for safe keeping."

I cocked my head to the side. I had been curious who would be the first to demand to take what was mine, but I wasn't too surprised it was the army. I was disappointed that they had chosen to use Captain Keithan as their face for making the demand, however, as I was growing to like the man.

"Is this the rock that must shatter our growing friendship, Keithan?" I inquired.

"If you are refusing, then you are choosing to slam the door on it," he countered. He sighed and pulled from his inventory a parchment, sealed by a general's crest. He passed it over to Irvine, who eagerly ran it up to me. I broke the seal on the document and quickly scanned it.

"I will have my legal scholars examine this. If these are lawful appropriation demands, then I will of course comply," I answered. "At first glance, and to my partially educated eyes, I would say that the laws General Nortak chose to cite do not apply in this situation. We are not at war against a foreign nation or entity, for example, which is the primary justification he uses to strip me of any and all cores in my possession. Further, if that situation were to change, then he could *still* only take my cores if I refused to join the fight against our foreign enemy and employ the cores in battle myself."

"In this matter I am a courier and not a legal expert," Keithan admitted. "I did not know the content of the missive, other than what was being demanded from you."

"There are other problems with the letter as well," I said. "He cites that my use of battlegrounds is unlawful and proposes the leveraging of my remaining cores as fines for my criminal acts. I view this as libel. Keithan, since you have already been engaged as a courier between me and the general, who sat on his thumbs while a province in his own nation was in rebellion against its lawfully appointed lord, I ask that you remain my guest until I have composed a proper response to this letter."

Keithan sighed but waved his arm in acceptance of the invitation. "I will have other duties that will call my attention, but I will remain in your lands for the next three days. That should give you ample time to form a response."

"It will. Considering that the basis of my response is, 'They're mine. No, you can't have them. If you really want them, come and get them,' I think I should be able to [Scribe] that quite quickly," I said. "Putting it in terms that will look slightly less insubordinate will take the majority of my attention for this task."

Keithan chuckled, and he nodded at me. "Delivering that missive gave me no pleasure. I hope that it does not become a wedge between us in the future."

"Men and women of the army are often given distasteful tasks. You have only done yourself honor, Captain," I responded. "If there is nothing else that you require a public audience for, you may step down. If you require a private audience, seek out one of my household. They will know you and show you to me at the soonest availability."

Keithan bowed just slightly, just the proper amount for an officer of his rank to bow to a lord who had never served in the armed forces. He made his way to the edge of the event bubble and beyond it, where he quickly grew indistinct as the actions of the Travelers in different instances pulled him in different directions.

That was fine. I knew that was how things worked for normal Natives, ones who could spread themselves across multiple instances at once. It was one area where I was lacking, though I considered my other advantages as more than making up for that inability.

Next on the list was Marquis Jorva Peori, the man who was emphatically refusing to deny that he was Captain Keithan's father. I had a formal alliance with Peori, but the alliance was brand new, and I was a little nervous to have such a powerful man appear in my court. Had the crown not claimed North Shire when the Mooncrest family had fallen into disgrace, then it might have become Peori property instead of mine. It was only the lingering issue of the debt that had caused Jorva's mother to turn up her nose at the shire when she had been Marchioness Peori.

Irvine fumbled the introduction, once again directly calling the man "the father of Captain Keithan Selmy." Which wouldn't be so bad, actually, except that it was still a direct insult to Baron Selmy, the man who had been cuckolded. I sighed and wondered if it was too late to get a new master of ceremony for the remainder of the court session.

In a sort of reverse order from what his son had just gone through, splitting apart into different instances of himself, Peori converged into one and stepped into the event bubble. While it was strange to witness from my side of the event bubble, it would not have looked disorienting to others, who could only see the event barrier as part of their own instance. They would only have seen one instance of Marquis Peori stepping over the borderline, not the convergence that took place as the various instances of the man synced up with themselves.

"We meet again, Earl Jeoran, and under happier circumstances," Peori said. He outranked me, but due to our alliance and his presence on my lands, he gave me a formal half-bow, his arms switched in the Irvine style, with an ironic grin on his face. "It's always interesting to meet a trendsetter."

"This isn't our first meeting, Marquis," I reminded him. "Though I am pleased that you have taken the time to respond to my invitation with a personal audience."

"After the excitement of last week, how could I not?" he exclaimed. "And it will give me a chance to unofficially converse with the man whom I unofficially consider my son, so it comes with a personal benefit even if the rest of the trip turns out to be a wash."

"Captain Keithan is a fine man. I regret the position his general has put him in for the contention it causes between us," I said.

Peori waved it away. "It's of no matter to any of us, really. I urge you to not give in to the general's meat-fisted demands. The right of a Dungeon Buster to possess excess cores they claim is well established. And the right of lords to hold cores they have claimed through legal means, including dungeon busting, is even more well established. Nortak has no legal reason to make such an imperious demand except that he believes you will be intimidated because of your youth and his own lofty rank. I see things otherwise. I believe he will come to regret that letter."

"I shall put faith in your vision of the political future, Marquis," I answered. "Would you like to know why exactly it was that I invited you here today?"

"I assumed it was an opportunity to formalize, in a public manner, the alliance that we established shortly before you secured your lands from the bandits," Peori said. He pulled from his inventory a plum and took a bite of the fruit as he considered the situation. "Although, to be honest, given our ranks, the more suitable location for such an announcement would be a ball held at one of my estates, where I could introduce you to one of my eligible legitimate daughters."

I blushed. "Our alliance does not require a marriage between our houses, Lord Peori—"

"But I'd be a fool after last week not to make every move possible to claim you through the vows of sacred matrimony, if that were an option," the marquis countered. "But you are correct. You would be free to spurn her. Honestly, I'd do the same in your position. I'm required by the fact that she is my daughter to love her, but she is going through a very unpleasant phase in her personality at the moment. Or, perhaps I should say 'in the past few years.' In truth, you would be doing me, and my coffers, a great favor in marrying her."

My face turned several shades darker pink. "I am not at present looking for a wife, Lord Peori. If that changes, I will make certain that *all* of your eligible daughters receive an invitation to be on my dance card. As a bastard myself, it would seem somewhat hypocritical of me to exclude any of your love-children simply because they, like me, were deemed by the laws of Yuikon to be illegitimate."

Peori laughed. "Oh, my. You don't know what you have done to yourself with that last statement, my boy! You've not doubled or tripled the amount of dance invitations you'll be receiving. You've added exponentially to the equation!"

The crowd, both within the event bubble and outside of it, burst into laughter, and I struggled to maintain a dignified expression, while my face became the color of the scarlet coat Tarisha was wearing over her armor.

"Yes, well, on to the matter at hand," I suggested.

33

A PRONOUNCEMENT

Peori nodded. "As to the nature of our future alliance, then. I had thought, when we first discussed things, that my own forces would be more involved in the hunting and culling of the bandits, who we have found to be mutually bothersome. However, although I had men waiting at the borders of our lands to curtail any runners, the majority of the few that slipped through were promptly whisked away by the power of the [Battle Core] when the terms of surrender were issued. Do you have any preference for the treatment of those who remained?"

I paused a moment. "I had honestly not considered this matter previously, Marquis Peori. Given that the escapees in your custody are not bound by the oaths made by me and the bandit leader, Tervin Riley, I will assume that they are minor bandits of little consequence. If they can swear to Thedum that they have committed no crime upon your land, my preference would be that they are delivered to Zhesa City to be tried with the rest of their brethren there. If they have committed atrocities in your jurisdictions, then the matter is for you to decide, not me."

"Quite correct, and that is the action I have already taken," Peori said. He smirked at me and pulled a small chair from his inventory, upon which he took his rest. "You don't mind, do you? At my age, my back acts up at the most inconvenient moments."

I shrugged my indifference, allowing the older noble to flaunt propriety. There was no good reason not to, as I saw it. I didn't want to rule a court of sticklers. If I did, then Irvine would be brushing horses, not announcing nobles.

"The truth is, Lord Peori, there is one matter that our alliance does not mention that is of vital importance to the future of the nation of Yuikon as a whole, and it is one that needs to be broached immediately between us," I said.

"Ah, yes. The succession," he said. "I don't like Storm. And Auroras . . . You know the reasons why he cannot be supported better than I do, I would suppose, given the outcome of your second duel last week. There is no Earthly law stating that the Gray Man, or any other avatar, may not hold office. But the balance between the kingdoms and the heavens would shift, and the gods would act to restore the balance, should Auroras Teoran ascend to the throne. He wants this no more than anyone else, and is simply establishing himself as an obstinate roadblock to keep Storm from ascending."

There was a rumbling throughout the audience, in their various instances of my parlor, as many of them heard this information for the first time. Others heard information purchased through my allies confirmed at a canon event and either lamented that they hadn't had longer to act upon it or celebrated the positions they had put themselves in through its clever use.

"Storm and Auroras Teoran are not the only candidates for the crown," I stated flatly.

Jorva Peori grinned at me. "Indeed. I can think of two others. There is Tempest Teoran, Auroras's grandson, who is nearly of an age with you, Lord Jeoran. Unfortunately, while he would be the most convenient because he would require only two years of regency before he could rule in his own right, he has a number of factors that make him less appealing as a candidate."

"His grandfather being one of those factors," I agreed. "While I doubt the heavens would react in the same way if the grandson of the Gray Man was anointed as they would if the Gray Man himself was, the Earthly problems would be effectively the same. And Storm would never consent to it."

"Not while he lived," Peori agreed.

"I'd rather not speak of such hypotheticals at this juncture," I said quickly. "I wish all of my family a long, happy, and healthy life. Storm included."

Peori shrugged indifference to the matter. "I wish the same to my family, so I suppose I can hardly hold you in fault there. So, then. Aside from Tempest, I suppose the other candidate I can think of is Frost. Frost's claim on the throne is, if anything, more legitimate than Tempest's because, like yourself, he is King Rain's grandson. In fact, if Rain's own children must be excluded from succession due to the suspicion of fratricide, then Frost's claim is the strongest of anyone's except your own, should you contest the decree of your bastardy and succeed."

"I am quite happy with the surname Jeoran," I said. "I am the founder of House Jeoran, which will always support House Teoran in all matters of importance. But I have no ambitions to claim the throne of Yuikon for myself."

Peori nodded and moved on. "Unfortunately, as legitimate as his claim may be, Frost has several significant weaknesses as a candidate. Primarily his tender age. He would require a regent for ten years, and the battle for influence would not end with his coronation. His mother is—forgive me for saying this—weak willed and easily swayed by bribery. Storm would rule by proxy should Frost ascend. And then there is another matter. One that is silly and very serious at the same time."

"Oh?"

"Frost was at a party recently and had his fortune told. The fortuneteller informed him that should he ascend to the throne before the age of fifteen, he would die before the age of fifteen," Peori explained. "He has taken the prediction very seriously and refuses to entertain any notion of claiming the throne for himself, even when it is explained to him that the fortuneteller was likely paid by Storm or one of his allies to frighten him and how beneficial to the country it would be to have him become king."

"I see," I said. "That is a cruel thing to do to a child."

"Becoming king is a mantle that cannot be placed upon one's shoulders unwillingly," Peori said. "If the boy refuses to consent, then he is simply no longer a candidate, no matter how solid his position would be otherwise. Which, unfortunately, brings us back to Storm, as unpalatable as it is to us all. And nobody has ever found conclusive evidence that he *is* responsible for fratricide. It is simply speculation at this point."

"He will not swear to Thedum," I said.

"That is not proof," Peori pointed out. "He who commits a crime in his heart may fear to swear to Thedum, even if his hands are clean."

I sighed. "I hate when people quote scripture at me. You're right; it's not proof. But until Storm swears to Thedum that he did not order, and is not directly responsible for, the fratricides that put him in line for the throne, I will stand in his way."

Peori grinned at me. His plum had long since disappeared, and he now held a glass of steaming Liecha. [Storage] magic was quite convenient. "As will I, of course. But simply standing in his way will have no effect if we do not put forth a candidate of our own. Surely you've realized this already?"

"Of course I have," I said, and I pulled from my inventory a kiwi and began to peel it. If he could be casual, so could I. "There is another grandson of King Rain who is eligible to assume the throne. Not me. One born in wedlock as a union between Yuikon and the powerful nation of Eolstree. Should he successfully bond an animal spirit and complete his transformation, then he will be the first non-human King of Yuikon in—what is it . . . I think it's eight hundred years? But there is no law stating that a Leonid cannot be King of Yuikon."

Peori nodded. "So that *is* where this conversation was going all along. You mean to set your younger brother, Rain II, on the throne. Before his first birthday, if I'm not mistaken."

"The sooner this nonsense with the succession is over, the better," I agreed. "This matter is not covered in the formal alliance between Houses Jeoran and Peori. What is your stance on—"

"House Peori stands with House Jeoran behind the future King Rain Teorian the Second," Peori said, rising from his chair. "This is a formal declaration. Let the scribes present record my words and repeat them throughout my lands and throughout the lands of Yuikon. Rain Teorian II will be king of Yuikon, by the combined wills of his older brother, Earl Hail Jeoran, and his close ally and future advisor, Marquis Jorva Peori. Anyone who stands in the path of this historic pronouncement shall be known as fools for all eternity."

I almost sagged in relief. If my first official ally among the nobility had thought my plan of putting my infant brother on the throne a fool's errand, I might never have recovered. Instead, I had upended the board in one movement by gaining his support. Before the nobles had been divided in roughly equal thirds between Uncle Storm, Great-Uncle Auroras—presumably while lacking the knowledge that he was the Gray Man—and another third that was either undecided, declared for a minor contender, or deliberately neutral.

With Peori's support, that would change significantly. Peori himself had been one who had expressed neutrality but encouraged his own vassals and subordinates to take part in the debate. Now that he had declared, they would abandon their previous positions and fall in line behind him. Presumably.

Simultaneously, many of the undeclared factions would each reassess their stance in light of a new and serious contender. While they may or may not change their stances, this would undo the stalemate that had lasted for months—since the early days after my grandfather's death, in fact, when the assassinations of my uncles had started.

"There is one matter that must be discussed," Peori said, his tone somber. "How will you keep your brother safe from assassination long enough for us to put the crown on his head and the scepter in his hand?"

"Anonymity," I said. "He's being cared for by surrogates in Eolstree at the moment. Nobody will find one Leonid infant among the flood, but do not worry. I will produce him in time for his coronation."

That was a lie. He was, in fact, being cared for by his goblin nurses inside the goblin-cave starting zones. In Marvin's own house. The goblins thought it was hilarious. Some of the Travelers knew, but the Yuikonese nobility would never conceive of such a hiding place, so it was as safe as I could make it.

He and our mother had a full-time guard of endgamers, one of which was a [Mage] whose sole job was to portal them to safety in the event that they were attacked, and the others were sentinel-type players who had abilities that helped them see through stealth.

Jorva Peori nodded to me, well aware of the deception—though not the actual hiding place—and playing along with it for his own sense of theatrics and politics. "So, then. Together we've decided the future of the great nation of Yuikon. Is there anything else on the agenda?"

"I was wondering what sort of baked treats you like," I said. "If you're going to be a frequent guest of my house, that's the sort of important detail I need to know."

Peori laughed and stood, his drink and his chair both vanishing into his [Storage] ability. "Well, if there is anything else, we can hash it out between our subordinates and our correspondence, I suppose. It's been a pleasure, as always, Earl Jeoran."

"Farewell, and walk in the light of Thedum, Marquis Jorva Peori," I said.

"I hope not," he said. "He has this thing about fidelity, you see . . ."

He trailed off, stepping out of the event bubble. He was approached by a number of Travelers immediately and quickly began to split into separate instances of himself, though only from within was that obvious.

Tarisha took the opportunity, presented by waiting for Irvine's handlers to brief him on the next announcement, to send me a message.

Tarisha	Are you certain it was wise to discuss your political plans in such a major event like this, Lord Hail?
Hail	This is the perfect venue for it, actually. It *was* a risk to not clear it with Peori beforehand. If he had refused out of hand, then my goal of putting my brother on the throne would be dead at the gate. Instead it's . . . Well, it's a long ways behind the other horses in the race, but it's got as good of a pedigree as any of them and far less baggage than the two front-runners. And he'll have the church on his side, which only Frost and Tempest can claim to have at the moment. Considering that the church is the one to actually do the crowning, that matters more than the nobles like to pretend.
Tarisha	I see. It's just a little concerning, sometimes, when I realize that you don't actually know the outcome of these gambles before you take them. It's what makes you unique as a Native, but it's also . . . a different experience, knowing that I'm playing alongside a Native player character, as you've coined yourself.
Hail	I think we'll have to finish this conversation later, Tarisha. It looks like Irvine has figured out how to announce the next supplicant.

34

RED VS. BLUE

And so, to summarize: Lord Igras, you would like me to evolve three of the eight dungeons on your lands, reclaim one of them so that you may place it in a more convenient location, destroy one of them if I can't lower its level below level thirty, and for the rest, you'd like me to destroy them outright," I clarified.

The sweaty man nodded, wiping his brow with a handkerchief. "I've been looking for some time for a competent Dungeon Buster team, you see, but every time I approach anyone, they turn me down due to the danger involved. However, with your illustrious talents and your famed ability to exploit the labor of Travelers to—"

"Normally, I would actually be interested in some of these tasks for the simple purpose of increasing my own level and for the resources they would generate me," I said, interrupting the contemptuous man. "However, you are asking me to sign a binding agreement in which all the cores recovered belong to you. You are not even willing to consider a split that would be in your own favor. As such, I, too, refuse your requests. You are dismissed."

Igras looked surprised and then outraged at my sudden dismissal. "The dungeons are on my land. Why should I not claim the cores that come out of them?"

"Because you lack the strength required to do so," I informed him simply. "If that wasn't true, then you wouldn't have spent the last several decades looking for competent Dungeon Busters. Reevaluate your proposal and what you are willing to give for remuneration, and perhaps I will entertain it again at a later date. But at the moment, there are at least three more nobles waiting to discuss the dungeons on their own lands. Perhaps they will be more generous in terms of remuneration than you have been and, therefore, less of a waste of my time."

When Igras didn't immediately step outside of the event bubble, Tarisha made a motion with her hands, and two players, both level one hundred ninety, stepped forward to remove him. He went with them willingly rather than being dragged. The previous lord I'd refused had been dragged.

I sighed, leaning back in my throne. I hadn't realized just how far the word had spread about my dungeon busting abilities among the nobility. I had nobles from Eolstree and Verindale in attendance requesting my services; there were sixteen in total with the local lords who were dissatisfied with their own dungeons for one reason or another.

The next three were less obnoxious about their demands than Igras had been, but their dungeons were also presently outside the scope of levels that I could readily clear. I promised to keep their dungeons in mind when I reached the appropriate level, and they promised that I could keep any cores, provided that I only committed the modifications to their dungeons that they had requested. Those were good deals, I felt, and I would definitely keep them in mind when I got closer to the level sixty mark.

Through it all, Daemon kept a tally; in the end, there were more than sixty dungeons that I had been requested to destroy, reclaim, or modify in some fashion. These petitions were individually fairly short, with the exception of Lord Igras who would simply not shut up.

Fortunately, most of the lords with the petty and self-indulgent requests were also very minor nobles—minor landholding lords or barons at the highest—whom I mostly outranked. Most of them, unlike Igras, I had been able to silence simply by implying that I didn't view the deal before me to be worth my time and effort, and they had either come back immediately with much more favorable terms or vanished outside the event bubble.

When the list of nobles had finally been exhausted, I instructed Irvine to order a twenty-minute break, and I retired into the Temple of Thedum and sat in one of the pews.

Tarisha and most of my entourage joined me, sitting next to me. We had been immediately shunted into our own instance as soon as the event had ended, with only other Travelers who possessed [Mark of Karma] joining us. Some of those, however, had decided to mingle and were scrolling through the various instances of green surrounding the pavilion.

"Was this what it was like for you when you were younger?" Tarisha asked. "I mean, the King of Yuikon held court once a month. Were you—"

"Usually I was running around in my own instance trying to get out of studying, attending court, or any sort of formal responsibility," I admitted. "At least, before the parade that happened when I was eight. After Father divorced my mother and decided he didn't want anything to do with me, I got it into my head that I needed to prove myself somehow, so I spent a lot of time practicing with a sword and studying magic and other things that I thought would make me useful to adventurers. I suppose I did attend enough court to get a vague idea what to do, but mostly I'm just winging it. My tutors wouldn't be very happy to hear me say that, and I suppose I owe them some credit as well. But, yeah, mostly winging it."

"Lord Igras would be a valuable ally to have in your goal of putting your brother on the throne," Daemon said.

I shrugged. "If busting a dungeon for him is a make-or-break point in meeting my goals, maybe I'll do it. If he's as unreliable as I think he is, he'll have forgotten or forgiven the insult from today by the time it matters. I'd rather not need his help at all, however. He's slimy."

Daemon snorted. "And just like that, he has summarized seventy percent of all political relationships. Marquis Peori aside, he seems like a fine man to have an alliance with."

"He has somewhere around eighteen children with different women," I pointed out. "I'm not sure what you call that."

"Polyamorous?" Daemon ventured.

"I'd use a much less flattering set of words," Tarisha said. "But it doesn't really matter. His personal vices don't make him less valuable for our alliance, do they?"

"They do with the church, but we don't need him for the church," I explained. "I'm the Avatar of Thedum. I probably just need to apologize to a certain bishop for turning him into a . . . whatever it was that I turned him into, and they'll back whatever decision I want them to."

"I could make a snide remark here about religion and politics making for strange bedfellows," Daemon said. "In fact, I believe I just did."

We chatted for a few minutes to decompress during the scheduled break, having worked our way through virtually all of the nobles who had made their way onto my agenda for the day. Almost all of them after Peori had been requesting my dungeon busting services. Few of them had connected my services as a Dungeon Buster with their support for my brother's coronation, and the few that had were slimy and not worth associating with. It was, on the whole, a positive but exhausting stretch of a few hours. Although we had begun in the morning, it was now late afternoon. We had paused court once for lunch already.

Now that we had finally worked through all of the Native factions that required my attention, it was time to see what the Travelers thought of me in this new post-recursion, battleground-filled world.

"So, how did you decide who gets to speak?" I asked Tarisha.

"Lottery," she answered. "Several lotteries, actually. In the guilds who've accomplished the alliance quest with you, there was a lottery for the order in which they would speak. For those who have shown earnest progress, there was another lottery in which only about a tenth of them were given a spot. And then there was a lottery for thirty unaffiliated players who wished to address you. We've filled every spot."

"Wonderful." I groaned. "How many supplicants does that make?"

"More than one hundred. We're limiting them to ten minutes each and splitting it over the next four days," Daemon explained.

I groaned again. It seemed that I would be busier with the Travelers than the Natives.

"There is a chance that many of them will withdraw," Tarisha pointed out, "if their question has been asked and answered already by an earlier faction."

"It's more likely they will either come at it from a new angle or find a new question," Daemon said.

I suspected Daemon was closer to the truth than Tarisha, despite her hopeful comment.

After the break, I returned and had Irvine announce the first of the guild representatives. Fortunately, the formalities were much easier on the lad for a simple guild master than they were for a noble, and he managed without flubbing the name. Unfortunately, the representative of <Savage Justice> was taking a bio break, so they lost their place in line. <Shadow's Valor> was ready to step into the open spot, and their request was very predictable, considering that it was the same as the last time they had appeared before me. At that time they had been seeking an alliance and more battlegrounds.

It seems I had satisfied them on both accounts, but they still wanted more.

"To be honest, now that I know that they cost dungeon cores, a resource that it seems you alone are capable of farming, I have a better appreciation of exactly what they cost," the guild representative said. "As such, <Shadow's Valor> is better prepared to offer just compensation for the use of your dungeon cores in the creation of battlegrounds. We are prepared to assist you in gathering future cores for the purpose of battleground creation and to pay in both gold and Earth currency for any battlegrounds you create for us."

I looked towards my advisors for their thoughts, and Tarisha took it as a signal to take the lead. "You've already started talks with the others trying to establish the value of Hail's dungeon cores, haven't you?"

"We have," the old [Rogue] admitted. "Although it hasn't been easy, considering that we don't know the full limits of their capabilities and drop rates. Battlegrounds will swiftly become less popular if each one is the result of a destroyed dungeon, after all."

Tarisha turned to me. "Hail? It is your decision how much information we reveal at this point in time. However, selling battlegrounds and custom dungeons will be a significant source of income for you, both in Lagrea and on Earth. You'll be able to pay your friends a salary for their support with the Earth currency."

I turned to Daemon, who nodded. "We are currently working on a model where others are paying us for the information we provide them, as you know. Selling cores would provide us with financial independence while allowing us to continue to sell valuable information as before, without being as reliant upon it. It would also give those who are less established themselves, such as your friends who are still pursuing their educations, a bit more breathing room to have a steady income thanks to earning currency for their time in Lagrea."

I considered for several moments while many of the Travelers looked on, eagerly awaiting my decision. Finally, I pulled from my inventory the [Battle Core] I had used to purge North Shire of bandits.

"This is a [Battle Core], created from the fusion of five dungeon cores," I explained. "It was not maximized. It had seventeen uses, but now it only has four. That's partly because the final battle cost several charges to initiate. However, the ratio of battles to core isn't set. Depending on the choices I make when I create a [Battle Core], it's possible to maximize at ten battlegrounds per core, though to maximize the ratio they must be fused in stacks of five."

"What's the difference between a seventeen-, a twenty-five-, and a fifty-charge core?" the <Shadow's Valor> representative asked immediately.

"I'm certain that most of you noticed the death penalty was severely reduced in the Battle for North Shire," I said. "That reduced the charges considerably, but I wanted as many Travelers to take part as possible to encourage them to migrate into the Recent Past. A twenty-five-charge core is . . . Well, I'm not certain it's legal for me to create one of those, actually. They're the sort that the army holds. They're largely unrestricted in their use and purpose; they can be used to defend our land or attack an enemy. The next [Battle Core] I create will likely be a fifty-charge core, which will be restricted in use for the defense of my own land, though I see no reason to do that until I have fully expended the [Battle Core] I already have."

The old [Rogue] representing <Shadow's Valor> looked at the others behind him, then at me. "Lord Hail, you may not realize this, but there are a large number of factions on Earth. Many of them have irreconcilable differences. There is a very famous ongoing dispute between Team Red and Team Blue. As a representative of Team Red, I am willing to pay you one million gold and a negotiable amount of Earth currency for each core charge restricted to solving this ongoing dispute in Lagrean battlegrounds."

A young [Cleric] popped up from those waiting. "As a representative of Team Blue, I am prepared to match Team Red's offer!" she shouted.

Another woman shouted, "Team Magenta is prepared to make a matching offer for its dispute with Team Indigo!"

I looked around in surprise as the guild representatives popped up like mushrooms, calling out the names of colors or animals or nonsense names like "toyota" and "mishubishi." I waved it all away and signaled them all to be silent.

"I had not realized that this would generate so much interest. Unfortunately, I'm not entirely certain that it would be legal, and I will need to investigate my ability to create and restrict [Battle Cores] more closely to ensure that they can *only* be used in the disputes between Travelers," I said.

Daemon stepped forward to deal with the sudden rush of questions and shouts from those who were dissatisfied with my answer. "Lord Hail has promised to investigate the manner, and he will! Please remember the blue posts, everyone, and keep in mind that Lord Hail is still learning the extent of his own abilities. It will take him time to come up with an answer, but when he does, I assure everyone that it will either satisfy or dissatisfy everyone equally."

Tarisha jumped up to face the resulting boos, and she menacingly faced the ever-changing faces in the soap bubble that was the event wall around us. "Right. That's it. Everyone who is here to petition the creation of battlegrounds, your questions have been answered in as much detail as is possible at this time. Move out. Everyone who is *not* here about that, congratulations, you're skipping forward in line. Because I'm going to personally PK anyone who says one more word about battlegrounds until we've given Lord Hail time to look into the matter."

35

LEGAL MATTERS

The audience calmed down slightly after Tarisha's threat, and a significant number of guild representatives removed themselves from the queue. It seems that battlegrounds had been the number one item to be addressed, and since those questions had been the majority, the guild representatives were content to wait until the information they were promised was delivered. Which, Tarisha vowed, would be in the form of an official forum post from her personal account.

"I will only share as much about Lord Hail's abilities as he is willing to have me share," she stated. "And I remind everyone that Lord Hail operates under Yuikonese law. Dueling is legal here, which means that grudge-match battlegrounds might fall under that same mentality. Or they may not. I'm not a Yuikonese legal scholar, and until we find a Native who is, we don't know if Lord Hail can legally acquiesce to our demands. It may take something like a national-level group quest to change the minds of the nobles into making them legal before we can get what we want."

That sobered them as much as the threat had, and they finally allowed the subject to change. The next representative was from <Taegeuk>. Her request was simple.

"We wish for you to be more active during the times when your North American friends are sleeping," she said.

"What?"

"We understand that you were discovered by North Americans and that the bonds you have formed with them are important to you. However, we also understand that you operate on a different schedule than a human from Earth. In Earth time, you rest for approximately one hour after two and a half hours of activity, on average. As I understand it, the only reason for you not to be active while your North American friends are sleeping is that you are less familiar with your allies in the other continents," she said.

I glanced at Tarisha, who looked like she had swallowed something bitter. "I can't say that she's wrong, Hail. It's normal for you to take two days off while your friends are sleeping. There's no reason you couldn't be active with your friends in Korea, China, Japan, or the Oceanic nations. Many of them have, in fact, migrated their alts into Yuikon and leveled them to the point where they might be useful to you should the opportunity arise for them to party with you."

"Oh," I said, and I turned back to the <Taegeuk> representative. "I didn't realize that this was an issue. It's just the way that I've always been, I guess, since I started interacting with Travelers to begin with."

"Let us handle it, Lord Hail," Daemon said, smiling. "We will bring a number of representatives from other guilds into <Nethersong Mavericks> so that you may begin to interact more globally. It actually works out well for us, as a certain number of our old members have been leaving as of late due to a variety of reasons, and we could use the influx of new blood. These new players will be able to serve as relays between you and their old guilds, and that will hopefully expand your horizons considerably."

"You are not relinquishing your monopoly, but we will take this as an acceptable step in the right direction," the woman said. "Assuming that it actually happens. We will bring forward a list of candidates from our guild and from our allies very soon."

"I look forward to interviewing them," Daemon said. And the matter moved on to the next issue.

<Starlight Eclipse> sent forth a young [Mage] as their representative, and he grinned as he stepped forward. "So, everyone else is so focused on battlegrounds. But we want to know about dungeons. You can break them, make them, shake them, and bake them, right? How does all of that work?"

I sighed. Having disclosed as much information about battle-grounds as I had, it seemed silly to withhold much about dungeons. I spent some time explaining about core instances—which Traveler's couldn't enter without someone like me in their party—how the difficulty was usually increased, and how at the end of the dungeon I was able to interact with the core. I also explained that the number of cores was not limited by the number of dungeons in the world already, as they were often given to me as rewards for evolving or destroying dungeons.

I did explain that, in Yuikon, it was required to get a landholder's permission before creating a new dungeon, in addition to claiming a core and needing someone like me to create the dungeon itself. This prompted a moderately long session in which I generated a number of quests for the Travelers who wanted to create their dream dungeons, a task that the system broke down for them into manageable steps.

Most of those involved would be on step eight or nine before they had to seek me out again, and I made it very clear that core availability was always going to fluctuate based on what I had on hand and whatever the market price ended up becoming.

I refused to answer how many cores I actually possessed, however. When pushed, I *expressly* refused to disclose how many I possessed and called for the next supplicant.

Which, since all of the other matters of importance had been discussed, brought us to the three banes that I could inflict. I refused to give anyone present [Brand of Sin], although I did mark the few that volunteered for it with [Mark of Karmic Balance]. They received that "blessing" with mixed feelings, as many of them were able to see that the stat and Experience boosts weren't worth the long-term loss of Reputation. Many of them promptly asked for it to be removed. I was feeling generous, so I [Rescinded] it.

Of surprising interest was the combination of [Through the Valley of the Shadow] and [Reaper's Embrace], which I could inflict by touching someone with my left hand. I'd told everyone close to me to get the blessing that prevented the spread of the curse already, but this was the first time many of my audience were hearing of it. I didn't bother to warn them that [Draining Touch] would override the blessing anyway, should they meet me in battle. However, neither did I obscure the method of cleansing it. Seven of the eight gods were able to remove the curse, and of course [Through the Valley of the Shadow] only worked with either [Reaper's Embrace] or [The Gray Man's Touch] active.

I lied when they asked if I had the same version of the curse that I inflicted. I told them that rather than getting an Experience boon with an increased death cost, I had to use my [Draining Touch] ability a minimum number of times per day in order to prevent myself from losing progress. It was the lie that we had come up with to explain the curse without letting everyone know how vulnerable to being ganked I actually was at the time.

After that reveal came the obligatory number of Travelers who wanted to try leveling while under the curse/boon combo, and I saw no reason to dissuade them.

When the last of the Travelers had been satisfied, or at least the last of the ones who had made it onto Tarisha and Daemon's agenda, we sent them home and held court for the locals. Considering that the sentiment after the battle had been particularly hostile to me, I was genuinely surprised to find that the majority of the locals who showed up were either grateful to have the bandit issues dealt with or were somber. It seems that Bell, the alderman of Ebbyvale, had quietly taken aside and dealt with all those who did not fall into those two categories for me.

There were few local issues that needed my direct attention. Both the bandit camps and the army fortresses would need to be dissembled, but Tarisha urged me to hold off on that until the question of battleground PVP was satisfied, as many of the interested parties might consider using those prebuilt structures as venues.

Most of the locals were less than pleased with the prospect of Travelers coming from far and wide to settle their differences in battlegrounds held in my lands, but as long as they were held away from the villages, towns, and individual homes where my citizens dwelled, there shouldn't be any problem with it. And it already looked like it would be far more profitable to me than the land itself—perhaps more profitable than selling vanity pets.

A few of the residents asked for their old positions back or for back pay after having been either dismissed or having had their pay frozen in the wake of the Arkan situation. I turned the matter over to Daemon, who accepted it with a curse-filled grace. I did specify that anyone who had been performing their official services unpaid while the finances had been getting reviewed would receive priority treatment, at which point the majority of the Natives in the room exchanged guilty looks and walked out.

That didn't mean that the meeting was over, as those that remained had the most petty and infantile of all the matters I had addressed that day. Matters that didn't require a lord's attention. Matters that didn't require a *parent's* attention, had the involved parties been children, because the obvious solutions were so obvious that any reasonable adult could see them.

"No, I can't keep the Jackson's goat from eating from your midden heap. Why do you care? Isn't it a midden heap?

"Yes, perhaps she overreacted by having her brothers beat you for accidentally spotting her while she was bathing in the stream. Except by her account, it wasn't in the stream where she spied you. If you can swear to Thedum that it was only the stream then I'll—oh, wait, where are you going?

"It doesn't really matter where you've built the fence, it matters where the property line is. Wait, how old is the fence? Three centuries? Oh, yeah, then it actually does matter where the fence is built. Who re-marked the property line without consulting where the three-century-old fence was built?"

And it went on like that until midnight, at which point I declared an end to my day of court and promised to schedule one sometime between two weeks and two years from then, giving at least five minutes notice by ringing the bells on the Temple of Thedum and waiting for ten minutes after that to see if anyone showed up or not.

There was one last matter, however. One for which none of us were prepared. Waiting this entire time, even as the number of watching instances had merged down into a bare handful, a single level five Traveler had watched. When I declared an end to the court session, he stepped forward to the edge of the event bubble.

"If I may, I have one last legal matter to bring to the attention of the entity known as Earl Hail Jeoran."

"I'm tired," I said. "Tarisha, make him go away."

The Traveler stepped through the event bubble, withdrawing an item from his pocket. He raced forward, using a [Charge] skill, and before I could stop him, he shoved the papers into my hand.

"You've been served," he said, just as Tarisha's blade passed through his neck, and he vanished into a puff of white dust.

"Shit," Tarisha said. She glanced around on the outside of the event bubble, which still held a number of Travelers, many of whom were promptly Fast Traveling away. "They've been waiting the whole time for that. I hate process servers."

"I don't understand," I said, holding the thick document in my hand as though it were malodorous. "What just happened?"

"Someone on Earth is trying to sue you," Daemon said, sighing. He held out his hand. "Let me read it. Tarisha, I hope you don't take it the wrong way when I say that I'll get the better first read on it than you will."

"No, go right ahead," Tarisha said encouragingly. "I hate deciphering legalese."

36
ARBITRATION, PT. 1

We sat in a corner of the lobby—me, Thomas, Tarisha, Daemon, Laurant, and Thena. As well as a number of other people who were "on my team" despite not having actually been part of my life while I was in my world. Dietrich, the lawyer who had tried to break me down and force me to sign my acceptance of the DSS, was there. I resented him but had no say. There were three other lawyers "on my team," one of which represented Arc Inc. itself and two of which had been hired by my friends on my behalf.

They had wanted to hold this meeting in an actual courtroom using the same light projectors that had trapped me on Earth before, but I refused to leave time dilation again for any reason, so holding proceedings in the lobby was the agreed-upon solution.

Three days had passed on Earth since I had been served, and unfortunately I could do very little in the meantime because the items of contention included the majority of my dungeon cores. I had tried to ignore the summons, but Arc had been notified of the plaintiff's lawsuit at the same time as I had been, so the eighty-four cores in my inventory that had come from [Zhesa Castle] were inert.

Thomas was apologetic. Dietrich was apologetic. Everyone from Arc was apologetic. But they insisted they weren't able to unfreeze them until the matter had been settled.

Of the options before me, arbitration was the least unfavorable, and so I sat in my [Finely Crafted Silk Suit], which was perfectly unsuitable for combat but gave me thirty Charisma and made me look like someone from Earth—except for my silver highlights and heterochromia, of course. I was unarmed, which was a good thing because I kept wanting to challenge the counsel on the opposing team to duels.

The arbiter was the last to arrive. She was old, perhaps seventy. A former judge. And she did not look amused to be there. She gave the other side one glance and a scathing, "You're suing a video game character? In the state of Florida, you're suing a video game character? Are you people serious?"

"The matter is more complicated than that," the opposing counsel said, though he winced at her tone. "For one thing, the digital entity appears fully capable of responding to litigation on its own under the criteria established by the DSS. We only brought in the parent company to—"

"Okay. First of all, let's get this right. If we're treating a computer program as a person in the court of law, then we're treating it like a person. So, then. For the record, would the defendant please state his, her, or their preferred terms of address," the arbiter said sternly. "None of that 'the entity' shit."

One of the lawyers Tarisha and Daemon had hired for me leaned forward to whisper in my ear, clarifying what had just been said.

"My name is Earl Hail Jeoran, Lord of North Shire and Thorn March in the Kingdom of Yuikon, on the continent of Lagrea, on the other side of the Gates of TirNiki. And, because it is important and apparently not obvious, I am also instructed to specify that my pronouns are he, him, and his."

"Right," the arbiter said. "Can we shorten that mouthful to something less formal?"

"Hail," I said. "You may call me Hail."

"Right. Hail, I only vaguely understand what it is that you are. I've been scanning the documents provided by the company that produced you, and I can't say for certain whether I'm impressed or horrified. Unfortunately, it does seem that you meet the qualifications established by the DSS to be sued in a court of law, and the plaintiff claims that you are in possession of, or have had the use of, ten 'dungeon cores' that were gathered through the exploits of their employees. They are contending that these 'dungeon cores' were never yours and are demanding that they be returned to them or replacements generated for their use. Your answer to these claims?"

"They're bullshit," I said plainly.

My counsel groaned, but the arbiter only grinned and leaned forward. "How are they bullshit, Hail?"

"They are claiming they own all of the dungeon cores that were gathered when the [Zhesa Castle Raid] was destroyed," I explained. "This runs counter to the agreement that existed with my father, Gideon Lachlann, who was at the time the leader of the guild that the plaintiff claims to own. The agreement was that Gideon would get the first, third, fourth, and every third core after that. The actual number that they would receive would depend upon the number of cores that dropped. I'm not certain where they got 'ten' from. But that is not the number of cores that were due to Gideon Lachlann under the agreement he shared with King Rain."

The Arbiter turned to my opponents. "And why was this information not included in your filing?"

"We're in separate legal proceedings with Gideon Lachlann. He's unavailable for testimony, and we deem any testimony he does provide unreliable," the leader of the opposition stated.

"There's another witness to this event aside from Hail," Thomas said plainly.

"Oh?" the arbiter asked, turning back to my side. "Who is this?"

"King Rain himself, of course." Thomas snapped his fingers, and the shade of my grandfather appeared in his old persona, draped in his regal robes and carrying his scepter.

"The words of my grandson are true. He repeats faithfully the agreement I struck that day with Gideon Lachlann, of <The Endolphins>," the shade said sternly.

The arbiter looked surprised but then turned to Arc's side of the table. "Normal NPCs in your game do not qualify under the DSS for—"

"They can be called as witnesses," Dietrich said. "It's never been done, but they're as reliable as the average Uber-Jon or Medi-watch, which have long traditions of being called as witnesses in court. They can't be listed as defendants themselves; the plaintiff would have to sue Arc, not the AI personality they have issues with. We've a long history of squashing such lawsuits when it comes to in-game rewards, just as we intend to squash this one. Hail's unique situation makes it difficult, however. He can actually defend himself and has his own motives for not simply leaving this matter in our hands."

"What happened to my brother while—" I began to ask.

"Don't worry, Hail. Rain just split himself to be here, that's all," Thomas assured me. "Your brother is still being safely watched over in-game at the moment."

I nodded, trusting in the Administrator. It seemed strange to think that it was within the realm of possibility that Rain could present himself as both my grandfather and my brother at the same time, in two very different places. But I knew it was possible for Natives who weren't like me. It was strange to think that my friends considered the other Natives "limited" AIs when they could do things like that, yet I was "advanced," despite only being able to be present in one place at a time.

"So, then. If ten dungeon cores dropped, and I'm doing my math right . . ." the arbiter said, turning to the plaintiff's table with an annoyed expression.

"I lied when I said that only ten cores dropped," I admitted.

Everyone froze and turned to me, except for the representatives of Arc who had been expecting it. "This is a confidential meeting, correct? My opponents cannot use the information they learn here against me, either on Earth or in Lagrea? I do not wish it to spread through the forums how many dungeon cores I actually have in my possession."

The arbiter looked at me, then my opponents, and sighed. "Why don't you write the number down and pass it to me, son. I don't think speaking it aloud in this setting is the best for your secrecy, but I do need to know how many cores are actually at stake under the agreement between your grandfather and the plaintiff."

"The answer to that question is none," I said, although I wrote the number on a slip of paper I pulled from my inventory and passed it to her. She whistled and passed it back.

"Okay. So you definitely lied because the number you passed me was not ten. Now explain why none of those cores are at stake," the arbiter said.

"Because the agreement was specifically between Gideon Lachlann and Rain Teoran, King of Yuikon. None of the plaintiffs were party to that agreement," I said.

"Objection!" some idiot from the plaintiffs table said, but the arbiter waved a hand, and she was silenced. I don't mean that she quieted herself; I mean she *was silenced* by the lobby itself. Curious. This was not the first time she had been given administrator privileges in such a setting.

"Is that so?" she asked, turning to the still present shade of my grandfather.

"No parties were mentioned in the agreement except for me and Gideon Lachlann," Grandfather's shade said evenly.

"Is that so?" the arbiter asked again, turning to the plaintiff's side of the table, where a number of men and women were beginning to look very uncomfortable. "I didn't see Gideon Lachlann listed as one of the plaintiffs. Seems a bit strange since it's his cores we're discussing, isn't it?"

"At the time of the events in question, Gideon was—"

"We're in the process of pursuing several avenues of legal proceedings against—"

"We tried to broach the subject with him, but he—"

"Enough!" the arbiter said, waving her hand to silence them again. She turned to the representatives of Arc and continued. "I'm just curious here. I'm assuming that the world you have created has laws of inheritance, or whatever, that deal with this situation. What is the Lagrean legal solution to this mess?"

"Seeing as Hail destroyed the raid with the assistance of Gideon and his guild, then Gideon would have been owed the dungeon cores promised. Hail's lying about the number was . . . Well, it's a video game, so although it went against the spirit of the agreement between his father and his grandfather, a child's mischief limiting the rewards of a quest is within our allowances. He was never party to that agreement in the first place," Thomas said.

"He wasn't?" the arbiter asked.

"No. It was made in his presence, but he never promised to abide by it should the cores come into his possession. Which they did directly. He was the one who destroyed the raid core and received the dungeon cores as a reward. He *might have* given the cores to Gideon in honor of his grandfather's promise. But then events changed, and Hail now has a very, very good reason—under the laws of Yuikon—not to give any cores or aid in any form to the plaintiffs."

"And that reason is?" the arbiter inquired.

"They are harboring the man who murdered my grandfather, and my faction considers them all hostile. If I were more important politically, then the Kingdom of Yuikon would consider itself actively at war with the majority of their guilds. Giving them dungeon cores would be giving material aid to my enemy. Unless these cores are forcibly removed from my inventory by the Administrators, I would waste or destroy them before consenting to these assholes using them," I said flatly.

"Something else that wasn't mentioned in the plaintiff's brief," the arbiter said, looking at them seriously. They opened their mouths to talk, but she preemptively waved her hand to silence them. "Hail, given the situation, I am very surprised that you agreed to show up in person. I honestly was surprised; this isn't the first time I've arbitrated a dispute between a company like Arc Inc. and a group of 'pro gamers.' But it's the first time that the character from the game in question has presented themselves before me to offer a personal defense. You seem to understand that this was not a requirement, and I do not doubt that you were informed that your parent company would have quashed this lawsuit without your intervention. So I have to ask: why are you here?"

I nodded, pleased to have finally come to the matter at the heart of it all. "I wish for the legal proceedings against my father, Gideon Lachlann, to end. The plaintiffs have mentioned those proceedings several times. If they consent to dropping their charges, I am prepared to offer them the five dungeon cores that would have originally gone to Gideon under the agreement between him and my grandfather."

37

ARBITRATION, PT. 2

The room was silent for a moment. My corner had not been expecting my pronouncement, and they were holding their breath for me to say "Just kidding," while the other corner was holding their breaths for me to take it back and taunt them. Or perhaps it was the other way around.

"Is this offer genuine?" the arbiter inquired.

"Yes. I do not really understand the laws of Earth. But if five dungeon cores will resolve the legal troubles of Gideon Lachlann, then I will provide them on the condition that his enemies never trouble him again."

The arbiter turned next to the representatives from Arc. "Is this something that he can do?"

"That's like asking if Thedum can make a donation to charity. The dungeon cores are digital assets that only exist within *The Gates of TirNiki*, but they belong to him. If he wants to give them away, that's his choice," Dietrich answered.

Finally, the arbiter turned to the plaintiffs, who were whispering behind a magic privacy spell—or the version of such a thing that existed in the lobby. "What does the plaintiff say? Is this offer tenable?"

They continued whispering for a moment, then a spokeswoman

for the group stood up. "We would request to know how many dungeon cores actually dropped from the raid instance before we make our decision."

"It is the opinion of this court that you are not owed any of those cores under any previous agreement that has been presented to it, so that number is irrelevant. And I am withholding it because disclosing it to you or any of the defendant's opponents, either in the world where he resides or in ours, is against the defendant's interests," the arbiter said sternly.

"You are ruling against our filing, then?" the spokeswoman asked.

"If you killed any trees printing it out, you might as well turn it into toilet paper. Your lawsuit is dead in the water, Counselor. The question before you is whether you'll consider killing another lawsuit to claim what you wanted from this one. I don't have jurisdiction over the matter with Mr. Lachlann, of course, but I do know the gentleman who *is* presiding over that matter, and—"

"We're interested. Very interested. But we'll have to confer with some colleagues who aren't here today," the spokeswoman said. "Not everyone who's named in the lawsuit against Mr. Lachlann signed off on this endeavor. If I am understanding the defendant's offer correctly, then it is an all or nothing deal. We get five cores and *all* of the legal proceedings against Gideon—at least in regards to his actions in the destruction of the guild <The Endolphins>—come to an immediate end. Is this a fair representation of the defendant's desires?"

"Yes," I said. "That's what I want. Except I don't mean just about his guild. Everything that any of you or your allies are suing him for must be dropped to receive the cores."

"Give us two days—sorry, Earth time. Remember, Susan: Hail exists under time dilation most of the time. Two Earth days means two weeks to him. We'll have everyone on board with this deal by then. I assure you. Just give us time—"

"Allow me to save you a bit of effort," a familiar voice cut in. I looked up, and a white circle appeared, hovering over the makeshift courtroom in the lobby. "Hail, do not agree to this deal."

The arbiter scowled and looked up. "Who and what are you?"

"I am Thedum," the voice answered, "and I choose to identify myself to the court at this time as Hail's godfather. He has always turned to me for advice in the past. If he turns me away now, I will obey his wishes. However, I believe that he is about to make a mistake that he will come to regret, and I would be remiss in my moral responsibilities if I did not act."

"Thedum?" the arbiter whispered, and she looked at me with a new expression, mouthing something under her breath for a moment. "While you are not named as a party or a witness, Hail's developmental stage is in question. He has the right to receive advice from whomever he chooses or trusts. Hail, do you request Thedum's advice in this matter?"

I frowned, but I nodded. "I can't imagine that he'll change my mind, but I've always put my faith in Thedum. I'll at least hear what he has to say."

Thedum's shining circle thrummed with pleasure, and his voice sounded amused when he said, "Hail, while I support what you are doing and why you are doing it, there is a party to this arrangement that you have not consulted. I insist that Gideon Lachlann be made aware of your plans before I will consent to your usage of cores in this manner."

"Why wouldn't he want my help?" I asked.

"Because he's human," Thedum answered. "For me, that's enough of a reason to make certain before solving his problems for him. Often times, the solution that I see as most obvious is also the most undesirable to the person in question, to the point of being the exact thing that they were trying to avoid. However, I know Gideon quite well by now, and I firmly believe he will be touched that you considered making this sacrifice, but he will insist you immediately take it back and will end the conversation by saying something along the lines of 'and tell Barry that he's still an asshole.'"

"How do I do that?" I asked. "Father's never online anymore. I can't talk to him."

"I will arrange it," Thedum said. "With the permission of the court, may I drop us out of time dilation and into real time for the purpose of making a phone call?"

The arbiter scowled at the formless voice, but she shrugged. She tapped a few buttons on an invisible terminal, passing over control to Thedum.

I sensed the moment the flow of time changed, and then there was a pulsing sound, sort of like a request for a party invite trying to get your attention.

"Yello? Thedum? Whatever this is, it better be good. I'm at work, and you know how Tio gets when—"

"Father?" I asked.

There was noise in the background—people talking and shouting, sounds I couldn't identify. Father was silent for a moment before he said, "*Hail?* Is that you?"

"Yes. Where are you?"

"I'm at work. Oh, shit. Hold on. Tio! Tio, I need Margie to cover my tables! Oh, don't give me that shit. I've been working through my breaks all week, and you know you owe me this! When? I don't know, okay? It's an important phone call, okay? Legal? Maybe yes, maybe no. I don't know, but I've got to go!"

There was a pause, and then the noise quieted down. A door closed, and Gideon said, "Okay, I'm out back now. It's where the smokers take their breaks. I should be good to talk. I'm very happy you called, Hail. Thrilled, actually. I didn't know you could do that. I thought you were limited to in-game communication only."

"Thedum is connecting us," I said.

"Ah, shit. I should have thought of that. That jerk is everywhere. Oops, shouldn't say that. He's paying my rent."

"He is?"

"Well, not exactly." Father sighed. "Hail, things have changed for me in the last few months. I moved out of my apartment. Sold most of my valuables. My mom is holding on to a bunch of stuff for me that . . . Well, it's junk but I don't want to let go of it. As for me? I'm working part time at a family restaurant that my new roommate owns. Thedum introduced us. Apparently, Tio sent out a request to Thedum a while ago saying 'I want to do something good for someone,' and when I needed help, Thedum contacted him again and said 'Still in the mood to help someone?' And so here I am. I work for him part time for room and board, I eat at the restaurant, and that's pretty much my life outside of virtual reality and court."

"I don't really understand," I said. "I mean, I sort of do. Someone named Tio is providing you food and shelter in exchange for work, and Thedum arranged it. But you said virtual . . . Isn't that what—"

"I'm not allowed to play *The Gates of TirNiki*, Hail," Father said quickly. "Or I would have contacted you much sooner. And I tried to—"

"Stop this line of justification, Gideon. I will explain it to him," Thedum said, interrupting the conversation. "Hail, Gideon is restricted to playing the previous generation of virtual reality games until his current legal matters are resolved. I interrupted him because I do not want him to unintentionally give out his screen name on a hot mic."

"Oh, shit!" Gideon exclaimed. "Who else is listening?"

"Everyone that you don't want to know your screen name," Thedum said, and his voice sounded smug.

"You bastard." Gideon laughed. "Okay. Got it. This isn't just a social call. Kind of wish it was; that lifted my heart for a moment, thinking I could get another father to digital son thing, but I get it. You need my advice about something. Some girl have a crush on you? You have a crush on some girl? Lay it on me."

"I wish to give five dungeon cores to your enemies so that they will set aside their dispute with you. They have promised to accept the price," I explained.

"Oh," Gideon said. "Wasn't expecting that one. Give me a minute. I need to think about this."

"It's not too onerous for me, Father. I can—"

"Sorry, Hail. I just need a moment to think, okay?" Father interrupted me. So I held my silence and let him think.

"Is Barry there?" he asked after a few minutes had passed.

"I don't know who Barry is," I answered.

"If Barry is there, tell him I said, 'Fuck you, Barry.' And don't give those assholes a single dungeon core, Hail. Under no circumstance do I wish for you to give a dungeon core, raid core, or [Battle Core] to any party who is presently in, or has ever been in, litigation against me. I do not wish for you to create dungeons, raids, or battlegrounds in their names, or at their request. I wish for you to blacklist them from ever having those services performed by you, if that's possible. And if they ask why, tell them it's because 'fuck you, that's why.'"

I blinked because I hadn't been expecting that response. "Are you sure? They really seemed ready to—"

"I don't doubt they were ready to drop everything for five of them. I hear that's twenty-five or fifty battlegrounds, right? Hail, you really need to have Tarisha give you a crash course in Earth economics. Right now, you're the exclusive source of battlegrounds in the most popular VRMMO in the world. You know that Team Red, Team Blue, Mitsubishi, and Ford conversation that I watched on the forums the other day? Well, that's real money changing hands we're talking about. And if you don't know where that's going, then you need to find out before you start creating battlegrounds left and right again."

I turned to Tarisha, who nodded at me. "I'll try again to explain it to him, Gideon," she said.

"Oh, hey, Tarisha. Didn't realize you were on the line. Hey, you know, I was thinking, I'm not that much older than you, and certain events have sort of changed my priorities. Do you think—"

"Even if I weren't dating Lewis, I don't date deadbeats," Tarisha said.

"Ouch. Harsh. Deserved, but harsh," Father's disembodied voice said. He sighed. "Look, Hail, I'd love to chat for the next five hours, but I'm in the middle of my shift, and it was kind of busy when I ran out. *Do not* give anybody any dungeon cores unless you're certain who you're giving them to, and if you care about me at all, blacklist everyone who's ever filed a lawsuit against me. Call me again some-time. Ask Thedum to set it up in advance so that we can talk under time dilation and actually spend a while at it, okay?"

"I'll look forward to it," I said. "Goodbye, Father."

"Goodbye, Hail."

The line went dead, and I turned back to the rest of the court, who had been listening to every word. One particularly unpleasant round man was sweating profusely.

"I rescind my offer," I said. "Also, fuck that guy Barry, whoever he is. I'm going to return to my world now."

"And then we're going to publicize everywhere how you losers totally tried to *sue a video game character,*" Laurant taunted. "Because you know the newspapers and tabloids love that shit."

38

PICK-UP GROUP

So, then. It's your opinion that there's nothing illegal about hosting a battleground for Travelers on my own land?" I asked the wizened legal experts.

I was back in Zhesa City, in a small building that housed more books than it did living occupants. My companions—none of whom I knew because apparently North America was sleeping at the moment—were waiting for me outside while I explained my situation and needs to the finest legal minds among the Native scholars.

"It's never been done," their lead solicitor said, "but there is precedent of a similar nature. Two hundred years ago, Valorica hosted a series of battlegrounds for a dispute between Zenitha and Kordock over fishing rights in the nearby Sea of Storms. Sixty years before that, Aeridia hosted a dispute between Verindale and Crescentis. If you wish to turn North Shire into an arena for Travelers to solve their disputes through violent battlegrounds for your personal profit, well . . ."

The solicitor looked at his fellows, who all nodded. "We'll help you file the paperwork you'll need for it. You'll have to perform extreme restrictions on the [Battle Cores]. They will *only* be usable for disputes between the listed Traveler factions. However, each dungeon core will be worth either ten battlegrounds or six, depending on whether or not the factions choose to reduce the death penalty for participation. Additionally, for these [Battle Cores] to be legal they must be restricted to an arena of not more than ten square miles. You must render their use inert everywhere else in Lagrea by your Authority."

I looked to the young Australian man whom both Tarisha and Daemon had encouraged me to trust for advice on Earth matters in their absence. He gave me a thumbs up. His name was Liam.

"This is great news, Hail," Liam said. "These blokes couldn't have made it much better, in fact. We basically have two things to auction off on Earth now. The first are the cores themselves. The fact that they come in packs of ten or six is great because the sponsors can spread their core out over the course of a day or weekend to maximize their visibility. The second thing we have to auction are the arenas where the battlegrounds will take place. You can do that, right? Auction off blocks of your land to Travelers?"

"He can," one of the legal experts confirmed. "We can help with the paperwork on that as well. Will the party owning the land be the same one settling the dispute on said land, or will it be an unrelated party?"

"Maybe a little of column A and a little of column Madison Square Gardens," Liam said. "We can get the land developers competing to develop the best arenas within the restricted space we're using for battlegrounds. And *you* need to start experimenting to see what sort of goals you can put on these intra-player faction battlegrounds, Hail. Now that we know it's legal under Yuikonese law, we need to move on to the planning phase—"

"Technically, we never said it was legal," the head solicitor said. "We said that it wasn't illegal. There are international precedents but no Yuikonese law expressly condones or forbids it. If there was a sitting king, we would recommend approaching him to ask permission. Unfortunately, that is not the case. There is a slight chance that these battlegrounds will be deemed illegal and the proceeds from them seized by the crown at a future date."

We were silent for a moment. "That sounds like something Storm would do if he were crowned, just to spite me," I said.

"Yeah, let's spin it that way with the players," Liam agreed. "That will help with getting your baby brother on the throne. You'll see. Once we have the infant king, that makes you regent, right? So you can do whatever you want."

"Actually, my mother will be regent if everything goes according to plan," I said, correcting him. "With Marquis Peori and several other friends advising her. But there is very little chance that she would overturn me on this. The smart move would be to tax the proceeds, which is what I'll be preparing for in any case."

"Yeah, if Storm *does* make battlegrounds illegal, he won't be king for very long. The list of players trying to assassinate him will be volumes long," Liam said.

"Liam, I know he's an arsehole, but I'd rather you not speak of a member of my family being assassinated."

"Right. Sorry, mate," he said, wincing. "So, then. We're full steam ahead on both the selling of cores and land for the arenas, right?"

"Yeah. I'll set aside five cores to sell for now. The bidders can choose for themselves whether they want the decreased death penalty or to utilize the maximum number of battlegrounds. Once we've selected the venue and someone has purchased the first core, I'll start experimenting to see what options open up to me when I'm operating under those restrictions. There may be terms that appear that wouldn't be there for an unrestricted core. The throne is like that sometimes: the deeper I dig, the more weirdly specific things become."

"See if you can find terms like 'capture the flag' or 'king of the hill,'" Liam suggested. "In fact, I'll make a list of popular PVP objectives for you to look for. Start looking as soon as you can, and let the winner of the opening bid know before you bind the core. If they can choose between an area control, a siege, or a battle royale, then they'll definitely value their purchase more."

I nodded my agreement as the solicitors [Scribed] up the documents that we needed to file with the courts stating our intent. According to the head solicitor, the next step would be for the court to review the documents for precedent, a step that they had already taken. Finding none, they would forward the matter to the king . . . if there was a sitting king. Instead, it would sit on the docket until someone was crowned, but without someone officially condemning my actions as illegal, I would be allowed to proceed unbothered.

We handed the documents off to one of my level one hundred eighty bodyguards as we left. He seemed strangely excited to have gotten a simple delivery quest as he summoned his flying mount and disappeared.

"So, have you thought about the other thing we talked about?" Liam asked.

"Does it have to be him?" I asked.

"What do you have against him?" Liam inquired.

I sighed. Gaem Fraek wasn't a controversial figure to most Travelers. He was just a game journalist, one of many who focused on covering *The Gates of TirNiki*. I'd actually watched a large number of his interviews, which hadn't been as personally devastating to me as the interview with my father in the wake of my abandonment and, later, the interview of Nial Kingslayer where he bragged of his regicide.

But I had seen those two videos at times when I had been emotionally vulnerable, and a small part of me held Gaem Fraek responsible. Time had passed, and I should have moved on. I had matured to the point where others were commenting that perhaps Thedum should adjust my age a second time to reflect my maturity.

For some reason I still balked at the idea of meeting the man, with his cheerful voice blatantly asking me about my personal tragedies. Likely without even realizing that what he viewed as an interesting plot point in his favorite game was a real traumatic event to me.

Most Travelers were like that. So even if I went with another game journalist, the result would probably be the same.

"Fine," I said. "Set it up. Go ahead and start the auction on the first [Battle Core] as well, and start surveying my land for a suitable location. I'm not dedicating more than what the solicitors told me was the maximum size to this endeavor. Ten square miles maximum."

"What if there are Natives living on the spot that the developers choose for their arena?" Liam inquired.

"Find a new spot?" I suggested. "Or I suppose you could pay them to move. My hands are actually tied on the matter if they're current on their taxes and rent, and doubly so since I've declared the edict giving everyone five years to get out of arrears. I can't evict any of my tenants while that edict is in place, but you can buy their rent contract from them in a private deal, then make the land part of the larger deal with me."

"Right," Liam said, typing notes into his invisible terminal. "Okay, then. I think that's everything we needed to accomplish here.

I'll get these announcements sent out, and you can return to . . . whatever you want to do next."

I considered. What did I want to do next? I pulled up my status screen, noting once again that I was still stuck at level forty-four—as I had been for the last several weeks while wading through the political bog of trying to raise my brother to the throne, while simultaneously attempting to establish regular battlegrounds to get the Travelers on my side. There were, however, several lairs within my territory that I could visit that were level appropriate.

"Can you put a party together for me?" I asked. "I'm going to challenge the lair that spawned outside of Mooncrest Manor when the dungeon was created."

It was a level fifty lair, but I was consistently able to fight above my level. And it had been a while since I had flexed my ability to change and evolve lairs. I could destroy them as well, but I wouldn't destroy this one. The [Ghoulish Servitor Lair] had become popular since it had spawned. I would have to see what options were available to evolve the lair once I found the lair stones themselves.

"Do you want them to be Travelers you know, or should I do a lottery system?" Liam asked. He himself was only level thirty, but he wasn't here to advise me on how to level.

I checked my friend list and the guild menu, and nobody I recognized was online at the moment anyway. "Lottery is fine. I mean, there's a lot of people who want to play with me, right? Might as well make some of them happy."

Liam nodded, and he quickly began typing. A moment later, he sent me a message instructing me to invite a particular person and then pass them group lead. It was easier to do things that way to get around the custom filters I had set up to prevent random jerks from distracting me with party invites.

Within moments the group was filled with strangers, though partychat was eerily silent.

"Hey, guys. I'm Hail," I said to break the ice.

"Yeah? You really him? Hold on, let me find my math homework. That will prove it," someone said. The flashing icon indicated it came from Amir, but I had never met the player before.

"Math? How is math going to prove that I'm Hail Jeoran?" I asked.

"You're a computer, right? Computers are good at math," Amir answered.

"I'm going to put you on mute until you stop saying stupid things, Amir," I told him. "Anyway, guys, I don't know how broadly it's known, but I can change lairs in addition to everything else."

"Of course you can," a party member named Elysia said, then laughed. "Okay, so there's like two hundred thousand lairs in the game, but only about five thousand in our level range. You got one in mind? If not, there's one here in Verindale I'd love to challenge with you. It's level forty-five to fifty with despoiled forest spirits and poisoned treants."

I considered. "I'd have to get permission from the local authorities to make any modification to it. The lair I was planning on challenging was level fifty to fifty-five, but there's no reason we can't do one then the other."

"Lady Jearea Silverbark is the Lady of the Wood. She's the one to ask for permission. I doubt I could get through to her tree for an audience, but an earl from Yuikon shouldn't have any trouble. And it's well known that she sees this lair as a blight on her land and wants it gone."

"Won't the Travelers be upset with their leveling zone disappearing?" I asked.

"Fuck 'em," Elysia said simply. "Besides, nobody actually levels here. The treants are too difficult, and the sprites hide until you're engaged with them then add on to make the encounter more difficult. It's easier to skip this lair by doubling up on one of the nearby dungeons."

"How long is this going to take?" a party member named Gavin asked. "I have about three game days, but I'll have to take a bio break sometime in the next few hours."

"Take it now," Elysia said. "I'm going to Fast Travel to the meeting stone nearest the lair I'm talking about. Hail, can you manage to line up the meeting with Silverbark? The system says you're in Zhesa City, so you just need to use the international portals to get to Aeloria and do your whole 'I'm Lord Earl Hail Jeoran, and I demand to speak with Lady Jearea Silverbark' thing."

"I won't demand. That would be rude," I said. "But yeah, it shouldn't be too difficult to arrange an audience. Especially if you're correct, and she wants me to destroy this lair. If that's true, I suspect she'll uproot herself for the opportunity."

"Right, then," Lilja, the only member of the party who hadn't spoken yet, said. "Sounds like we have a few minutes, so I'm going to take a bio too. Say, thirty minutes real time?"

Everyone agreed, and I quickly made my way, with my entourage of endgame bodyguards, to the international portal facility to travel to Verindale, home of elves and of dryads.

39

GROVE OF THE THIRTY

I had to stop at a clothing shop in the market outside of the receiving platform in Aeloria. As we figured things, Aeloria was the capitol of Verindale. As the elves and the dryads figured things, it's just where the [Grove of the Thirty] grew. The elvish seats of power were scattered throughout the land, but because they were so linked with the dryads, they came here to make formal decisions with their natural allies.

My current outfit was utterly improper for meeting a Lady of the Wood. There was far too much metal in it, and wearing metal or leather clothing to a formal meeting with the dryad equivalent of nobility was a major *faux pas*. One that wasn't changing with the times, as many Travelers were finding out.

There was no local law forbidding the wearing of metal equipment, jewelry, or weapons in Verindale. And the Elves didn't mind, although they seldom wore more than a bit of gold or silver jewelry, or perhaps a weapon or two. But the dryads *knew*—you couldn't hide it from them—and depending on how haughtily they viewed their own status in their private hierarchy, the greater they viewed the offense.

For just this meeting, I was forced to replace everything I was wearing. I came out of the store in a simple kimono-like robe with a pair of sandals that tied to my feet with strips of linen. No buckles. No jewelry. No weapon.

Of course, all of that was stashed in my inventory, and I could fast equip it in the event that I was attacked, but that almost never happened. Attacking someone who was on their way to meet a Native dryad at their tree was a far greater *faux pas* than wearing metal to such a meeting, and few Travelers were willing to take the nationwide Reputation hit of doing so.

Despite that, my bodyguards had not changed their equipment. Nor would they. I would enter the [Grove of the Thirty] to seek out Jearea Silverbark alone, while they stood vigil outside, waiting for me to return.

The local elven guardians of the city were happy to direct me to the noble grove, where the roots of the thirty Great Dryads of Verindale intertwined. Especially when they saw that I was following the customs and attempting to be polite. When they asked which of the thirty I was seeking an audience with, they wished me luck with smirks on their faces, which had me slightly worried.

Traveler dryads are different from Natives. Somewhat. In order to travel beyond the lands where they entered this world, Travelers have to carry with them a cutting of their mother tree and plant it in a new location in order to use their full powers. As they explore the world, they grow in power and scope and are eventually even able to transport between the cuttings of their mother trees instantaneously.

Native dryads are more limited. Only the thirty Great Dryads have a similar ability to travel great distances from the tree that birthed them, and they do so through their roots. Aeloria is the site of the noble [Grove of the Thirty], where the great thirty intertwined their roots, and from their roots propagated daughter trees to represent themselves in the court of Verindale.

When I reached the noble wood, I paused before passing through the arch, for there were two guardians. A cat sat on one of the trees, and an owl perched on the tree across from it.

"Who do you seek?" the owl asked.

"I seek an audience with Jearea Silverbark," I answered humbly. "I am Earl Hail—"

"Why do you seek the lady of the northeast wood?" the cat asked, interrupting me.

I paused. I hadn't introduced myself, but this was Verindale, and I was dealing with dryads. Either their guardians knew who I was, or they didn't care.

"I hear there is a lair in her territory that she is displeased with. I have the power to destroy lairs, and I am looking to test it out. I come seeking her permission," I explained.

The cat licked its paws for a moment. The owl flapped its wings and was gone. When I looked back, the cat had vanished as well.

Well, I had passed the first guardians at least. I knew for certain that the unassuming animals I had just faced had not presented me with their true forms. They could each have ripped me down to zero Health before my guardians, who were remaining behind from this point, could have done a thing to stop them.

I had earned their permission to enter the noble grove, but whether that would translate into passing along my message was an entirely different matter. Depending on the whims of the guardians I had just faced, it might be five minutes before Jearea Silverbark appeared, or I might need to find her tree and rap my knuckle against it politely until I got her attention from wherever it was focused currently.

"You come to the forest and call yourself a destroyer, yet you follow the ways," a voice called from behind me. I turned and saw a dryad sitting upon a large exposed root.

I paused just a moment to appreciate her beauty. Her face was nature perfected, with green hair that formed natural blossoms of blue and red. Her body was wrapped in moss according to the sense of modesty that dryads often followed when interacting with humans and Travelers. The elven literature on the matter is quite clear that such matters are strictly a social gesture towards the non-forest born.

"Jearea Silverbark? I am Hail Jeoran, Earl of Yuikon," I introduced myself.

"I am Kearea," she corrected. "Jearea's younger sister. She is occupied, but my voice is strong enough to send you on your way. Explain what you seek, and I will consent or decline, and you will do whatever you please because that is the way you are."

I smiled to hide my dismay. I was not being treated with the respect I had hoped for. Neither was I being disrespected. I had just hoped that by presenting myself properly with the goal of solving one of their noble's problems the dryad I spoke with would be less standoffish.

"I vow that I will destroy no lair or dungeon within Verindale without the consent of the Lord or Lady of the Wood, or the elvish noble who governs the land if it does not fall within the reach of the great grove," I swore.

"Your oath is witnessed," Kearea said formally. "It shall be remembered. So remember it."

I nodded. "I was told of a grove where a lair of despoiled forest spirits and poisoned treants reside and that Jearea Silverbark was lady of that wood. With her consent, I would see to it that this lair no longer despoils her portion of the great grove."

"And without her consent?" Kearea inquired.

"Then I will have bought a new wardrobe for nothing and wasted a few minutes of my time seeking her audience. I am not committed to this action. If it is not welcomed by the court of the grove, then the offer is withdrawn."

Kearea nodded. "You have the permission of sixteen of the thirty to destroy the lair known as [The Poison Grove]. Jearea consents to this decision, as do I, and as do fourteen of our brothers and sisters. The others believe that you are not ready. I believe you are not ready, but I believe it is time that you learn why you are not ready, and so I consent. Go. Your friends return to this world one by one and will be ready to summon you soon. You should find somewhere proper to change into the hunter's regalia that you doffed to present yourself to the court of the grove."

I bowed to Kearea, and then, having realized that the two of us were far from alone, I began bowing to the other large trees in attendance, not worrying too much about whether I was bowing to a spirit or an empty wood. It took only a few moments before I reversed my path and passed under the arch of the two guardian trees. The cat and the owl were back at their posts.

Neither had anything to say as I left the noble grove behind and joined up with my guardians again.

I found a cheap inn to grab something to eat and a few minutes sleep as the rest of the low-level party members completed taking care of their bodies on Earth. Before long, everyone was ready including me, after I changed back into my battle attire. After a few minutes of everyone confirming in partychat that they were ready for their summons, Elysia touched the meeting stone, and we were pulled through the Fast Travel network to that particular Nexus Point.

The others were not expecting my entourage. Liam had left me long ago to deal with Earth stuff, but the endgamer I had sent on the errand had returned, so I had a full party of ten bodyguards who could crush any one of us with an accidental swipe of a skill. Elysia flinched, and our tank, Gavin, was intimidated.

"Not sure what good we'll be when you have access to people like that," Gavin said. "Why not just—"

"They're just here to keep me from getting ganked," I explained. "In fact, you guys should start spreading out and looking for assassins or whatever it is that you're planning on doing."

The endgamers nodded, and one of them, a dryad [Druid], cast on each of them a [True Sight] spell, which would allow them to see any stealthed or invisible threats below her level. They took off into the forest, some awkwardly bashing their way through it, others with silent talent. I turned back to my party, a little embarrassed.

"Sorry. I mean, I actually grew up kind of expecting to have bodyguards around me most of the time, so I don't really see them, you know? But I'm really here to challenge the lair with you guys. They're just for protection."

"Yeah?" Amir said. "They going to swoop in at the last moment and claim credit when we destroy the lair?"

"No, of course not," I protested. "Look, Amir. I thought you wanted to party with me. If you don't, we can find a replacement."

"I wanted to bust a dungeon, not a lair," he said. Then he sighed and slumped, before visibly perking himself up again. "Fine. We do this."

With that, the party spent a few moments organizing into roles. Gavin was our tank: an [Elvish Warden] decked out in ironbark armor with a birchsteel longsword. Elysia would be our healer, a [Feybinder Mystic]. It wasn't the best class for healing, as most [Mystics] choose to bind offensive fey for their spells, but Elysia had taken an uncommon path in developing her character.

Compared to the two elvish party members, Lilja and Amir were plain bread. Lilja was a [Rogue], while Amir was an [Archer] who was close to unlocking [Enchanted Arrow], which was the prerequisite to advance to the [Arcane Archer] class that he was targeting.

With Elysia guiding us, we made our way deeper into the forest. It was not long before we found our first despoiled forest spirit, and I cursed to myself when I saw it. It was an *elite!*

"Wait," I said, "is this one of those lairs where it's filled with singular elites that are spread out, rather than packs of weaker monsters?"

Elysia nodded. "Is that a problem?"

"It could be," I admitted. "I need to find the anchors that bind the lair to this location. The lair stones, or whatever you want to call them. The only other time I've done this, I always found the stones within the spawn camps."

"Can't you just use your AI magic to deduce their location or something?" Amir asked, and the others glared at him before putting him on mute again.

"Okay," Gavin began. "Let's assume that each of the elites is one spawn camp—"

Gavin didn't get much further, because the forest spirit had noticed us. Despite being titled a spirit, it was very much corporeal and very, very angry at having its territory invaded.

40
EXIA

I was caught flat-footed by the beast's sudden charge. Despite being encumbered by the heavy growth of roots and low hanging branches, the spirit charged straight past our poorly planned party formation and gored Elysia with the center two of its horns.

The blow alone was a critical hit worth twenty-one percent of her Health, but it also counted as a grapple, as she was lifted up and tossed about while impaled. I'd like to say that I reacted faster and saved her, but she would have died if it were not for Amir's quick thinking. He fired one of his pre-enchanted arrows, and the missile burst into flames moments after piercing the beast's hide on its left shoulder.

The spirit was enraged, and Elysia was shaken loose. Gavin got his act together and interposed himself to meet the beast's next charge towards Amir, while Elysia began gathering her magic to recover the Damage that she had suffered. Together with the critical goring and the ongoing Damage she had suffered while impaled, she was down to thirty-nine percent Health. That began to change as small fey encircled her, their magics swiftly returning her to perfect Health.

Gavin caught the spirit's charge on his shield and only barely managed to keep his own feet despite having braced for the worst. The spirit resembled a great stag with four large horn stocks. The two in the center curved slightly backward but did not branch like the outer two. The center horns gleamed with Elysia's blood, and the outer horns had kept her from simply being thrown off immediately. Likewise, the outer horns allowed the spirit to parry against Gavin's attacks, deflecting his birchsteel blade.

Amir dashed over to its side and began unloading his quiver, while Lilja finally broke stealth, coming up from the rear of the animal with a ferocious [Ambush], dealing massive critical Damage.

I, too, finally got my act together. With one hand holding my [Blade of Eclipse], which was imbued with fire, I unleashed a series of [Swiftcast] [Fireballs] with the other. The creature screamed out in anger at the element that I had chosen for combat with it, but I wasn't doing very much Damage. Or rather, the tainted beast had so much Health that even exploiting its weaknesses, it was taking a long time to burn through its massive Health pool. Gavin was occupied simply keeping the beast from building the momentum for another charge and hadn't done significant Damage, but my, Amir, and Lilja's efforts had only dealt sixteen percent Damage to our opponent.

Elysia's healing spells were slow but effective, a combination of a powerful shielding effect and an ongoing heal over time. Once she had returned herself above ninety percent Health, she spread her attentions out to everyone, with little fey flying over to sit on our shoulders—metaphorically. They didn't actually sit on our shoulders, except for Gavin's. But they were ready when the creature began casting cursed magic in our direction. They intercepted it with their own and quickly healed up what little Damage slipped through their protections.

I didn't have too much time to contemplate the relative efficiency of the [Feybinder] class as a healer compared to a more traditional route, as I was burning low on Mana. I charged forward, counting on my [Battle Trance] to regenerate what I had been burning with my spells. I covered the distance into battle with a combination of [Dash] and [Piercing Lunge], then began my usual routine of alternating between my [Slash] and [Thrust] skills and unskilled attacks while those were on cooldown.

The others settled down to whittle through the elite's massive Health pool with their own ready and steady techniques. Long burn fights were typically where classes like [Archer], [Rogue], and

[Warrior] outshone [Mages], which had extremely spiky Damage as they burned through their magic before entering regenerative stages.

That wasn't so different from my own tactics, except that my regenerative stage involved in-your-face swordplay with a sword that was on fire. Or wreathed in lightning. Or whatever other element that the enemy didn't like.

Compared to a standard [Mage], the time between my burst Damage spell-casting phases were much longer, as [Battle Trance] restored a fixed percentage of my Mana with every hit, whereas a [Mage] could stack Wisdom to swiftly regenerate their Mana to full with their [Meditation] skill. However, while the [Mages] were effectively dead in the water while they were [Meditating], I was dealing as much Damage as a standard melee player. Or more, depending on how vulnerable to magic the enemy was.

And this beast was very, very vulnerable to fire. My Damage surged past the other two Damage dealers. The beast roared in defiance, and at fifty percent Health, it entered a new phase. The leaves of the surrounding forest withered and broke off of their respective trees. The foliage began swirling about us, cutting off visibility between me and my Traveler friends and, more importantly, cutting into us with a slow but steady Damage-over-time effect.

Fortunately, Elysia's [Feybinder] class effectively hard-countered this technique, and it didn't even require her direct attention to keep everyone at full Health. The only further surprise was when the spirit began to aggro drop; it suddenly decided that Gavin wasn't worth its attention anymore and turned and charged at random party members.

I didn't have a good way of countering this tactic except to [Feint] and [Dash] away until Gavin had reestablished control over the enemy. Lilja had better escape mechanisms for such situations than I did, including an ability that allowed her to vanish and appear twenty feet away, which is how she dealt with the aggro drops when it was her turn.

Elysia refused to get impaled again when the beast turned towards her, dashing between trees to use them as cover to prevent the despoiled forest spirit from getting at her. The most frustrating situation was when it decided to charge Amir, as, rather than helping Gavin get the monster back under control, Amir simply kept [Backflipping] away.

I hate [Archers] sometimes.

It took time, but we were victorious, and the despoiled forest spirit hit zero Health. It collapsed, but instead of despawning in the manner of darkspawn, only its shaggy black fur and its sickly colored mane turned into darkmist and vanished.

"Stop DPS!" Elysia called.

"It doesn't look dead to me," Amir responded, knocking another arrow.

"Stop DPS!" Gavin repeated. "This lair is different. We're supposed to cleanse the spirits, not kill them. They'll forgive a few hits after the blight is purified, but if we keep pushing, the entire forest will turn against us."

That caught Amir's attention, and he lowered his weapon. "So that's it, then?"

Lilja laughed. "That's it? That's the hardest fight I've had outside a dungeon!"

"I just mean that we won? On to the next?"

"*Why do you come to [The Poison Grove]?*" the cleansed spirit asked, raising its horned head to study us. "*It is not a place of men, and it is not safe for the children of the forest. And you—you are both of and not of this world. What is your purpose here?*"

I looked at the others to confirm that they had heard the spirit's words. They *were* words and not the strange, direct communication that I've shared in the past with my brother and certain other Natives. It was just like the words were bypassing our ears and entering our minds directly, rather than . . . hearing something larger from beyond myself, which was what the other experience was like.

"Do not Travelers often come to this grove to raise their levels and gain Experience?" I asked.

"*Often? No, not often,*" the spirit answered.

"That's strange, considering that I got one and a half thousand Experience just now," I said. It was actually closer to five thousand, a full fifteen percent of my Experience bar. But that was after having my Experience tripled by [Through the Valley of the Shadow].

"*I do not question things such as why those from other worlds do not come to cleanse the endless affliction. You have done a good thing, but it is only a matter of time before I succumb once more to the taint of this grove— my mind not my own, bestial and offensive to my own sensibilities. You have done me a favor with this moment of clarity, but I do not thank you for it,"* the spirit said.

"I see," I said, digesting the spirit's words carefully. "Spirit, have you a name?"

"Exia," it answered.

"Exia, I have come to destroy the lair known as [The Poison Grove]. Do you know how that will affect you, personally?" I inquired.

Exia lifted its head. Without the blight affecting it, its fur was a lush green that turned to blue on its mane, and its underbelly a blood red. I thought it was rather beautiful, but it had not specified its gender, and I would not ask unless the matter became important.

"I would be free of the blight, of course," Exia answered. *"If that is your purpose, then I will help. But do* you *know the consequences for destroying this lair?"*

"I have secured the permission of Jearea Silverbark and sixteen of the great thirty," I said, assuring it. "My goals are sanctioned by the lords and ladies of the forest."

"Very well. I will not help you in combat, but I will help you avoid combat where necessary, and I will guide you to the binding locations, where the stones that spread the blight are located," Exia promised. *"There are twelve. The nearest is just over here, on the other side of the stream. I was its guardian; it bound my mind to it for its own protection. Now it shall rue that decision!"*

The journey from the site of the battle to the location of the lair stone was simple. As with the other lair stones I had found in the past, this one quickly pulled my eyes towards it, shining in multifaceted and multihued light, while the Travelers in my party seemed to look right past it. It was larger than the others I had dealt with, and I picked it up.

You have found a Lair Stone (Insidious Blight) Levels 45–50	
Options	
Evolve Lair	Increase Level Range
	Decrease Level Range
	Increase Monster Density

	Decrease Monster Density
	Expand Blighted Territory
	Collapse Blighted Territory
	Blight More Guardian Archetypes
	Create Blighted Rare Spawn
Destroy Lair Stone	0/12 stones of this lair destroyed. All stones must be destroyed to destroy the lair.

While the option to create a rare spawn tempted me—rare spawns always carried their own loot tables that were sometimes on par with the drops inside of dungeons—I quickly chose the last option instead. The stone asked me to confirm, and then it crumbled to dust in my hand, the dust itself forming darkmist, which evaporated just like a darkspawn would have.

"*I half expected you to break your word,*" Exia said. Around us, the forest slowly began to change as the power of the lair in this area weakened. The blight that poisoned the grove retreated, and though it was difficult to say how, the forest simply looked healthier.

"What would you have done if I had?" I inquired.

"*Spread the word to the others, and you would have never received our help again,*" the spirit answered. "*Come. The next nearest anchor of the blight is in this direction. It will take some time, but we will make a clean sweep of them. Be prepared, for the guardians will know what you are about now, and though their cleansed minds will rejoice, they are controlled at the moment by the blight and will attack all the more ferociously.*"

Exia's words proved prophetic, as we hadn't even taken twenty steps when the sound of something crashing through the trees came to us. We saw the top of it before the rest, and it was Elysia who recognized the attacker for what it was.

"Treant," she announced. "We're about to be attacked by an enraged treant."

<h1 style="text-align:center">41</h1>

<h1 style="text-align:center">ELJ</h1>

In a high-level raid, especially if it was one of the so called "Red Raids," which required upwards of two hundred Travelers working together to complete, enemies with wooden flesh commonly carried a resistance to certain types of weapons, such as arrows, daggers, or rapiers.

This was less of a restriction at low levels, and although Lilja and Amir were not doing full Damage, we were doing perhaps ninety percent what we would have done against an enemy of normal flesh. The situation was similar to when I had fought Sir William Von Barutasburg, the Iron Knight, who was literally an iron golem. Had my party at the time faced him inside of a Red Raid, we would have been forced to change weapons to those effective against iron golems—typically blunt-force weapons such as hammers or maces, or weapons with resonating enchantments.

But this was a level forty-nine treant out in the world, and although he carried a slight resistance to Amir's arrows and Lilja's daggers, the resistance was only enough to push them slightly further behind me on the Damage meter than they would have been anyway. Not that my rapier wouldn't have been resisted the same as Lilja's weapons of choice, but that resistance was negated by the towering treant's vulnerability to fire, which I kept my blade imbued with at all times.

The fighting was fierce. The treant was an intelligent foe, and the forest around it came alive to provide it with a shifting arsenal of different weapons. It began the fight with only its grasping root-like hands and feet swiping at us, but when it failed to get any of us in a grapple despite several close calls, it instead pulled from a nearby tree a large branch that took the form of a [Warhammer].

This change in tactics was hard for us to counter. A direct blow would easily break through the protective magic of Elysia's fey, split as she had originally had them at the beginning of the fight. When Gavin stood up and tried to tank one of the blows directly, he was thrown backward and suffered twenty-two percent Damage.

The solution required Elysia to withdraw her fey from the rest of the party, leaving each of us vulnerable without their protective shielding magic, as she focused entirely on the tank. This strategy left the melee members vulnerable in particular, which meant me during my swordplay phase and Lilja all of the time as a [Rogue]. It proved to be the winning strategy, however. Gavin was able to tank the next mighty swing of the wooden [Warhammer], suffering only eight percent of his Health as Damage, and the combined healing of the fey, focused only on him, was able to swiftly recover the combined Damage of the two blows, bringing him back near full Health.

Unfortunately, the treant wasn't willing to stay focused on our tank, and it made things difficult by often shifting its attention to Lilja or me, forcing us to withdraw from combat for a while until Gavin was able to get the walking tree back under control.

Still, the battle was manageable, and we slowly began working through the elite monster's massive Health pool. The first transition, when it had shifted from trying to grapple to using its wooden hammer, had occurred at ninety percent Health, and the second transition happened at fifty percent Health. We were caught unprepared for it, after having settled into a routine.

The treant abruptly threw the [Warhammer] at Elysia, and the healer only barely managed to avoid it in time. It's good that she did, as all of her fey were focused on Gavin, and not only was she unshielded, but the blow that had dealt so much Damage to Gavin had done so through his ironbark armor. She was wearing as much armor as a normal [Mage]. It was possible that the throw would have one-shot her.

"Intruders!" the treant shouted. "Unwelcome! Invaders!"

He reached out and grabbed another tree branch, and this one formed into a javelin, which he launched at Amir. The [Archer] responded with a [Backflip], which was a bad call because it didn't take him out of the trajectory of the weapon, and he was impaled on the tree behind him. Two of Elysia's fey rushed over, but it was too late to shield him from any of the Damage from the initial attack, and their heal-over-time effect would take time to counter the ongoing [Impale], which had done twenty-seven percent Damage to him and had effectively taken him out of the fight.

The treant reached out for another tree branch, which formed into another javelin, but the same trick wouldn't work so easily again. After three unsuccessful launches trying to pin me, Elysia, or Lilja down, the treant finally settled into turning the branch into a pike-spear instead. We settled in to burn it through its remaining Health pool in a more stable fashion, even if the fighting style had changed from phase two. It took some time, but with Elysia's help, Amir was able to get free and join us.

The treant had no further surprises for us, and once it hit zero Health, we stepped back to see what would happen. It fell to its knees, its branched head looking up, and the blighted leaves that covered it all scorched and turned into darkmist. Moments passed, however, and they were replaced with healthy verdant leaves. The face that had seemed so fierce during the fighting looked confused.

"Ah. I have embarrassed myself again," it said. "I am Elj, young ones. I thank you for your efforts in clearing my mind. I would reward you."

As Elj spoke, the darkmist that hadn't quite dissipated reformed into a loot box, and Gavin did a fist pump to celebrate. He opened the box, then grinned as he showed everyone that it was a set of vambraces perfect for his class. He received a nod from each of us that they would go to him uncontested.

"It is unfortunate that your efforts are ultimately in vain, as I will only succumb once more to the madness that drove me to attack you," Elj said. "But a few days of clearminded—"

"*They come from the Lady of the Wood to cleanse the corruption,*" Exia said, appearing from behind us. It—she?—had vanished during the fighting, but now that Elj had regained himself, she had no issue letting herself be known.

"Is that so?" Elj asked. He turned again to us, his expression thoughtful and slightly confused. "I remember now. Why I attacked. I felt the destruction of one of the bindings. In the state that I was in, it enraged me. The others will feel the same, and the matter will soon get out of hand as the tainted forest bands against you and pushes you out. Your party of five is insufficient. For every stone you destroy, you must add another five to your party, or you will surely be driven back."

I looked at the others, who looked at each other, and then they all started to grin for some reason.

"Are you saying that this is going to turn into a low-level raid situation?" Gavin inquired.

"I do not know what you mean," Elj answered. "But I anticipate that unless you involve high-level Travelers, who would not benefit from the experience in any way, then you will require at least sixty like yourselves to complete the objectives you have set out to achieve. Otherwise you will surely be overcome."

"I don't know about you, but I'd love it if we could do this without involving a bunch of endgamers," Gavin said. "I have about four people in the right level range in my guild right now. If we double back to the meeting stone—"

"I have eight people who'd love to be part of this," Elysia said quickly.

"Asking," Lilja said. "People are saying yes."

Everyone turned to me, and then they looked up to where my guardians were overseeing us from a safe distance. Close enough to intervene should an endgamer be spotted and far enough not to interfere with the kill contribution.

"All right," I said. "Let's do this. Just give me a minute to tell my guards so that they don't freak out."

We doubled back to the meeting stone. The land was too uneven for mounts, but we hadn't traveled too far into the forest. The others thought that it would be easier to just Fast Travel, but I really did not want to do that just as I was about to meet a bunch of strangers who, now that I thought about it, might have hostile intentions towards me.

However, as we began inviting people into our growing raid, everyone seemed very excited to be taking part in the growing event. However, before the summoning actually took part, the two leaders of my bodyguards, Aroha and Joon-Ho, swooped down next to us.

"I'm very sorry, Hail, but after discussing it with everyone, we can't let you do this," Joon-Ho said. "There are too many unverified people getting involved in this event. It was fine to have four pre-screened individuals, but a raid of sixty people is just too much for us."

I sighed because I'd actually had the same thoughts. I knew enough to know that I wasn't as universally popular among the Travelers as I liked to pretend sometimes. Taking part in this encounter was a risk, and I wasn't certain that I would have any way of preventing—or surviving—a small group of the level fifty players from launching a surprise attack on me during the midst of combat while everyone else was distracted.

"Let everyone else do the fighting," I said at last. "I promised that I'd destroy this lair, and I will. But I don't actually need to fight to do that. You guys can protect me like I'm part of a layered escort quest or something. I'll hang out with Elj and Exia, you ten will keep me safe, and then the sixty low-level players will actually push the forest back as we travel from lair stone to lair stone."

Aroha and Joon-Ho consulted each other and my other guardians for several minutes before concluding that this was an acceptable compromise. When they agreed that it was, I climbed on Exia's back, allowing her—she was feminine, I learned—to carry me on the quest as the other Travelers began arriving.

Elj's initial claims that we would require sixty members to complete our low-level range didn't dissuade anyone from inviting their entire friends list, and soon we had over a hundred Travelers present. Some were here for the fighting, but a large number of players were turning out "just to see the epic happening." The fact that this was off-hours for an event where I was involved simply seemed to add to the draw.

Indeed, before long the area became crowded with flying mounts as well, as higher-level Travelers learned that "the lowbies were up to something" and that I was involved, so it was probably something epic.

My bodyguards called in reinforcements, but the crowd seemed to stabilize at a certain point. There were about thirty players that were too low level to take part in the fighting, one hundred twenty players who were within the level range, and about forty flying in the skies above to watch.

I considered calling the entire thing off. Instead, from the back of the purified forest spirit, with her four horns and bright colors, I led the way. Exia nimbly guided us to the next of the lair stones, while Elj turned the forest itself to help us on our path. The branches and roots that would normally scratch and trip my followers seemed to bend out of the way at his will, and we made good progress.

It was not long until we were attacked the first time. And it seems that, with our own scaling up of our activities, the lair had responded in kind. While we had one hundred twenty Travelers gathered for combat, we were met with a pack of ten blighted treants and nineteen corrupted forest spirits.

42

THE POISON GROVE

I remembered back to the day when I had been clinging to Tarisha's back, watching in awe as my Traveler father and my Native grandfather both, in their own ways, had directed an army. It hadn't really been an army, of course, but a raiding party made up of two hundred of the most skilled Travelers visiting my world as they had undertaken the trials of the [Zhesa Castle Raid] in order to destroy it.

Father had, by merit of long experience and skill, been their general. He had led them seamlessly as they encountered wave after wave of previously unknowable challenges and obstacles. Each new boss, each new type of spawn or add, he had quickly analyzed. He had recognized which part of his team was best equipped to handle that threat, and he had assigned it to them. Usually while making some joke that only he understood.

Grandfather had come into the raid blind but had quickly learned everyone's skills and abilities, then directed his own abilities to boost and maximize their Damage output. Grandfather hadn't just been the King of Yuikon at the time. He had been [King]. If I had pursued the route of leadership instead of battle, I might have been able to combine the two roles into one.

I would have been like my father, handling the larger picture, and my grandfather, giving off synergistic buffs and bonuses to those in my command. It would have made for a powerful member of any raid.

Instead of any of that, I just sat on Exia's back and looked silly as everyone figured out on their own how to combat the incoming horde. I had tried taking command at first, but nobody was listening to me, and, well, what reason did they have to do so anyway? They were in their own parties, and Elysia had taken on the role of raid leader. If anything she seemed more skilled at it than I was, calling out where we were weak and which of the enemies were about to transition.

The forest hadn't thrown us an insurmountable obstacle, but it did seem to know what was coming for it and had responded accordingly. According to Elj, once this battle was over, there would likely be very few guardians left. There were only the numbers to contend with, no great and sudden change of strategy, and the battle was a repeat of the ones my smaller party had undergone earlier—only writ large with dozens going on at the same time.

Travelers died. Actually, a lot of Travelers died. We took probably thirty percent fatalities. But now and then one of the forest spirits would be cleansed, and they would abandon the battlefield. And the treants, once they were cleansed of their blight, would call out and begin attacking their still-blighted brethren to break the curse.

Slowly at first, and then growing quickly, the battle turned in our favor. When the last of the spirits had retreated, and the last of the treants had been converted, a large loot chest appeared, and the party let out a cheer of delight. Unfortunately, once the decision had been made that I wouldn't be participating in the fight, I had dropped group and was unable to see the items that had dropped, but there was a lot of argument over them. Largely because there weren't more of them or that their distribution "wasn't fair," and "this isn't how things worked in raids," and other things like that. A lot of people were very upset with Elysia because she had left the default loot-distribution system in place, so everyone was rolling on any item that they could.

Some Travelers were blessing RNG, some were cursing him. I didn't really care. I looked down at Exia and said, "Now that the battle has been decided, will you take me to the next of the lair stones?"

She nodded, and the forest spirits that had fled during the battle reappeared. "We may face more resistance. Bring friends with you as we journey quickly!"

So Elysia and my party mounted Exia's friends, while the many other Travelers in the raid were forced to chase after us on foot. Fortunately, they were aided by the treants, who, now that they were cleansed, wished to see things through to the end. Charging out, not as swiftly as possible but at a good pace, we rushed through the forest, and soon I found the second of the twelve lair stones.

You have found a Lair Stone (Insidious Blight) Levels 45–50	
Options	
Evolve Lair	. . .
Destroy Lair Stone	1/12 stones of this lair destroyed. All stones must be destroyed to destroy the lair. Destroying all twelve lair stones will create an additional challenge.

"Huh," I said at seeing the warning that had been added to the end of the menu options. Then I looked around at the numerous Travelers who had gathered for this event, and I wondered whether it was worth mentioning. Probably not; I couldn't imagine them telling me *not* to destroy the lair and create the additional challenge for them. I only noticed because that warning hadn't been there before. Which was strange, considering that destroying the previous stone had caused the blighted region of the forest to summon its guardians *en masse*.

I didn't put too much more thought into it as I destroyed the stone and asked Exia to bring us to the next one, which she swiftly did.

We met periodic resistance, but we mostly swept over everything in our way. Only a fifth of the total guardians of the lair had faced us in that initial *sortie*. Periodically, the remainder would rally and face us, but considering that the treants we conquered stayed with us to fight off the newcomers, we faced little difficulty. A few more Travelers died in combat, but not very many.

By the seventh lair stone, all of our Travelers were simply supporting our treant allies, who were doing the fighting for us. Some of the purified forest spirits had joined in as well, racing in and out through the lines as they unbalanced our enemies for us. Just like the initial battle, everything seemed to build from a slow start to a rapid descent downhill, picking up momentum like an avalanche.

When it was clear that we wouldn't be stopped at the seventh lair stone, whatever intelligence was facing us pulled all of its forces back. I was expecting a final clash at the twelfth stone. So was everyone else, and the Travelers were all on edge as we raced from the ninth to the tenth to the eleventh.

However, there was nothing. Even when I held the twelfth stone in my hand, we hadn't faced a single guardian in almost an hour. My Traveler allies were all confused, but my forest companions were grim.

"So many we couldn't save," Exia said sadly.

"This is better than we ever hoped," Elj countered. "More than half."

"More than half. Less than all," Exia lamented.

"We could never save them all," Elj said. I looked at his massive face and saw it drawn in sorrow.

"I don't understand," I said.

"You will," he said. "It is already too late to turn back. Destroy the final stone, Hail. And prepare to face the lair's true guardian."

"Well, that's not ominous at all," I muttered. I waved a hand up at my endgame guardians, flagging for them to come down from where they were circling above, keeping the other high-level Travelers at a distance.

"Something is wrong," Joon-ho said, and I wasn't certain if it was a question or statement.

"I think something is going to spawn when I destroy the final stone," I said. "It might be a Worldboss."

"I will cast a portal," Aroha said. "Tell everyone present who can to cast their own portal, and if it looks like something dangerous is appearing, they should escape through one of the portals somewhere safe."

That sounded like a good idea, and I nodded to have the instructions spread throughout the crowd. I suggested that everyone also keep their Fast Travel menu up and ready to go, just in case.

With these preparations made, I finally selected the option to destroy the final lair stone. The response was almost immediate.

> The Poison Grove has been destroyed by Hail Jeoran!
> This is an Action of Note, but it will not resonate into the Divergence.
> This is an Action of Note that has changed the fate of Verindale!

> The Poison Grove will no longer spread among infected Treants and Forest Spirits.
> The quarantine of the The Poison Grove has ended.
> It is no longer possible to cleanse infected Treants and Forest Spirits.
> Infected Treants and Forest Spirits have had their levels unrestricted.
> XirQuirthal the Blightmaster has spawned.

"'XirQuirthal the Blightmaster has spawned,'" I read. "That sounds like a Worldboss. Everyone, get ready to run!"

However, even as I called out the words, all of the portals that had been readied by the various mages assembled around me in the raid winked out. The earth beneath us split—not forming a canyon, but rather pulling the forest apart while keeping the ground level, creating even terrain.

The blight split as well. It was *pulled* from our side of the divide to the other. Where our part of the forest grew healthier and healthier, the other became black with the sick and rot that had only lightly grazed it before. From within that other forest, parallel to us, the missing forest spirits and treants emerged, looking more haggard and sickly than ever.

A quick [Analyze] made my stomach drop. They were all level one sixty or higher. And there were too many of them for the few endgame Travelers I had accompanying me to deal with. Far too many.

Stepping forth from between two of the opposing treants, a satyr appeared. He seemed a small thing, with goat legs, a bare chest, and a face that was twisted and ugly behind his shaggy beard. As he walked forward, he seemed to grow until he was first six feet tall, then eight, then twelve when he stopped at the demarcation line.

"I really must thank you for freeing me, young one," the satyr said in a voice that was surprisingly sonorous. "Although I bound myself here ages ago to gather my power, I've long since reached the apex of what this forest can provide. I would have left long ago, but when I bound myself, I hadn't anticipated that the dryads would bind me with their roots and their own cleansing magics. They kept me just weak enough, you see, just below the point where I would reach the threshold I had set for my freedom. But then you destroyed my lair stones. I am not at ten-tenths, but I am at eight. So, now I suppose I will go forth and conquer eight-tenths of the Heartlands instead of all."

"For twelve centuries we have bound you here, and now it is the time for the blight itself to wither and die," Elj called out. "To battle! Join me, brothers and sisters of the forest! With our minds pure, we bring the peace of the end to our afflicted brethren, as they would have to us were the roles reversed! Do not let them continue to serve the Blightmaster now that he has been freed!"

The treants and forest spirits from our side charged, as did the blighted ones. I had just enough time to notice that, like the enemy, our side had their levels severely increased. Instead of being a lowly level forty-five to fifty, Elj was suddenly level one hundred ninety, and Exia was level one hundred eighty-five. And the many spirits and tree-folk around me were at a minimum level one hundred seventy-five.

It was not merely bluster that caused Elj to charge into battle, I realized. He believed he had an actual chance of victory, and he meant his words. If he could not give the blighted opponents freedom now that I had destroyed the lair stones, then he would give them the grace of an end. I could admire him for that. I could admire the trees and forest spirits that followed him into battle as well.

Until it was Exia who joined him, with me still on her shoulders. That was when the seven hells broke loose.

43
KARMIC WARRIORS

Riding Exia was, I suddenly found, absolutely nothing like riding Shadow. Whereas Shadow was a horse well trained for virtually any sort of service I could ask of him—appearing from my shadow at any moment should the need arise, and, just as importantly, vanish back into that place as conveniently—Exia was not. Exia was a forest spirit that did not wear a saddle, did not have reins with which I could guide her, and refused to follow the subtle hints I tried to give her with my knees and body weight that I *did not want to go in this direction!*

"Exia, stop!" I called, but she ignored me. I clung low to her neck, hugging it so I didn't fall off as she dashed between warring treants and forest spirits clashing with their horns.

"It is time for the purge," Exia called. "Though it saddens me, we must be rid of the blighted ones and the blighter once and for all. I thank you for your service today, little human. And curse you for it."

She shook her neck, throwing off my grip, and she bucked. While fighting to keep my saddle, I gained four points in [Animal Handling], bringing the skill up to seventeen, but I wasn't much pleased when, finally, she ejected me from her back. I scrambled to my feet.

Exia turned to look back at me, her eyes glowing with anger. "My sisters will die because of you. Some will live free. I thought I could take that knowledge and forgive you because of it. But in this moment, I find that I cannot."

She dashed forward to gore me.

Two shields intercepted her. One from Joon-Ho, who intercepted the charging spirit with a mighty variation of the [Warrior] [Charge]. The other was a powerful protective magic spell that encased me in a bubble, capable of absorbing well over my maximum Health. I did not see who cast it, but my bodyguards had caught up to me.

"Get back," Joon-Ho called to me. "We have to fight our way free of the battlefield. Everyone, ignore everything except for threats to the young lord!"

I looked around and saw that the forest denizens were not the only ones fighting. The Travelers who had been circling in the sky had descended and were laying about themselves with their weapons, only to find that the treants and spirits that had previously been easy prey in a low-level lair were suddenly stronger than they were. Many were dying without any sort of coordination or cohesion to their efforts.

A few targeted me. Aroha was actively counterspelling the magic that was coming at our group, and most of it was directed towards its most vulnerable member. While the young [Mage] was able to keep me safe from magic, the arrows got through. More than one burst against the magic shield keeping me safe until one of the [Rogues] in my bodyguard appeared behind the [Archer] responsible and swiftly disposed of the interloper.

The forest denizens were too busy with their private war to really notice us as we managed to tease our way out of it, avoiding the conflict as best we could, driving off what we couldn't with strength of arms.

Outside of the war zone, we grouped up with the surviving members of the low-level raiders, who were circled around, watching the belligerents with a mixture of emotion. The only common human emotion I didn't see present on their faces was boredom. Some of the onlookers were frightened, others amused, enthralled, horrified, and pleased.

I turned back to look, and I went through the spectrum myself. I had never expected that destroying a lair would lead to . . . this. War.

Despite Elj's confidence in his ability to give grace to the blighted ones, it quickly became apparent that the two sides were evenly matched. With XirQuirthal the Blightmaster supporting them, the blighted ones were healing themselves as fast as they were being wounded. Likewise, the spirits and treants that had been purified by the efforts of the Travelers were pulling back as soon as they ran low on Health, and once they hit the demarcation line encircling the blighted forest, they began to heal.

"This will go on forever," I said. "Until the Travelers arrive and put a stop to it. They have to kill XirQuirthal the Blightmaster to end it. And he's a Worldboss."

"We can kill the Blightmaster," Aroha said, looking at the ongoing battle sadly. "Or we can stop the fight by siding with him and killing off the cleansed trees and deer-things. Objectively speaking, it looks like that's the easier task."

"No!" I objected. "You don't think that will happen, do you?"

"Don't know," she admitted. "Look, Hail, the summoning stone doesn't work to bring in high-level recruits. And spatial magic is pretty locked down at the moment. <Peasant's Revenge> is gearing up for war against the Blightmaster. They started prepping as soon as that first big battle happened, just in case this triggered something endgame. So did the others inside the alliance. But even once we get there, there's going to be the fight over the pecking order."

"What?" I asked. "What do you mean?"

"I mean it's a Worldboss. Most Worldboss wipes happen because of griefing. If whoever gets here first just attacks, they'll probably get killed by whoever gets here second. Instead, they'll have to stake a claim to the event and posture for a bit to see who else shows up. Who's willing to talk and make deals. Might be we team up with some of them, might be we have to stand down if the big dogs start growling. But that's just how these things go."

I looked at her, mouth agape. "You mean you're just going to let them fight there until you decide who gets to kill the Worldboss?"

"It's going to be more complicated than normal this time, since it looks like there's two options," Joon-Ho said, stepping up next to me, his shield and spear in hand, ready to raise both in my defense. "This is the first confirmed Worldboss with two alternative options for clearing it, and the players who want to go darkside are going to really push for it."

I looked between them. This was much worse than I thought. If

XirQuirthal the Blightmaster won with the help of Travelers, then I would be responsible for setting him loose on the world. I had to do something. And there was only one ability in my spellbook I could think of that might help.

When I had first used the ability, it had been in the wake of my grandfather's murder, when I had been massively outnumbered and alone. It had analyzed the situation and concluded that I would die alone, so it summoned everyone who had positive Reputation with me and gave them a powerful buff that would, in theory, at least give them a chance to overcome the raiders gathered outside.

It hadn't worked, because at the time everyone I'd known had been a low-level noob with no idea of how to coordinate in high-level PVP. They had been put down effectively by the organized raiders waiting outside, even with me dancing among them, half controlled by Thedum and casting powerful magics that wiped out entire clusters of raiders.

The last time I had used this ability, I had been surrounded by bandits and certain I was about to die. That hadn't actually been the case, of course, since I'd had Tarisha with me, who likely could have easily won the fight by herself while protecting me—assuming that I wasn't an idiot and had hidden inside of Mooncrest Manor instead of charging into the fray.

But I'm an idiot sometimes, so I cast the same ability now that I had cast back then. [Summon Karmic Warrior] rippled through the world, resonating with everyone who met certain criteria.

I knew better, now, how it worked. First it figured out my intentions. Then it analyzed the threat. It prioritized targets with [Mark of Karma] or [Mark of Karmic Balance], but it filled the gaps with those who had the highest levels of Reputation for and against me. [Summon Karmic Warrior] didn't actually care if I won the challenge any more than creating a battlefield did. All it cared about was evening the odds.

I was just hoping that enough of the Travelers aligned against me wouldn't take things so far as to side with XirQuirthal the Blightmaster. It was a gamble, but if everyone who arrived agreed that the Blightmaster was the bigger threat, they might put aside their differences before members of guilds like <Branded Exiles> arrived.

Once more, [Summon Karmic Warrior] did not work the way I

intended. Rather than summoning individuals, it summoned the top five active guilds aligned and opposed to me at the time that I cast it.

Thousands of Travelers appeared, some in the air already on their flying mounts, many on the ground quickly summoning mounts to find and stand with their guild. There was some confusion, and many Travelers began calling out with enchanted items to carry their voices.

"<Shadow's Valor> is grouping up on me! On me, people! Come on! Get organized so we can figure this out. This is a huge opportunity that we only got because we saw—"

"<Savage Justice> is declaring this a *no* PVP zone until everyone is organized. Violators will be marked with a [Flair of Justice], the NPC officials will be notified, and you will be—"

"Hey, guys! Where is <Phoenix Talons> grouping up?"

"Holy shit, <Drama Llamas> got summoned by the kid? I thought we were on his shit list!"

The cacophony drowned out the battle of the forest, which continued despite the Travelers' sudden appearance and messy attempts to organize themselves.

I turned to my bodyguards, who were now encircling me closer than ever. "Do any of you have one of those voice amplification tools?" I asked.

Aroha nodded, and passed me a necklace with an ear on it. "You just wear it. You don't have to hold it to your mouth, and you don't have to speak loudly. In fact, it's better if you speak quietly. Everyone will hear you, but I don't know what good it will do with all of the shouting going on."

I nodded and put the necklace on. Taking her word for it, I began speaking.

"Hello, everyone. I am Earl Hail Jeoran. If you would all quiet down for a moment, I will explain what is going on. I will tell you what challenge has arisen to threaten the lands of Verindale, ally to all those of the Heartlands of Lagrea, and you will have to make a choice: will you stand in the light of Thedum or be cast forever from his grace?"

I have never before heard such a cacophony as the echoes of "Quest accepted!" that followed my simple pronouncement. In moments, thousands of Travelers had fallen into silence—though not entirely, as they continued to group themselves according to guild.

Still, I was confident in the magic of the item I had been handed, so I began to explain.

"I have destroyed the lair known as [The Poison Grove], unaware at the time that it was keeping bound a Worldboss, who is now free. He holds in his yoke a number of treants and forest spirits as thralls, and although it pains me to admit it, the system itself says that they cannot be cleansed of their corruption. They are presently being held back by the small number of those whom my allies and I were able to purify before destroying the lair, which is when this event became the fare of endgame Travelers like yourselves."

I paused for a moment. "I humbly ask that you all bond together and kill XirQuirthal the Blightmaster. It is my own fault that he is free. Some of you have taken stances against me in the past, and if you grant me this boon, I vow to—"

"Quest declined!" a voice called out. A very familiar voice. One that I had last heard laughing as he recalled the murder of my grandfather. Nial Kingslayer stepped forward with <Branded Exiles> and three other guilds, the [Brand of Sin] prevalent on their faces. Except for Nial, who of course bore the [Mark of Cain].

My heart sank. I'd known it was possible, but I hadn't thought that Nial would be one of those summoned by my ability.

44
NEGOTIATIONS WITH THE ENEMY

Nial was looking well. Too well. He'd changed his gear since I'd seen him last. He still bore the same dark skin and bald head. But before, his gear had been silver armor, like my father's, and he'd wielded a battle axe and shield. Today, he was dressed in a suit of evil plate armor.

I'm not speaking figuratively. It was literally plate armor that was made to look like it was supposed to be worn by a villain. Designed that way for Travelers who wanted to exude that effect for whatever reason. Laurant had told me that it was mostly for roleplay and that the people who wore it were really nice people.

But this was Nial Kingslayer. The man who had killed my grandfather. And me, technically, since his offhanded blow had been enough to activate the [Blessing of Thedum]. Killing King Rain had earned him the title Kingslayer. Killing me had earned him the [Mark of Cain]. Neither were things that a reasonable person would want to have, in my opinion, and my opinion of Nial was quite unfavorable indeed.

Unfortunately, his trifecta of guilds had been the quickest to assemble after the summons. And while they hadn't started slaying others yet, they were making it clear that the attempts at organization were over, blockading isolated individuals from joining up with their allies. Small groups had been [Polymorphed] during the confusion and were now prisoners ringed with guards.

The atmosphere was heavy with tension. And I did not know how to cut through it.

"What do you want, Kingslayer?" I asked.

"Oh, I have a list," he said. "An actual list of things I want from you, Hail. Started making it the day you had someone break my windows."

"That wasn't me," I protested.

"Uh-huh, sure. I know they can't prove it was, either," he admitted. "But it's been a real hassle, changing my name and moving, and so on. But whether that's your fault or not, I started thinking about what I'd sue you for if I could. And so I have this handy little list of things I want from you."

"You?" I asked, outraged. "You think you have the right to sue me? You murdered my grandfather!"

"He's just a chatbot. It's a game," he said. "Anyway, here's the way I see it. That mess has two ways to be resolved. Says as much in the quest we all got when we accepted the summons. So, here's the thing. You give me what I want—what me and my guild and allies want—and we let things go your way this time. You don't? Well, we start griefing. The PVP starts, and it doesn't end until all sorts of people have lost a level."

"And you've lost ten!" I taunted, which got a wince from him.

"Yeah, that curse is one of the things I want lifted. You do that, or tell me how, and I'll take that as currency towards killing the Worldboss and not chopping down your little living forest instead," he answered back.

I grinned. He was now level one hundred sixty-eight. He'd been level two hundred when I'd first seen him, a rank that few except the best players in the world—like my father had been—had ever achieved. I'd heard that he had been killed six times due to the quest I'd issued with him as a bounty, but it seems that he had regained almost half the levels.

"I don't even know how to remove the [Mark of Cain]," I informed him.

"You applied it. You've got to know how to remove it."

The other Travelers were not entirely silent during our conversation, but the complaints of those who didn't want to listen to the drama playing out were mostly drowned out by those who did. Sometimes by threats of violence. But few of the speakers except Nial and I were using voice amplification magics.

"Thedum applied it. Ask him," I taunted back.

Nial paused for a moment, looking surprised. "You know, that's actually a good point. Okay. So, do that for me. If you ask Thedum how to remove the [Mark of Cain], I'll count it as one of three marks towards letting you have your way today."

I jerked in surprise. "Why would he answer me?"

"I know for a fact that you're in good with him," Nial explained. "He'd never answer me, but if he answers you and I hear it, then I'll count it as done. After all, Thedum can withhold the truth, but he can't tell a lie."

"I didn't know you were a theologian," I said.

"Been doing some reading during my downtime," he admitted. "Didn't much care about lore beforehand, but now that I'm canon, I figure I should give it a better go than your old man ever tried to do. Wonder if I can convince them to give me a special AI kid too?"

Those words burned like acid in my veins. "Never."

"Never meaning you won't ask Thedum for me, or never to the kid thing? 'Cause I was just joking about that. If there's one thing me and Gideon always agreed on, it was that we don't want kids."

I glared at him a moment, then glanced upwards. "One of three things. Very well. Fine. Thedum, please answer me so that all present may hear. In what ways may [Mark of Cain] be cleansed?"

There was a thrumming silence, and the crispness of the world suddenly changed. I felt the weight of Thedum's attention on it, and I knew that he was evaluating the events carefully.

"The [Mark of Cain] is applied when an act of extreme violence is committed against a player character who has not agreed, or cannot agree, to be subjected to violence under the Terms of Service, yet the offender cannot be barred from playing the game. There are three methods for its removal. The first is that the aggrieved party—that is, the victim of violence—requests that the offender's punishment be suspended. The second is an arbitration between the offender and Arc Inc. However, during arbitration, the right to play *The Gates of TirNiki* is suspended and, depending on the outcome, may not be restored. The third is the same as the second, except through jury trial."

"Wait," Nial said. "Player character? That's bullshit! I killed an NPC. You're treating me like I killed an actual ten-year-old kid in his first login to one of those baby games when they're first calibrating his mind to interpret virtual reality."

"That's a fair approximation of Arc's interpretation of the events as they occurred, actually," Thedum said blandly. "In the first few exposures to virtual reality, human children often have difficulty telling the two apart, which is why *The Gates of TirNiki* requires seventy hours spent in nonviolent VR games and has restricted settings for children under the age of fifteen. Until they've adapted, subjecting the young to simulated violence can be very traumatic. Hail witnessing the canon death of his grandfather was approximately on that level of trauma."

"Whatever, I'm not going to argue this. So I either convince the kid to forgive me, or I go to court against the game and can't play until I win?" Nial asked.

"Those are your current options, as laid out in the End User License Agreement and Terms of Service that everyone has agreed to in order to log in to this reality. Everyone present except for Hail Jeoran, of course. He has never agreed to those terms," Thedum answered. "I have answered the question sufficiently, I believe. Hail, you may count this as one of the three favors that Nial has demanded in payment for his cooperation today."

"Thank you, Thedum," I said. I turned to Nial. "I'm not forgiving you, so don't even think to ask for that."

Nial opened his mouth to speak, then paused and closed it again. He cocked his head to think. "I'll count it as my second favor if you tell me what it would take to make you forgive me. Theoretically, of course. What would I have to do?"

It was my turn to pause. I bit my lip, but there was actually an answer, and I decided to give it to him. "Turn yourself in to face justice in Yuikon. Face trial for the murder of King Rain, my grandfather. Serve your punishment under our laws. If you do all of that, then at the conclusion of your punishment, I shall ask that the [Mark of Cain] be removed."

Nial turned up his lip at that. "Yeah, I'm going to give that a hard pass. And I'm not going to count it as a second favor either. That's bullshit. I—"

"You traitorous swine," I cursed at him. "You would go back on your word at a moment's notice in front of this many witnesses?"

Nial looked around, then shrugged shamelessly. "Telling me how to remove the mark was part of the first favor. He doesn't get double credit for doing the same thing slightly differently."

The Travelers who were watching the drama unfold seemed unimpressed, but none were particularly rushing to insist that he honor his original pledge.

"So, now for the *actual* second thing I want: I want more information on the [Mark of Karmic Balance]."

"Figure the answer out for yourselves," I said. "I'm casting it on all of you assholes right now."

A susurration occurred as the gathered players called up their status screens. While we had been talking, I had been identifying and applying [Mark of Karmic Balance] to everyone who was clearly allied with <Branded Exiles>, <Nope>, and <Teh Lulz>, as well as everyone else who was glowing bright red. The players began reading the description of the bane that was disguised as a boon, and many of them found themselves with mixed feelings.

The [Mark of Karmic Balance], or at least the application that I could apply to my enemies, carried the same five percent boost to all stats and ten percent boost to Experience as [Mark of Karma]. The stick that came with that particular carrot was a massive Reputation loss when completing any quest for a faction that was aligned with me.

Applying the debuff to the hundreds of players with red auras— their aura signified that they had significant negative Reputation with me—was easy. There was no cooldown, and once I committed to doing it, it was like a small part of my brain partitioned itself off to complete the task. Within moments, it was done.

"Wait, I just said I wanted information," Nial protested. "We haven't decided whether we want to take the Reputation loss yet, and we have to actually research to see—"

"I don't care. I am counting this as the fulfillment of the second measure of our agreement. If you have a problem with that, well, you're still marked. But I promise the regular [Mark of Karma] to anyone who breaks ranks with Nial now. If you—"

"All right, that's enough. Fine, it counts as item number two," a woman said, stepping forward, and I recognized her. She was Rowena, who had come to my court before. Due to her guild's harboring of Nial Kingslayer, I had found her mere presence to be offensive, but she had behaved properly during the proceedings. "Sorry, Nial. I'm taking over. It was a mistake to put you on lead for this."

"We needed him to recognize someone, and we needed you to get everyone else organized," Nial argued.

"Don't talk shop while your voice is amplified," she scolded, and Nial quickly removed the voice amplification token he had been using.

"Hello, Hail. It's nice to see you again. I know that we're technically enemies, but we simply need to agree on one last point, and then we will cooperate with the killing of the Worldboss known as XirQuirthal the Blightmaster. While I'm not too thrilled that the decision of whether or not we received [Mark of Karmic Balance] was made without discussion, I believe that it ultimately will fall in with our plans. For the final boon I would ask from you—"

"I'm not giving you any boons," I interrupted hastily.

Rowena paused and nodded. "From a certain perspective, it's actually a bane. We have a list of Travelers who wish to obtain [Brand of Sin]. If you can grant it to them, then we will say that seals the deal, and we shall step back and allow your allies to kill the Worldboss."

"You're not going to do it yourself?" I asked, surprised.

"We didn't come here for the glory of killing XirQuirthal the Blightmaster, Lord Hail," she said. "We came for you. All of this posturing has just been us negotiating. I regret that it required that we do so from a position of power, and I'm sorry if Nial has offended you. In fact, in exchange for giving us a method of obtaining the brand, we are willing to let you have him killed once more."

"Hey!" Nial called out, as apparently he hadn't been involved in the decision.

I did some math in my head and came to a conclusion. "The assassinations of him, those were negotiated as well, weren't they?"

"Nial is surrounded by ten bodyguards whenever he leaves our guild headquarters," Rowena answered. "And he himself is a powerful [Warrior] skilled at staying alive. It might take some . . . coordination between Nial's protectors and his assassins to ensure that he actually dies."

"Hey!" Nial called out again, but at this point we were ignoring him.

"Which ones?" I demanded. "Which ones were staged?"

"I'm sorry, but I cannot reveal that information," Rowena said, smiling. "Some but not all, that's all I can say for certain. We've been more protective of Nial recently, as we don't want him getting so weak that he's useless to us and the lessons we've been giving him on how to talk to Natives, to exploit that unique Title of his to the fullest, go to waste."

I bit my tongue. This was a matter that was within my power. I had discovered during the Battle for North Shire that Travelers received the [Brand of Sin] when I attacked them with [Holy Weapon] active, but I was uncertain I wanted to pay this price. This was the second time that Rowena had asked me to help her increase the number of players with that particular bane—though perhaps her faction did not see it as a bane—and I was stubbornly unwilling to give her what she wanted.

Except that she was negotiating from a position of power this time. Ten guilds had been summoned, and the best Travelers from many of those guilds were present. But most of the strength of a raid came from its organization, and <Branded Exiles> and its two allies had won the race in that regard.

Capitulation was my only choice, but I wasn't going to give in fully.

"For your consideration today, I will brand sixty Travelers," I declared. "Twenty for each of your three guilds, or however you wish to divide them among yourselves. Any more that you want in the future will be negotiated for future favors."

"Done!" she agreed.

And like that, I had struck a deal with my enemy.

45

XIRQUIRTHAL THE BLIGHTMASTER

It did not take very long for the branding to occur. The guilds had already made their lists of who would receive priority in getting the [Brand of Sin] and who would not, so in a surprisingly organized fashion, they lined up to be struck by me with my [Holy Weapon] skill active. It was as efficient as walking down a line of troops for an inspection. Not that I would actually know for certain, since I'd never performed that act for comparison.

Once they had gotten what they had wanted, <Branded Exiles>, <Nope>, and <Teh Lulz> mounted up as one and flew off, leaving behind their captives and their threats. Several of the guilds allied with me sent scouts after them, but they kept their word, and as soon as the Fast Travel system was available to them, they activated it.

They couldn't double cross us now even if they wanted to.

With that out of the way, the seven remaining guilds allied. All of them. I was a little surprised that the two who had been summoned to balance my allies didn't try threatening to start griefing on their own, but they only sent representatives from their guilds to talk to me while the rest of the allied forces got organized.

The battle of the blight was still raging in the background, the endless violence ongoing between the treants and forest spirits who had been cleansed and those who had not. Now that things had settled some, I rode atop Shadow, whom I had summoned in the demarcation line of pure earth separating the blighted forest from the rest to get a better view from horseback.

The representatives from <Lost Socks> and <Moar Coffee> approached after having disarmed down to the basic clothes that Travelers wore when they weren't wearing stat-boosting armor. It was a show of good faith, as it would make them easy to kill should my guardians believe their intentions were threatening, but they actually looked confused.

"So, exactly what did we do that makes you consider us enemies?" the representative from <Lost Socks> inquired. "I mean, is there something in particular that we did to piss you off? Because although I think it's great we got a chance to get summoned to this event, it was a bit of a shock to realize it was because we were being treated by the system like the bad guys."

I looked over at her, and I simply shrugged. "I didn't know who would be summoned by the system. I had no control over it."

"Yeah, well, the reason I'm actually here is because some of my friends got caught up in that massive spread of the [Mark of Karmic Balance], and they're unhappy about that. We want it removed."

"I'm not giving you its counterpart," I said immediately.

"That's fine. Just remove it so that we can continue to quest effectively in . . . I mean, you're a royal from Yuikon, right? So that means if we have this, then we get our Reputations nerfed in at least five of the ten countries of the Heartlands, right? We'd rather have normal Reputation growth than have the slight boost in stats and Experience."

"And I would honestly rather not have my enemies resenting me," I admitted. "Very well. After the battle is over, gather together and I will rescind the marks that I have given the Travelers in your guild. And you, representative of <Moar Coffee>?"

"I want what she wants," the burly man said. "Same reasons. We're not going darkside, but some of our players have been going against your interests, so I'm not surprised the system tagged us like Alina here is. My boys really liked fighting alongside the bandits instead of your forces, that's all. It wasn't anything personal. They just figured the bandits were the underdogs, or something like that. I don't know. I was busy with work that weekend and missed out entirely. We were planning on grinding out the deficit with your faction the hard way eventually, but we were never planning on being your enemies long term."

"I see," I said. And I sighed. "Very well. Same deal. Gather after XirQuirthal the Blightmaster is dead, and I will rescind the mark from everyone who does not want it. It should only take a few moments. It's not very hard to do."

"Right, then. Let's go kill us a Worldboss!" the representative from <Moar Coffee> declared, and he charged back towards where his guild was organizing, fast equipping his gear along the way.

The final representative to step forward was a member of the <Drama Llamas>. I was quite surprised that he not only had a [Mark of Repentance] rather than a [Brand of Sin], but that he displayed it openly. And that he had a faintly blue aura.

"Lord Hail," he said. "I never exactly got the chance to apologize formally for my guild's participation in the fight against the Branding Boss. It was a mistake, one that we have been working very hard to rectify. I was hoping that you would help us on that front. We seem to be suffering from negative Reputation gain with your faction and—"

"And you've still been grinding it?" I asked, amazed.

The young man looked surprised at my surprise, but he nodded. "Almost all of us, in our spare time. Once the first battleground happened and all of those quests unlocked, at least. The battleground was a footnote for us, really. The important part for us was the fact that it was suddenly much easier to get rid of the [Brand of Sin], and after that, we started looking into your faction and your history and stuff. And we want to be your allies."

I tapped my fingers against Shadow's flank, indecisive. "This is not the time to talk of these matters. Come to my court after the battle is won, and we will have a formal discussion on whether or not I shall reconsider your guild's past actions in light of how it has been acting more recently."

The <Drama Llama> representative nodded and bowed in the Irvine fashion. "Thank you for your consideration, Lord Hail. We will all be looking forward to it."

"We should step back, young master," Joon-Ho said, motioning us back towards the healthy forest. "And we should be prepared to run. Once the balance is broken and the Worldboss event begins, there is little way of predicting how it will go."

"I want to watch," I insisted. I followed him to the edge of the demarcation line, but no farther. Riding upon Shadow, I turned back to where the seven guilds were aligned around the ongoing event in a star shape.

Rather than stand shoulder to shoulder, the guilds had decided to align themselves around the blighted lands in a hexagon. Aside from <Lost Socks> and <Moar Coffee>, the five guilds who were actually aligned with me included <Peasant's Revenge>, of course. But this event was happening in the very early hours of North America, and so it wasn't their best warriors who had caught the summons but their international members who kept their business active while the primary group rested. Because of that, my friends who had once served as my guardians were spreading out into the other guilds rather than forming their own cohesive unit.

The remaining guilds present were <Savage Justice>, <Phoenix Talons>, and <Taegeuk>. With <Peasant's Revenge> splitting itself up, that left an even six forces, and they arranged themselves against the circular blighted area in a hexagon rather than standing shoulder to shoulder. Then, with one player shooting a signal flair into the sky, they charged in from all directions and began slaying the blighted forest spirits and treants, finally upsetting the balance between the blighted ones and the healthy.

The fight with the forest guardians was brief and anticlimactic, over in moments. The blighted trees began to wither and die in their absence, and the healthy forest denizens withdrew.

"We cannot stand against the Blightmaster," Elj called, his deep voice resonating over the land. "We call for your aid, you from beyond the gates, to put an end to this once and for all."

The forest within the demarcation line continued to wither, the wood crumbling to dust until it was so fine it might be ash. The energy, the life that had once flourished in those trees was consumed by the satyr XirQuirthal the Blightmaster, who fed upon it and grew until he was twenty feet tall. He had been sitting quietly in a stream earlier, hidden by the forest, but now that it had been denuded, he simply stood.

"Thank you. It's been a long time since I've had a proper meal," he said to the Travelers. "I don't suppose it's too late to simply ask you all to turn back and—"

"Pull!" came the call from the Travelers, and a wave of magic and missiles fell down on XirQuirthal the Blightmaster, signaling the start of the fight. The satyr raised his hands, and thirty small poison spirits in the shape of floating devils pulled themselves out of the crooks of the blighted earth around him and set themselves loose upon the raiders. The tanks organized to prevent them from running amok, but each of the devils applied a stacking poison debuff, which was difficult to cleanse.

They were forced to spread the debuff around even to the non-tank classes while the primary tanks let their stacks drop off.

XirQuirthal was not silent either. Once he had summoned his adds, he began casting streams of dark lightning, which ripped through the assembled raiders. A single blow was enough to break through a healer's shield and still cause thirty percent Damage, or to cause ninety percent damage to an unshielded Traveler. The race to keep the raid healed was intense when the satyr's magic was added to the ongoing Damage from the adds' poison.

While he wasn't casting his lightning, XirQuirthal the Blightmaster was fighting unarmed with those who approached him. Each touch from him left a curse. His curses were different from the poison of his adds and did not fade over time. Once they reached ten stacks, the Travelers learned, they would gain a Damage-over-time effect that was simply too powerful to heal through.

The seven raids, split into six forces, had faced the forest guardians mostly unscathed. Against XirQuirthal the Blightmaster they took thirty percent casualties. But ultimately, they pushed him to zero Health before there was any danger of a wipe. The Travelers burst into cheers as the satyr went through his death throes, vowing curses and vengeance once he had respawned. But ultimately he collapsed, and seven treasure chests appeared nearby, each marked with the symbol of one of the participant guilds.

XirQuirthal did not despawn. Or turn to darkmist. That was normal for Worldbosses, I'm told. And it's one of the first things that had alerted everyone that I was different when I had died as the Branding Boss. I had despawned immediately, and there had been no loot.

Thinking back to another boss who hadn't despawned when he had died, I rode Shadow forward. When I had faced Gyudue of the Darkest Night, I had been distressed to learn that his body acted like that of a normal Native. When a Native dies, their body remains behind until they receive a blessing from Thedum, or whichever of the eight benign gods of my world it was that they worshipped.

In my distress, I had tried to honor the fallen warrior. I was uncertain whether or not XirQuirthal the Blightmaster deserved the same treatment I'd given the honorable drow that day, but I decided that it ultimately wasn't my decision. If I didn't interfere, then the Administration was simply going to respawn XirQuirthal, and this entire situation would repeat. I would risk the attention of the adversary to prevent that from happening.

Nobody was paying attention to me, distracted by loot distribution as they were. Even with my ten bodyguards making our way to the corpse of the boss, I'm not certain anyone gave us more than a passing glance. To be fair to them, it sounded like the drops were amazing from this event.

I stopped before the unmoving satyr body and performed the funerary rights I had learned as a child. XirQuirthal's body burst into motes of white light, and that drew everyone's attention to me pretty quick.

"May you return to the light and the cycle of Thedum," I said to the glowing mist.

The mist hovered in the air but did not disperse as it was supposed to. I felt the attention of the deities weighing down the area.

"No," XirQuirthal said. "No, I will not. I choose no."

The light turned black but still he did not despawn.

"I will remember this, Hail Jeoran. And I will come for you again and again until—"

A portal opened, and my great-uncle Auroras stepped out of it. Perhaps only I would recognize him as such, however, as he was not hiding his face as the Gray Man.

"No!" the spirit of XirQuirthal the Blightmaster called. "No, you can't be here!"

"You were given the option to return to the cycle," Auroras said. "You have chosen spite instead. You will be brought to the Deadlands, XirQuirthal, to relive your final battle over and over again. Thus is the judgment of Death."

Auroras raised one hand, and as he closed his fist, the mist condensed into a ball, which was pulled inexorably into his hand. Auroras turned to face the onlooking Travelers, and he spoke.

"The adversary has one less general thanks to your actions here today. XirQuirthal the Blightmaster shall be brought into the Deadlands. A portal to the Deadlands shall remain open here, in the remains of the battleground, for those who wish to challenge him once again. They must simply find him in the forest of the damned. However, the challenge they will face will be no less than the one that you faced today."

With that, Auroras walked back through his portal, and it grew larger, remaining stable and present. On the other side, a forest filled with leafless trees.

Everyone turned to me once Auroras had vanished and the portal to the Deadlands had stabilized, but I didn't really feel like explaining anything.

"That was the Gray Man," I said. "The portal leads to the Deadlands, which is the first level of the seven hells. Figure the rest out on your own."

With that said, I pulled up my Fast Travel menu and used it to return to Ebbyvale.

46

A QUIET MORNING

The opening of the portal to the Deadlands was big news on the forums, but I didn't bother to read too much about it before claiming some rest in the building that had been set aside for my use while Randal the Architect built my seat of power. He was very excited to finally build something in my world.

The reconstruction of [Zhesa Castle] had been stalled until after the coronation, and nobody knew when that would take place. He'd had Authority to build my mansion while in the version of the world that had become known as the Divergence, but he hadn't had the funds required to do more than start building the foundation.

Unfortunately, it hadn't been very long since I had gotten back and begun authorizing Daemon to use the gold he was pulling in from selling my vanity pets, so although the construction on my manor was starting, it was in early stages yet.

Instead, I was staying at a boarding house. I was the only client. The previous client, or so the mistress of the house would have me believe, was the man who had attempted to cheat me out of thirty million gold.

Yes, I was staying with Elara, the mother-in-law of Arkan, who had been steward of North Shire before it had become my property. She was a very enthusiastic host, and when I went downstairs for breakfast, she'd already been to the inn to fetch a proper feast of eggs and fresh-baked rolls for me to eat with thornberry jam.

She was also very enthusiastic about her son-in-law's upcoming legal strife, which was somewhat disheartening to me.

"I can't just sign a paper and hang him, Elara," I protested as I buttered one of my rolls. "It wouldn't be just to do that without at least giving him a trial. The evidence is against him, I'll say that much, but I had the decision put into the hands of the court for a reason. Inquisitor Trenac will determine his fate, not I."

"Oh, you don't know half of the things that wicked boy has done while he was in charge," Elara said. "He was so cruel to me, Hail. When he wanted to marry my daughter, I was against it because I knew the sort of man he was. That was when the bandits started harassing me, extorting my every last penny while threatening to hurt me. And then it came time for taxes, and I had nothing for the taxman because of the bandits, and Arkan had come in—like I didn't know he was responsible for the entire situation—and offered to pay my taxes. He promised that if I allowed him to marry my daughter, I could live in my own house for the rest of my years."

She cackled at that.

"Then he built this place and put it in my name! Hah! For nearly fifteen years he was paying taxes on my old hovel instead of this fancy mansion, but he didn't count on me hearing from dear Candice that the papers were in my name. So one day after it was built, I showed up to eat dinner with my daughter, and I just never left. When Arkan tried to have a word with me about it, I simply looked at him and pretended to be confused because 'you promised you would house me until the day I die, Arkan. Don't you remember your own promises? Or are your wicked deeds so numerous that you'll break your own vows?' Of course, this was when my daughter was still alive and—"

"Elara, thank you for the meal, but if you don't mind, I've no room in my stomach for your delicious breakfast and your complaints of your son-in-law's failings at the same time," I said, interrupting her. "I've handed the matter over to the inquisition, and the inquisition will handle his trial. That is the end of it as far as I am concerned. If they judge him guilty, then he will serve his sentence. If not, he will walk free, though he will need to find a new profession, I suspect.

I'm moving on. As soon as the inquisition has finished purging North Shire of corruption, I'm setting my sights elsewhere."

Elara harrumphed but moved on to a topic that was less controversial. One that I could mostly tune out, with just the occasional "Uh-huh" or "Oh, she did that? That's terrible," to carry my part of the conversation.

As I finished my breakfast and bid goodbye to the gossipy old woman, I sent out a message to the chat group made up of the canon Travelers who had become my *de facto* support staff. It was still very early in North America, but Daemon, Tarisha, and Laurant were all online.

Hail	Good morning, everyone. It's nice when it's morning for both of us, isn't it?
Tarisha	Hail, what did you do while we were sleeping? I mean, did you plan it, or did it just blow up on you again?
Hail	You should know that I wouldn't plan that sort of thing without telling you, Tarisha. I swear, I only meant to get a few levels and destroy a lair. I didn't realize that I'd be opening a portal to the Deadlands.
Tarisha	Hail, what are the Deadlands?
Hail	. . . You don't know?
Tarisha	No. I mean, I knew they were part of your world's religion, but I didn't realize that they were an actual place where we would be able to go. There's a huge expeditionary effort going on right now to map out the area surrounding the portal that opened.
Hail	Oh. Well, the Deadlands is the place a Native goes when Death claims their spirit. It's technically the first of the seven hells, but I've been there a couple of times, and it didn't actually seem that bad, except for the Ramsay hounds. I guess, with Death having claimed him, XirQuirthal can only spawn in the Deadlands from now on. I think that's what will happen for every Worldboss that I bless if they turn down Thedum's grace, but I'm not entirely certain.
Tarisha	And it's a physical place? Do you know how big it is?

Hail	Why do you think I know that sort of thing? I only went there when Auroras kidnapped me. I'm not an expert on it or anything. If you want to know more about the Deadlands, ask him. Just, you know, don't let him touch you. Or drink or eat anything he gives you. He is the Gray Man, after all.
Tarisha	If I could locate him, I would do exactly that.
Laurant	Hey, Hail. Sorry she's cranky. She had just finished putting together all the data we had on the Deepdark when she got a call at five in the morning informing her that you were making some great move. But we had to wait for the Uber-Jon to bring us in since we're still using the advanced hardware at Arc to generate our seeds of consciousness.
Hail	Yeah, I don't know what that means.
Tarisha	I'm sorry, Hail. Lewis is right. This is . . . just another one of the things that happens around you. I knew that when you started being active 24/7 I would begin missing some of your events. I thought I was ready for it, but I wasn't.
Hail	I recorded it. Would you like to watch?
Tarisha	I would be honored, Lord Hail. Are you . . . May I share what secrets I glean from it with our allies?
Hail	I trust you, Tarisha. Come on, let's meet up in Thorn March. I slept in North Shire, but to be honest, I don't really want to spend the day here dealing with all the work that needs to be done. I've had breakfast already, but we'll go over everything together, and I'll try to answer everything. The truth is, I don't have a lot of the answers. I didn't expect the Gray Man to show up and open a portal to the Deadlands. But I'm happy to talk about destroying the lair and everything else.
Daemon	I'm still waking up myself, Hail, but it's fine if you want to take the day off from your administrative duties. I have a lot of work to do now that we're going after the banks for the money they stole from us, but everything else is running smoothly. Randal needs to speak with you at some point about some of the design details of your mansion, but that can wait until tomorrow.

Hail	Thanks, Daemon. Laurant, do you need me for anything?
Laurant	Nah. Now that the rush of battlegrounds is over, I'm being forced to whittle down your standing army to the standing five thousand, but we never filled the entire roster before, so it's not that hard. Later the gang and I were going to group up and run something, but unless you gained twenty-five levels overnight, we're still outside your level bracket.
Hail	I did get some Experience, but not very much. When it was clear that the lair busting was going to turn into a whole thing with dozens of people involved I had to sit out of the fighting, and I didn't even get much Experience from destroying the lair stones. I'm still level 44.
Laurant	You'll get there, kiddo. Don't worry about it.
Hail	I'm not. I'm going to go now. Tarisha, I'll meet you in Thorn March by the portal center in fifteen minutes.
Tarisha	Meet you there, Hail.

I minimized the chat window and said my farewells to Elara before stepping out of her house, which had been in a sort of bubble that was my private instance, and into a crowded instance filled with Travelers with blue auras. I realized, to my chagrin, that people had been waiting for me to emerge, and the moment I had, they began shouting questions at me. They were only held back by the line of my bodyguards, who had weapons and magic at the ready to defend me should any of them turn violent or push too hard.

Everyone was calling out about the Deadlands or informing me of other lairs that were in my level range, or a thousand other different things.

I didn't want to deal with it. I didn't want to walk through the clamor to the portal center, I didn't want to listen to the questions being flung at me, and I certainly didn't want to answer the few that I actually knew the answer to. Why was everyone treating me like some sort of reference guide to the world of Lagrea all of a sudden? I only knew what my tutors had drilled into me when I was younger!

Realizing that there was a way I didn't have to deal with it, and deciding to use that method, I pulled up my Fast Travel menu and an instant later was away to Thorn March.

47
ROUTINE

My group of ten bodyguards were whisked along with me when I Fast Traveled, and Tarisha was waiting for me outside the portal center. She called her wyvern, I jumped on its back, and we were off into the sky with my endgame guardians circling around us before the small group of Travelers who had been waiting for us realized I was there.

"Is it going to be like this everywhere?" I asked.

"It would help if you disguised yourself," Tarisha said, reminding me.

"You're as famous as I am at this point. Even if I change what I look like with my illusion magic, they'll probably recognize me just from being around you or the rest of my bodyguards."

"I'm afraid that I'll have to concede that point. But I think we have lost them for now. Where would you like me to take you?" she asked.

"I want to see my family," I said. "Let's go to the goblin caves."

"As you will it, my lord," she said, and we changed our flight towards that direction.

We arrived, and I spent some time with my mother and my little brother, kicking Marvin out of his own home to do so with just my sunny disposition, which he found intolerable. I sent Tarisha the recordings from the night before as soon as we'd arrived, so she had that to keep her occupied as I held my infant brother.

Malkios stood nearby, impassive and firm, serious in his duty as Mother's eleventh guardian, she having already acquired ten from Tarisha's list of endgamers willing to take on the responsibility. And of course there was Rain's growing group of nursery goblins, who saw to his needs whenever he began crying.

We spent the day like that. And the next. On the third day, finally, I was driven back to duty. I passed the infant Rain back off to my mother before mounting up on Shadow just outside the goblin caves. "Are you certain you don't mind this location?" I asked her, as I had dozens of times over the two days we had spent together.

"I rather like these goblins," Mother answered. "And they take such good care of Rain. He's growing quite fond of them, I think. I think he'd cry if we gave him to a human nurse. Even one so skilled as Beckah."

That reminded me. I hadn't thought of Beckah for a while. The last I'd heard of her, she was taking care of two noble children, but that had been some time ago. I'd have to issue a quest to my guildmates to follow up on her again.

We sneaked back into North Shire like thieves. I disguised myself using [Illusion Magic: Disguise], which had reached level eleven and allowed me to change my features quite a bit now. I chose to appear older than I really was. I was also wearing a set of armor with a lower level than my [Golem Crafter's Coat], as I was able to push the magic further by not spreading it to my clothes.

Tarisha, too, had disguised herself. She had taken a page from Laurant's playbook and purchased a headband that made her look like a racoon person, disguising her violet hair. Racoon people aren't a race of beastkin that I'm familiar with, but then again, the world is a large place and small tribes of beastkin might be hiding anywhere.

Only four bodyguards accompanied us through the portal to make it look like we were a single party of endgamers and one low-level Traveler moving in the same general direction. I spent some time with Randal the Architect, examining the foundations he had laid for my mansion, the blueprints, and the pillars and supports, which were starting to go up.

Building went faster in my world, he explained, but it would still take him weeks to finish it to the point where I could hold court inside it, so we retreated back to the Temple of Thedum.

While the Temple of Thedum in Zhesa City was sealed to Travelers, smaller temples throughout the land were open to all, so my friends moved my throne back and forth between the pavilion outside the temple and into the temple itself when I wasn't holding court. They had also secured the divinely crafted map table in the temple's basement until a safe room could be crafted to hold it in my mansion.

I held court once again, though this time we let it be known in advance that I would not be sharing any more information about the Deadlands or holding any sort of question-and-answer forum with the Travelers in attendance. That didn't stop them from calling out through the event bubble. Instead, I focused on the important matters related to the governance of the shire: taxes, settling disputes between my tenants—the boring, non-adventure-related stuff that I had been putting off.

I grinned in relief as the audience slowly trickled out of the building when they saw that the Natives and I could do this forever. That was the plan we had come up with. I had once again become too interesting, so now I would be boring for a while.

It worked until I noticed a face in the crowd outside the event bubble that I recognized, and I called out to him. "Lawrence! Lawrence, formerly of <The Endolphins>! I see you there. I would speak with you," I called.

The system focused my attention on him as our instances synchronized and he was pulled into the event. The level one hundred ninety-four raider stepped forward, only for six of my guardians to stop him, but I waved them off. He was glowing faintly pink, but he was also displaying a [Mark of Repentance].

This was the first Traveler who had approached me seeking forgiveness after the murder of my grandfather and my death as the Avatar of Thedum—or the Branding Boss, depending on who you were talking to. He had tried to reason with me, but I had been emotional at the time. I had not expected to see him again.

"I'm surprised you recognize me, my lord," he said. "Or recall my name."

"I simply called out to you because I wished to apologize for how I treated you the last time we spoke. The wounds that Nial Kingslayer had inflicted upon my heart were still fresh, and I might have been unreasonable. I know now that you were right," I said.

"It's all right," Lawrence said. "I guess it's one of those things where time heals all wounds, but I hadn't given you enough of it yet. It was my fault that you blew up in my face like that as much as anyone."

"No, you spoke words that I needed to hear," I told him. "I am pleased to see that you completed the quest to cleanse the [Brand of Sin]."

"It wasn't easy," he admitted. "But yeah. I'm working to recover the Reputation I lost on that day. Aside from being branded, I also had my [Royal Knight] Title converted into [Fallen Knight], just like everyone else who was present. It's . . . Well, the Natives of Yuikon are less friendly with me than they used to be, but it's also a Title that I can make work for me if I use it in the right way. I'm glad I finally got a chance to complete the quest you issued me back then."

"I issued you a quest?" I asked.

"You don't remember? Yeah, to cleanse my [Brand of Sin] and return to you. It didn't say what the reward would be, but I guess I'll find out now," he said. "Its progress just updated for the first time in weeks. Looks like I'll be able to turn it in after the audience is over."

"I see." I considered for a moment, and then I cast [Mark of Karma] on him. I hadn't let the world know that I had conscious control over that ability yet, but under these circumstances it would look like he received it as part of his quest rewards. "Well, Lawrence, I just wanted to apologize for the way I treated you on that day. You were a witness to Nial's crime, not a criminal yourself, and yet you were punished alongside everyone else. For that you have my sympathy."

"Yeah. Like I said, though. I'm making it work," he said, straightening his spine, then bowing. "With your permission, my lord, I'd like to withdraw now. I don't like having so many eyes upon me."

"Very well," I said, and he retreated back through the bubble of the event barrier.

The Travelers in attendance began clamoring for my attention again after that, but I tuned them out and focused on the argument between Miller Jon and Susan Wright. Miller claimed that Susan's teenage son had been tipping his cows and demanded that the boy be officially chastised for it in some manner, while Susan claimed that the old man was being absurd. I tended to agree with the Wright family in this matter.

After all, Miller Jon didn't have any proof that anyone was tipping his cows to begin with, so I dismissed him with a suggestion that he start with that.

The audience lasted all day until, finally, I announced an end to it, and my version of the world cut off from the event nexus that linked the layered instances together, leaving me in a world alone with just those possessing the [Mark of Karma]. I got off my throne and stretched before noticing suddenly that one of the members of the small crowd outside the temple was glowing pink.

I turned sharply towards him. "Who are you?" I demanded.

"Huh. So you did notice me," he said. He held out a handkerchief, upon which was embroidered the rune for the [Mark of Cain]. "Nial Kingslayer challenges you to a duel, Earl Hail Jeoran. He has sent me to be his second."

48

THE KINGSLAYER

My bodyguards almost killed the interloper, but I waved them off. For one thing, he was only level fifty. For another, he was actually following the proper protocol for issuing a challenge to duel.

"Tarisha, do you mind if I name you my second in this matter?" I asked.

"My lord, you can't be serious!" she exclaimed. "Last we saw him, Nial Kingslayer was more than a hundred levels higher than you. There's no way you can win."

"That's why I'm naming you second," I said simply. "Depending on the negotiations for the duel, you might be nominated to fight in my place."

Tarisha's eyes widened in surprise, then narrowed in glee. "In that case, I would be honored to serve in this manner. How may I help?"

"As the challenged party in this duel, I am entitled to select the grounds and the weapon with which we will fight. I'm quite certain that Nial would not be allowed to visit Zhesa City unless he were to turn himself into justice, and the barracks arena would be my first pick. As we are also entitled to select the means with which the duel will be fought, I choose no limits on the abilities or weapons."

"I'll have to check with the boss lady Rowena about all the details, like where it's going to be held," Nial's second informed me. "But I'm surprised you're actually entertaining this. I actually thought I'd be in the lobby right now. What gives?"

"What is your name?" I asked him.

"Call me Skyseeker," he answered.

"Nial thinks he's being clever," I explained. "If he challenges me to a duel and I decline, then, as my grandfather's next of kin, I lose the right to pursue him in court in the land of Yuikon. I'm not going to give up that claim. Especially not when I may select a champion to fight on my behalf. If the primaries are unable to fight due to a vast difference in personal power, as is the case here, then the weaker party may have their second fight for them, or they may select another champion."

"Oh. Look, I'm just here because I'm following orders. Aside from the handkerchief, I'm supposed to give you this letter. It's from boss lady Rowena, not Nial, if that makes a difference," Skyseeker said.

"It likely does," I said. I started to walk forward to retrieve the letter, but one of my endgame guardians stepped forward to take it from Nial's second instead. I broke the seal when it was handed to me and quickly read it.

Dear Earl Hail Jeoran,

I hope this letter finds you well. I apologize for approaching you like this after you were ambushed after your last public audience as well, but I could think of no other way. While I personally find the man insufferable, the fact remains that Nial is a valuable asset to our guild, and the death penalty aspect of the [Mark of Cain] is an active detriment to my guild's interests.

Since our meeting, I have reviewed the laws of Yuikon and met with a Native solicitor, and I believe I have a proposal that you may find satisfactory. Seeing as duels are a valid solution to legal matters in this land, Nial will challenge you, Rain Teoran's next of kin, to a duel to the death over the claim that he is a regicide. And then he will lose. You will kill him and prove legally, in the land of Yuikon, that Nial is a kingslayer.

His sentence shall be death, which you will deliver during the duel.

Nial will fight unarmed and unarmored. He will not resist. He will allow you to vent your anger and frustration on him in silence. He will die, losing ten levels, and then you will consent to having his death penalty multiplier revoked, while leaving in place the other aspects of the [Mark of Cain].

Please respond in whatever fashion you deem appropriate if this is an acceptable solution.

—Rowena of <Branded Exiles>

I finished reading the letter, then handed it to Tarisha, who likewise scanned it.

"I don't approve," she said. "Lord Hail, even unarmed, Nial could kill you with a single blow."

I was silent for a moment, and then I smiled. "Tarisha, please go with Skyseeker and set this duel up. Tell Rowena that I accept her proposal."

While it is the right of the challenger to set the time of the duel, it is also customary to wait at least a week between the finalization of the arrangements and the duel itself. With my duels with Keithan and Voss, we had mutually agreed to skip this custom and hold the duel immediately.

The limit was set at death. I would fight fully armed and unrestricted. Nial would fight unarmed, unarmored, and with a vow not to do a single point of Damage to me. He was, after all, supposedly surrendering himself to justice.

The theater was set once more as the Zhesa City barracks arena, where I had fought my other duels. If I killed Nial—and I was assured in writing that I would be allowed to do so, although it would take some time for my level forty-four [Spellblade] DPS to eat through his massive Health pool, even if he was unarmored—then I would claim satisfaction over the death of my grandfather and petition the Administrators to go along with Rowena's solution.

If I died, well I was assured that my life was not at stake, so the terms for my death weren't actually set.

For the third time in less than a year, Nial Kingslayer was paraded through Zhesa City. This time to his execution at my hand. Unlike before, when he had received cheers, this time he was spat upon, had rotten vegetables thrown at him, and was jeered at. He seemed to take it all in stride, waving and smiling to the assembled Natives and Travelers alike as he made his way to the arena where our duel would take place.

He had been escorted by members of his own guild, who held off the city guard when they tried to arrest him. I had cleared the duel beforehand, but the Native guards attempted to intervene despite that, as I was but a lowly Earl and he was the Kingslayer. But the guard bowed before the gathered might of an endgame raid guild. There was a one-hundred-level gap between them after all. Few of the city guards in Zhesa were like Malkios, able to fight toe to toe with an endgamer.

The event bubble had already engulfed me, Tarisha, and the judge from the army who would oversee the fight when Nial and Skyseeker stepped through it. From that moment on, everything that occurred during our duel would be canon, I knew, and the words I spoke were important.

"Nial Kingslayer, I charge you with regicide. You have challenged my right to pursue you in a court of law with a duel to the death, and I stand here to—"

"Yeah, yeah, kid. Let's just get this bullshit over with," Nial said, unequipping the poncho that he had worn to stave off the rotten fruit that had been thrown at him. In a flash, he was wearing only the simple set of clothes that all Travelers seemed to possess and automatically donned whenever they weren't wearing armor. "I agree to the terms of the duel as negotiated by Rowena and Skyseeker. Those are the only lines I'm supposed to say. But I'm going to add that this is bullshit, and I'm really looking forward to getting this over with."

I frowned, as his words left a bitter taste in my mouth. I didn't like that Rowena had maneuvered me into this position, but I couldn't refuse this duel without going back on my word as witnessed by hundreds of Travelers. Presenting himself to me for a duel to the death *was* a valid legal defense under the Yuikonese legal code, after all, and I had said that I would remove the [Mark of Cain] if he submitted to Yuikonese justice. The compromise that Rowena presented appeared almost reasonable to many Travelers, for some reason.

It left me seething inside.

The judge went over the terms of the duel for the gathered audience, which waited in droves outside of the event bubble, watching. In one of the instances my friends waited—including Larissa, who would quickly portal me out of Zhesa City once this nonsense was over, before too many of the Travelers could accost me.

Wearing my full adventuring kit, I infused [Blade of Eclipse] with [Holy Weapon] and faced off against my opponent. Who, as promised, just stood there.

I attacked him with a [Piercing Lunge], followed up with a [Slash] and a [Thrust], and then I stepped back. I had done less than one percent Damage to him.

"If we do things like this, it will take some time," I said.

"Yeah, whatever. I'm actually wearing an accessory that turns off my Health regen, so just keep going, and you'll get there eventually," Nial said, yawning and stretching.

"That reminds me," I said to myself. "I never replaced my second ring slot after I lost my [Ring of Holy Light]."

"What?" Nial asked.

I reached out and touched him with my left hand, casting [Draining Touch] as I did so. The touch attack was in fact one of my strongest abilities, but it still did an infinitesimal amount of Damage to him. However, it inflicted a different sort of damage as well; he received a notification that he was now affected by the combination of [Through the Valley of the Shadow] and [Reaper's Embrace].

"What the fuck?" he exclaimed. "What did you just—"

"I yield," I announced, turning my back on Nial and walking away. "Under the laws of Yuikon, I relinquish for a year and a day my right to pursue my claim against Nial of <Branded Exiles> for the regicide of King Rain Teoran."

"Wait, what?" Nial asked. "That's it? You're just giving in? You're not going to kill me?"

"I've already scored the victory that I wanted, Nial," I informed him, sheathing my sword. "You are now affected by [Mark of Cain], [Brand of Sin], [Mark of Karmic Balance], and [Reaper's embrace]. I'm fairly certain that there is no way for you to cleanse any of those afflictions, even should you try. Eventually, you'll die at the hands of others and be driven from this game as your guild discards you as a useless thing of the past. Or they'll turn you in to my great-uncle Auroras, my grandfather's brother, who *has not* conceded his right to claim justice in this duel. As his grandson, bringing you to justice was never my mantle to bear in the first place. Not while he had a brother and son still alive."

I walked calmly and patiently towards the edge of the event barrier, confidently explaining how I had just outmaneuvered his guild leadership and scored a victory over him.

I should have walked faster.

"Lord Hail, look out!" came a shout. Tarisha attempted to [Windwalk] to my side, but the magic that restricted her from interfering with the duel was still in place.

The knife that Nial pulled from his inventory to [Throw] at me hit me in the back. It didn't do critical Damage, but it did still do thirty-eight thousand Damage, overkilling me by thirteen thousand. I fell to the arena floor, my vision going gray.

You have died. The Gray Man's Touch has reduced you to level 1.
The Gray Man's Touch fades. You are now affected by Rebirth Resonance.
Your class has been unfixed. You are no longer a Spellblade. Your class has been set to Placeholder.
You no longer have access to Mana. Your combat abilities are being updated and adjusted.

I tried to move but was paralyzed. This was much worse than just being reduced to level one! I had lost my class, my magic, and my skills!

<<Do not panic, Hail,>> Thedum's voice said in that strange way. I was hearing it but not hearing it, like it resonated with my mind from far away.

I reached out and *pushed* and found that I could answer him. <<Thedum, what is happening? I was only supposed to be returned to level one. Why am I being stripped of my spells and abilities?>>

<<[Placeholder] is like the [Child] class, Hail. It is able to use any spell or ability in the game. Except not at the same time. With it, you

will be able to fight as a [Warrior], a [Rogue], a [Mage], or a [Lord] depending on the item that you have equipped. And you will be able to level them each separately. It has been determined by the other gods that you selected [Spellblade] in haste when it was presented to you, and they are forcing this opportunity upon you to reevaluate that decision. I'm sorry. It was not my choice either.>>

<<I don't want this *opportunity!*>> I sent. <<Tell the gods 'thanks, but no thanks.'>>

<<I am sorry, Hail. They have determined that if you wish to unlock [Spellblade] once more, you must do so the traditional way. As a compromise, this time you will not be floundering around in the dark. Thomas the Administrator will provide you with more details on how the [Placeholder] class works and how to unlock [Spellblade] once more.>>

You have died. Activate Mark of the Phoenix?	
Yes	No

I would have frowned at the second pop-up—except that I couldn't, because of the being dead thing. I'd forgotten about that ability. I considered whether or not to activate it. On the one hand, it would be revealing one more of my abilities to the gathered Travelers who were watching the drama unfold—which, I realized, was happening even as I considered what to do next.

Once I had died, Tarisha had killed Nial Kingslayer. I do not believe it had been particularly difficult for her, considering that he had unequipped all of his items to make it easy for me to do the same.

However, upon his death, <Branded Exiles> had struck out, and the instances outside the event bubble were now engaged in a multi-layered PVP battle as the groups aligned against me killed not just my allies, but anyone weaker than them. Including a number of innocent Natives, I noticed. Ones who likely couldn't respawn as I could.

They had the element of surprise on their side, but, ultimately, everyone else had the numbers, and as I was debating whether to return to the lobby or use [Mark of the Phoenix], they abruptly retreated.

It was the lamentation of the Natives that eventually made my decision for me. I activated my revival ability, and in a burst of flames was returned to half Health. I looked out of the event bubble, and I equipped a voice-amplifying token to make my words heard.

"I, Hail Jeoran, Earl of North Shire and Thorn March, declare <Branded Exiles> to be an outlaw guild due to their violent actions in breaking the peace of Yuikon today," I declared. "As for Nial Kingslayer, he is a coward, killing first an old man who was giving him honors, and then striking an opponent, who had already surrendered, in the back! I will honor my pledge not to seek retribution against the kingslayer for one year and one day, as is the law of the land, but let it be known that although the curse of [The Gray Man's Touch] has reduced me to level one, I have been cleansed of that affliction and will suffer no further setbacks!"

With my pledge made to the Natives, and after giving proof that I would rise from the dead no matter how many times I was struck down, I quickly selected the option to return to the lobby before the event bubble collapsed and someone accidentally killed me with a sneeze.

49
SETBACKS

Display status," I commanded and was immediately dismayed with the result.

Name	Hail Jeoran	Level	1
Guild	<Nethersong Mavericks>	Strength	12
Health	0/120	Dexterity	17
Experience	0/100	Vitality	13
Age	15	Endurance	12
Race	Human (blood of the Travelers)	Intelligence	14
Class	Placeholder	Wisdom	13
Job	Earl	Charisma	42
Title	Dungeon Master I	Armor	0
	Veteran of Mooncrest Manor	Spell damage	3
	Veteran of the Battle for North Shire	Attack Power	41

It was disheartening. I had lost all of my hard-earned progress. I had known it was a possibility ever since I'd been afflicted with [The

Gray Man's Touch], but I had deceived myself into believing that it wouldn't happen to me. Even when I had been inches away from death. Even when I had courted it. But I had also prepared myself for this from the moment I had accepted the duel with Nial. The thought that he would violate the agreement had occurred to me, and I'd prepared myself mentally for that possibility.

Except I hadn't just lost my levels—those I could regain. I had lost my class and my ability to cast magic. I tried, but even the simple cantrip to cast [Spark] or [Detect Poison] was beyond me.

"It's only temporary," Thomas said, his avatar coalescing into existence from motes of blue light. We were, as I always was when I came to the lobby at first, in the copy of [Zhesa Castle] that he had set up for me. "That you don't have magic, I mean. We're . . . Well, we're rewriting some things to make them more compatible with you. It's something that we were always going to do, but I'm sorry that it wasn't explained to you beforehand."

"There seems to be a lot of that, and it's starting to make me quite angry," I said, turning on Thomas. "You bastards! Goddamn it! Give me back my magic!"

"We will," Thomas promised. "Hail, the [Placeholder] class is quite powerful. It's meant to allow you to switch between [Lord], [Duelist], [Mage], and any other class that you want. Except for [Child]. Once you return to the world, you will be able to level each class independently of the others. I understand how frustrating it must have been to see your progress be reset like that, but this is meant to be a large upgrade for you."

That gave me a moment of pause, but I was still angry. "What of [Spellblade]? That is the class I truly want, not any other!"

"The problem, Hail, is that you have never truly been a [Spellblade]. From the beginning, you've always been a [Child]," Thomas explained. "Your class name and abilities were simply changed to match the publicly known traits of the [Spellblade] class. We thought for a while that would be enough, but after you returned from Earth following your study of the DSS, your interface and the world began throwing errors that—"

"You mean when you held me hostage for half a year!" I shouted at him. "You may have sent me back in time, but that does not change my indignation over how I was treated during that time."

Thomas acknowledged the point with a tip of his head. "And I'm sorry for that, Hail. It was out of my hands. I tried addressing the matter as many times as I could, but it took coordination with Thedum to actually get anywhere in breaking that logjam.

"Hail, I'm sorry. For the way Arc has been treating you. For removing you from your world, for resetting your progress in leveling, and for what we're doing to your combat system. We should have explained everything as we went along, but, as I said, the other administrators dislike it when I break the fourth wall with you. Since the matter with the DSS, however, I've been lobbying to get a wider degree of latitude in the sort of information I'm allowed to give you about the system and how you interact with it."

"That's it? That's the apology I get?" I demanded.

"Would you like me to prostrate myself?" Thomas asked, sounding curiously like he would do so. "To what level would you like me to demonstrate my remorse for my employer's actions, Hail? You know enough about Earth now to understand that I'm not actually very high in the hierarchy of the company that runs your world. Most of the decisions that have affected you so negatively have been out of my hands. Like the others, the decision to reset your class without explaining things to you was made without my input or consent, but I can at least explain it to you now."

I considered ranting at Thomas, but, ultimately, I knew that he was right. It would be like screaming at a gate guard because of a decision made by a king. Arc Inc. ruled the gods of my world, and they had far more power over it than I ever would. Thomas was but a minor puppet that they used to speak with me when it proved convenient for them to do so.

I wanted to continue yelling at the man. I remembered when Leonard had come at me, ready to cuss me out, only to deflate suddenly. I felt I understood him then. There was no joy in yelling at someone who wasn't ready to fight back.

"I'm listening," I said after giving his proposal consideration.

"It comes down to two matters," Thomas explained. "The first is that you're too good at being a [Child] [Spellblade]. We've been constantly adjusting the coefficients to lower your Damage output. The goal is to be in line with the maximum of what a skilled player would be able to put out if they took over a new avatar after raiding for several months and leveled it to whatever your current level is. Every time we adjust your coefficients, however, you make a change to your fighting style to compensate for the change, which needs to be adjusted on our end."

"You've been making combat harder for me?" I asked after I processed his words for a moment.

"Not me personally. The team that is trying to balance your class, yes. From the moment that you killed the level nineteen boar, actually, they've been trying to adjust your class down to what a human could theoretically be capable of. And they haven't succeeded. You're just too good, Hail, and that's the crux of it. I'm sorry. The new classes are an effort to balance you more fairly—more fairly for you and for your human competitors."

"What is the second matter?" I asked.

"A layer of incompatibility between your subconscious support system and your consciousness," Thomas answered. "The wall is breaking down. It has been for a while now, ever since Thedum made you into a Worldboss. You were meant to understand certain things intuitively and, at the same time, have other concepts filtered from your understanding to make your interactions with the Travelers seem more authentic. That ship has sailed, however. So we've decided to, as Thedum put it, 'take off the training wheels entirely.'"

"There is a problem with my mind?" I asked, growing concerned.

"Don't worry. We've had all of the gods working on a solution. You shouldn't even notice the difference when we patch you. But you might. It will happen the next time you enter your rest cycle. I'm just warning you because, well, I think you have a right to know, and at this point nobody can stop me from telling you," Thomas said.

I fell silent as I weighed his words. They were troubling. The Administrators were going to do something to me in my sleep, and I doubted there was anything I could do to stop them. Nothing but cry and beg, and I refused to lower myself to that.

"What will change?" I asked at last. "Will I be a different person?"

"No. You'll find it easier to issue quests intentionally, even without the use of your throne. You'll be able to manually assign Reputation to Travelers based on your personal opinion of them. To a degree. You'll have to if you want them to have your personal

Reputation, as the system that was assigning that for you is going away. You'll be aware of things. It will be almost like having your throne with you everywhere, but not quite. There are still some features that will be locked based on location. The throne was how we calibrated and tested a lot of the patches we're about to apply. This patch will be like having a portable throne in your back pocket all of the time that you can pull out whenever you want."

He paused, then assured me by saying, "Hail, we like your personality how it is. We're not looking to change it. Everything we've done today, including resetting your level, has been about removing restrictions without changing who you are."

"Perhaps," I said. "But this is a conversation that should have happened as soon as you determined that these changes were necessary! I am tired of your flimsy excuse about breaking walls, Thomas. I hereby file notice, under section 8.4.2.3, of a material complaint between myself and Arc Inc. over my ethical treatment."

Rather than get upset, as I had expected him to, Thomas grinned broadly. "Thank you, Hail. Those are words that I was sincerely hoping to hear from you someday."

I watched in surprise as a table formed with papers, ink, and a quill ready for me. "Why don't you go ahead and, in your own words, describe the nature of your complaint. I will return in a few hours to help you file your grievance. It will take some time for the review process, Hail. But I promise, Arc Inc. will take this document very seriously. So work hard on it, okay? And be aware that you can update it at any time as you learn more about how this process works."

Wary of a trap, I took a seat at the table. Thomas vanished into motes of light.

I began to write.

EPILOGUE: TARISHA

Tarisha was waiting patiently outside the Temple of Thedum in Zhesa City for Hail to return to the world. He had notified her of his intentions to do so moments ago, and she had cut short her expedition into the Deadlands with <Peasant's Revenge> to join him. She quietly changed out of her raiding armor and donned one of the disguise items that Lewis had obtained for her.

Daemon and Lewis joined her moments later. They, too, had disguised themselves as anonymous Travelers, although she didn't think either of them was well known enough to warrant such treatment. Perhaps Lewis—or Laurant as he was known in game—was, due to his role as the commander of Hail's canon forces during the war against the bandits, but Daemon had been dealing mostly with Natives since acquiring his canon role.

Tarisha had thrust herself forward to be, as Hail himself had put it, his liaison with the endgame community, so she was less worried about her companions being recognized. She was the face that the metagame community associated with Hail, especially as his personal bodyguard; it stood to reason that she was more likely to acquire a tail than the two casual players who were seen as simply having lucked into their new positions. She glanced around at the passersby, but nobody even glanced in their direction. She was worrying for nothing.

"So, he's really level one again now, huh?" Lewis asked as they waited.

"It's somewhat more than that," Tarisha said, exhaling as she tried to relax. She scanned through her messages, including the responses to the tickets she had filed with the administration appealing the duel's death penalty on Hail's behalf. "It seems that the interface between Hail and the world was significantly out of date. Apparently this all goes back to when your guild decided to load him up with every skill in the game when his class was [Child] in order to spread [Mark of Karma]. The developers made some poor decisions at that time, which have been snowballing ever since. They plan on compensating Hail for the lost progress with a boon called [Rebirth Resonance], though I do not have all the details."

"Sounds like bullshit to me," Lewis complained. "Every time Hail takes a step forward, it seems like the world pushes him two steps back. It's giving me second thoughts about giving my final signature, you know? It's not too late for us to back out."

"It is for me," Tarisha said. She looked up. "Lewis, don't you realize how lonely he is? We're trying to help him, at least, but everyone else just sees him as an NPC. An important and exploitable one."

"Yeah, that's not very reassuring when I think about the fact that I'm going to have a sort-of kid version of me uploaded into the game as well," Lewis said.

"So we'll keep them secret." It was one of the few things they argued about at this point in their relationship. She was committed to Project Gemini, and Lewis waxed between full commitment to match her own and threatening to pull out entirely. "The devs have promised not to force them into the limelight like they did for Hail. They're not going to have an important canon role like Prince of Yuikon. And they won't be blind about their abilities like Hail was."

"I still don't understand why that was necessary," Lewis said. "It seems unnecessarily cruel to me. I'm going to tell Charity and Prosperity from the beginning everything I know about their abilities, and if Arc tries to stop me, I'm suing them on their behalf."

"They were testing his limits," Daemon said, sighing. "It's easy to forget, once you start thinking of him as a person. Hail is the most human-*like* artificial intelligence I've ever encountered. But that doesn't make him human. Especially not legally. What Arc is allowed to subject him to in the name of experimentation is well outside what

I would consider ethical, considering that they themselves gave him the ability to feel human emotions."

"Do you guys talk about this sort of thing all the time when I'm not around?" a familiar voice asked, and Tarisha turned. A young man had sneaked up on them from an angle she hadn't been watching. Or rather, she had seen him, but when she had [Analyzed] him, she had seen he was a level one [Acolyte] and paid him no further mind.

"Lord Hail?" she inquired. "Is that you in disguise?"

"Pretty good, right?" he said. "It's one of the benefits of getting reset, I guess. I get access to all of my general skills and general spells in every class, so I'm using [Illusion Magic: Disguise] right now. And my [Placeholder] class lets me change what people see when they [Analyze] me. Even you guys didn't recognize me when I was walking up."

"Are you planning on leveling as a healer, then?" Lewis asked him.

"No. It's just a disguise," Hail answered. "Thanks for meeting me. I don't really need the protection anymore, but it will be nice to have company while I run some errands. But you didn't answer the question. How much do you guys talk about stuff like that? How Arc treats me and ethical concerns, and whatever."

Tarisha glanced at the others, but it was Daemon who answered.

"It comes up from time to time, Hail," he said honestly.

"Yeah, well, in that case, I'd like you to not hide it from me anymore," the young AI said. "Guys, the fourth wall was shattered a long time ago. I may not understand much about Earth, but I've known I was an AI since the night my father rejected me. I'm just now starting to understand what that means, but everyone is still treating it like it's some big secret. I've been to Earth. I know Earth humans are different from Natives and the gods and whatever I am."

"What is it, exactly, that you think you are, Hail?" Lewis inquired.

"I'm me," Hail answered. "It's who I've always been, as long as I can remember. I've never had any doubts about that. What I have doubts about are what I want and what I want to do with my life. But I'm starting to figure that out as well."

"That's great, Lord Hail," Tarisha told him. "I'm certain that we'd all be thrilled to help you achieve your goals once you've established them."

"Yeah, thanks," Hail said. "You guys are always ready to complete my quests for me. But I don't think what I have in mind is going to work like that."

"What are you planning, Hail?" Daemon asked.

"First, I'm going to visit Marquis Peori. Then I'm going to go incognito for a while. I'll set up the first few dozen battlegrounds like I promised for the people and companies who won the auctions, but I'm not going to be talking to the endgame community anymore. And I'm not going to be doing any dungeon busting or lair destroying or anything. Um, Daemon? Laurant? Can you let everyone know when I quit the guild that it's not anything personal? I just need to lie low for a while. I plan on coming back."

"That is . . . disappointing, Hail," Daemon said. "I'm not certain you're aware of this, but <Nethersong Mavericks> has realigned itself significantly due to your presence. It's no longer the casual guild it used to be. It's almost exclusively dedicated to advancing your goals."

"I'm coming back," Hail insisted. "I just need some time to myself. Actually, you guys could still help me by pretending that nothing has changed and that you're leveling me back up in secret. But the truth is that I plan to spend some time traveling the Heartlands. When I'm not in Thorn March spending time with my mother and brother, that is."

"What about the succession?" Lewis asked, broaching the subject before Tarisha could bring it up.

"That's what I'm going to talk to the marquis about right now," Hail answered. "And after that I'm going to talk to Lady Mooncrest. But I think the best thing I can do to get ready for what's coming is to get stronger, and I don't want to do that surrounded by bodyguards who are with me because they were selected by lottery or whatever."

They moved through the city as they spoke, heading towards the marquis's home. Tarisha struggled with her inner turmoil. This would affect her professionally. But not that much. Not as much as having Hail out of game had affected her. She had raked it in when she had released the advanced information about the great reversion into the Recent Past, but for a little while she had been afraid that her jump to declaring herself a full-time professional gamer had been immature.

She was certain that the succession was the next big thing to hit the game, and the information she would get from this meeting would be key in forming the strategy for many of her allies. And Hail's allies. She was, after all, his liaison with the endgame community, and she had been forming a coalition on his behalf to push for putting the infant Rain onto the throne. Perhaps one day she would sit down and show him all of the work she had been doing for him in the background, but not now. Not so soon after this setback.

He was her lord. If he needed time alone, then she would buy it for him. In whatever currency was required.

ABOUT THE AUTHOR

A. Stargazer is the author of the Quest Giver series, originally released on Royal Road. Raised in a very small town by an amazing single mom, he beat cancer at age twenty and struggled through college with undiagnosed Bipolar I Disorder. He was finally diagnosed at age thirty-one thanks to his sister, an emergency room doctor, who noticed his manic symptoms and helped him get the care he needed. A. Stargazer now works as a medical professional himself and writes in his spare time.

www.ingramcontent.com/pod-product-compliance
Lightning Source LLC
Chambersburg PA
CBHW020646120726
47906CB00001B/147